Die To See Tomorrow

POULOMI SANYAL

Connect with Poulomi Sanyal

Website: https://poulomi-sanyal.weebly.com/

Twitter: https://twitter.com/sanyal_poulomi

Facebook: https://www.facebook.com/authorPoulomiSanyal/

LinkedIn: https://www.linkedin.com/in/poulomisanyal/

To follow latest updates, insightful blog-posts, book-signings, giveaways and promotions, sign-up to the author's newsletter at:

https://poulomi-sanyal.weebly.com/news

ISBN-13: 978-1-7753950-6-5

DEDICATION

"It was the best of times, it was the worst of times, it was the age of wisdom, it was the age of foolishness, it was the epoch of belief, it was the epoch of incredulity, it was the season of light, it was the season of darkness, it was the spring of hope, it was the winter of despair."
—*Charles Dickens, A Tale of Two Cities*

"If you want a picture of the future, imagine a boot stamping on a human face—forever."
—*George Orwell, 1984*

"It is a civilizational wake-up call. A powerful message—spoken in the language of fires, floods, droughts, and extinctions—telling us that we need an entirely new economic model and a new way of sharing this planet."
—*Naomi Klein, This Changes Everything*

OTHER BOOKS BY THE AUTHOR

Colour Me Confounded

The Thought Warriors Series
Book 1: The Coming of Kalki
Book 2: The Curse of Gaia
Book 3: The Frozen Saint of Baikal

Songs of Ennui: Poems

PRAISE FOR COLOUR ME CONFOUNDED

"Written in simple and lucid language with economic use of words, she puts forward the life of modern women as it is, minus the embellishments or the jargons of feminism and alternative living."—*The Statesman (Kolkata, December 9, 2018)*

"I applaud Poulomi Sanyal for crafting a work that captures the subtle complexities of women's lives. I look forward to reading more of this author's future works." —*J.G. MacLeod (Author)*

"Excellent work and incredible writing by Poulomi Sanyal!" — *Steven Nedeau (Author)*

PRAISE FOR THOUGHT WARRIORS BOOK 1
THE COMING OF KALKI

CHAPTER ONE

Aquila raised a glittering ampule of clear liquid to the light streaming in from the window of his tiny trailer cabin. A rainbow reflected off its surface filling him with a longing—a desire to inject himself with the fluid that shimmered inside. He resisted the urge and set the vial down on an end table before turning on the TV, where a broadcast was only offered on select days of the year.

Today, multiple channels blazed on at once because it was 4th March 2524, the silver jubilee of the United World Forum's Joint Resolution. Aquila flipped through the channels as all the news networks around the globe featured the regional versions of what this day meant to them. It had been a hundred years, since the mission to build a habitable world on Mars had gone up in flames, literally as well as metaphorically.

Over-population was still humanity's biggest unresolved problem. The United World Forum's Joint resolution of 2499, forbade the development or use of technology for medical purposes. All the stalwarts nodded their heads, put on their most austere expressions and agreed unanimously that artificially extending human longevity did no one any good. But what about technology for defence? The attendees of the forum were all too eager to pay lip service to the inherent senselessness of wanting to kill from a distance, the brutality of slaughtering in the millions, even under the pretext of defending one's own.

But the silence of the unspoken words in the room had been palpable as the world leaders sneaked furtive glances at one another, thinking up the most humane way to voice their concerns. The world clearly had too many people at a level that it could no longer sustain. This crisis meant that a storm was brewing in the horizon. It would not be long before the nations of the world clashed against one another over resources. Without weapons, how would a nation survive if such a time were to arrive?

At the age of fifteen, Aquila had watched the live-feed of the 2499 forum from his mother's trailer. It seemed like an eternity had passed between then and now, without any significant changes in this discussion. Weapons of mass destruction were still in vogue, though not as frequently in use as say, a couple of centuries ago. However, the rate of mortality due to natural causes had seen a substantial uptick as a direct consequence of the forum's resolution.

That is how he had lost his mother. To an evolved variety of cancer.

Aquila still remembered the moment. The herbalist at the local hospital had been tending to his mom for days, but by then even she had turned somber and teary-eyed.

"Do you think she will last the night?" Aquila had asked.

"It doesn't look likely," the herbalist responded, wiping a solitary tear from her eyes.

Aquila stayed next to the bed all night. With each rise and fall of his mother's chest, he held onto hope that the next one was forthcoming. But then, just about an hour after midnight, a little gasp followed by deathly stillness. The smell of the room still haunted him. The myriad herbal concoctions, the incense, the oils, all mingled into one, the stench of mortality.

At nearly seven-thirty in the evening, Aquila fingered the little ampule of ethanol on his end table that would supply him with his daily doze of buzz.

Nah, he thought. *Today I'll have the real stuff!*

Bending forward, he reached down to the bottom shelf of the mini-fridge in his cabin, and pulled out a reclining bottle of a 150-year-old rye whiskey of his favourite variety. It was a hundred degrees inside his trailer cabin, even with the fan on, and he could really use the chilled drink.

He poured himself a couple of shots and recalled how he had come across that rare bottle a few years ago, while still an intern at the Ministry. The bottle came from the last batch of confiscated liquor, auctioned out to civilians, when the production of drinkable alcohol was finally declared illegal by the International Taskforce for Food Crop Conservation.

At the end of the auction, there were still a couple of bottles left that no one had wanted. A lot of activists had gathered around the auction venue, booing the auctioneers and guilt-tripping them into dismissing the whole event in a symbolic gesture supporting Food Rights' Activism. In the end, the pressure being too much, the auction had to be called off. Not a soul wanted to bid on the remaining bottles. Some buyers were even seen outside the building, emptying their expensive alcohol into dumpsters, to roaring crowd applause.

In the confusion, Aquila, while assisting with the auction, was asked by his manager to hide a couple of bottles inside his backpack and get out of there, before the crowd stormed in and smashed everything to smithereens. He had done just that. Thankfully, no one noticed him sneak out, pushing through the masses and making for the bus stop. He had done nothing with the bottles for quite some time. He wondered every day, why his manager did not ask about the bottles or order him to return them to the Government repository.

When nearly half a year went by, his internship almost over, he realized that his manager had probably forgotten all about the contraband in this newbie employee's possession. Several times, Aquila thought about reminding him. He even knocked on his manager's door late one afternoon to do just that.

"Who is it?" the elderly official had responded.

"Umm ... it's me Aquila."

"Oh, rather late for you to be still at work, isn't it, kiddo! C'mon call it a day. We can talk tomorrow."

"If you say so," Aquila had mumbled, but mostly he felt relieved. He realized, he never wanted to have that conversation to begin with. This constant tug-of-war between his urges and his conscience was killing him.

The next day, his manager had forgotten all about this matter as usual, and Aquila decided to finally put it to rest. Ever since then, the bottles had been his, and no one had ever questioned it. Aquila drank them sparingly, knowing that they were the last few extant bottles of potable alcohol available anywhere on the planet.

He relaxed into his favourite armchair and reclining it, put his foot up on the suspended foot stool that hovered at its base. That internship at the Ministry, back when he was a strapping young man, had later secured him the permanent position he now held. It was a competitive world, crippling under the pressures of overpopulation and food scarcity. Naturally, Aquila was happy to be gainfully employed in such an important Government position. Without this role, he would have probably had to slog away at a dead-end job in the agriculture or conservation industry, the only two viable sources of income available in the present-day society. Unless of course, you were in politics.

Aquila descended from the migrants, who had once fled in a north-easterly direction to the vast stretches of land, previously occupied by the mighty Russians. Like many others, they had been ousted in droves from the erstwhile nation of The United States of America, during the Great Deluge of 2389 and the subsequent desertification that consumed much of their homeland. It is believed, that his family had originated from the western part of the United States, from a region known as California, where the magnificent floating nation of Calamerica now resides.

Aquila took in a large gulp of whiskey, churning it inside his mouth deliciously to take in all the flavours, before swallowing it down ceremoniously. The alcohol stirred up his appetite, but it had been a long day and he felt too tired to move. He sank back further into the comfy couch and lovingly rubbed his whiskey glass against his cheek, letting the coolness soothe his skin.

A loud knock jolted Aquila back to reality. He hurried to the door and peeked into the security camera affixed to its edge. A burly man, possibly in his mid-thirties, stood there with his bushy eyebrows furrowed and an overly serious expression on his face.

Aquila opened the door and was about to ask for identity, but the burly stranger had already started speaking.

"Deputy Secretary General of Conservation Affairs, Aquila, Division 2, Subdivision 15J?" The man read in a deep voice from his hand-held tablet. Looking up from the tablet he stared inquiringly in Aquila's direction.

"That would be me," Aquila replied, squinting slightly.

"I have a warrant, Sir. You are under arrest."

"Wha ... who ..." But before Aquila could form a coherent sentence, a pair of robotic handcuffs soared through the air and magnetically latched themselves around his wrists. A gravity beam lifted him about a foot above the ground, pulling him in the direction of the security vehicle that stood less than fifty feet in front of him.

"Wait, *stop*!" Aquila screamed. His captor pushed a button and the gravity pull receded, but held Aquila locked to the spot. "What is it?" he asked, raising an eyebrow.

"Who are you? You're not in uniform! I'll call the authorities on you so fast ..."

"Sir, we are the International Satellite Police. We don't have uniforms. You've been summoned for trial by the ..."

"International Conservation Council ... no way!" Aquila let out an audible gasp.

* * *

Carina fished out her pre-processed, state approved, high-energy dinner from the pantry and set it down on her little dining table. She laid out a plate for herself as she carefully removed the food from its temperature regulated, bio-degradable packaging and emptied the contents onto it.

The meal looked unappetizing at best and dismal at worst. Just as dismal as her current mood. Carina didn't like eating alone but Mizar, her partner of 7 years, was travelling for work this week. Carina didn't know whether this was a blessing or a curse. Mizar was still lovely and just as radiant as the day they had first met. Yet something about her fundamental nature seemed to have changed. Something had awakened inside of her lately that had turned her into a stranger in Carina's eyes.

Carina raised her right hand and waved it in front of her, tracing a symbol in the air with her index finger. The wall ahead lit up immediately as the news channel started to play in 3D.

"More unrest ensued in the east today with the food crisis mounting rapidly in Southern Indochine. Thousands of angry demonstrators surrounded the Food Ministry headquarters ..." The audio was momentarily interrupted by a little beep as the feed from the news channel flickered twice, indicating an incoming call. It was Alrakis, her young aide at the Ministry and her most trusted confidante in recent times. Carina swiped in the air with her finger and accepted the call. The face of a friendly young man in his late twenties appeared. He had soft, genteel features set with sapphire blue eyes that felt bottomless if you stared into them.

"Evening Alrakis. What's up?"

"Good evening, Ma'am. You asked me to report on any unusual activity, and I have a recent one to report."

"Oh?"

"Yes Ma'am. A high-profile detainee cell is being prepared

for tonight. I've been asked to receive and transfer the top-secret prisoner to his cell by no later than midnight tonight."

"Top-secret, huh? This doesn't sound good. Who do you think it might be?"

"I have no idea as of yet, and when I do, I'll probably be sworn to secrecy with a secrecy chip. So ..."

"Busted if you reveal it."

"Literally, yes." Giggled Alrakis, although cringing a little at the thought of getting blown up for revealing a secret of this calibre.

"Alright, thanks. I'll let you go. Don't want anyone to get suspicious."

"No. We don't. Were you planning on coming here—"

"I'll decide in the morning." Carina cut him short. "Best not to speak of this any further."

"As you wish. Have a pleasant evening, Ma'am."

"Likewise." Carina flashed him a hint of a smile through the corner of her lips before switching off the feed with a flick of her fingers. She was in no mood for more TV. Too much was on her mind. She got up hastily and started clearing the remnants of her half-eaten dinner. She needed to turn in early tonight. Tomorrow was going to be busy.

* * *

Aquila woke up in a small chamber with walls of dazzling white ceramic. He squinted, his vision disoriented and head throbbing. He was lying on a miniature bed suspended from the rear wall of the room. Pushing himself up on his elbows, he inspected his surroundings—a stark little cabin about ten feet in either direction. Completely empty, apart from the tiny bed, almost a berth that he was lying on. No doors or windows, toilet or sink in sight.

Aquila rubbed his eyes and sat up on the bed. *Where the hell is this place,* he thought.

"You are in the VIP cell of satellite station 17R3," boomed an electronic voice.

"What? Who are you? You can hear my thoughts?"

"You were speaking out loud, I'm afraid," the voice responded with mechanical politeness.

"I see, but you didn't answer my question. Where exactly am I?"

"I'm not here to answer questions."

"Wait, that's crazy, because you just did! So, will you or will you not tell me what the hell is going on here?"

There was silence.

"Hello! Hello, can you still hear me?" Still nothing. Pin drop silence. Nothing stirred.

"Damn it!" Aquila growled, balling up his fists and striking the wall next to his bed in frustration.

"Do not attack the vessel or else I'll sound the alarms," the mechanical voice warned in a sing-song voice, still as polite as ever.

"You're funny, aren't you?"

"I'm not programmed to be funny."

"But you're programmed for conversation? So why not tell me where the feck, I am?"

There was no response. Aquila sat up and suspended his legs from the edge of the bed, taking in his surroundings. The last memory he had was of being dragged into a security vessel and stuffed inside a capsular-cell. They must have drugged him inside that cell. For obvious reasons. The whereabouts of the satellite police stations were for the most part hidden from the general public. But if he was being summoned by the International Conservation Council (ICC), could it be …? No, it sounded impossible. The headquarters of the council were half way between the earth and the moon. They couldn't have just brought him there. No civilian he knew of, had ever seen this location, let alone been captured by the Council. The offences they tried for were high international crimes of such magnitudes that ordinary civilians could never accidentally

8

implicate themselves.

Aquila rested his elbows on his thighs and held his head between his hands, sighing deeply. He could think of nothing to do, but wait for answers. The throbbing in his temple had eased, but now his stomach growled. He hadn't had dinner and had no idea how much time had elapsed since he grabbed a light lunch at work, the afternoon before his arrest.

There was a beeping sound and the wall of resplendent white, right across from him, parted revealing the entrance to his cell. A robot, about four feet tall glided in. The door closed behind it.

"Good evening," the robot greeted.

"Err … yes. I wouldn't say good, but evening it is, if you say so."

"I'm here with your dinner," said the robot in a suave male voice, ignoring Aquila's snide remark. The front panel of the robot opened up producing a tray containing an unappetizing-looking meal. The robot picked up the plate and touched a point on the wall that was exuding a faint green light. A collapsible tray-table opened up. The robot set the dinner plate expertly atop it, before swerving around to look at Aquila.

"Your trial will be tomorrow at 11 AM. Do you have access to a lawyer?" it announced.

"Tomorrow … tomorrow … what day are we today?"

"Saturday, the fifth of March, 2524."

Shit, I lost a day!

"SIR!"

"Yes?" Aquila was jolted back into reality.

"Do you or do you not have access to a lawyer?"

"I don't believe … what am I being charged with, anyway?"

"I'm afraid I cannot answer that question. I'm the superintendent of the VIP cells here at the International Conservation—"

"Council!" Aquila completed with a gasp.

"Yes, that's correct. I have no information on the condition of your arrest or charges laid. However, I am able to request legal aid on your behalf should you so require. Appearing before the Council tomorrow without representation is not particularly advisable."

"I can imagine. Yeah, I'd like a lawyer if you could arrange for one."

"Certainly." The robot pressed a button on its chest and a small tablet emerged. With both hands it typed rapidly into the tablet for about two minutes and finally looked up at Aquila, nodding slightly.

"A request has been put in. Should a lawyer agree to represent you, they will be here tomorrow morning prior to your trial, so that you may have a few minutes to discuss your case before you appear—"

"Discuss what *case*, though?" Aquila interrupted. "I don't have any idea what's going on here …"

"Your file has been submitted for review to the available lawyers. Should one of them choose to represent you, they would know all the details pertaining to your arrest and charges. You can, at that time, discuss the matter with them directly."

"How exciting. And what if no one volunteers to represent me? What then?"

"Then Sir, you'll appear for trial at the appointed hour tomorrow, and your charges will be announced to you at that time."

Aquila got up from his bed and walking hastily up to the robot knelt before it so that his face was level with its head. The robot glided back instantly, moving about a foot away from him.

"There's no need to sound the alarms," Aquila assured. "I just want to know my situation here. Do you have a phone that I could use to consult with my own counsel? My personal equipment seems to have been confiscated," he said, as he searched his pockets.

"I do not provide that facility. You'll have to wait for your lawyer to arrive in the morning, should they wish to represent you."

"Aight." Aquila stood up, exasperated. The robot turned to leave.

"Wait, where do I sit?" Aquila called after the guard. "And, there's no toilet—"

The robot turned around in a whisk. "The bathroom is on your right." He motioned to the wall in that direction. Then, he zoomed over to that area and touched a faint green light on the wall, opening up a portal into a small adjoining room that served as the toilet for this cell. "Your chair is collapsible," the robot continued as he fingered a spot on the floor next to the tray-table. A little stool rose from the floor in an instant.

"I'll be here in the morning to escort you to your trial," it declared before turning briskly and zooming out of the room. It left behind a deafening silence in its wake. Aquila no longer felt the urge to eat. The dinner was probably cold anyway. He took a bite off the burger on his plate.

Is it real beef? Nah, that stuff's for the super-elite. It's probably just synthetic beef. At least better than the cricket-based, high-protein burgers they serve at the office cafeteria.

Aquila gulped down his glass of water, leaving behind what remained of his burger on the tray. Nothing seemed to stir his appetite this evening. He hobbled back to his make-shift bed and collapsed into a fitful, restless sleep.

* * *

Aquila was running so fast his legs ached, yet *they* were still on his tail. The cops. No idea why they were chasing him. And then, he fell. He tripped right over the ledge of the sidewalk and fell. Except, it was not a sidewalk he was on, but a bus, hovering over the city on his way to work. Where did the cops go? He had lost them. He grabbed a seat at the back of the bus next to a shrouded woman. He turned his head to look at her face. She looked familiar. But deathly pale. *Who is she? Who is she? Oh my God!* Recognition dawned as he broke into a cold sweat.

"Mom!" he screamed. She was not moving, breathing, talking. Just then, there was an announcement.

"6 AM ALARMS. 6 AM ALARMS. ALL PRISONERS ARISE."

Aquila woke up with a jolt. The announcement had stopped.

Guess it's the day of my trial, he thought, rubbing the sweat off his forehead with his palm.

He desperately needed a shower. He rose slowly, feeling light-headed from not having eaten much in the last two days. Taking a couple of seconds to steady himself on his feet, he made for the enclosed bathroom. It had a tiny shower. That would have to do.

The water in the shower was too cold and only came on for a couple of minutes. But even that felt like a luxury. Water usage was so severely curtailed since the last century that showers no longer ran seven days a week. Each neighbourhood had its own running water days. Aquila didn't know how that system worked up here in this spaceship. Nevertheless, he felt fresher and more awake. He needed to be alert for the hearing, and that was all he could think of. When he came out of the bathroom, he found a plate of what looked like breakfast, waiting for him at the tray-table, and the remnants of last night's meal had disappeared.

Aquila sat on the collapsible stool and ravenously gobbled down a few pieces of dried fruit and bread. He was about to wash it all down with a glass of water when the door to his cell opened unexpectedly, and a lady walked in. She was in her mid-forties, medium-height, jet-black hair that ran down her shoulder in dainty waves and a pale brown complexion.

"Ahem." She cleared her throat, wearing a stern but not unkind expression.

"Oh, hi," said Aquila, taking a swig from his glass of water to gulp down the contents of his mouth. "Nice to meet you. I can't believe they sent an actual person!" He got up and extended his hand to the visitor.

"A what?" The lady looked offended.

"Oh, I'm sorry. I meant, I was expecting a trained bot. But I'm glad you're here. I thought I'd be all alone this morning."

"I'm sorry? You're making no sense. My name is Carina and I am—"

"My lawyer. Nice to meet you! And thanks for agreeing to represent me. At such short notice, I thought no one would."

Carina gave out a small chuckle. "Oh, I see. You think I'm a lawyer. I'm afraid I have bad news. I'm no lawyer."

"Oh!" Aquila clenched his jaw, feeling both embarrassed and anxious at the same time. "I'm sorry," he blurted.

"That's alright."

"Who are you then? I interrupted you back there."

"I'm the Secretary of State of Calamerica."

"Whaaaat? No way!"

Carina, flicked him a half grin and extended a tablet in his direction. "Now, if you don't mind signing here. I can get you out." She indicated the bottom of a form with her index finger.

Aquila found himself trembling a little. What the hell was going on here? Felt like serious stuff. How could he take it all so lightly? He gulped, extending his hand to accept the tablet but his hand shook violently, and the tablet landed with a clang on the floor. Aquila winced and closed his eyes, expecting to see the device in a hundred pieces at his feet, but when he opened them again, lo and behold, the tablet was still intact.

"Unbreakable, eh?" He asked, bending to pick it up promptly.

"Yep. Now, if you would please …"

"Yes, of course!" Aquila scrolled through the form. It was not as much a form as a legal document. He was agreeing to some things, disagreeing to others. It made him nervous. He didn't have time to read all this.

"Err … umm … it's a lot of stuff. What am I signing away here? Do I need to read all this?" he asked, tentatively.

"If you wish, but we only have ten minutes. I need to get you through the checkout protocols within the next hour, if you want to get sent on your way home today."

"Oh, I see. Okay then, let me ask you something. Why are you even doing this? Why are you setting me free? I don't get it. Any of it."

"You probably realize there has been a misunderstanding. Your arrest was a misunderstanding. I'm here to clarify that with the authorities. With your signature on this release form, you'll be agreeing to my explanation of the situation that clarifies your innocence. It exonerates you. You just need to acknowledge my conclusion. That is all."

"I see." Aquila's brows furrowed. He was in no mind to argue with the second most powerful delegate from one of the world's most powerful nations. Yet, he did not feel convinced that signing the document without reading it would be the wisest thing to do. What choice did he have though, given the situation? He thought for about thirty more seconds and quickly made up his mind, roughly capturing his fingerprint on the signature line, providing his consent to whatever the hell was written on that form.

"Thank you." Carina nodded curtly, accepting the tablet back from him. "Now if you'd follow me." She motioned with her hand urging him to follow, before speeding out the door.

CHAPTER TWO

Alrakis paced anxiously inside the meeting room, waiting for Carina to arrive. He checked the time again. She was already half an hour late. This made him nervous. Did the plan not work? The door to the meeting room opened, and a middle-aged man poked his head.

"Sorry, I didn't realize this room was taken," he said, shaking his head when he noticed Alrakis pacing inside.

"Oh, that's alright, Botein. I have it for another half hour. If you can wait."

"Might as well," Botein replied in a gruff voice. "All the rooms are occupied, and I figured since your door was half open, that I might just be in luck. Your meeting ended early or something."

"They're all booked, eh? Unusual. It's never this busy. Wonder what's up."

"Me too. Anyhoo, I'll leave you to it then." He turned to go, and then pivoted quickly, as if remembering something. "Who you meetin' by the way, if I may ask?"

"You may not!" Alrakis guffawed. "Joking. But not really. I'd rather not disclose that. Hope you understand. That's why I got a high security room." He smirked.

"Sure. I'll get out of your hair then. In case I bump into your top-secret guest and blow their cover." Botein smiled dryly before walking out the door.

This time, Alrakis made sure to lock the door behind the intruder. Five more minutes passed, and then finally the hologram phone in the meeting room beeped. Incoming call. Alrakis answered it promptly and Carina's hologram appeared immediately in front of him.

"Ma'am." He bowed, ceremoniously.

"There, there. You don't need to be so dramatic." Although Alrakis was considerably junior to her in rank, Carina enjoyed a somewhat jovial relationship with this budding new talent on her staff.

Alrakis smiled his signature crooked smile. His dimples immediately denting. "So, did it work?" he asked.

"Yeah. Sort of."

"Dare I ask what that means?"

"Well, he's free, if that's what you're asking."

"And? Is there more? Can you share?" asked Alrakis with a worried expression across his features.

"Not at the moment, no. What about you? Did you find out anything?"

"I did. It's bizarre ..." Alrakis trailed off.

"Well, go on ..."

"Yes, just gathering my thoughts. Our ally says he used his most reliable agent. They had the highest levels of security clearance. Not sure what went wrong."

"Did the agent get to the files, at least?"

"Nope. That's the thing. The bizarre part. They were denied access and that's when our bureaucrat over here was flagged down and arrested," Alrakis explained.

"Aquila."

"That's the one."

"They claim that his credentials were used in the breach," Carina confided.

"I don't understand. Our ally denies it. The agent he used

was a completely different person."

"Strange!"

"Makes me doubt the reliability of our source."

"Same."

"Do we want me to investigate?" Alrakis asked, frowning.

"We should, but right now, we have greater priorities with the debate on the Armaments Resolution around the corner."

"Do we know when that'll start?"

"No, but soon. We need to be prepared. Everything hinges on how the politics plays out around this issue."

"I'll get cracking then."

"Yes, please. Oh, and by the way ..."

"Keep it under wraps?"

"As always."

"Yes, Ma'am!"

* * *

Aquila woke up in his trailer without any sense of the date or time. Something was beeping next to his bed. Voicemail. He touched the sensor and the hologram of his boss, Fornax appeared promptly, tiny, twisted and irate.

"Aquila, you have missed three days of work now. This is my final warning. If I don't see your ass at work tomorrow, you can say goodbye to the Ministry," he hollered.

Wait, why haven't I been to work? Aquila wondered. There were dozens of other messages all from the same person. Aquila rubbed his forehead and squinted to scan his surroundings in the mellow half-light of dawn. His empty whiskey glass lay on a floating stool in front of his armchair.

"Geez, how much did I drink?" he wondered out loud. Then, like a bolt of lightning, the memories flashed through his brain, they coalesced and settled in a nebulous mass. He began to recollect. There were inconsistencies and holes in his memory, but now he knew for a fact that he had been arrested, miraculously released and possibly returned to his residence in the dead of the night.

He checked the time on his trailer's virtual assistant; 6 o'clock.

I should get my ass to work, he thought, rubbing his eyes. *I'll have a hell of a lot of explaining to do when I get there!*

He dressed quickly, gulped down a frozen breakfast and hurried to catch the seven o'clock bus to Conservation Plaza. He arrived at work one hour early and thought he would use the time to prepare a brief for Fornax. Depending on what his boss already knew, Aquila would have to make up a believable excuse for his absence. There was no way he was going to spill the beans about his arrest. He didn't trust Fornax enough for that. And given what he just went through, Aquila no longer felt like trusting anyone.

He walked up to his office building's employee entrance, churning various ideas in his head, trying to formulate a believable alibi for his unexplained absence. Distractedly, he gazed into the retinal scanner for access, as he made to enter the lobby.

BAM!

His face smashed against the massive double-panelled, bulletproof glass door.

"Ow!" Aquila cried, rubbing the bridge of his nose. "What the hell?"

"Access denied," replied the robotic, saccharine voice of the scanner.

"Denied? You're kidding right?"

"I don't kid."

"Let me try again. Maybe the retinal image was hazy." Aquila stared squarely into the scanner's rectangular face, almost burning a hole into it with the intensity of his glare.

"Access denied."

"Are you serious?"

"I'm always serious!"

"Do you know what's going on?"

18

"Yes. You're holding up the line, Sir."

Turning his head, Aquila noticed a queue starting to form. The faces behind him snuck irritated glances in his direction. "Damn it!" Aquila exclaimed. "What do I do now?" he asked, throwing up his arms and aiming the question at no one in particular. But the scanner was a piece of artificial intelligence and it immediately assumed the question was directed at it.

"You can go to the general reception and make an inquiry with the receptionist if you wish," it responded. "But now, I must ask you to step aside," it added.

Aquila cursed under his breath and moved away from the scanner. He tried to remember where the general entrance to the building was. The last time he had entered the Ministry through those doors was when he had come here as a strapping interviewee right out of college. The building complex was massive like most other government offices of this age. So, it took a while for Aquila to navigate his way through the structural jungle and arrive at the fancy front lobby.

He entered like a commoner with no ties to the Ministry or one who sought to build those ties from here on. The lobby was starting to get crowded at this hour. Through the busyness, Aquila could see a single, solemn-faced, human receptionist seated astutely behind the front desk, answering questions, wearing a perfect poker-face. He hurried over to accost her.

"Good morning," he said brusquely. "I'm Deputy Secretary General Aquila of Division 2, Subdivision 15J and I'm being denied access to my department. Could you please look in to this matter urgently, and get me back my access? I have pressing issues I need to attend to at work today." Even as he spoke these words, Aquila felt his pulse quicken and his lips quiver.

The receptionist turned her dignified, impassive face towards him and nodded. "Certainly, Sir. I'll look into it for you. Please face the scanner on your right."

Aquila did as he was told.

The receptionist's face grew thoughtful as she peered into the display cast across the section of her desk hidden from Aquila's view. "Hmm," she said, after a moment's deliberation. "It appears that you no longer work at the Ministry," she concluded, looking directly into Aquila's eyes for the first time.

"Ridiculous!" Aquila thundered, slamming his palm on the desk.

The receptionist flinched.

Aquila continued; voice hoarse. "This is *not* how the Ministry works. There cannot be termination in absentia! That isn't the law. To fire a high-ranking government official, you need to serve a proper–"

"I'm sorry, Sir," the lady interrupted, "who said anything about a termination?"

"Huh?"

The clerk turned to her display and searched for the wordings on Aquila's file. "It says here, Sir, that you've voluntarily tendered your resignation on the instant of—"

"*Voluntarily?*"

"Yes, that's what it says."

"Now, why … why would I do that?"

The receptionist shrugged, appearing genuinely confused. "I don't know, Sir."

"I wish to see Chairperson Fornax, the head of my division. Immediately!"

The slender lady behind the reception desk momentarily lost her composure and averted her eyes from the furious man in front of her. Hastily scanning the display on her desk, she looked up. "I … am … afraid that's not possible … uh … until tomorrow." She gulped.

Aquila drew in a ragged breath. "Tomorrow it is, then. Can you give me a time?"

"How about 9 o'clock?" she replied, checking Fornax's calendar.

Aquila frowned. *Fornax is particularly nasty in the mornings,* he thought. *But what choice do I have?* "Alright," he said. "Please, book me in." He turned to leave, realizing with a sudden sinking feeling that he didn't have anywhere to go.

Aquila walked around aimlessly for a while and eventually found himself outside the building's massive front doors. There, towering over the rush-hour pedestrian traffic, stood a thirty-foot stone statue of Laura Westfield, the teenage climate activist of the twenty-fourth century, who died providing tsunami relief to the victims of the Great Deluge.

The day was starting to warm up really quick, and Aquila felt the weight of heat-induced languor in every cell of his body. Surrendering to the lethargy, he plopped down on the platform at the foot of Laura's statue. In front of him, across a courtyard, stood a glass-panelled building shaped like a giant wave. Lifelike and accurate in its most intricate details, it was a symbol of the horrors the Great Deluge had brought upon humanity. It housed the offices of the Water Conservation Department. Reflected in the glassy wall of the building, just below the crest of the wave, was Laura's youthful face, angry, determined, frustrated. Aquila stared at the image feeling a tinge of irony. Here she was, guarding the gates of the all-powerful Ministry of Conservation, which would never have existed had it not been for the efforts of the likes of her. Yet, that attempt at conservation came too late and at the price of her martyrdom.

Maybe this was the mantra of the universe we lived in. For some to thrive, others must be sacrificed.

Is that what happened to me? Aquila wondered. *Was I getting in the way of something, and they had to get rid of me?* Aquila shook his head to dismiss these annoying thoughts. Around him the city buzzed with activity. The primly dressed genteel bureaucrats strode past with an air of affected busyness, their faces unreadable, their movements robotic. Not one of them so much as bothered to glance at Aquila as they hurried to get to their respective meaningless jobs. Seated at the feet of the legendary Laura Westfield, Aquila felt helplessly alone.

The world was teeming with people, its population exploding like a runaway popcorn machine. Yet, with every new individual that came into existence, the bonds that bound him to all the others of his kind were becoming weaker. Aquila scanned the faces of the people that passed by. They were like little islands floating with the currents of the time, isolated, self-contained units, not connected to anything or anyone. Not bothered even to learn the names of their neighbours. If he disappeared right now, who would notice? He might as well have been a part of the statue that stood behind him.

Aquila sighed and rubbed his eyes. Soon it was going to get too hot for him to sit out here in the open. Reluctantly, he stood up. He heard a familiar voice in the distance and quickly swerved on his feet. Someone was waving at him, and calling out his name from the door of the Ministry. Before Aquila could react, the man had rushed up to him, huffing as he caught his breath. It was his colleague, Dorado, a man he considered a friend and confidante. Or was he? Aquila could no longer be sure.

"Oh hey, buddy," said Dorado, panting, "I just heard the news."

"What news?" Aquila asked, feigning surprise.

"You know … about your … uhm … resignation."

Aquila caught the hint in his friend's voice. Dorado knew something. He cleared his throat. "I see," he began and waited for Dorado to make the next move.

"What are you doing this evening? Say at around seven?" Dorado asked, lowering his voice.

"Umm … nothing, I suppose."

"Good. I get off work at six, and I can come right over. We can chat then, okay?" Dorado looked around to make sure they weren't being overheard. Then he winked lightly, like it was a signal.

Aquila nodded. "Sure. See you then," he replied.

"Good. Now, go straight to your trailer, alright? And don't wander about till we chat tonight," Dorado locked his friend in a firm stare. Then he affectionately patted Aquila on the shoulder, before turning around and rushing off towards the Ministry's entrance.

CHAPTER THREE

Rush hour had passed, and the sun was beating down on the concrete jungle like a raging inferno. Aquila wiped beads of sweat off his forehead with the sleeve of his shirt and looked around him. The traffic had cleared and the street in front of him was deserted. He figured it must be close to ten, which was when the last buses plied in the morning. He headed to the bus stop to catch a ride back to his trailer, before the day-time service ended. Otherwise, he would have to wait until four—when the evening traffic resumed—to get back home. The other option, walking or renting a bike in this sweltering heat, did not seem too palatable.

Aquila was the only passenger on the last morning bus back to his trailer complex. It felt weird. Ever since his childhood, Aquila had learned the basic rules of city life in the twenty-sixth century. Buses take you downtown in the mornings and bring you back in the afternoons. During the in-between hours of maximum ultraviolet exposure, lives and livelihoods are confined inside of doors. Minimizing the hours of traffic, minimizes pollution and energy consumption. Everything was about conservation. Everything.

Fine, he got that. Of course, part of that system always included the buses that plied in the reverse direction during rush-hour—the ones that came back to the trailers from downtown in the mornings—just like the one he was sitting in right now. But Aquila never considered that part of the equation. He assumed that everyone simply went to work in the mornings and returned in the evenings and never the other way around. Today, his solitary bus ride back from work was turning his entire simplistic existence on its head. He was starting to see his world from a flipped perspective, the countercurrent version of reality.

He disembarked at his stop onto a deserted sidewalk and stared languidly at the horizon. A milk-of-magnesia-coloured sky stared back at him, taunting him with its sulphur-dioxide-impregnated haziness. To his right, was the path that would lead him straight to his trailer field, now overgrown with a grassy cover crop that was planted every four years in rotation with the cash crops that were farmed there. Once the winter crop was ready for planting, their trailers would have to move to a winter location—a field that was currently growing its share of summer produce.

When Aquila was a boy, his grandfather would read to him from children's books of the twenty-first century. It made him nostalgic, Grandpa used to say. Though nostalgic for what, Aquila could never tell, since his grandpa had never lived in the twenty-first century. Aquila's favourite memories from those books were the descriptions of villages and countryside, where endless fields stretched to the horizons all year round. There, stalk upon stalk of golden wheat swayed in the mellow breeze, and sunflowers unfurled row after row, with their smiling faces turned towards the sun. Now, such fields dedicated to farming throughout the year were unheard of, if at all they existed.

When did it all come to this? How did we mess up our world so bad? Aquila wondered as he walked in the direction of the canteen trailer. He had never ordered his lunch ration at his home canteen inside the trailer field before. He worried that he would not be allowed to do so when he tried. Approaching with mild trepidation, he tried to appear nonchalant as he swiped his food card at the canteen's kiosk, expecting it to be rejected.

There was a beep.

Aquila sucked in a breath in anticipation.

But instead of the rejection he feared, a food tray opened up invitingly. Breathing a sigh of relief, Aquila glanced over the available menu and grabbed a juicy looking sandwich from the pile along with a pack of dried fruits and nuts. Maybe it was due to the stress from the last few days, maybe the smell of the fresh bread in his hands but either way, Aquila felt famished. He ripped into his sandwich as he walked to his trailer without waiting to get back home. With the food in his stomach, his mind felt dull and foggy. So, all he could think of when he entered his trailer, was to curl up for a nap.

Aquila awoke to the sound of footsteps outside his window. He started for a second before remembering that he was expecting a visitor. He checked the time; almost six thirty. Before he could get up to straighten his clothes, the visitor knocked twice.

"Coming!" Aquila hastily ran his fingers through his ruffled hair and tucked in his shirt, before opening his front door.

Dorado walked in wearing an uncertain half-grin. He was one of those guys who seemed to have perpetually tousled hair. There were the signs of light stubs on his amicable face. He was still wearing his office clothes, a long-sleeved white shirt with the sleeves now rolled up to the elbows and dark pants. "Did I wake you?" he asked, as his eyes scanned Aquila's tired frame from head to toe.

"Hmmm? Yeah ... I mean no."

Dorado grinned and plopped into the nearest chair, setting a tote bag down on the floor next to his feet. "Good. I brought dinner. But we can eat later if you aren't hungry."

Aquila was still kind of full from his lunch. He hesitated and then nodded. "Are you?"

"Nah, I can wait. Come, have a seat. We have stuff to discuss.

Aquila smiled and grabbing his favourite armchair, he turned it around to face his friend. Relaxing into it, he put his foot up on a floating stool. But he remained silent, contemplative, and wondering what this visit was all about. After a moment of awkward silence, still hesitant to broach the subject, he raised a fist to his mouth and coughed into it, as if to clear his throat.

Noticing this hesitation, Dorado leaned forward in his chair and comfortingly patted his friend's knee. "Hey buddy, I know how you feel," he said. "But I want to cut to the chase and tell you that you can trust me. I know everything," he added, lowering his voice.

Aquila was startled. He furrowed his brows and looked searchingly into Dorado's eyes; confusion written all over his face. "What ... do you mean ... know everything?" he stammered.

Dorado pursed his lips, becoming thoughtful. "You know. About what happened. Why you resigned etcetera." He gestured with his hands and shrugged.

"Umm, yeah ... that," Aquila nodded, not sure how to proceed and unconvinced that he could trust Dorado enough to tell him the truth.

"You look like you don't remember much, do you?" Dorado continued, scrunching his face sympathetically. "Well, I don't blame ya. They say you were pretty hammered when you confessed everything. Good thing you did though, 'cause there would've been no way out, come hell or high water, if you'd tried to break into that database while sober!"

Aquila couldn't take it anymore. He was confused out of his mind. He sat up straight and threw up his arms. "Broken into what *database*?" he asked in frustration.

"Look, that's not important. What's important, is that you need to go. Immediately! Leave the country."

"WHAT? That's outrageous!" Aquila stood up abruptly and started pacing up and down. His heart raced inside his chest. Beads of sweat were gathered on his brow. He swerved around and fixing his friend with a firm look, said under his breath, "I have a meeting with Fornax tomorrow morning. I'm not going anywhere."

"No!" Dorado rose from his chair. He walked to his friend, and grabbed him by the arm. "You are *not* meeting with Fornax. Not tomorrow. Not *ever*. Do you understand?" His voice sounded severe and gravelly.

"But why? What have I DONE?" Aquila's exasperation was palpable.

"Buddy, they found drugs in your system. You know that, right? The illegal stuff. And alcohol, of course ... and then the ... the ... security breach—" Dorado sputtered. "Listen!" Dorado grabbed his friend by both arms and shook him emphatically. "Do. As. I. Say."

"Are you trying to say that in a drug induced haze, I accessed secure information, got caught and resigned?"

Dorado released his friend and sighed. "Confessed your mistake and resigned." He hung his head dejectedly. "So, you really remember nothing, eh?"

"Nope. But why?" Aquila murmured.

"Why what?"

"Why did I confess to all this?"

Dorado threw his arms up and shrugged. "I dunno." And then after a moment's pause, "It was a good decision though. Looks like you still had some of your wits about you. If you weren't on drugs, that kinda crime could've gotten your ass locked up for eternity."

Aquila rubbed his chin. "But they'll still arrest me. For the drugs, I mean," he mused.

Dorado nodded in agreement. "That's why you need to get the hell out of here. And soon."

"Leave the county, you say?"

"Yep."

Aquila shook his head in disbelief. "I still don't get it."

"What don't you get?"

"Why did they send me back home? Why not take me into

custody?"

"My friend, that's not the Satellite Police's—"

"Jurisdiction."

Dorado nodded; his face grim.

"Crazy!" said Aquila throwing up his arms.

"True. But this is just the tip of the iceberg," Dorado whispered releasing a breath.

Aquila whisked around to meet his friend's eyes. "How do you mean?" He frowned.

Dorado dismissed the question with a wave of his hand. "Later," he said. "All in good time. But now, what do we do about you? Do you know where you could go? You know, to hide out a bit until your offences are time-barred?"

Aquila dug his hands into his bushy curls clasping fistfuls of them between his fingers, as he paced back and forth. "Shit! Shit! Time-barred? That's like—"

"Five years. The Statute of Limitations is five years," Dorado supplied. "So, do you?"

"Do I what? Oh, right … no … I can't think of anywhere I could go for that long. My family left the United States ages—"

Dorado lifted his hand to stop him mid-sentence. "I know." He paused. "In any case, you would need a serious enough reason to leave the country and loads of money. A sponsor. A powerful one …" he mumbled almost to himself. Suddenly, his eyes lit up and he snapped his fingers. "Got it!" He pulled up a chair and sat down, resting his elbows on his knees. "I have just the place for you." He flashed a wicked grin.

Aquila raised his eyebrows, looking incredulous. "What? How?" He dropped into a chair as he spoke, a frown written across his face.

"Remember how I returned last year? From a project abroad?"

Aquila narrowed his eyes. "In Indochine. Yes? But what's that got to do with me?"

"Ah! Hear me out, my friend. Hear me out."

"I'm listening."

"Well, that project needs more people. I'm really close to the guy in charge, The District Manager. If I can get him to requisition you, you'll be outta here in no time. Security clearances and all."

"Hmm. I see. What about the charges against me?"

"It'll take a day or two for the Satellite Police to hand over your files to local authorities. They're super bureaucratic. By then you will be long gone." Dorado checked the time on the trailer's control centre. "It's not even seven. If I call tonight, you can leave by this time tomorrow."

Aquila wiped the sweat off his forehead and relaxed into his chair becoming thoughtful.

"What are you thinking, buddy?" Dorado asked with a slap to Aquila's knee.

"I'm thinking ..." Aquila chewed his lower lip and continued. "I'm thinking ... why are you doing this for me? What's in it for you?"

The muscles in Dorado's face tightened. "Because." He rubbed his forehead and looked Aquila straight in the eye. "We are living in dangerous times, and I want to make sure someone out there will have my back if I ever need it one day."

"So, you're trying to put me in your debt?" Aquila laughed.

"Something like that." Dorado shrugged, grinning ear to ear.

"Fair enough. Shall we eat? I'm hungry!"

"Oh yeah, of course." Dorado stood up to unload the dinner boxes from his tote bag and set them on the coffee table.

"So, tell me," Aquila said, biting into a sliver of synthetic roast beef, "what is this project that you're sending me to?"

"Oh, it's a huge conservation project. You'd be perfect for it. They have all the farmlands down there. You know that right?"

"Yeah, I do. So, drip irrigation stuff?"

"You got it! And there's climate control too. It's a huge enterprise. You'll see when you get there." Dorado replied between his munching.

"Interesting. How did you get sent up there?"

"Oh, it was all Orion's idea ... you know the District Manager? He's a pal of mine. We grew up together. He's been at that project for a decade now."

"Good for you. But as for me, I dunno ... I've never been abroad, don't know anyone there ..." Aquila sighed. "It's a bit daunting, to say the least."

"Ah c'mon! You'll be fine. Much better in fact, than in jail," Dorado assured with a chuckle.

"True that!" Aquila guffawed in his natural lighthearted way.

"Besides, they have *real* booze down there," Dorado added with a sly grin before taking a sip from a bottle of boring water.

"You don't say! How come?"

"Oh, it's still legal down there. One of the few places in the world where it still is. Supply is limited, of course. But the officers get access. So, you should be fine."

"Interesting, I didn't know that. I mean I've studied a lot of world history and never came across—"

"Speaking of history," Dorado interrupted, "I almost forgot! You're a history buff, aren't you?"

"Yeah, kind of. I mean, why do you ask?"

"Perfect," Dorado exclaimed, slapping his knee. "Oh, you're gonna love it there. They have a real treasure for history enthusiasts like you. Have you ever been to the world history museum in Moscow?"

"Have I *ever*? Yes, of course. I used to be up there all the time when I was younger. One of my favourite haunts, when I need a break from life."

"Then you'll know what I'm talking about. Do you remember the section with the historical archives of each country from before the Great Deluge?"

"Indeed," Aquila replied enthusiastically.

"Did you ever notice something off about those records?"

"Umm ... I ... how do you mean?"

"Okay, let me cut to the chase," Dorado said. "You see, all the great cities of the world that sank during the tsunami, managed to salvage most of their historical records till that point and save them for posterity. All but one. The complete history of the French city of Paris, and by extension that of France, has never really been recovered. The museum mentions this in their French history section. You must have known this?"

"Ah okay! Yeah, I knew that. So what?"

"It never struck you as odd?"

Aquila shrugged. "No. Why should it? It happens with history. Sometimes things get lost."

"Hmm. But why only *specific* things? The entire history of Paris isn't lost. Anyway, if you hear the rest of the story then you'll understand why I think this whole business is pretty odd."

"Go on then. Enlighten me."

"Alright. So, about ten years ago an unmanned military aircraft exploded in mid-air over the Pacific Ocean and its remains were never found. You've probably never heard the news because it was such an insignificant event back then, with no real damage or loss of life, that the media never covered it. The only reason I know is because, a diver from Orion's team inspecting their sea water distillation system, discovered the wreckage, while I was working down there. Orion immediately sent a few more divers with him to check out the site and bring back anything that looked valuable." Dorado paused for breath.

"This is getting interesting. Go on."

Dorado smiled. "Well guess what they found underwater!"

"The missing records?"

"Part of it. Yeah. Only some digital files with holograms. None of the real artefacts, like paintings etc. that went missing, but still a significant bit of digital stuff."

"Hmm. So did they hand these over to the museum?" Aquila asked.

Dorado leaned forward and began in a near whisper, "No, of course not ..."

Aquila frowned in confusion.

"It's sensitive material. Orion ... well, he's kept it under wraps until he figures out what to do with the stuff."

"You mean, he plans to wield it like a bargaining chip?"

"Maybe." Dorado shrugged. "So, keep it to yourself, okay?"

"Sure. Does his team know?"

"I don't think so. Not many know besides me. Only the ones he trusts."

"Interesting."

"It is. But my point is, if you can gain his confidence, then he might show them to you. Knowing that I trust you and all," Dorado explained.

"Should I ask him about it?"

"Not right away. Wait a bit. Feel him out. If you think you've gained his trust, then you can tell him that I told you about the God of War files. He'll know what you mean and probably share it with you."

"God of War files, eh? Why do they call it that?"

"You'll find out when you see the tapes." Dorado winked mischievously.

"Now you've really piqued my curiosity." Aquila chuckled. "So, when do I go?" he added with a grin.

"Right. I better get started with that then. What time is it?" He checked the time. "Seven thirty," he said, getting up. "Let's call it a night, my friend. I'll talk to Orion and get the ball rolling for you as soon as I get home. In the meantime, get packed and wait for my message. You might need to leave tomorrow." Dorado patted his friend's shoulder and flashed him a half grin before rushing out the door into the foggy dusk outside.

CHAPTER FOUR

"Aquila didn't sleep a wink that night. After packing a couple of bags with the essentials for his impending journey, he lay on his back with his arms folded under his head, staring at the ceiling just like he used to as a boy, especially in those grim few months following his mother's death. He thought about Dorado, his words, their friendship, the incredibly kind offer he had made—one that could save Aquila from a great deal of undeserved harassment. They had known each other for a while, but never before had Aquila contemplated on the nature of their friendship. He had no need to. But now, it was different. He was on the brink of embarking on a potentially life-altering journey, based on the assurance of this man. So, he had to decide if he trusted him. And he had to do it soon.

They had met years ago, when Aquila first joined the Ministry, shortly after his internship. More than a decade had passed. Yet, Aquila had never really sat down to reflect on how much he trusted Dorado or even how much he actually knew the guy. Yes, they were in the same department. Yes, he was exceptionally smart. Very dependable. Everyone trusted him. But was that enough? What if it was all a front, a façade? And behind it, who knew what kind of a deceptive monster might lurk?

Aquila broke out in a cold sweat. His apprehensions distressed him. Standing up quickly, he began pacing up and down the room with his arms folded behind his back.

"Calm down, calm down," he whispered to himself. He drank a glass of water and leaned forward to set the water bottle down on his bedside table. As he did so, an object caught his eye. He picked it up. It was a framed 3D image of his mom, smiling just as he remembered her. Picking up the frame, he smiled back at her and his eyes welled up. The same hazel eyes as hers. He remembered what she used to say to him about people.

"Trust no one," she always said. And when he objected, she would smile that very same kindly smile and ruffle his hair.

"A person's face is a mirror to their soul," she would then explain. "Look at a person's face. I mean, really look. Deeply beyond their external features. Then you'll know. In your heart you will know if they're worth your trust. People wear many masks, but if you can train your eyes to look beyond that mask, then you'll pierce right through it and know what they're really about. You will have discovered their soul. Do you know what I mean?"

Back then, Aquila did not know what she meant. But off late he had become more perceptive. Reflecting on this piece of wisdom he tried to picture Dorado's face—his chubby cheeks, the amiable assuring grin that lit up his amber eyes, his dirty blonde hair that seemed to appear ruffled at all times. He could not remember ever having seen any malice there. And then there was that incident some five years ago, when he had had his back at a team meeting after Aquila's weekly report had failed to satisfy the fastidious and exacting Fornax.

Aquila paced some more and furrowing his forehead, recalled other happy memories with his friend; the after-work conversations over alcohol, the weekend trips to the mountains, the laughter, the games. Sometimes there were others with them, but somehow Dorado and Aquila had often found themselves in each other's company at events. In a world teeming with people, true human connections were so few and far between, that Aquila had always imagined himself to be a lone wolf. He was probably not alone in thinking this way. This seemed to be the mantra of the generation. But now, after this brief reflection, something inside his heart lit up. A realization was born—a feeling of love and brotherhood. For the first time in his life, Aquila felt that he was not completely alone. He had a friend. At least one friend he could trust. And that friend was Dorado.

Having quieted his nagging trust issues, Aquila sat down at his writing desk and leaned forward on his elbows with his head between his hands. He knew right away that there would be no sleep for him that night. He had a lot of questions to ask Dorado before he set off on his new adventure. And then, there was the matter of settling his affairs at home. He would be gone a long time, so he couldn't leave everything in disarray as he ran like a coward, a thief. He bent around his desk to pull out his tablet from his luggage and started making notes. He jotted down the things he needed to sort out before he left the country, in the sequence that they occurred to him in his anxious frame of mind. Before long, he dozed off, slouching over his folded arms with his forehead balanced on the tablet.

* * *

When the phone rang at the break of dawn, Aquila nearly fell off his chair. It took him a second or two to gather himself before he answered the call. Dorado didn't waste much time getting straight to the matter at hand. Everything was arranged. Orion was excited to have Aquila on board. Aquila's trailer home would be subleased out. The belongings he decided to leave behind were to be stowed away in safety. Dorado would take care of all that. And finally, did he have any questions?

"Oh yes, important point," Aquila responded. "I need to see the paperwork."

"The paperwork?"

"For the assignment, I mean. The terms, the pay etcetera. You know, the usual jam."

"Ah, for sure. I already sent them to you and I hope you don't mind, but I took the liberty of sharing your résumé from our files with Orion …"

"No, I don't mind. Not at all. Do I need to send you the signed—"

"Offer? Yes, you need to send it back, but not to me. You'll see that I've copied Orion. Once you've reviewed everything just sign and send it back to him."

"Great. How much time do I have?"

"Well, Orion needs the offer back by noon, but your flight isn't until the evening. So, you still have time to pack."

"Oh, I'm already packed. Will you come and get me when it's time to leave?"

"No. It's safer if we meet at the airport. Your flight is at eight, so I'll be in front of security at seven, to see you off. Sounds good?"

"Ah wait, did you say security?" Aquila asked in a tensed tone.

"Yeah, why?"

"Oh, I mean … the thing is …"

"What's up buddy? You sound unsure … oh I get it! Are you worried about harassment?"

"Kind of, yes. Where are you? At work?"

"Me? No, of course not! I'm at home. Took the day off to plan your escape!" Dorado laughed out loud. "So, yeah you can speak freely. What are you worried about?"

"I wonder if they're looking for me. In which case, going through airport security might be an issue."

"Got it. But you don't need to stress out about that. Orion's project has its own private transport for executives and top officials. I guess you've never flown before, so let me give you the basics about airport security. It's not centralized. Each entity with an air passage clearance, handles its own security. Orion's men will check his carriers and he's too high up in the system for the local government to mess with his protocols. So, you're in good hands. Orion is no Fornax, mind you. He's a real big shot!"

"I see. Well, that's certainly a relief. I'll see you at seven then?"

"You bet. Ciao, for now!" And with that Dorado hung up and left Aquila with his paperwork to complete.

* * *

In the evening, Aquila hired a private cab for the first time in his life, because he didn't want to risk being seen by too many. It cost him a fortune. He knew that private cab costs were kept artificially inflated in order to discourage their frequent use. Still, he didn't expect it to cost him more than half of the cash he was carrying with him on his journey. Anyway, it couldn't be helped. He had to escape unnoticed and the window was closing fast. Sitting in his cab, he jolted a little at this thought. Here he was, planning an escape. An *actual escape*! The words repeated themselves in a recursive loop inside his head. He had never imagined having to become a fugitive. Yet, such was his fate and he didn't even know why. He would have to find out. But now was not the time to ask such questions. He would have enough time during his long exile in Indochine. His contract was signed. Five and a half years. Yes, that was plenty. He paid his driver and disembarked with his luggage.

It was six o'clock when Aquila reached the airport. He still had an hour to kill before Dorado's arrival. He dropped his luggage off at the public locker and proceeded to wander around the terminal. It was a moderately sized airport. Around a dozen daily flights plied in and out of it, and not more than fifty people milled around the terminal building at this hour. So, Aquila got quickly bored. He had heard about the famous aircraft museum—featuring pre-World War VI commercial and military planes—tucked away in the eastern wing of the building. He decided to go there to kill time.

Fortunately, the museum was open. It was the hundred-year anniversary of the International Resolution on Commercial Aircraft Ban, so extended hours were in place. Of course, air travel had already trickled to a minimum before the ban was instated, but the Resolution was the final nail in that coffin. The remaining commercial carriers were given Government handouts to pay pensions to their staff and shut down their operations by the end of that year. Centuries of lobbying by the aerospace industry came to naught in the face of the rising current of green activism. The remaining carbon intensive aircrafts in their inventory were relinquished to the Government, to be displayed in museums such as the one Aquila was about to tour. Aquila was impressed with their collection. Airbuses, Airhippos, Airwhales, they had them all—from twenty-seater domestic models to three-storied, thousand-seater Airwhales of the mid-twenty-fifth century. They even had some of the older solar-powered models that served as an inspiration for the modern-day crafts.

Aquila wrapped up his museum visit in about half an hour, picked up his luggage and headed to the security clearance area. Dorado was waiting for him with a broad grin on his face.

"You made it!" He chuckled, extending his arms for a hug.

"Yes, it looks like I did," Aquila replied with anticipation in his heart.

"Here, I brought you something for your trip but you mustn't open it till you get there. Promise?" He asked, handing his friend a soft bundle, the size of a cushion, inside a buttoned-up cotton bag.

"What is it?" Aquila asked, pressing the packaging to get a feel of what might be inside. "Clothes? Shoes?"

Dorado shrugged. "It's a surprise," he said shyly.

"But why can't I open it?"

"You can. After you get there, that is. If you open it here, you won't appreciate its value. Trust me on this one, buddy," he explained with a friendly pat on Aquila's back. "Now, let's get to business. You brought your trailer keys and the lease etcetera?"

"Ah, yes! Where did I put it?" Aquila bent over his backpack and started searching its main pocket. "Here, you go." He recovered the small envelope he was looking for and extended it to his friend.

"Perfect. It's almost time. So, I'll let you head to security. Just follow the sign that says, 'Project Redistribution' and you'll find Orion's staff. Nervous?"

"A little," Aquila confessed.

"Don't be. I was pretty nervous too when I left, but I came back a changed man. You'll change too, and you'll be the better for it." Dorado assured with a wink.

"Alright then. Hopefully, we'll stay in touch."

"Of course," said Dorado, raising his hand to his forehead in a farewell salute.

Aquila shook his companion's hand and turned towards the security gate. He didn't have to go far, before a uniformed woman greeted him from behind a kiosk.

"Your name?" she asked with a straight face.

"Aquila."

"Aquila, what?"

"Huh?" Aquila looked up at her with a perplexed expression on his face.

"I mean, do you have a last name, Sir?"

"Umm, no. Whoever does, in the twenty-sixth century?"

"Oh, where you're going, plenty still do," she replied in a matter-of-fact way. "Please look into the scanner."

Aquila turned his head to the retinal scanner and saw a tiny dot of light across his visual field.

"Okay, you're good. Please step onto the walkway," the lady concluded, pointing Aquila to the movable path to her left.

Before Aquila could do as he was instructed, a small robot arrived with a luggage cart attached to its rear. "How many items of luggage?" it asked him in a rather monotonous voice.

"Umm ... two. Just this and this." Aquila pointed.

The robot glided forward and began hauling the bags onto its trolly as Aquila stepped to his right and alighted the movable walkway.

Noticing this, the lady in the kiosk lowered her head and whispered into a microphone. "Activate implant scan." Aquila barely heard the words before his walkway began to move.

He arrived a few feet away, in front of the door to a small chamber. The walkway led Aquila into the chamber and stopped. The door closed behind him. The doorway leading out of the chamber had already been shut. Aquila was trapped.

Aquila was aware of the process of implanting and always feared it. People were implanted for security purposes all the time—top military brass, government officials entrusted with classified state secrets, law enforcement personnel, politicians, high profile criminals and so many others. But Aquila was not that important, so he had nothing to worry about. Yet somehow, he felt an uneasiness creep up his gut. Did he have a chip implanted somewhere in his body that he did not know about? Beads of sweat appeared on his brow and his heart thundered against his rib-cage.

To calm himself, he focussed his attention on his own image reflected off the glass-like chamber wall in front of him. He had gained a bit of weight lately, as was evident from the gently undulating landscape around his tummy. His tan complexion had darkened a shade or two—to a golden, honey-brown. His frequent field visits for work might have contributed to this. His hair was beginning to grey around the sideburns and right above his temple. But other than that, he was still pretty energetic and healthy. A towering six feet of muscle interspersed with a few unwanted layers of not overly cumbersome fat. His face was still handsome and youthful, set with a square jaw and expressive hazel eyes beneath its long dark lashes.

"Commence scan," said a disembodied robotic voice, waking Aquila from his reverie. He gulped once. Twice. A beam of light scanned his frame from head to toe and then his outline appeared on the wall in front of him, replacing his reflection that had been there a second ago. Aquila took in the electronic image. It was a milky white recreation of his physical shape enclosed inside a dark border. It resembled an image from a children's colouring book. As he was smiling to himself at this thought, a blinking red dot appeared near the figure's right wrist, and an alarm sounded inside the chamber. The door from which Aquila had entered opened, and a security guard marched in, armed with a rod-like instrument.

"Your right hand, please." The guard had a gruff voice.

Aquila wiped his brow with his left hand and extended the other for examination. The guard grabbed his wrist in a firm grip and roughly turned it over. "This might tingle a bit," he said, as he placed the tip of the rod on Aquila's wrist. He then dragged the rod—which appeared to be a scanner of some sort—across the wrist three times. The scanner emitted a pulsating beep. Aquila held his breath and closed his eyes. He felt a sort of static flow through his arm.

After a minute, which felt like an eon, the guard looked up and spoke.

"All set. You can proceed to boarding." He turned and walked out of the enclosure. The door exiting the chamber opened, and the walkway started to move again. Aquila let out a deep sigh. His first hurdle was over.

The wait at the boarding lounge was brief. Aquila seated himself with half a dozen other passengers, as their aircraft taxied down the tarmac towards its appointed gate. In a few minutes, they were ready to board, and no further security screens were conducted. Before proceeding to his flight, Aquila took a moment to check out the rest of the passengers. There were four ladies and two other gentlemen travelling with him that day. They were all dressed in business attire and seemed not to know one another. Among them, a petite lady in a sunny floral top and pleated skirt attracted his particular attention. She had an oval face with a small, pudgy nose with soft dark brown hair that fell in ripples around her shoulders. She was not conventionally beautiful. Yet, there was a tender radiance in her features and a glow in her jet-black eyes that held Aquila's gaze a tad longer than was appropriate. Realizing this, he blushed and averted his eyes at once. He then trotted awkwardly to board his flight.

Once inside, Aquila noticed that the aircraft was a standard issue unmanned model, with a couple of robots in the crew for company. The interior of the craft however, exceeded all his expectations. For starters, there were individual compartments with lockable doors for each passenger, all equipped with their own attendant request features. Aquila's cabin contained a plush twin bed with fluffy pillows and a duvet, a coffee table, an armchair and an entertainment station. The compartment was redolent of lavender and potpourri. A large window decked the far wall of the room, offering magnificent views of the open skies beyond. The lavishness of this arrangement alone, assured Aquila of the power and position his new manager undoubtedly commanded. He felt a little awed by this, but at the same time he felt fortunate to have been offered this role.

"Sir, would you like any refreshments before take-off," an attendant glided in to ask.

Aquila whisked around from gazing out the window to shake his head in response. "No, I'm fine."

"Alright, Sir. Call me if you need anything. We'll be taking off momentarily," the robot announced, before gliding out of the room again.

Aquila closed his cabin door and made himself comfortable on the bed. On a screen in front of him, a holo started playing with the takeoff guidelines. The lady in the visual informed her viewers how to activate their magnetic seat-belts, how to exit the aircraft and how to disengage their cubicles—which doubled as flotation pods—in case of an emergency landing on water. The robotic cockpit then took over, welcomed the guests, explained the features of the flight and predicted a flight time of a little under six hours, depending on the weather. It discussed the seemingly never-ending list of onboard entertainments, pointed out where to find the vessel's extensive menu for the two meals included, and finished by wishing everyone a very pleasant flight.

Once the announcements were over, Aquila switched off the broadcast and fastening his seatbelt, relaxed into his bed with a pillow under his head. In a mere six hours, a brand-new life would begin for him. He wanted to use the interim period to simply process his thoughts and nothing else.

CHAPTER FIVE

A t the other end of the world, Alrakis arrived at Carina's floating mansion in Revolution City a little before seven—almost at the very instant that Aquila's flight took off from Moscow. Although a Calamerican like his superior, Alrakis did not live in the capital city or rather could not afford that luxury, given his pay-grade. Nevertheless, his closeness to Carina ensured that he was a frequent dinner guest at his Secretary of State's lavish residence. He scanned his wrist-chip at the entrance, letting the massive glass doors of the dome-shaped mansion spring open at once.

This was Carina's personal home, but as long as she remained in office, it had to be leased out to the Government, as the official residence of the nation's second in command. Carina however, had been very strict about the terms of the lease she had given them. There was to be no Government snooping, no tapping of communication lines and no security personnel other than the ones she approved of. In other words, complete freedom and privacy within her own home was to be guaranteed. At first, there had been some opposition from top officials, but eventually they relented. A lifelong activist and patriot, Carina was known for her fiery temperament and her beloved status among the people. No one with an iota of political wisdom expected to offend her and get away with it unscathed.

Alrakis strode into Carina's living room, wearing his typically playful grin, to find her lounging in an armchair, nursing a tea cup between her palms.

"Evening," he said, with a little nod.

"Good evening. Been a while since the last time we met, eh? How have you been?" Carina's voice was gentle but firm and exuded a confidence, not uncommon among politicians of her rank.

Alrakis shrugged. "Not too bad, I suppose."

"You look tired. Anything wrong?"

Alrakis rubbed his forehead wearily. "Nothing out of the ordinary, but yeah, I haven't slept much in a while. Plus ..." He looked up and flashed Carina a coy grin. "... I haven't had lunch. I thought there would be food," he concluded, as he mockingly scanned the room for the missing edibles.

"Tch tch! Cocky as usual!" Carina broke into a laugh. She set her cup down on a coffee table and rose from her seat as she spoke. "Come, they're probably getting it ready as we speak."

Alrakis followed his hostess out of the living room and into the adjacent dining hall where dinner was being served. A robot was setting the table, as lovely aromas emerged from the kitchen door behind it. Seeing them enter, the robot issued a routine greeting, seated them at the table and promptly excused itself in order to fetch their dinner.

The prim little robot promptly returned with a loaded tray and started arranging the courses across the dining table in a buffet-style setting. As it did so, Alrakis noticed that it was a male. The design was humanoid, similar to most other models of its kind, and it was organically grown to resemble a living entity. But what struck Alrakis, was a tiny red patch just under its left ear that indicated self-regenerating capability. It was certainly an advanced feature in domestic robots and unsurprising that Carina would have one on her staff, but this was just her kitchen help. Not a security robot or body guard. Alrakis wondered if it could mean that all her staff were in some capacity trained to defend her, if the need arose. He was about to ask her, but the robot interrupted him.

"Dinner is served, Madam, Sir. Bon appétit." It bowed formally and spun around before promptly leaving the room.

Alrakis' stomach growled, as the fragrance of the freshly made dinner filled up his senses. He quickly lost his train of thoughts and started to fill his plate instead. Carina too helped herself to some of the food. It was a strictly vegetarian fare as was customary in her household. But today was special since she was entertaining a guest after a very long time. Naturally, she had ordered some of her chef's special items. Biting into a rather juicy honey-roasted carrot, she sighed with satisfaction.

"Mmmm ... it's so good to eat real food once in a while, isn't it?" she asked.

"For sure," replied Alrakis, gulping down his salad. "I know why *I* don't eat well, but who's stopping *you* from eating like this everyday?"

Carina looked up with a sad smile but said nothing.

"Something troubling you?" Alrakis asked.

"No," she replied. Then after a short pause, she continued. "I rarely eat down here anymore, you know ..."

"Oh? How come?"

Carina shrugged. "This table is a bit much for me alone. I have a smaller dining area in my study, where I eat packaged meals on most days."

"Ahem, it's probably not my place to ask but ..." he paused to search for words.

"But what?"

"I mean, what about Mizar? Doesn't she eat with you? I know it'd suck to eat down here in the big hall all by yourself, but when Mizar—"

Carina raised her hand to stop him mid-sentence. "There's no Mizar," she said abruptly.

"Whaaaat? You ... you ... broke up?" he asked, lowering

his voice to a sympathetic whisper.

"No. Not exactly. Not in so many words, at least. But she hasn't been home in months." Carina bent over her plate to reach for some couscous. "She's been busy reporting on international affairs, she says. Apparently, that's what's keeping her out of the country. But my gut tells me otherwise."

"How do you mean? She could genuinely be travelling for work, no? I mean she *is* a journalist after all!"

"True. And she's been away before. If you think about it, ever since we've been together, she's travelled every couple of months at least. And been away for ten … fifteen days at a stretch. But this time was different."

"How so?"

"One morning, I woke up, and she had left. She didn't tell me anything in advance, didn't leave a note. Didn't even call right away. It took her a week to bother to explain herself. Even then, it was very cursory. Like it meant nothing. Like I was nothing. Nobody." Carina sniffed as a lone tear glistened on her right cheek. She quickly wiped it with the back of her palm.

Alrakis reached out and gently squeezed her hand with his. "I'm sorry," he said softly. "Did she explain why she left so abruptly?"

"She said it was a top-secret project, and her life could have been in danger. Or even mine." Carina paused to drink some water. "I understand that. Of course, I do. In my profession, my life is almost *always* in danger. But why hide it from me, when I have access to the world's greatest security and intelligence networks? In fact, discussing it with me would've been to her benefit. I could've protected us both."

"So, you think she was lying?"

"More like hiding something …"

"What do you think it might be? Did you have a fight? A disagreement? Could there be someone else?"

"Oh no, no. I don't think it's anything like that. Nothing personal at all. I suspect it might be political"

"*Really?*" Alrakis sat up straight in surprise. "But I always thought she shared your political views. How did you even end up with her if she didn't?"

"She did, indeed. To a certain extent obviously. No two people can ever hold the exact same views on any topic, can they? So yeah, we did have the same values and so on. But there are nuances. It's not so simple. Her upbringing has been very different from mine, after all."

"I see. So, she's not from Revolution City then?"

"She kind of is. Her family moved here when she was a teenager. They're originally from the American Republic. They come from a long line of heartlander farmers."

"You don't say! So how come they came here?"

"They defected during the Farmer's Revolt, when the Government put them on a watchlist for inciting insurrection."

"Oh! Did they still have farms up there?"

"They did, but production was at rock bottom due to ground-water shortage, and they couldn't compete with the prices from the huge establishments in Indochine. The influx of produce from The Redistribution Project, at dirt cheap prices, was severely impacting their bottom line. The corporates were at their heels trying to run them out of business or to buy them out for a pittance. So, they joined the revolt, but the authorities started cracking down real hard on the dissenters and ..."

"They moved here."

"Yep. The Government confiscated their land and put out arrest warrants. They applied for refugee status and settled down in Revolution City."

"Defectors from the Republic, eh? That's pretty bold. Do you think some of that sentiment still lingers in her mind? Like the idea that the heartlanders are the true patriots and we're a bunch of traitor secessionists over here in Calamerica?"

"Maybe not in such strong terms, but yeah, I've often wondered about it. And then, there were some hints from her too. I dunno ... either way, I think it's our politics that's driving a rift between us."

"Hmmm. That *would* certainly make sense. The secrecy etcetera ... would make sense in that context," Alrakis mused, as he rubbed his chin. "*But,* for your sake and hers, I do certainly hope you're just worrying too much over an innocent business trip."

Carina shook her head in frustration. "I hope so too, but I doubt it. You know I'm not the worrying kind, right?"

"Gotta agree with you on that one." Alrakis chuckled.

"But enough about me. What's going on with you? Why haven't *you* been sleeping well?"

"It's nothing. The usual. It's been stressful lately, as you know."

"Hmmm. I see what you mean. A storm is brewing. I can feel it in my bones."

"By the way, speaking of a storm, what ever happened with that bureaucrat? He's dropped off my radar."

"You mean, Aquila?"

"Yep, that one."

"They're off his trail as far as I know. He should be safe for now."

"Good. I was worried about him," Alrakis confessed, as he wiped his mouth with his napkin and set it down beside his plate. God, I need a steep drink," he added with a guffaw.

"Well, I have some punch." Carina's lips curled into a sly grin.

"With *real* alcohol?"

"*Of course* not! What do you take me for? An opportunistic hypocrite? I was one of the first people to fight for the ban on potable alcohol, you know? And now, you expect me to toss out a lifetime of activism to indulge in the very thing I fought to eliminate?"

"There, there. Calm down, will you?" Alrakis consoled. "I don't support using food crops for alcohol production, either. I mean, what a gargantuan waste of resources! I thought ... well, never mind."

"Were you thinking, I had some lab produced booze up

here?"

"Maybe." Alrakis shrugged. "But nah, those are super expensive to mix in a drink. The affordable ones are injectable-only. So yeah, just ignore what I said and tell me what's in that punch of yours." He chuckled, his eyes dancing.

"It's a light opioid. I also have cannabis. What do you prefer?"

"I'll go with the cannabis, if you don't mind."

"Sure, I'll order some." Carina leaned forward to ring for her kitchen help. "Do you want to have it out on the balcony? I could use some fresh air ..."

"That'd be lovely," Alrakis replied as he got up.

When Alrakis stepped onto Carina's balcony, the sun had just set, and the azure expanse of the Pacific Ocean was tinted with a blood-orange hue. He moved closer to the railing that surrounded the half-moon-shaped hanging structure and gazed into the distance. Before him, he saw other dome-shaped buildings with baby blue roofs, suspended like soap bubbles on the sleepy waters. Some of these buildings were nested like the compound eyes of gigantic sea-insects, lurking just beneath the waves. Others were almost translucent and often glowing with other-worldly phosphorescence. Sometimes, one dome was connected to the next with a covered passage that looked like the bridge of a pair of eye-glasses. Other domes stood all by themselves like the torn petals of water lilies. Their collective lights reflected from the water like a million floating candles. For as far as his eyes could see, such bubbles of human habitation erupted from the ocean's bosom like the pimples of civilization. The endless city unfolded before him and extended to the horizon. Alrakis could not tear his eyes away from this mesmerizing scene. Consequently, he didn't notice when Carina appeared behind him carrying two goblets of punch.

"Hey," she said, lightly touching his upper arm. "Punch?"

"Yeah, thanks," he replied accepting the drug-laced drink. He took a sip and turned to admire the view. "Beautiful, isn't it?" he murmured.

"It sure is!"

"Oh, look! What are those?" he exclaimed, pointing to the western horizon, where a flock of something could be seen splashing in and out of the water.

Carina squinted to focus on where he was pointing. "Flying fish, I think. We're seeing them a lot lately, since they banned all the boats."

"Fascinating." Alrakis grinned ear to ear.

Carina sipped her punch and leaning over the railing, sighed deeply. "It certainly is. And why wouldn't it be? It's our capital. The oldest city in our realm," she said.

"Indeed, it is. It's like what, a hundred and eighty years old?"

"The new city, yeah. But Revolution City existed even before Calamerica. When California officially seceded from the USA, Revolution City was founded as the seat of the movement. The first city of the secessionists, really."

"Yeah, I knew that." Alrakis winced and stuck out his tongue.

"Of course, you did." Carina winked. "When the Great Deluge happened and the other coastal cities were flooded, despite their walls and dams—"

"That's when the other states seceded and Calamerica was born. Yep, knew that already. My history's a bit rusty, but I retained all the basics."

"You better have!" Carina admonished. "You work for the Government. You represent our nation. It's your job to know these things."

"Among others," Alrakis replied, looking slightly abashed.

"Have you ever seen the city from the sky?"

"Of course, I have. Why?"

"I mean from really high up? Like a satellite station for example?"

"I … don't believe so … I'm usually too busy when I'm up at a satellite station to find time to enjoy the view."

Carina scrunched her face at this remark. "Is that a dig at me, Alrakis?"

"Oh no, Ma'am. I would never *dare*!" Alrakis replied in mock alarm.

"Anyway," Carina resumed with a playful grin, "as I was saying … from the sky, the city looks like a pair of eyes with blue irises. Because of the way the suburbs have grown around the center."

"Wow! I didn't actually know that. Is that where the nickname for the city came from? The Eyes of The Nation?"

"Of course! Why don't you come to live down here? To the capital? It will make you feel more connected to the heart of our politics and history."

"Me? On *my* salary?" Alrakis laughed out loud. "It's a pipe dream."

"Hmmm. How about if you move in here? I won't charge you rent. Mizar's gone and I could use some company. Besides, we have plenty to do before the Armaments Resolution. It'd make sense to have you around."

"Ha! You're funny."

Carina turned around to look him directly in the eyes. "I'm not joking," she said with a straight face.

"Oh, you aren't? Hmmm … but that would be unprofessional, no? Being roomies with your boss?"

"In a normal situation, probably. But as you know, we have our mission. And The Underground. It's an unprecedented time and situation."

"I agree. But you don't think it would raise suspicion? Or risk exposing The Underground?"

"You're my top aide. It's not unusual to want to have your aides close before a huge international resolution gets debated. What happens after the Armaments' debate is a different story, but we can cross that bridge when we get there."

Alrakis nodded. "I see your point." He fell silent for a bit. "Alright, you've convinced me. And truth be told, I did always want to live in Revolution City. So, why not now?"

"Exactly." Carina smiled and turned towards the ocean. Then, closing her eyes she breathed in the warm salty air. For the first time in a long while, she felt a deep and abiding sense of calm.

CHAPTER SIX

S hortly before daybreak the following day, Aquila's flight landed at the Lucknow airport, in the heart of Indochine. He opened his cubicle door to find his attendant robot waiting to see him off.

"Good day, Sir," it said. "Here's your disembarkation suit." And with that, it shoved a lumpy package into Aquila's hands and whirled off into the next cubicle.

With this bundle under his arm, Aquila made for the exit ramp and was the first to land on the tarmac. He stepped out of the hermetically sealed ramp and gasped.

He was choking.

He seized his throat with both hands and sucked in large mouthfuls of air. His throat burned. His eyes were on fire. He collapsed to his knees and tried to scream.

"Gahh," was all that came out of his mouth.

Then, there were strong arms pulling him to his feet. "Sir, you didn't wear your suit?" A voice was screaming from his side.

He was being pulled back onto the ramp. An oxygen mask was strapped to his face. Air, fresh air at last! Aquila breathed in, greedily filling his lungs to capacity. Everything started to come back into focus. He noticed a man standing next to him.

A real man, not a robot. But he was strangely dressed. The man spoke.

"Mister Aquila?" he asked.

"Yes, that's me," said Aquila from under the mask. Looking up, he realized that the other man was also masked. Additionally, he was wearing a safety suit of some sort.

"Please Sir, put on your suit. The exposure wasn't deadly, but could've been avoided." The man pulled out a hazmat suit from the disembarkation package and handed it to Aquila.

The suit was made of sinolium, a very comfortable and airy material, offering advanced levels of protection. The head-piece had a transparent window for the eyes and an opening below it to accommodate an oxygen mask. Aquila got busy putting on his suit and mask. When he was done, the other man came up to him to make sure the gear was securely fastened. "Why didn't you put it on earlier?" he then asked.

"I didn't know I had to," Aquila confessed.

"Didn't you listen to the landing instructions?"

"No. I fell asleep."

"Okay, that explains it. Come, the District Manager must have sent someone to pick you up."

"You mean Orion?"

"Correct. Please, follow me."

Aquila followed his escort out of the exit ramp and stepped onto the tarmac again. This time, he was breathing fine. He looked around him to find that he stood inside a much larger airport than the one from which he had departed. Yet, surprisingly enough, it was a lot emptier. In fact, there were no other aircrafts in sight at that hour. Despite the lack of traffic however, the airport was heavily militarized. Aquila didn't understand why such security was necessary, but he didn't feel comfortable asking his companion. Instead, he asked him about something else that he found strange.

"Where is everyone?" he said.

His escort looked confused. "Ummm … yours was our only flight today, if that's what you were asking."

"I see. And where are my co-passengers?" Aquila turned his head from side to side, scanning the area as he spoke.

"When you had that ... er ... emergency earlier, they were led out through the other exit. They must've left by now." He looked curiously at Aquila and held open the door to the terminal. "You're new here, eh?" he then asked.

"Ha! I am. I'm sure it wasn't hard to guess, given my actions earlier." Aquila chuckled.

His companion smiled before leading him into a small room with a glass door and a single empty couch. "Please wait here, Sir. I was asked to fetch you. Someone from your team will meet you shortly."

"Thank you." Aquila sat down on the couch and extended his legs.

The man left with a curt nod. But Aquila didn't have to wait long, before another man with a stocky build and broad shoulders entered the room, striding confidently. Although most of the man's face was hidden behind an oxygen mask, friendly dark-brown eyes greeted Aquila from under his hazmat suit.

"Welcome, welcome, Aquila," he said, extending his hand. "A pleasure to meet you!"

Aquila grasped the extended hand and smiled. "The pleasure is all mine, believe me. You must be—"

"Orion. I'm Orion."

"Oh!" Aquila was startled. "I didn't expect you to come personally ..."

"*Of course,* I would," Orion assured. "Any friend of Dorado's, is a friend of mine."

"And likewise."

"Besides, you're my second in command and I couldn't possibly—"

"Whoa! Sorry to interrupt, but what did you just say?"

"About what?" Orion asked, puzzled.

"About me being the second in command ... I thought I was the Chief Conservation Officer."

Orion nodded. "You certainly are. And over here, that's the number two guy on site. Reporting directly to me, the District Manager. I thought Dorado explained all that to you, the hierarchy. No?"

"I don't believe we spoke about that," Aquila replied, shaking his head from side to side. "Nevertheless, I'm honoured. I don't know if I deserve—"

"Oh hush!" Orion interrupted with a dismissive wave of his hand. "No need to sell yourself short. I've seen your résumé. And dear God, what recommendations!"

Aquila furrowed his forehead in confusion.

"Oh, don't look so confused. Come, our ride is waiting, and I just got a message that your baggage is getting loaded up."

Aquila followed Orion out of the room and into a mostly empty lobby where two people, who looked like airport staff, sat behind a desk. Scanning the perimeter of this room, Aquila realized that it was not empty at all but just as heavily guarded as the rest of the airport. At least a dozen armed military men stood along the walls, and two others manned the door leading out of the building. Aquila tried not to look at them or feel intimidated, but under his layers of protective clothing, his heart beat faster than ever. He kept his head down and walked briskly out of the building, with Orion lagging a few paces behind.

Outside the terminal, there was a strip of paved area. Beyond this, a narrow, reddish-brown and dusty road winded into the distance. On this dirt road, stood a kind of two-seater cycle-rickshaw with a robotic driver. It was a jaunty little vehicle, painted in bright yellows and greys. The robot was a modern model, by design a female, and of organic variety. Behind the covered seating area of the rickshaw, a luggage cart was attached. One of the military guards from the airport was busy loading Aquila's suitcases into this container.

"That! We're going in *that*?" Aquila pointed to the rickshaw and asked in disbelief.

"Why? You don't like it?"

"No, no … it's not that. Don't get me wrong. I'm thrilled. It's just … I've never seen a thing like that before. Except in history lessons. They still exist?"

Orion laughed amiably. "Yes, absolutely they do! Over here, it's a whole new world. You'll see."

"Trust me, I'm already seeing. Seeing more than I can comprehend, to be frank."

"I bet! The driver you see is a new addition. They used to be driven by the farmers when I first got here," said Orion, as he walked towards their ride.

"How awful!"

"It was. I was horrified and immediately ordered these robots to be delivered instead."

"You did the right thing."

"Thank you. Get in, it'll be a fun ride. I promise," Orion said, letting Aquila board before him.

The seats inside were comfortable, and Aquila was tired from his journey, so he leaned back and yawned. "Gosh, it was a long flight."

"You think so? We have faster planes, but I usually prefer to use these luxury models. They are optimized to balance comfort versus speed. Also, it helps ease you into the jet-lag. I get massive jet-lags with the super fast crafts."

"Jet-lag?"

"Don't tell me you don't know what a jet-lag is?"

"I'm sorry. I'm a rookie flier."

"Ah, I forgot. Dorado did mention that. Well, you'd fit right in with everyone else on the farms. They haven't flown before either. Precious few can afford to, in this country."

"It's pretty much the same back home. Flying is for the elites. "

"I agree. Still, there are many more people who can afford it in the west. Here, you'll be lucky to find a handful. Just the top execs and statesmen. That's it."

The rickshaw had started to move forward and Aquila noticed that the ride was a lot less bumpy than he had anticipated. Peering out his window, he realized why that was the case. The road they were driving on, although a dirt road, was made of compressed soil which gave it a smooth appearance. It was nearing dawn. A faint yellowish glow crept up the edge of the horizon, while a thick smog hung in the air. It felt like a resident smog. Like a rowdy tenant who once leased these lands and refused to go away. The topography around the road was barren and rocky. Almost completely devoid of life. Here and there, a stray cactus raised its thorny head or some dry grass grew in patches. They drove on in silence for several miles, until they crossed a moat. On the other side of the moat, Aquila could see what looked like small shrubs that grew denser, as they approached a thick forest. Orion spoke first.

"When we get to those shrubs over there, you can remove your oxygen mask," he said. And with that he began unfastening his own headgear.

Aquila proceeded to do the same. In a minute, the top of his suit came off and a pungent gust of air hit his nose. It was a lot less suffocating than what he had encountered at the airport, but there was still something chemical about it. He rubbed his nose and looked at his manager, who seemed to be completely at ease with this environment.

"What's that smell?" Aquila asked, wrinkling his nose.

"Ah, long story. It'll go away slowly as we enter the forest. Then, once we're inside the district, it's completely fresh air."

"Geoengineering?" Aquila asked.

"Absolutely. And that's why you're here. To oversee all the components and suggest improvements."

"What kind of mechanisms are you using at the moment?"

"Oh, you'll get a full run down at your briefing tomorrow, but there's plenty of stuff going on. Air filtering with suction pods, cloud generation, fog control, ocean fertilization, drip irrigation, rain-water harvesting, you name it and it's there."

"Wow, that sounds like the complete climate-control and conservation package. Who pays the bill? And why?"

"It's paid for by a coalition of western countries, as per the terms of an agreement brokered by the International Conservation Council. So that's your 'who' part. As to the 'why', it's complicated, but the short answer is farming. This region already produces more than half of the world's food crops. And we're increasing our capacities every day. With your help, we can grow even faster."

"I certainly hope so! But I can't believe I had no idea about this project until now."

Orion shrugged. "It's not your fault. We don't live in the days of mass access to information like the early millennial generations. These days, it's hard to disseminate information like this to the masses. There are too many restrictions against launching new communication towers and satellites. As you know, it's all about finding an equilibrium between communication and environment. We just don't have the means to communicate that much. And then, there are secrecy requirements. Most people are just like you. Completely in the dark."

"Thanks for the pep-talk," Aquila said with a burst of laughter. "I want to know more. What was this agreement? Why was it signed? What are the terms? All the details."

"All in good time." Orion smiled. "And by good time, I mean tomorrow," he finished, as their vehicle rolled into a verdant forest filled with tall, leafy trees.

"Fine with me. And what's the agenda for today?"

"Today? You want to start working right away? Eager chap, aren't you!" Orion guffawed.

Aquila blushed and smiled shyly in response.

"I didn't put anything on your agenda for today," Orion continued. "You'll be jet-lagged. You need to get accustomed to this environment too. It's very different here from what you're used to. You can take this day to acclimatize yourself before we start talking business."

"Thanks, I appreciate it."

They were deep inside the forest by now, and the freshness of the air hit Aquila's lungs like a rejuvenating bath. He smelled musky foliage, rain-soaked grass and crisp wild flowers. He heard song birds twitter in the trees. The first rays of the sun trickled in from gaps in the foliage, like the fingers of an unknown divinity, reaching down to bless mankind. He was in paradise.

"What an enchanting place," he whispered, as he gazed all around him.

"Hmm. Enchanting is exactly right. Enchanting, because it's an *enchantment*. The reality is what you'll see beyond the periphery," Orion grunted.

"I'm sorry, I don't understand," Aquila confessed, turning to scan his manager's face for clues. Orion looked disappointed, angry perhaps, or a bit of both. Aquila did not know the guy well enough to tell.

"Oh, you will. Give it a few days," Orion mumbled. "Ah, we're almost here. Do you see the buildings at the edge of the forest? That's where we're going," he added, changing the subject.

In a few minutes, they had made it out of the forest and were heading down a slightly wider and lightly paved road, towards a couple of cabins surrounded by kitchen gardens. The rickshaw pulled up in front of the second, slightly smaller cabin.

"This is it," said Orion getting off the vehicle. "Your quarters while you're here. Mine is the one we just passed. I'll walk home and get some breakfast, if you don't mind. Please settle in. Catch some rest. Get some food. You have two house-robots assigned to you. They're inside and can help you with whatever you need. Sounds good?" Without his headgear, standing in the first light of dawn, Orion looked like a shimmering angel. Getting a full view of his face for the first time, Aquila noticed the high check-bones and rugged, careworn face of a once handsome man. Behind the ruggedness of his features, he noticed a certain kindness in his eyes.

"Sounds splendid." Aquila nodded. "And where do I report for tomorrow?"

"Report, eh? You'd do well in the military, I daresay!" Orion laughed out loud. He clutched his belly and bent over as he continued to laugh. Aquila stared on in amusement. Finally, he straightened and patted his deputy on the back, "Your ride will be here at eight tomorrow morning, to take you to the office. It's not far. About three miles out. You have a packed day tomorrow, so I suggest you catch up on all the rest you need."

"Ha! I don't think I'll be resting much. But I *could* use some food alright." Aquila rubbed his tummy as he spoke.

"Well, your kitchen is stocked. Just let your help know what you'd like. You should try the fish! It's freshly caught from the Ganges over here."

"You've got to be kidding me!" Aquila exclaimed. "You actually have real fish? I've never tried any …"

"You'll love it then. We export two thirds of the fish the world consumes, and the perks of that? We get some for ourselves as well."

"But how do you get any fish? Ocean fertilization?"

"Correct. We cultivate them using river and ocean fertilization."

"Brilliant! What about beef and poultry?"

"Nope, no beef. That's forbidden here, like most other places in the world. Too energy-intensive. Poultry, some, but with heavy restrictions. Ah, but the thing we *do* have that's most enticing of all is potable alcohol. You'll find some in your cellar too. I took the liberty of ordering you some choice wines."

Aquila licked his lips at the words. "I don't know how to thank you for that. But I must warn you, it'll make me never want to leave!"

Orion roared with laughter. "You're a fine chap," he said. "Anyway, I'll leave you to it. Looking forward to seeing you at work tomorrow." And with that he waved goodbye and strode off.

Aquila's luggage had already been carried inside the cabin when Orion left. The rickshaw driver asked if he needed anything else, and when he said no, it drove away. Aquila sighed and entered his new home. It wasn't particularly large but definitely larger than his trailer. There were two bedrooms, one and a half bathrooms, a living room with an adjacent dining area and of course, a kitchen. The most beautiful aspect of the cabin however, was the large verandah at the back, with panoramic views of the forest. For a second, Aquila worried that wild animals from that forest could attack his home at night, just like in the period dramas. Then, he recalled having read somewhere that carnivorous animals had become extinct all over the world, and not just in Russia. He felt a pang in his heart at this realization. A part of him had hoped to see a living wolf or a fox or even a tiger some day.

Aquila spent an hour or so before breakfast, exploring the house and kitchen garden. To his delight, he easily located the tiny cellar stocked with the wines Orion had gotten him. This reminded him of his own contraband stash of whiskey, so he retrieved those bottles from his luggage and added them to the collection. After that, he ate a hearty breakfast and despite his efforts to stay awake, soon found himself falling asleep like a baby on a soft, fluffy bed.

CHAPTER SEVEN

Having spent his first day in carefree indolence, Aquila woke up early the next morning to start his new job with spirit and enthusiasm. He ordered a lighter breakfast, shaved and got cleaned up, donned his favourite black suit with a silver tie and headed to work in the rickshaw that arrived for him.

The road that had brought him to his cabin, extended onwards through open grassy fields for some distance, before broadening up into a large square, surrounded by several official-looking buildings. The buildings were not tall and much smaller in scale than his workplace back in Moscow. Other than that, they were similar in design and construction. Unlike the airport where he had landed, these buildings had no military presence. There were, however, security guards at the gates—one for each of the three largest buildings. At a distance, a fourth structure, similar to an airport hanger or storage facility, was visible, surrounded by a tall fence that secured its entire perimeter.

Aquila was dropped off in front of the largest building in the complex. He walked up to the door and used the retinal scanner to gain access. The rickshaw-driver had told him to arrive at Orion's office on the ninth floor for their morning meeting. Aquila took an elevator to the ninth and topmost floor and found himself directly inside Orion's spacious office. It had wall to wall windows on all three side, overlooking the river on the right and the forest on the left.

Orion was at his desk, busily flipping through some files on his tablet when Aquila entered. "There you are." He looked up. "I was just going through your security clearances. You'll need them around here. So, you were chipped back in Moscow, eh? What was it for?"

Aquila didn't know how to respond and scrunched his face in confusion instead.

"I meant the chip you had in your wrist," Orion clarified, noticing his employee's hesitation.

"Yes ... that ... well ... umm ..." Aquila rubbed the back of his neck in agitation. "Actually, I didn't know I had it, to be honest," he confessed.

"That's worrisome," said Orion gravely. "I mean for you, not me," he quickly corrected. "What do I care. My staff took care of it before they let you board. It's a standing instruction on my team. I don't admit outside snooping. But ..."

"But, what?"

"But if someone chipped you without your knowledge, that should get you concerned. I'm worried too, actually. My employees' well being and safety matter to me more than you can imagine, and knowing that you might be in danger worries me. We'll have to get to the bottom of this at some point, eh? What do you think?"

"I'd love to. But I have no idea where to start. I can't think of any suspect. Anyone who could have possibly wanted to track me without my knowledge."

"Maybe they weren't tracking you. Maybe they wanted something else. There are many kinds of chips you know. Anyway, I'm a bit of an expert on security topics, so I'd love to help you figure it out someday, if you like."

Aquila smiled gratefully. "I'd love that, Orion. Although it's not my biggest priority at the moment," he replied.

My biggest priority is figuring out why I was arrested. But maybe solving this, would solve that too, he thought but didn't say it aloud.

"Fair enough. Let's get to business now, shall we?" Orion rose from his chair. "First, I want to give you a virtual tour of the facilities. Then I have blocked off an hour, to discuss the purpose and end-goal of this project in detail. After that, we can have lunch. Let's go. The virtual reality room is downstairs."

They took the elevator to the eighth floor, which held all the conference rooms. It was mostly empty at this hour. Orion led them into the farthest room from the elevators. It was a medium-sized room with no windows and designed like a black-box theatre. There were a dozen seats for viewers from which Orion and Aquila chose a pair in the front row. Orion snapped his fingers, commanding the head-sets to descend from above. The lights automatically dimmed, and the show started.

The show didn't have an inbuilt narrator or guide. It was designed such that one of the viewers could assume this role and lead the remaining audience. Orion took the lead and guided Aquila into the District from the very forest they had crossed the day before. The show displayed a sign welcoming them into Project 15/8.

"Here we are. This is where we entered. Do you remember?"

"I do, yes. But what's Project 15/8? I thought this was Project Redistribution."

"Ah, you're observant! It's the same thing, Project Redistribution is intended for common usage and Project 15/8 is for the paperwork. But the locals call it neither. They have their own nickname."

"Oh, really? And what's that?"

"Project Independence Day!"

"Like that twentieth century movie?"

"Oh no, no. The number 15/8, whatever it might mean to

the bureaucrats, to the locals here, it means only one thing; the fifteenth of August which was traditionally their Independence Day. India's Independence Day, you know, before—"

"Before the Treaty of Lhasa and the formation of Indochine. I get it."

"Hey, someone knows his history!"

Aquila grinned broadly. "It's a hobby," he mumbled.

"Anyway, let's move on. Can't hang around at the forest all day." With these words, Orion led them along the same path Aquila had taken earlier, explaining what they saw along the way.

"As you see here, all this grass, you must have seen them on your way to work, they're for carbon sequestration. We alternate crop field with grasslands and add perennial crops in the mix."

"Makes sense," Aquila agreed. "And what do we use for fertilizers?"

"All organic. Compost and manure from the dairy cows. Our compost fields are near the forest."

"Ah! So that's what smelled so bad in the forest yesterday."

"You got it."

They moved further along the road and arrived at their current location. Orion explained that the buildings here were mostly administrative. The scientists and project managers were also busy at work at the various labs inside this complex. Outside of this little hub, there were just farmlands for as far as the eyes could see. In between the farms, there were some air and water purification plants, some atmospheric carbon capture and other technologies but no more office buildings or any other buildings for that matter.

"Come let's take a mini-tour of the farms and plants, shall we?" Orion announced enthusiastically.

"Would love to yes, but wait, before we go, what's that building over there. It doesn't look like an office at all." Aquila pointed at the walled structure that looked like an airport hanger.

"I almost forgot … yes, that one. That's our future!"

"Future? How do you mean?"

"It's where we're building the technology that will take over, when this region will no longer be habitable."

"No longer habitable? Why? But it's so well developed!"

Orion shook his head in dismay. "For now. But this is not sustainable. We can't maintain this artificial environment for ever. The cost is too much. And temperatures are rising fast."

"So, what happens when it becomes uninhabitable?"

"In all probability, this area will become uninhabitable by humans in a decade or so. Maybe less. But with the technologies we have in place, the crops—at least some of them—could still thrive. When that happens, robots will take over these farms and continue what we've started. That's what we're building and training in that shed."

"The robots?"

"Yes. And their control systems."

"But what about all the people who live here? What will happen to them in ten years? Another Deluge situation? Mass casualties? Refugee crises? That'd be terrible!"

"There there, calm down. We've thought about that of course. There is an evacuation plan in place. I'll explain it all in our meeting, right after the show. Now come, let me show you the nifty suction pod nests, that keep the air around here this pure."

The tour lasted another fifteen minutes or so. Bordering the office-area, they visited a tiny shopping strip, housing a variety of different stores. Beyond that, there were no more urban hubs. The entire district was just a sprawling network of farmlands interspersed with air filtration and other plants. Farmers could be seen hard at work in the fields. Much of the labour was manual and large machines were forbidden. All vehicles were of bi-cycle type or solar-powered. Even then, the number of vehicles were limited. Orion explained, that there was a total of ninety-eight farm units in his district, and each unit had its own shopping area. There were however, no other office buildings outside of their present location. Given the vastness of the enterprise, they only had time to see a couple of farm units. Orion assured that the others were almost identical, and Aquila would have plenty of time to visit them all during his tenure.

"So, that's it for the tour on my part," Orion said finally, switching off the show and removing his head-set. "Do you have any questions about the facilities?"

"Yes ... I do. There was something really odd. I saw all these farmers. Quite a few, eh? How many are there?"

Orion furrowed his brows and became thoughtful. "Ummm ... very many. I'd have to look up the numbers exactly, but there are thousands, why?"

"Well yeah, that's what I was getting at. There are all these people. So many of them. Thousands, you say. But where do they live? I didn't see any houses. None at all."

"Ah, fair point." Orion's face became sad. "They ... have colonies ... outside the farm-complex." Here, he paused and appeared to consider adding something more. A moment later, he decided against it and stood up. "It's almost time for our meeting. How about we meet in my office after a short break, say fifteen minutes?"

"That works for me," Aquila replied tentatively, still confused about what was going on with the farmers.

"Good. I'll have someone show you around. You can check out your own office or the cafeteria or just walk about."

Aquila nodded and stood up. "Sounds good."

* * *

Aquila spent the next quarter of an hour with a wizened, elderly lady, who identified as his and Orion's secretary—and whose name he immediately forgot—walking around the building and meeting various staff. He also saw the cafeteria and recreation room and of course, his own corner office on

70

the seventh floor with large windows on both its external walls. The highlight of the tour however, was an annexe building that housed the district's library. They didn't have time to go inside, but even from the outside Aquila got a feel for the vastness of the treasures it held behind its doors. It was also by far, the most attractive and well-maintained wing of the building. He made a mental note to visit this place often.

When Aquila returned to Orion's office with a cup of tea from the cafeteria, he found his manager engrossed in some documents again.

"Oh, is it time?" Orion asked, slightly startled. He checked his clock. "Very good, let's get down to business. Sit, please." He indicated the chair across from him.

"Thanks," said Aquila sitting down.

Orion sat up straight and folded his arms in front of his chest. "Let's get straight to the crux." His voice sounded authoritative. "Project Redistribution. That's what we are. That's why you're here. So, what is it?"

"Exactly. What is it?" Aquila agreed taking a sip from his tea cup.

"To explain that, let's dig into the past a bit. The Age of Globalization, you remember that? From history?" Orion placed his arms on his desk and leaned forward with a serious expression across his face.

"Yes, I know about that. Go on … "

"Okay, so during that age what was going on? Factories, factories everywhere. Unchecked capitalism. No Government regulations, none at all. It was all about maximizing profit, am I right?"

"Absolutely. It was disgusting."

"Well, that's another matter. But yeah, like I said, maximum profits. And how do you get that?"

"Cheap labour."

"Correct. So, all the factories were in countries they called the third world. Indochine was one of the hotspots."

"Yeah, I knew that. And then, pollution destroyed these

lands."

"Pretty much. As you saw for yourself when you exited your plane. Anywhere outside this geoengineered bubble—and that includes the airport—you'd need a hazmat suit to survive the exposure."

"What a terrible, terrible situation."

"True. But it didn't happen overnight, mind you. It's the result of centuries of industrialization and consequent urbanization. Now, even before the Great Deluge happened, a lot of activists blamed the consumerist west for inflicting this harm on the third world. Because, as you know, the factories here were owned by corporate America and Europe, and its products were meant for export to western markets. They were only *produced* here because it was cheap to do so!" Orion slammed his desk and stood up; his face visibly flushed. Till now, Aquila had not seen him this agitated.

"Yes, I am aware. The exploitation was quite pervasive."

"Correct. So, activists demanded compensation for the carbon debt. You know what that is?"

"I believe it's some sort of payment of damages for ruining another country's climate. But I thought that argument never went anywhere ..."

"Ah! That's where you're wrong, my friend. At first, you're right, it was going nowhere. But then the Great Deluge happened and it was a moral wake up call. Most of coastal India and Bangladesh went under the ocean—"

"And with it, all the arable land. The world's largest paddy fields ..."

"You got it!" Orion started to pace behind his desk. "But even then, the western countries did not own up to ruining the nations, where they built their factories. No damages were paid."

"That's what I thought was the case. Did something change in recent times?"

"Not everywhere. But certainly, in Indochine. You see, after World War VI ended in these parts with the Treaty of

Lhasa, the dynamics changed. The combined power of India and China strengthened the debate around carbon debt. Also, there were these vast lands, full of knowledgeable farmers, where food crops could be grown with a little outside investment. So, an agreement was struck and Project Redistribution was created."

"So that's the agreement you were talking about yesterday? The one which helps pay for all the geoengineering?"

"Exactly."

"What are the terms, and is there an expiry date?"

"I'll give you a copy of the agreement later, but the gist is that, a coalition of wealthy nations—you'll get the complete list—pay their climate debt to Indochine by funding this geoengineering. *But* this came with a pretty hefty price tag. It was determined therefore, that the cost would be more than the climate debt owed."

"And who pays for the difference?"

"We do. Our produce, that is. Almost 80% of what is produced here is sent back to the sponsor countries as the differential payment for the geoengineering."

"Wow, that's a pretty complex arrangement. But there's still one big problem."

"Which is, what?" Orion stopped pacing and turned around to face his employee.

"Basically, what happens when, like you said, this area become uninhabitable again? You mentioned some sort of rehabilitation earlier ..."

"Yes, that's the last bit of the arrangement. Each farm unit in my district has to fulfil a quota of produce to ship to the West. This quota is in the millions of metric tonnes range. And as soon as a unit reaches that quota, it is eligible to send all its workers to a safe place, a haven of sorts. A pre-developed city called Sanctuary City. There, they can live out the rest of their lives in retirement and receive pensions from the International Conservation Council."

Aquila shook his head vehemently. "I don't like this. I don't like this *at all*."

"And why not?" Orion asked in surprise.

"I don't know … just something about it doesn't feel right. Who's in charge of building this Sanctuary or whatever city?"

"The International Conservation Council, of course."

Aquila's jaw muscles tensed.

"You don't like them?" Orion raised an eyebrow.

"And who's paying for it?" Aquila asked, avoiding the question.

"The western countries are. The sponsor countries."

"Which countries are in that list? Wait, let me guess, Russia, The American Republic, The European Union and—"

"Calamerica."

"What about Canada?"

"They were in at first, but opted out." Orion smiled, as if reminiscing something. "I'm Canadian you know," he added after a pause.

"Oh? I thought you grew up with Dorado!"

"I did. In Canada. He moved to Russia when he was hired for a project."

"All these years I knew the guy and he never told me …" Aquila mused.

"Ha! Maybe, you should've asked!"

Aquila chuckled. "Yeah, I should've. But now it all makes sense."

"What does?"

"Why he's so friendly." Aquila paused, grinning from ear to ear. "And so are you," he added.

"I wouldn't be so quick to say that about me," Orion warned, wagging a finger. "Now, do you have any other questions?"

"Ummm … I don't think … oh wait, important question, when do all the farm units reach capacity?"

"Great question. The answer is different from unit to unit. Each one produces and exports at a different level, so some will finish earlier than others. The unit closest to our offices will be the first to get there, if things proceed as planned. I think they should be ready to move to Sanctuary City in a year or less."

"A YEAR OR LESS? That's really soon!"

"Better for them, don't you think? They're going for the good life after this."

"I suppose." Aquila shrugged. But in his heart, he felt a nagging discomfort about this whole arrangement and try as he might, he could not drive it away.

CHAPTER EIGHT

Carina sat in an armchair in her study, with her hands clenched together on her lap and her upper body bent forward. A couple of paces in front of her, Alrakis worked the holo-phone, trying to catch a flickering signal.

"Any luck?" asked Carina, her voice quivering with agitation.

"Nope. I had a tiny signal, but it's gone now."

"Are you sure you have the right band?"

"I'm pretty sure," he said. "... wait, I have something coming in ... hello, is anyone there?"

A crackling sound was heard, like someone stepping on stone chips. There was some static. Then, a faint broken voice filtered in. It sounded unnatural. Neither human nor robotic. More like an alien's words.

"I'm sorry, you're clipping," Alrakis said into the phone. "And we have no holo, no image at all, just the sound."

"Better?" replied the alien voice.

"Yes. Much better, but we still can't see you," Alrakis replied.

"That's fine. I turned off the holo. For privacy," the voice responded.

"Alright, no worries. How much time do you have?"

"Not much. Be quick."

"Okay, then …" Alrakis flicked a glance at Carina, who nodded her approval to proceed. "I'll get straight to the point. The situation with this Aquila, how did that happen?"

"I used impersonation gloves. They turned out to be his and he got busted."

"You didn't know whose they were, when you tried them?"

"Nope. We have a bunch of them. All top diplomats. We just know which department they work for. I tried the Russian Conservation Ministry and it turned out he did work there, but didn't have access. Where is he now? The bureaucrat?"

Alrakis took a second to make eye contact with Carina. Carina signalled him to go ahead. "He … let's say he's been taken care of."

"I hear there's a warrant out for him."

"I see and—"

"Sorry, my time's up. The call will drop soon …" the voice trailed off and was replaced by static. Some more crackling. And then, silence.

"Lost him," said Alrakis turning to Carina, when the call disconnected.

"Hmmm. Was it his real voice, you think?" Carina asked.

"Not a chance. He doesn't use his real voice. It's too dangerous. I thought he'd blur his face in the hologram."

"But he turned that off entirely."

"Yep! It's a pity. I always wanted to meet the mighty leader of The Underground."

"Don't worry, you're not alone. I haven't met him either," Carina assured.

"Or her. Some say, she's a woman."

"Could be. Or they could even be a couple. Very few actually know. Anyway, what did you make of the information?"

Alrakis frowned. "It's strange, don't you think?" he asked. "That he didn't have access. This Aquila guy," he clarified.

"Very strange." Carina shook her head from side to side.

"He was in a pretty senior role at the Ministry. And this is a conservation project with Russia as a sponsor."

"Yep. Should've been right up his alley."

"They tell us we can't have access, because that'd create too much political intervention. Apparently, it's only the scientists that are in the know for now. But he was a scientist ..."

"And a senior one too! So, what the heck?"

"Exactly. We need to find out more." Carina closed her eyes and massaged her temples with her right hand as she spoke.

"We can bring it up at the convention—"

"No. That'd lead us right into their trap. Whatever it is they're playing at, we need to beat them at their own game."

"How?"

"Secrecy. We uncover the whole thing without them ever suspecting."

Alrakis sighed and slumped into a chair. "I guess you're right," he agreed.

* * *

About a week into his new assignment, Aquila was at his office going through some maintenance plans for a drip-irrigation unit, when his elderly secretary—whose name he had finally learned—rushed into his office, panting heavily.

"Good morning," she said, trying to catch her breath.

"Morning, Lyra. What's wrong?" he asked, studying her compassionately.

"There's a lot of trouble in the Farm-robot Unit and I can't find Orion anywhere," she gasped.

"Oh, Orion is travelling to one of the central farms today. Didn't he tell you?"

"No Sir, he didn't! What do I do? I have the plant manager on hold at my desk ..."

"Okay, I'll take the call. Can you transfer the call to my

room?"

"Sure." Lyra turned to leave, when Aquila stopped her.

"Wait, do you know what exactly happened?"

Lyra threw up her arms and made a face. "No idea. But she said it was urgent."

Lyra left and shut the door behind her. In a few seconds, Aquila's phone rang and the holo of an intelligent-looking, portly, middle-aged lady appeared.

"Morning Aquila, I hear Orion is away?" she asked hurriedly.

"Yes, he's gone for the day, I believe. If it can't wait, then I'm happy to see if I can help."

"You bet it can't wait!" She shook her head disapprovingly. "I have a serious mess on my hands. One of my lead engineers is threatening to resign immediately."

"What on earth for? And if he must go, can we replace him?"

"I'd rather not replace him. He's an asset on my team."

"In that case, can we talk him into staying?"

"I've tried everything. It's not working, and that's why I called. Orion is a master mediator. Maybe he can make a deal or something ..."

"Hmm. In his absence, would you like *me* to give it a shot?"

"Could be worth a try," she said. "He says he'll walk out today in the middle of an upgrade we're doing. If he makes good on his word, the upgrade is doomed."

"Okay, I get the idea. So, what's the grievance? More pay? Better hours? Time off?"

"Ha! I wish it were that simple." She laughed sarcastically. "I think it's best if you come down to the plant, and hear it from him yourself. Can you come now?"

"Sure," said Aquila. "I'm in the middle of something here ... give me fifteen minutes and I'll come see you."

"Thank you. I appreciate it." She gave him a curt nod, before hanging up.

Aquila put away the files he was looking into, grabbed a

coffee and went straight to the Farm-robot Unit. The manager's room was right at the back. When Aquila arrived there, she was seated at her desk with the troublesome engineer across from her, arguing passionately.

"Hello," said Aquila to alert the present company of his arrival. The engineer turned to look, a grimace across his face. He was of medium height and sturdily built with broad shoulders, expressive dark brown eyes and shoulder-length, salt and pepper hair. The most striking feature of his face however, were his bushy, jet-black eyebrows that curved like millipedes over his long lashes.

"Hello there, my name is Aquila. I'm the new—" Aquila started.

"Yes, I know," the engineer replied as he stood up and shook Aquila's hand. "And I am Ramesh."

"Ramesh? What an interesting name! Is that also a constellation?" Aquila asked cordially, trying to ease the tension.

"No. We aren't all named after constellations like you folks in the west. My full name is Ramesh Dutt. Dutt is our family name that I inherited from my father, and his father before him."

"Ah, I see! I did hear about that tradition continuing on in Indochine, but now you've become the first person I met, who isn't named after a constellation. Which means, I'll never be able to forget you!"

"Ha! If you're trying to butter me up this way, then I can tell you it's not going to work," Ramesh said jovially. "But I have to say, I do appreciate your effort." Despite his words however, Ramesh looked a lot calmer than before.

"I try." Aquila smiled. "So, tell me, how can I make you stay?"

"If you can make me feel safe, I will. But I doubt that you can."

Aquila's eyes widened. "You don't feel safe here? Why is that?"

"Well, it's the damn robots. You know what they are, right?"

"I … er …" Aquila stuttered and looked at the plant manager for assistance. A plaque on her desk said that her name was Sabrina.

"You should see the robots," Sabrina offered. "Maybe you'll see what he's seeing. I certainly couldn't tell."

"Okay, can you take me to the robots?" Aquila turned to ask Ramesh.

"Sure. Please follow me." Ramesh beckoned with a wave of his hand, as he walked out the door.

They rushed along an immaculate corridor buzzing with activity. Workers could be seen everywhere, testing equipment, fixing wiring and soldering different parts. Some were at their desks developing software. Very few looked up from their work to notice the managers passing by. Arriving near the western corner of the building, Ramesh halted in front of a set of tall double doors of reinforced steel. He placed his left palm on a sensor-pad next to the door. The pad lit up and scanned his credentials. With a roaring sound the massive doors slid open.

It was dark inside the room when they walked in. The door behind them was closing fast and shutting out the remaining shreds of illumination.

"Lights," Ramesh called out in the darkness, and the room lit up.

It took an instant for Aquila's eyes to focus to the changed lighting. Then, he saw those menacing things. His jaw dropped to the floor.

"*Those?*" he yelled; his eyes as large as saucers. "How did *those* get here?"

"See, I told you," Ramesh said to Sabrina, who looked utterly lost. "You recognize them, don't you?" he asked Aquila with an air of vindication.

"Of course, I do!" Aquila acknowledged. "Killer robots. World War VI relics. But why are they *here?*"

81

"Wait, what did you say they were?" Sabrina now asked, gathering herself from her confusion.

"They're killer robots. Designed to identify and kill human targets during total war. They were last used by the Neo-Nazis during World War VI. But they were banned—"

"When the war ended," Ramesh completed. "But here they are now. In our backyard. So yeah, either we send them back. Or I'm out!"

Sabrina shook her head vehemently. "No, no, that can't be right. How do we know these are the same robots? They might just look alike! When did we get them?"

"This is the batch that came in last week. The ones we're supposed to be upgrading right now," Ramesh said briskly. "And *of course*, they're the same ones. You think I didn't do my due diligence? Come here, I'll show you," he added, beckoning them forward with a wave of his hand.

Ramesh marched up to a unit in the first row and stamped his foot on the ground to turn on additional lights in that area. "Look ..." He ran his hand along the robot's lower arm. "You see this? You know what it is?"

"High power laser death beam," Aquila promptly replied, before Sabrina could even open her mouth to speak.

Sabrina's face turned paler than chalk. "They ... they ... must have disabled those, right?" she muttered.

"Yes, that's what they told us. That's what their manuals say as well. But my question is—"

"Why weren't they removed altogether?" Aquila said under his breath, as he inspected the robot himself.

"Exactly," Ramesh agreed.

Sabrina was still shaking her head. Noticing this, Aquila turned to face her. "Sabrina, you need to stop being in denial, and call a spade a spade. I've seen enough World War VI material to know exactly what these things are, and what they're capable of doing." His eyes flashed with anger. "You can shake your head all you want while they're switched off, but once that laser turns on, it'll melt you into a bowl of mush before you could even say 'mush'."

"That's exactly right," Ramesh agreed, looking pleased with having made his argument. "Besides the lasers, their arms are also loaded with hundreds of rounds of ammo. Once a command kicks in, they can riddle a moving target with bullets from a distance of up to a mile."

"*Can* we send them back?" Aquila asked.

"I've tried. But I'm getting push-backs. I'm told they need to be repurposed. And hence the upgrade," Ramesh replied.

"Maybe I could try? Or Sabrina?" Aquila mused. Sabrina looked sheepishly at them without venturing to object.

"If we try that angle, then we should probably ask Orion," Ramesh suggested. "He'd have the most leverage. But I seriously doubt it would help. They told me that it was part of the agreement to repurpose the unused World War VI robots for this project. Since we've already signed on to it, we have no way out. Plus, as you can see, they've sent hundreds. How would they even replace so many so fast?" Ramesh sighed deeply and leaned against a robot.

"Darn it!" Aquila exclaimed. "I knew I should've read that entire agreement. It's too dang long." He clicked his tongue in disapproval. "Okay, tell me this," he continued after a moment's pause, "say we can't send these back. Say, even Orion can't. Could we at least disarm them? You know ... like by removing the laser and bullets ... I'm no defence engineer, but seems like that'd do the trick, no?"

Ramesh nodded. "That's the first thing I tried. I've got my best guy on this, and he's been trying all week. But no luck so far. Hang on, I can get him in here so that you can ask him yourself." He pulled his phone out from his pocket. "Send for Alan in the storage room," he ordered the phone.

A minute later, a skinny teenager with closely cropped, jet black hair and a jolly expression, skipped into the room. Despite his bony structure, he had the athletic frame of someone who was probably accustomed to hard physical labour. "You called me, Sir?" he asked gleefully.

"Ah, yes. Come here, my boy. Aquila, this is Alan Shi, a real wizard when it comes to gadgets. I have him on my team for exactly such instances as these. Alan, tell him what you found …" Ramesh trailed off.

"I'd love to, Sir," Alan said. Then turning to Aquila, "are you the new manager here?" he asked.

"Yes, my name is Aquila. So, you've been working on this, eh? You're just a boy!" He ruffled the kid's hair.

"No Sir, I'm eighteen." Alan blushed. "My father's a poor peasant here, but he can't work much anymore. Too old. So, Ramesh gave me a job."

"They could really use the cash," Ramesh explained. "Besides, he's a total whiz kid. You'll see. Tell him what you know, Alan."

"Yes, Sir," said Alan turning to the robot. "Here, you can see the laser unit is built into the arm. There are two ways of doing it, one—"

"Wait." Aquila raised his hand to stop the boy. "I don't need the details. I wouldn't understand. Just tell me this, can we remove the laser … like physically … or no?"

"It's not a separate module, but embedded in the armour itself. So, no Sir, we can't. Not without replacing the arm."

"Could we do that? Replace the arm?"

"In theory we could, but this beast is made entirely of platinum and weighs close to fifty tonnes. No replacement arm we order, would come anywhere close to that specification. And the weaker the arms, the less output we'll get from them in the farms. Meaning that we'll need more robots, by several orders of magnitude, to get the same productivity."

"That'd be unacceptable," Aquila agreed.

"How about having the laser and machine-gun modules permanently disabled? With hardware or software? Have you tried that?" Sabrina asked.

"Yes Ma'am, I can give you a complete report, but the summary is that, we can definitely implement a software latch that prevents the attack mechanism from engaging. But there'd be a catch."

"Which is what?" Sabrina moved closer to a robot and started examining it with both hands.

"It could be overridden."

Sabrina's curiosity was piqued. She flipped around and looked Alan in the eye. "How? Wireless upgrade?" she asked.

"That's correct. The AI we're uploading now to repurpose this to a farming mode, can be wiped out entirely, by wirelessly installing a new software to its hard-drive. Anyone with access could do it. The AI from the killer robot mode is still in existence. All you'd need, is to install that back on, and the safety latches would disappear, and our robot would flip instantly from farmer to murderer. A hacker could do it. Or a terrorist, perhaps." Alan shrugged.

"That's a really really dangerous situation," Sabrina finally admitted. "What should we do?" she asked, turning to Aquila.

Aquila rubbed his chin and nodded thoughtfully. "I don't know," he whispered. "Anyway, thank you, Alan, you've been a great help. You can go back to what you were doing. I'll discuss what to do next with the others and let you know."

"No problem, Sir. Do you want to see my full report?" Alan asked.

"Yes, please send that to all of us, will you?"

"I'll send it right away," he said as he ran off.

When he'd left, Aquila turned to Sabrina, "How do you think the authorities would respond, if we bring up these security concerns?" he asked. "You have experience dealing with them. Are they reasonable?"

"Nope. They'll probably claim that the alternative AI is in a secure location that cannot be breached."

"Ha! With a good hacker, anything can be breached. Everyone knows that." Aquila shrugged.

"Like I said, we're doomed." Ramesh sighed.

Aquila walked over to Ramesh and held him by the shoulders. "My friend, see what you did there?" he asked.

"What?" Ramesh asked, wearing a puzzled expression.

"You said, *we*. We are a team. You can leave us, if you like. But if you do, the rest of us are still doomed. You'll have left knowing that you abandoned us, the rest of your team. And if that's okay with you, then you're free to leave. I won't try to stop you. But if it weighs on your conscience, then stay, and I promise to fight for all of us to get this sorted out."

"Ha! Are you a politician or something?" Ramesh joked. "That was some speech!" He rubbed his eyes and found that they were moist. "I'm not going anywhere. But how do you plan on fixing this?" he added with a smile.

"I'm not quite sure yet, but I'll have a chat with Orion and then … then I need to read up on the terms of the act, that banned these robots … there might be something in there, that prevents even a repurposed usage … I'll have to see."

"That's a good idea. Certainly, an angle I didn't consider," Ramesh agreed.

"I'll also try to find more material on the robots, to see if there are any built-in hacks to permanently disable their military capabilities. In the meantime, please keep trying what you've been trying over here. We can meet every two weeks to catch each other up? How about that?"

"Sounds good to me," Ramesh said. "Sabrina?"

Sabrina replied with a thumbs-up.

CHAPTER NINE

A month later, Aquila found himself in the district's library hunched over the reading desk, digging through obscure instruction manuals. Yet, no solution to their killer robot problem seemed to be in sight. It was the Friday after a long week, and he was really tired. His biggest worry at this point, was not merely that a hacker or terrorist could attack them. It was that, something much more sinister could be afoot in the background. Why were these robots sent in the first place? On the surface, it seemed like a practical choice, since recycling was the order of the day. But this was no ordinary stash of recyclable equipment. This was a catastrophe in the making. Aquila wrung his hands in frustration. He leaned back in his chair, stretching his legs underneath the table. Then, he covered his mouth and yawned. He decided to wrap it up for the evening, and go grab a drink.

Getting up, he realized that his legs had fallen asleep. He walked around the desk a couple of times to restore his blood circulation. Just as he was about to pick up his stuff and leave, he thought he saw someone staring at him from the opposite end of the room. He turned in that direction. This section of the library was quite empty, apart from a single couch against the western wall, where a dark-haired lady sat next to a window. She was watching him from under her lovely long lashes. Aquila had a feeling that he had seen her before. But where? She smiled at him, and his memory was immediately jogged. They had flown in from Moscow together. He smiled back and was about to walk up to her to say hello, when a cleaning robot with a huge vacuum drove right in front of him, obstructing his view.

By the time the robot had moved out of the way, the lady was no longer at her seat. Aquila navigated around all the cleaning and edged closer to the western wall. He spotted the lady a few feet from the couch she had earlier occupied, walking down a corridor with her back turned towards Aquila. Aquila hesitated at first. And then, he decided to follow her. She was wearing a knee-length dress of gorgeous magenta, below which her pale and shapely calves flexed with each hurried step she took. She turned a corner and Aquila continued to follow. Right around the bend was a metal arch and beyond that, a set of doors. Before the arch there was another door to Aquila's right, probably leading to the outside. The lady had disappeared through one of these doors, but Aquila couldn't tell which one. He decided to try the one right in front of him, behind the arch.

He took a long stride and stepped through the arch. Immediately, an alarm went off, and the librarian came running. "Stay where you are," she said, gasping for breath.

Aquila did as he was told.

The librarian moved closer and deactivated the alarm. "Oh, it's just you," she said, finally noticing Aquila. "Sorry about that," she apologized, as she realized who Aquila was. "It's the restricted section. You don't have access?" she asked, looking surprised.

"I guess not," Aquila shrugged. He was just as surprised as her. Not because there was a restricted section in the library. Libraries often had them. But like her, he too couldn't believe he didn't have access.

"Hmmm ... that's strange. Do you need something from

there? I can check with Orion if he can get you a quick—"

"No, that's quite alright." Aquila waved his hand dismissively. "I'll speak to him myself. But thank you." He smiled and bowed his head slightly to take his leave.

He retraced his steps to the main hallway and decided to go see his boss at once. Not so much to get access to the restricted section, but because he badly needed a drink by now and could certainly use some company. He knew that Orion would still be in his office as he always was on Fridays. It was a ritual of his, to enjoy his first glass of whiskey at his own desk, before going home for the weekend.

Walking out of the library, Aquila made his way to the main elevators. In the quiet of the elevator, he remembered something he had long forgotten. Something Dorado had told him about certain restricted files in the library—historic documents that were somehow salvaged and kept there without anyone's knowledge but Orion's. The God of War files, Dorado had called them.

Oh! So, that's what the restricted section must be for! he thought.

He made up his mind to ask Orion about the files. Now that he had come to know his manager quite well, Aquila felt confident that he would be trusted with this secret. Besides, it would be a fine distraction to learn some obscure history, on the days when he got tired of researching robots. This thought brought a spring in his step, as he rushed to his manager's door.

Getting there, he found Orion lounging in his chair with a whiskey glass in his hand and soft music playing in the background. The sound of music drowned out his footsteps, so in order not to startle his boss, Aquila loudly cleared his throat.

"Aquila! You're still here?" Orion asked joyfully, turning his chair around.

"Oh no, I'd left. But now I feel like I need a drink. Just wanted to check if you'd like to join."

"You know I'd never say no to that. Did you want to head to the pub or hang out here? I have some more of this fine whiskey, if you'd like." He pointed to his glass.

"I'd rather go to the pub. I've been stuffed up in that library all by myself for way too long …"

"Tell me about it," Orion agreed. "Sometimes I wonder how you do it." He chugged his remaining drink and stood up as he spoke.

"Like I've said before, I'm worried to death about those robots, and until I solve this … plus I promised Ramesh."

"Yeah, yeah, I know. I admire your dedication, you know that?" Orion replied with a friendly clap on Aquila's shoulder.

Aquila blushed. "Thanks."

"So, are you getting anywhere with it?"

"No, not really. And that's the frustrating part. When they were deployed the last time—"

"During World War VI," Orion completed.

"Yeah, back then … back then … ah, I lost my train of thought …" Aquila shook his head. "But while we're on the subject of war, can I ask you a question?"

"Ask away!" Orion assured.

They walked out of the building and were greeted with a mellow gust of breeze across their faces.

"The thing is, before I came here …" Aquila started. "Dorado mentioned something that's in your possession. A treasure of sorts, you might say." He looked around to check if anyone was within earshot. Noticing no one else in the vicinity, he continued. "Do you understand what I'm referring to?" he asked, making a suggestive gesture with his eyes.

"I believe I do, go on …"

"Okay then, would it be safe to assume that you have begun to trust me enough to allow me to access that treasure … those files?"

"Ha! Of course, I trust you. Don't doubt that for a second. But why are you so interested in seeing them? I'm just curious. Indulge me, please."

"History is a passion of mine that has kept me entertained ever since I was a child. And I don't have that much to do around here. I figured it'd be a nice break from poring over all those robot manuals."

They had arrived at the only pub in the shopping strip adjacent to their offices, so Orion stopped before the porch to finish their conversation.

"Fair enough. Your love for history hasn't escaped my notice either. In fact, it's an asset to have on our team." Orion paused to smile. "Sabrina said, that's how you recognized those World War VI robots. That's impressive. After you." He smiled, opening the pub door for Aquila.

The pub was not particularly busy at that hour, but neither was it deserted. On Fridays there was always live music, which was an added attraction. There were about a dozen patrons scattered around the bar and at the various tables inside the establishment. A lively young couple was dancing right in front of where the band was playing in a corner. Overall, it was a merry little scene unfolding around them. A lot merrier than anything Aquila had ever witnessed back home in Moscow.

"Let me buy you the first round," Orion said, as they seated themselves at the bar. "What would you like?"

"Some beer would be great."

"Alright. I'll have the same. What's on tap?" Orion asked the droid at the bar.

The droid blurted out a list, and Orion ordered them two glasses of the district's finest honey lager.

"Mmm ..." Aquila made a delicious sound after taking his first sip. "Nice and refreshing. So, where are we on access to those files, Orion? You okay with it?"

"Tomorrow. We can go tomorrow." Orion sipped his own beer. "It'd be better during the weekend. Library's a lot emptier."

"Yeah, that works. What time were you thinking?"

"Let's say in the evening ... around five?" Orion asked, while searching his pockets for something. "Ah, shit," he said, after a futile search. "I forgot my phone at work." Then, downing his beer, he stood up. "Be right back," he said and left in a hurry.

Aquila sighed and ordered himself another beer. When his second glass arrived, he grabbed it and moved himself to a table closer to the band. The music was starting to get livelier as the night wore on. Quite a few people had joined in with the general air of gaiety, and some were clapping and swaying to the tune. He took a closer look at the folks around him. They were well-dressed and energetic. There was a certain polish in their appearance, that pointed to the abundance of wealth and privilege. Very unlike what he had seen among the few farmers he had met so far. He wondered where all the farmers were, or if they ever visited this business. He did not recall having seen them here on any of his previous visits either.

Aquila gulped down his chilled beer and became reflective. Despite the anxiety around the robots, he felt like his life had taken a turn for the better. Merely a month ago, he was living in a drab, mechanical city, trudging away at a boring job, not having seen any of the world beyond its boundaries. Then, he was suddenly a pawn in some twisted political game, a fugitive, an alleged drug addict running for his life. It had felt like his life was pointless. The fetters too tight around his neck. But everything changed from the moment he landed here in this strange, colourful country. He had made new friends. Found new purpose. He grinned to himself at this realization.

"Is this seat taken?" a female voice asked, bringing him back to the present.

Aquila turned his head towards the speaker to find the lady in the magenta dress, smiling shyly from behind his shoulder. "Ummm … no … please, have a seat," Aquila said, pulling up a chair for her.

"I saw you at the library. In fact, I see you there every day." The lady sat down on the proffered chair. "So, I thought I'd say hi."

"Great idea. Yeah, thanks for doing that. I'm Aquila. I'm new here and looking to meet the locals."

"Oh, I'm not a local either," the lady explained with a flick of her hand. "We were on the same flight here, remember? I'm Razzy, by the way."

"Nice to meet you Razzy," Aquila said, smiling with his eyes. "Now that you mention it ... yeah, you're right. You were on my flight from Moscow," he added with an air of nonchalance, that he didn't quite pull off. "So, you're a Russian, eh?"

"Ummm ... no, not exactly Russian, either. I'm actually American."

"American ... meaning from the Republic?"

At this, Razzy's face became remarkably stern. "There's only one America," she replied curtly.

"I guess you can argue that ..." Aquila started, but noticing the expression in Razzy's eyes, he decided to let it go. "Never mind. Hey, let me get you a drink. What would you like?"

Razzy relaxed into her seat and smiled. "The merlot here is really good."

"Great choice. Wait right here, I'll get you a glass." He strolled off to the bar.

Aquila soon returned with another mug of beer for himself and a merlot for the lady. "Cheers." He raised his glass to hers. Then, taking a long sip, he searched for ways to resume the conversation. He didn't have to try too hard, because Razzy was quick to break the silence.

"I take it you're Russian, then?" she asked.

"Yep, Russian through and through. My ancestors migrated there nearly a century ago, and since then we've been calling Moscow our home."

"Very cool. And what brought you to these parts?"

"Just business. Same as you. Do you work at a plant, perhaps?" Aquila asked, wary of giving away his designation, just in case she might be on his staff.

"No, no. I have nothing to do with the Project. I'm a journalist with The International Gazette. I'm here to work on a book."

"A book, eh? That sounds really interesting." Aquila

breathed a sigh of relief. "What is it about?"

"About the Project, of course." Razzy appeared bewildered. "It's a big deal you know. At the ICC, I mean. Once the rehabilitation begins, it'll be on every news channel. The hottest subject on everyone's lips. And when that happens—"

"You want to be right there with your timely and well researched book, am I right?" Aquila laughed, flashing a set of beautifully aligned teeth.

The single dimple on his right cheek caught Razzy's attention and she blushed. "You have a nice smile," she said, softly.

"Thanks! You're the only one who's ever said that."

"You're kidding!"

"No, absolutely not," Aquila lied.

"Ahem, not sure if I'm interrupting, but I brought a plate of fries for the table," Orion's voice boomed from Aquila's left.

"Hey, you're back!" Aquila exclaimed, spotting his manger. "No, not interrupting at all. Please do join. This is Razzy."

"Yes, I know," Orion said, with a half smile.

"I met him for an interview, a week after I landed here," Razzy explained.

"Plus, it's my business to know everyone who enters my district. Everything goes through me, all flight data, passenger lists, you know … everything," Orion said.

"That's true. How could I have forgotten? Must be the alcohol." Aquila laughed out loud. He reached over and grabbed some fries. Orion did the same. Razzy however, became a little withdrawn and fidgeted awkwardly, often glancing at Orion from the corner of her eye.

With more alcohol and as the night progressed, Razzy seemed to relax a bit. The three of them ended up hanging out at the pub into the late hours of the night, until Orion finally got up to leave. After he left, Aquila and Razzy exchanged phone numbers, promising to meet again over the weekend. Aquila went home that night, feeling like his broken pieces were finally starting to mend.

CHAPTER TEN

The next morning, Aquila found himself groggy and disoriented, struggling with a bad hangover. He woke up late, went for a jog and had a strong coffee spiked with a hangover tincture that he always brewed from scratch. This tincture was the real stuff. In about an hour, he was as fit as a fiddle.

With his headache eased, clarity set in. He realized that he had drunk away an entire month's ration of alcohol in just one sitting. Orion must have done the same. This would effectively ban them from buying anymore booze until the first of July, which was more than twenty days away. He still had a couple of bottles in his cellar, and Orion probably had some too, but their Friday night outings would have to be paused for now.

Considering that his social life here was already limited, this was an unfortunate situation. He was about to call Orion to grumble about their predicament, when going through his contact list, he noticed a new number. Razzy! He had met Razzy at the pub last evening, and they were supposed to meet again tomorrow. Life was not that gloomy after all.

With a newfound joy for life, Aquila had breakfast on his verandah watching the little orange and yellow-necked birds chirping in the nearby trees. After lunch, he called Dorado and caught up with the developments from Moscow. Fornax had apparently made his peace with Aquila's departure and was not asking any more questions about his whereabouts. There was still a warrant out for him, but it was not enforceable outside of Russia, just like they had anticipated. Already, Aquila was becoming just one of those petty offenders who became irrelevant to the authorities with the passage of time.

Hanging up the call with Dorado, Aquila felt blissfully at ease. He decided to take a short nap. He woke up just in time for his visit to the library. He had his tea and took off for his office complex. He couldn't recall, if they were supposed to meet in front of the library or in Orion's office. Taking an educated guess, he went directly to the library.

Orion was waiting for him when he arrived.

"How's the hangover?" he asked with a grin.

"All better now. But it was terrible when I woke up!"

"Really! How did you make it go away?"

"Oh, I have this tincture recipe that I've been using for more than a decade. It works like a charm!"

"You don't say! Looks like I need to borrow that recipe of yours." Orion paused as they approached the restricted section. "Or better still, can I get some tincture?" He frowned and massaged his forehead.

"Yeah, I can make you a bottle," Aquila said with a smile. They stood in front of the arch where Aquila was stopped the day before. "Should I pass?" he asked, indicating the arch.

"Yes, you can go ahead. I approved your clearance this morning."

Aquila passed without incident, followed closely by Orion. Orion touched the sensor pad on the door in front of them and let them inside. The door immediately closed behind them. It was a small room without any windows. In the center, there were three cozy couches arranged in a circular pattern around a low cylindrical terminal. The terminal had numerous touch-activated buttons for various functions such as activating holos, adjusting volumes and scrolling through files.

"This is it." Orion plopped into a sofa. "Our restricted collection. I had this terminal loaded with everything we could salvage from that wreckage … you've heard the story, right?"

"Yeah, Dorado mentioned the crashed aircraft that was discovered by your divers," Aquila confirmed.

"There you go. So, you know. Anyway, I had Ramesh work on the recovery. He loaded all the files he could restore, into a terminal. We stuffed that terminal into this room and put up all the security around it. That's how this section of the library was born."

"Interesting. What was in this room before that?"

"Nothing. It was just a reading room for those, who wanted a little more peace and quiet."

"Got it. And other than Ramesh and you, does anyone else have access?"

"Dorado did, when he was here. But now, it's just the three of us. So yeah, like I told you before; see what you want in here, but share it with no one. *Do you understand?*" Orion leaned forward and looked Aquila straight in the eyes to emphasize his point. "Not even that lady friend of yours. Especially not *her*. You can never trust a reporter with a scoop like this," he added.

"Lady friend?" Aquila frowned. "Oh, Razzy … I just met her last night. Can't really call her a friend."

"Well, things can change real fast," Orion said playfully. "But even if everything changes, some things must never. And this is such a thing. Breach this trust, and I'll have you banished from the Project."

Aquila laughed. "Aww c'mon, you don't seriously mean that!"

"Try me," Orion said with a straight face.

"Jokes aside," Aquila said, becoming serious. "I'm not sharing this secret with anyone. You have my word of honour."

"Good." Orion picked up a remote from a side table next to his seat. "Here, you can use this to bring up the full list of what's in there. There are thousands of hours of material, I believe. Watch at your leisure." He tossed the remote to

Aquila, who was sitting at the other end of the couch.

"Thousands of hours, eh? That's like paradise for me! Have you seen everything?"

"*Everything?* You crazy? I haven't got the patience. But I have a general idea of the kind of stuff that's on there. A lot of history. Some live footage from around the time of the Deluge. Go on, pull up the menu and you'll see," Orion encouraged.

Aquila used his remote to display the menu which appeared suspended over the central terminal. "Let's see, what do we have here … Siege of Paris … riots … more riots …"

"That's filmed during the weeks that led up to the tsunami … right before Paris was consumed by the sea,' Orion clarified.

"Ah, okay. And what is this … Renaissance … French Revolution … but that's like really really old? Who still cares about the Renaissance?"

Orion shrugged. "I dunno … historians?"

"Sure, but my point is, these files were stolen. *Stolen.* And then possibly dumped into the ocean. You think a bunch of snuffy old *historians* would do that? I mean, what on earth for?"

"You have a point. But to be honest, we don't know that any of this was stolen. They could've just been misplaced. After all, the Deluge was a chaotic event and when cities sank, a great deal of their wealth went down with them. Some were recovered and others, lost forever."

Aquila shook his head vehemently. "It's super fishy, if you ask me."

"It *is* slightly odd, I must admit, but you don't need to go looking for conspiracy in everything."

Aquila flicked his manager an incredulous look. "Is that right? Then how come you're keeping it all locked up in here like some pirate's treasure? You suspect something too. Just admit it!"

"Maybe I do," Orion admitted. "But I want us to keep an open mind. And not jump to conclusions. Makes sense?"

"Alright, I can do that. Let's see … what else have we got

here," Aquila said, as he continued to scroll. "Aus ... Auschwitz. What's that?"

"Ah, that's an interesting one. It was a concentration camp built during World War II by—"

"Adolf Hitler."

"Correct."

"Wait, I thought this material was all related to what used to be the French nation, but Hitler was from Germany ..."

"Exactly. And that's why I think this is the interesting part. Most of the resources in here are, as you said, from erstwhile France. With some rare exceptions. And this is one of the exceptions. Now, in terms of why it's in there, your guess is as good as mine. Maybe if you watch it all, you'll be able to figure it out. I certainly haven't!"

"But aren't you curious? Wouldn't you like to know?"

"Of course, I would. Why else would I be guarding these here in such secrecy? *They must mean something.* But I simply don't have the time or resources to uncover that meaning. Unless of course, you want to add that to your to-do list, with everything else you've already got on your plate." Orion laughed in a friendly, kind-hearted way.

"Yeah, given everything else ... and by everything else I mean killer robots ... that I have on my hands, I'd have probably turned that offer down. But this is not work. For a history buff like me, this is pure and perfect entertainment. Besides, I'm bored to death on most days. So, I'll try to figure this one out, if I can."

"All the better for us! If you can crack the mystery behind the existence of these files then, who knows, we can become rich perhaps."

"Ha! I dunno about becoming rich but ... I do want to make sure they aren't an augury of danger."

"Oh Aquila, you and your fear-mongering!"

"I'm not fear-mongering. Just being cautious. We live in complicated times."

"I do agree with you there," Orion nodded.

"And then look at what's on these files ... riots ... sieges ... *Hitler,* for crying out loud! Fear would be a completely justified emotion."

"Just because someone studies violence in history, doesn't mean that they are scary people. All of this could simply be study-material for a team or something."

"Again, with you and your historian theory!" Aquila cried out, his face sweaty and flushed. "I bet these files weren't with historians. Can't prove it yet, but that's what my gut tells me."

"Well then, go ahead. Do your research, and we'll see what you can find."

"That's the plan." Aquila relaxed into his seat folded his arms behind his head. "By the way, how much of this information is brand new? Like stuff no one's seen before?"

"A fair bit, I'd say. For example, everyone knew about Hitler and his concentration camps, but much of the details around the camps themselves were lost. Like Auschwitz. I'd never heard that name before."

"Me neither. Interesting."

"There's more like that. You'll find chunks of stuff in here that are completely omitted from other historical records."

"You're kidding!"

"No," Orion said solemnly.

"No wonder you think it's valuable." Aquila rubbed his chin, deep in thought.

"Anyway, you can come here whenever you like. Or stick around tonight even. Just keep me posted on any discoveries from this project. I'm ready for some dinner. Are you staying?"

Aquila's stomach growled at the mention of dinner. "Actually, I'll come back later." He stood up. "I'm kind of hungry, myself."

"Okay. Come join me for dinner, if you don't have other plans," Orion invited. "My chef is making a fine sea-food bisque tonight. It's more fun when you share the joy."

"Wonderful! I'd love to join. After you," Aquila said, holding the door for his boss.

CHAPTER ELEVEN

At dinner, Aquila did not ask Orion any more questions about the secret files, nor did they discuss about work. Instead, they bonded over some good music and ended the night playing digital chess. Aquila came home before midnight and went straight to bed, waking up fully rejuvenated the following morning.

It was a bright day outside, when Aquila ordered his morning tea on Sunday. He was looking forward to meeting Razzy that evening. Grinning to himself at the thought, he promptly pulled out his phone and sent her a voice burst, wishing her a good morning and asking her if she was still free. Then, he set down his phone and started planning his day. He wondered what they could do together on their first evening. Inviting her over to his place would be too forward. A restaurant might work better, but he had exhausted his monthly alcohol allowance. It would be rude, not to buy the lady a drink at dinner. He clicked his tongue. He was out of ideas. Planning a date was never his forte. He usually preferred to just go with the flow. As he finished his tea and set the cup down, his kitchen robot appeared by his side.

"Will you be going to the office today, Sir?" it asked.

"What? The office ... no ... wait, that's it! The office. I'll go to the office."

"I'm sorry Sir, but are you going, or aren't you?"

"I'm going, I'm going. But not right now. In the afternoon. Can you pack me some food?"

"Of course, Sir. What would you like?"

"Ummm ... let's see ... what do you have that's fresh?"

"Ah, there's plenty of stuff that came in about an hour ago. The catch of the day was a large bighead carp. We got some fresh plantain and beetroots. Some feta cheese straight from the dairy farm ... and some fine crabs freshly caught ... let's see and ..."

"Okay, I get the idea. That's plenty of goodies right there. How about you pack me a bottle of Pinot Grigio with some fish and crab cakes and ... um plantain chips? And how about some warm beet salad with feta? Can you have that ready by four?"

"Of course, I can. In an auto-heat basket, Sir?"

"Yes, please," Aquila said. The robot turned to leave. "Oh wait," Aquila called it back. "Please make it a meal for two." The robot nodded and rolled away.

Aquila stretched his back and relaxed into his chair. He would take Razzy to the recreation room next to their cafeteria. *Why didn't I think of that before?* he wondered.

The building would be completely deserted on a Sunday. The only two people who ever showed up to work on the weekends, were Aquila and Orion. And today, Orion was going to be at a plant, checking on the weather system. They had a weather event planned for this afternoon—a thunderstorm. If everything went well, the clouds would gather by around five-thirty. It would be best to meet Razzy before that.

They could watch movies. He stood up to look for his portable holo home theatre. Pulling it out of a drawer in his closet, he started flicking through the menu. He had a huge collection of holo-films on it. He got busy picking some good ones to suggest to Razzy later. He brushed past all the romances, rejecting them at once. Too cheesy for a first date. Instead, he shortlisted some dramas, a couple of thrillers, an action-adventure that he loved and a few classics. He popped the chosen holos into a separate folder, turned off his home theatre and packed it into a duffle bag.

After all the planning was done, he took his breakfast out on the verandah and sat down to get some work done. He answered some mail and checked on the plant controls to make sure the weather system was proceeding as planned. He looked up at the sky to confirm what the system told him. Far into the distance, the western horizon was starting to appear overcast. A fragrant, moisture-laden breeze was blowing from west to east, which would carry the clouds closer to him by the end of the afternoon. Everything was going off without a hitch. Then, his phone beeped.

Must be Razzy, he thought.

"Play message," he said to his phone.

"Message delivery failed," replied the phone in its unromantic voice.

"That can't be right," Aquila murmured. "How many attempts were made?" he asked his phone.

"Calculating attempts. Fifty attempts."

"Is the phone switched off?"

"Communicating with Razzy's phone. Communication successful. Phone is in on-state."

"That's weird," Aquila said glumly.

"I do not understand that command," the phone replied.

"No, it's nothing. Abort message," Aquila told his phone.

"Message aborted."

Aquila checked the time. It was just ten o'clock. He stood up with a jolt and started pacing around his verandah with his arms crossed over his chest.

"Why does it always happen to me?" he muttered, berating himself. "Did I come on too strong? Or am I too awkward. No, not awkward, more like aloof. Yeah, that's gotta be it. I'm just aloof. A nerd to the bitter end. Gosh, look at me behaving like a teenager." He shook his head in incredulity.

He took a couple of deep breaths to calm himself and went in to the kitchen to cancel the evening meal. Instead, he ordered a healthier dinner for just himself, together with a large mug of coffee to go. He made up his mind to leave for the library before the storm hit, and enjoy his evening digging through the God of War files.

* * *

When he arrived at the library, the sky was darkening fast. Terrible claps of thunder sounded from the large glass windows, filling the entrance hall with a transient, angelic light. There was not a soul in sight in the entire building, just as Aquila had expected. He appreciated this solitude. He didn't bother to turn on any of the main lights and headed straight to the restricted section instead.

Once inside the cozy nest of the secret room, he settled himself on a sofa and grabbed his auto-reheatable mug of coffee. He placed it on a side table along with his box of dinner. He found a floating stool to rest his feet and leaned back with his coffee in hand, as he browsed through the menu.

"The Siege of Paris, yeah this looks interesting. Let's start there ..." he mumbled before starting the holo.

Mobs could be seen in flooded streets looting various buildings—The Louvre, the Palace of Versailles, the Château de Fontainebleau, the Hôtel des Invalides and various other buildings that were not easily recognizable. Paintings were being torn off the walls, shattered ceramic and glass littered the floors, royal memorabilia were being pilfered. It was chaos and mayhem everywhere you looked.

"And there, we see a very rowdy group, breaking in through the windows," said an agitated narrator voice. "They are climbing on to the tomb. Nay, they are breaking it! An angry mob is breaking the tomb of Napoleon Bonaparte! The grave of the greatest French icon, the hero of a nation is being desecrated before our eyes! Oh God, what a terrible day … the paramilitary, as you can see, are trying to make their way into this area. They're clashing with—" Aquila switched off the holo.

"Napoleon Bonaparte? Who the hell is that?" he said to himself. He prompted the terminal to search for all the files sub-indexed under Napoleon, then Bonaparte, then Napoleon Bonaparte. The terminal found hundreds of entries in the search results. Aquila set down his coffee, lowered his feet and sat up straight.

"Very Interesting," he whispered. "All these years of studying world history, and I hadn't heard of him? A French icon, they said. What the hell is going on here?" He selected the first file he found under Napoleon and played it.

Now, he would have to examine them all.

CHAPTER TWELVE

Carina fiddled anxiously with an unruly strand of hair as she waited for her upcoming meeting. She had not seen the Chancellor since his return from the latest foreign trip, nearly a week ago. The debate on the Armaments Resolution was coming up, and he would certainly be overwhelmed with the preparations. She wondered if she should postpone her meeting until after the debate. But this was a critical issue, having potentially far-reaching consequences, if proven to be true. It would not be wise to delay the discussion.

She sat ramrod straight at the large oval desk in her luxurious office going over Alrakis' report one last time. Alrakis had never failed her before, so she trusted it with all her heart. But the real question was, what would the Chancellor say? There was a knock on her door.

"Come in," she said. "Ah, think of the devil ..." She smiled at her aide, who had just walked in.

"Are you ready?" Alrakis asked.

"As ready as I'll ever be." Carina sighed.

"Good. Let's go then. It's almost time."

Carina got up and grabbed her tablet. "Yep. Did you make sure he's meeting with us alone?"

"Of course. That's why we had to wait this long. For his schedule to clear."

"Excellent. When we get there, let me do all the talking, you understand? He loses focus when multiple people speak at once."

"Got it, Ma'am," Alrakis replied in his characteristically playful way.

Carina smiled in response, before heading out the door. Chancellor Cygnus, who was the reigning leader of Calamerica, had his office in the west-wing of the Presidential Mansion with Carina's chamber one level below it. Although Calamerica did not have a President, the Chancellor's house was still called the Presidential Mansion, in keeping with ancient American legacy. As the leader of the nation, the Chancellor lived in the east-wing of this building along with his family, whereas the west-wing was completely dedicated to official business.

As Carina walked down the corridor with Alrakis at her side, many heads turned to look at her. Her confident, straight-backed frame tended to cast an imposing aura over any room she deigned to enter. And so was it now, as she walked over to the elevators, comporting herself with utmost grace and dignity. Arriving in front of the Chancellor's office, they were led in by his secretary, who promptly left the room to give them privacy.

"Please, sit down," said the Chancellor in a heavy voice.

"Thank you." Carina and Alrakis said simultaneously. "And thank you for meeting with us," Carina added respectfully.

"Of course. I'm sorry I could only find fifteen minutes. I have delegates waiting, you see."

"No need to apologize, Sir. We do understand," Carina confirmed. "We'll get straight to the point."

"Yes please. I hear it's urgent?"

"Indeed, it is."

"Concerning the Armaments Resolution, I presume?"

"No, not at all," Carina said, casting a quick glance to her aide.

"What is it then? Go on …"

"Actually Sir, it's about the Republic. We suspect that they're pursuing an illegal cloning project."

"Cloning? I take it you mean human clones?"

"Precisely. Full grown human clones," Carina said with an ominous look in her eyes.

"That's a very serious accusation, Madam! As you know, it's prohibited as per the Treaty."

"Yes, I know. And that's why I said, illegal. I'm of the opinion that we should send an independent body of international delegates to investigate."

The Chancellor shook his head vehemently. "We cannot just do that without any cause. Do you have watertight substantiating evidence?"

"No, but we do have shreds of evidence that point to—"

"*Shreds* of evidence? Just *shreds*?" The Chancellor banged a fist into his desk. "No, no, no, we definitely can't proceed with anything that's short of conclusive …"

"But how do we get conclusive information about another sovereign country, without sending in an independent team?" Carina countered.

"That's not how things work in diplomacy. You should know that better than me. Given the tensions between our nations, if we request such an investigation and the team finds nothing, we're just asking to be kicked off the Conservation Council's permanent members' list."

"Yes, I do understand, but our spies—"

"Spies are spies. They exist to protect our nation from foreign threats. Let them do their jobs. Seeking international intervention based on a spy report would be imprudent. Besides, from the intelligence reports I've received so far, all attempts to create a complete human clone have failed. Even if I were to believe that they were trying to create human clones, our top scientists have claimed that such a venture would not succeed. The technique has not been perfected. Now, if we go poking our noses into a failed project, we are bound to invite more questions than answers."

"But Sir, you don't understand, if a successful project does exist, then of course our scientists wouldn't be aware of it. The experts that work in Area 51 are sworn to secrecy—"

"Area 51? You think that's where the project is based?"

"That's our hunch, yes."

"I find it quite impossible. Area 51 was destroyed during World War VI. I smell a conspiracy theory!"

"Officially it was, but … Sir, please give us a chance to explore this further. I don't trust all the official information we are getting from their government."

"Neither do I. But, like I said, until we have hard facts, it's just a conspiracy theory and we cannot call for international action based on conspiracy theories."

"Will you authorize the funds for us to continue our investigation then?"

"Depends. I welcome an investigation but first, I'd like to see the proposal. Budget is tight as you are aware, and we have other priorities. Send me your draft proposal, and I'll consider it."

"Fair enough. I'll have our Intelligence Department prepare a proposal by the end of the week."

"Good. I'm afraid that's all I have time for today," the Chancellor said standing up. "I'll look forward to your proposal." He extended Carina a handshake.

Carina and Alrakis shook hands with the Chancellor and took their leave, promising to be back to discuss their proposal next week. Once outside the room, Alrakis sighed.

"Think we should've told him about the impersonation gloves?" he whispered in Carina's ear.

"Of course not," Carina replied almost inaudibly. *We cannot compromise The Underground;* she thought to herself.

CHAPTER THIRTEEN

E very year on August 15th, Aquila's district celebrated Independence Day. Although India was no longer a sovereign country, the inhabitants of this district carried on the tradition of their ancestral land and modified the celebrations to resemble a harvest festival. This made sense, because August was typically the time when the summer crops began to be harvested.

Aquila had learned that the locals had another reason for continuing to mark August 15th as their Independence Day. It was a tribute to their project, Project 15/8, which accidentally or not, had the date 15/8 built into its name. Project 15/8 was to bring about their salvation, their economic independence, to be precise. Once the project was over, they would be freed from their current economic hardship and transported to the paradise colony of Sanctuary City, where they would receive lifelong pensions. Project 15/8 would set them free. Hence the festivities continued each year on this auspicious day.

This year was Aquila's first, and he was excited to participate. He had been invited to one of the largest farm units near the center of the district, to inaugurate the celebrations. He arrived there bright and early and was greeted by a cheering crowd of farmers clad in a variety of exotic costumes and headdresses. He waved to everyone as he mounted a podium to deliver his opening speech. Scores of people, young and old, waved back and tossed their hats into the air in greeting. Aquila had never addressed a crowd before and was slightly daunted by the idea. He decided to keep it short and honest.

"Good morning, everyone!" he said to the gathered audience. "It's so wonderful to see you all assembled here today. The harvest season is upon us. And our Day of Independence is also around the corner. Very soon, we will be reaping our last harvests here for Project 15/8 and sailing to brighter shores. Metaphorically of course, but you know what I mean. Soon, all our hard work will be rewarded and we will once again be truly free. So, while we can, let us make this day worth remembering with our music and laughter and merrymaking that continues into the night. I don't want to keep you here any longer. Go now and make sure to have a great time!" With that he smiled, waved and stepped off the podium to a roaring applause.

Finishing his speech, Aquila went about surveying the area around the podium. It was set up like a fair with little stalls selling their edibles and colourful wares. Interspersed between these vendors were magicians, folk dancers and musicians performing their gigs and being replaced by other groups of performers, some in costumes, others with painted faces and bodies. The air was redolent with the scent of freshly fried fish and chocolate covered pineapples. The entire farm was vibrant with the infectious energy of the festivities.

After watching some of the performances and trying a few snacks from the stalls, Aquila met with the unit's plant manager and walked with him to the lunch area.

"A beautiful day, isn't it?" Aquila remarked, looking all around him.

"Yes, it really is," the plant manger replied. "Is this your first time at this farm?"

"In fact, it is," Aquila confessed.

"And? What do you think?" his companion asked with a sweeping motion of his arms.

"Well … I haven't really seen much of it yet … only this region. But so far so good." Aquila shrugged.

The plant manager glanced at the buffet area, before turning back to face Aquila. "Looks like it'll be a bit longer for the buffet to be ready. Do you want me to give you a little tour? We have some wonderful drip irrigation going on in the maize fields over there," he said, pointing to his left.

"Yeah, that'd be fantastic. Let's do that."

They turned left and made their way towards a dirt road between two vegetable patches. In the distance, they could see the tall stalks of corn swaying in the wind. It was a clear, cloudless day that was starting to get rather warm. Aquila rolled up his sleeves and undid the top two buttons of his shirt to cool down. They walked at a leisurely pace, stopping to inspect the vegetable patches and making sure the cultivable land was being fully utilized. Aquila was satisfied with what he saw and conveyed his sentiments without hesitation.

Finally, they arrived at the edge of the corn field. From where they stood, it looked intimidating—like a gigantic maze with narrow paths in between, where one could easily lose his way, never to be found again.

Aquila laughed at this realization. "After you," he said to the plant manager. "I feel like if I go in first, I'll be lost in no time!"

"Ha! I don't blame you. The maize fields can be confusing, if you don't know your way. Come, I'll show you the neat network of drippers and micro-spray heads going on in there," the manager said, as he jogged into the field.

Aquila followed right behind, trying to keep up with his subordinate. He had hardly made it a few feet, when he tripped over something and fell to his knees.

"Watch it, that's my set up!" yelled a female voice from behind a row of corn. Hurried footsteps advanced towards Aquila.

"Razzy?" Aquila exclaimed, getting back on his feet.

Razzy's cheeks flushed crimson. "Oh," she said meekly. "I ... um ..." She bit her lip.

"Do you have permission to be on this field, Ma'am? Can I see a permit?" the manager came up to ask.

"Yes *of course* I have a permit," Razzy replied in an offended tone. "I'm a reporter with The International Gazette," she added, extending her hand in greeting.

"Nice to meet you," said the manager with a nod. "And do you know her, Sir?" he asked Aquila.

"In fact, I do, yes."

"Here's my permit," said Razzy as she flicked her wrist and displayed the access band around it.

"Thank you, would you like to join us on a survey of the irrigation system?" asked the manager with a smile.

Razzy dismissed the offer with a wave of her hand. "I'm sorry, I can't. I'll have to set this up all over again. The camera got unplugged and the mount fell over ... but ..." She looked meekly at Aquila before continuing. "I'm wondering if I could talk to you later ... maybe after lunch? I'd like to—"

"Actually, let me help you fix the set up," Aquila interrupted, noticing where this conversation was heading. "It was my fault. I knocked it over."

"Oh, you don't have to, but if you *want* to ..." Razzy trailed off, grinning sheepishly.

"Yes, I do want to," Aquila assured and then turning to the manager, "How about I meet you in the lunch area, in ... say ... fifteen minutes? And you can give me your tour after lunch," he said.

"As you wish," said the manger with a slight nod. "I'll wait for you near the buffet table."

Once the manager was out of ear shot, Aquila turned towards Razzy with his hands on his hips. "So," he said frowning. "Where do we start?"

Razzy smiled, brushing away a stray strand of hair from her eyes. "How about we start with me telling you that I owe you an apology?" she said coyly.

"Is that right? And what exactly for?" Aquila teased.

Razzy chuckled and made a silly face. "I mean it. I'm really sorry. That day, I got called into something important. I had no phone coverage the whole day. But I should've returned your call later. I wanted to. I really did. It just felt awkward to make excuses after disappearing like that and … the longer I waited to call you back, the harder it became to explain away my situation." Delivering her monologue in one breath, she stopped to heave a sigh.

"Hey, shit happens, okay? No need to get all worked up about it," Aquila said comfortingly. "I'm glad we had a chance to clear it up though. To be honest, I was kind of worried about you. But then I thought you're a reporter, so—"

"Ha! Yeah, we have precarious lives for sure. Precarious and unpredictable," Razzy interrupted. "Still, I have no excuse. What I did was rude, and I'm sorry."

"Apology accepted. Now, shall we get to work? What was it you were setting up here?"

"Ah yes, a time-lapse holo-recorder."

"To capture the irrigation mechanism?"

"No, of course not. In my industry no one cares about irrigation. It's too boring. I am trying to capture smoke patterns."

"*Smoke patterns*?" Aquila asked in amazement.

"Yeah, from the Black Lands," she said matter-of-factly, while turning her back to Aquila and pointing straight ahead.

"The what now?"

Razzy whirled around like a ballet dancer at this question, her eyes as wide as pizzas. "Are you telling me you've never heard of the Black Lands? Beyond this field?"

"Ummm … this is embarrassing …but I believe I haven't," Aquila confessed.

"Good God! How much time do you have? Come, I can show you," she offered.

"How far is it from here?"

"Less than a mile."

"Okay, let's go then. I'm sure no one will mind me being a few minutes late for lunch."

"Right. Follow me. The path in here is confusing, but I've got sensors set up that'll show us the way."

"Smoke sensors?"

"Correct," said Razzy, as she trotted forward. "The smoke will start getting stronger as we get closer. Not enough for us to smell it, but enough for the sensors to pick up and image. The micro-environment inside the Project almost keeps the smoke out entirely. That's what I'm trying to capture with my imaging—how the smoke levels drop exponentially as soon as we enter the Project."

They almost sprinted through the corn field, winding and curving in accordance with the sensor placements along the way. In a few minutes, they arrived at the edge of the field, panting and puffing and trying to catch their breaths. Aquila bent double over his knees to take in a lungful of oxygen, before straightening to behold the sight in front of his eyes.

"Holy shit," he said, pointing in front of him. "Is that it?"

Razzy nodded in the affirmative. Standing now at the edge of the maize field, they saw several hundred meters of barren land ahead of them on a downward incline. Beyond that, a charred, skeletal forest stretched on, till what seemed like the end of the world. They could hear crackling sounds coming from a very great distance. And plumes of smoke darkened the distant horizon, where the forest seemed to blend into the sky.

"I think you can smell it just a tad over here, at the edge," Razzy said, sniffing the air around them. She plopped down on a soft tuft of grass, with her knees folded in front of her.

Aquila went to sit beside her. Then looking up at the forest, he said, "How did that happen? Forest fires?"

"What else? At first, before Project 15/8 was envisioned or funded, there was an effort to revitalize this area and facilitate carbon sequestration with acres and acres of planted forests. You know, to try and salvage this land, and make it somewhat habitable again—"

"Habitable and cultivable, I presume?"

"Correct. Years of industrial exploitation of this region had killed the vegetation completely. Nothing grew anymore. Rain was scarce. As the weather warmed up, dry desert terrain was threatening to swallow up every last acre of these lands."

"So, these forests were planted?"

"You got it! It was progressing quite well, as you can see. Full grown trees covered all of that area in front of us. But then, it got hotter still and drier and the forest fires hit. And now, this is what remains."

"I see. I can still see smoke inside. Some smaller fires continue to flare up, I suppose?" Aquila enquired, shading his eyes with his hands, and gazing into the distance.

"Yep. There are drones up there in the sky, continuously putting them out. It's an exhausting and expensive business."

"When the Project was built, why didn't they bring the Black Lands inside its climate-controlled zone?"

"It was already too far gone to salvage at that point. The cost to benefit ratio wouldn't have made sense either. Instead, they planted the other forest. The one that you passed on your way here from the airport. It's much smaller, but it's something." Razzy shrugged.

"I see. So do you have your sensors inside the Black Lands as well?"

"Oh, no. Can't do that. It's forbidden. Too poisonous in there. Once the forest fires kicked in, something rose from the earth that was not simply smoke. There were some chemicals in the soil that burned up along with the trees. The vapours that got released—and are still being released with the smaller fires—are quite deadly."

"So, no one is allowed to go in there at all?"

"No, you can go. With the proper protective suits, which are really hard to come by. But planting sensors is out of the question. There are laws against that."

"Interesting. I'd really like to know how bad it's still in there. Like air and soil quality-wise."

"Why? You think you can salvage it?"

"Well, that's my job, isn't it? I'm a conservation engineer. Reviving lost resources is my forte. Besides, I want to figure out, who did this to the earth? And make them accountable."

"Isn't that what the climate debt is all about? Project 15/8 is the reparation they paid for the damage. The first world countries. What more accountability do you expect?"

"That's what I have to find out!"

"Don't even think about it," Razzy cautioned.

"And why not?" Aquila turned to flash her his most radiant smile.

"No good can come of it. Plus, you could very well die in there. Some people have."

"Ha! I'm not afraid of death," Aquila said, as he stood up. He extended a hand to Razzy to help her to her feet. "Shall we get some lunch?" he added.

CHAPTER FOURTEEN

When Aquila returned home that evening, he could not stop thinking about the Black Lands. He stayed up late that night, lying on his back and picturing the charcoal-streaked devastation play out all over his ceiling. Thankfully, it was Friday and Razzy had promised to meet him for lunch the next afternoon. This time he did not even have to plan their date. Razzy had been the one to suggest that she could meet him at his residence. She even promised to bring some food. But given what had happened the last time, Aquila decided to take all her assurances with generous helpings of salt.

The next morning, Razzy called to confirm that she was indeed planning to come over for lunch that day. She wanted to know if he liked stews. She was going to make some for him. Aquila should have been excited. He could not remember the last time an actual human being had cooked something for him. Cooking was not much in vogue in Russia. It was too energy-intensive to have individual homes set-up with fully-equipped kitchens. The community kitchens that served their daily rations were a great deal more effective, and everyone just went with that model without asking any questions. Today would be different. Yet, Aquila could not muster up the enthusiasm he had expected to feel. His mind was preoccupied the entire morning.

After breakfast, Aquila found his agitation giving way to determination, as a resolution started to form. He needed to find a hazmat suit. He remembered the one he had dawned on his way here from the airport and started looking for it in his bedroom closet. After fifteen minutes of literally turning his bedroom upside down, he could not locate it anywhere. So, he summoned his house-robot.

"Do you remember the suit I wore, when I arrived here for the first time?" he asked.

The robot took a second to search its memory bank before responding. "Yes, Sir. I have located the memory. Would you like me to describe it for you?"

"No, I remember it too. I just can't find it. Do you know where it might be?"

"Ah yes, certainly." It paused again to search its memory. "It was a standard issue, military-grade protective gear that belonged to the airport authority. By law, it was to be deposited in a pick-up box for security equipment the following morning. You'll be glad to learn Sir, that I have followed protocols and returned it to the pick-up box number three hundred and seven at eight hours and fifteen minutes on Tuesday—."

"Jesus Christ!"

"I'm sorry, Sir. Did I make a mistake?"

"No, no ... you did alright. It's just ... I wasn't aware of that requirement."

"I apologize for not having informed you of that legislation. Normally, it is stipulated on the packaging for such gear, but sometimes people do not notice it."

"Yeah, I have no idea what was written on it. Anyway, the bigger question is, what do we do now?" Aquila mumbled mostly to himself, while cupping his chin and furrowing his brow.

The robot looked quizzically at Aquila, as if not sure whether it was expected to respond. "Would you like me to order you one from the Project?" it then asked tentatively.

"You can do that?"

"I certainly can, Sir. The current wait time …" It paused to calculate. "Is one hundred and thirty-eight days," it said.

"Holy!" Aquila shrieked grabbing fistfuls of his hair in agitation. "Why this long?"

"Hold on Sir, let me query the system … I'm getting a message that there is a shortage of supply."

Aquila made a mental note to ask Orion about this situation on Monday. He dismissed his robot with a sigh and got to work clearing the mess he had made, while searching his closet earlier. He spent the next quarter of an hour arranging all his clothes back on the shelves where they belonged.

Disappointed and tired, he was finally about to walk away, when a fluffy cotton-bag lying inconspicuously in a corner, caught his attention. It was the gift Dorado had given him at the airport, right before his departure from Moscow. Aquila had stored it lovingly inside his closet as a reminder of their friendship, without ever having opened it at all. As soon as he landed in Lucknow, the bizarre and hectic new world had sucked him in so completely that he had forgotten all about it. But now it stared at him endearingly, begging to be opened.

Aquila pulled the bundle from its hiding place and ripped it open with alacrity. He could not believe his eyes when he saw what was inside. It was a high-quality hazmat suit of the finest material, fully equipped with helmet and mask. The only thing missing was an oxygen cylinder, which he could easily procure from one of the unit's hospital wings. A memory flashed into his mind—of Dorado asking him not to open the gift until he landed in Indochine.

"If you open it here, you won't appreciate its value," he had said.

Truer words could not have been said. Dorado must have known he would need it. But how? Did he visit the Black Lands as well? What did he find there? Aquila had to ask his friend these questions, but not yet. Not until he figured out some things for himself. Until then, it was important to act alone and keep his agenda under wraps.

His robot arrived. "Sir, you have a visitor," it said.

Aquila checked the time. It was almost noon. Razzy had come after all. "Yes, let her in please," he said. He tossed the bag back into his closet and closed the door. "Oh, before you go," he called, beckoning his robot back. "Could you order me an hour's supply of oxygen from a hospital wing? You know, the portable tanks?"

"Yes of course, but why Sir? Are you unwell?"

"No, I'm quite alright. Just need it for a project. When do you think I can get it by?"

"Checking with hospital ... I can get one delivered in an hour," the robot confirmed.

"Perfect, thanks. You can go. And please get the door."

Razzy was standing in Aquila's living room holding a steaming pot of stew, when he came out to meet her. She was dressed in delicate colours, a flowing lavender skirt of ankle-length, and a baby-blue tank top with frilly shoulder straps. The full-length skirt made her look slightly taller. Her hair was done up in an artistic top bun with a few stray strands curling around her temple. She looked other-worldly. Aquila smiled warmly and took the pot from her to hand it to his kitchen robot.

"So, you came?" he said laughing.

"Of I course I did. I'm not a flake, you know. Last time was ... well work is work and—"

"Yeah, I know. I was just messing around. No need to get emotional or anything," Aquila interrupted.

"Ha! I've never been accused of being emotional. Not once." Razzy grinned, sinking into a couch.

"Is that right? Me on the other hand, I cry like a baby every time my neighbour plays with his dog or when the wild flowers bloom in the spring."

"I can't tell if you're being sarcastic," Razzy wondered out loud, observing Aquila closely with her head cocked to one side.

"No, absolutely not! But enough about me, can I get you something to drink?"

"I usually don't drink during the day ..."

"I meant something non-alcoholic," Aquila clarified.

"Oh sorry. Yeah sure. What do you have?"

Aquila flicked his fingers to summon the kitchen robot. "Could you please tell our guest what kind of non-alcoholic beverages we have today?" he asked it.

"Why, of course. Would you prefer a cold beverage Ma'am or a warm one?" it asked turning to Razzy.

"Cold, please."

"Alright. We have fresh mango juice, iced-lemon tea and a farmer-made sherbet today, Ma'am."

"Oooh sherbet! I'll have the sherbet."

"A fine choice," said the robot, before turning to Aquila. "And for you, Sir?"

"Same for me, thank you."

The robot returned in a few minutes, carrying two ice-cold glasses of sherbet on a tray, together with some crackers.

Aquila grabbed a glass and sank into an armchair, becoming absent-minded.

"What's wrong?" Razzy asked, taking a sip of her drink.

"What? Nothing. Why?" Aquila replied, sitting up and looking slightly startled.

"You seem distracted."

"Oh, that. It's nothing," said Aquila, glancing at his phone to check the time. "Are you hungry?"

"Yeah, a little bit."

"Good!" Aquila clicked his fingers to summon his robot. "Could you please set the table for lunch?" he asked.

"Most certainly, Sir," the robot replied, bowing politely. "And your oxygen cylinder has also arrived. Would you like me to bring it here for you?"

"Ah, right. Yes, please take it to my bedroom, thanks." Aquila replied in a hurried tone, before turning towards Razzy.

"Shall we?" He motioned with his arm to invite her to the dining table.

Razzy set her empty glass down on the coffee table and rose with a swirl, her forehead puckered questioningly. She glided towards Aquila, and looked into his eyes saying, "Oxygen cylinder? Are you okay?"

"Yeah, I'm fine. It's just … err … you know, let's talk about it over lunch, alright?"

"Sure. But now I'm kind of worried."

"Oh, there's no need," Aquila assured with a wave of his hand.

They sat down at the dining table and allowed the kitchen-robot to load the table with various dishes, including the stew Razzy had prepared. Once the robot left, Aquila cleared his throat.

"So, yeah help yourself. I can't wait to try your stew. What's in it?" he asked with a smile.

Razzy did not smile back. Instead, she arched her eyebrows and bit her lips while flicking Aquila a piercing look, as if in an effort to fathom him.

"It's a root vegetable stew," she said, after a moment's silence. "Originally, I'd learned to make it with beef, but since we don't have any beef over here …" She reached forward and served herself some spinach salad.

"I see," said Aquila, ladling some stew into his soup bowl. "I hear that beef is a lot more abundant in the Republic. All we ever get in Russia is—"

"Synthetic beef. Yes, I know. But why are you avoiding my question?"

"Which question?" Aquila looked genuinely puzzled.

"Why are you stocking up on oxygen cylinders? I mean … you're not obligated to tell me. We hardly know each other, but I can't help feeling concerned. Should I be?" she asked, working her way through a mouthful of spinach.

"No. Like I said, there's no cause for concern. I just need it for work."

"Then why did you have it delivered to your home? Wait! You're planning to go to the Black Lands, aren't you?" she shrieked, dropping her fork on the plate with a clink.

Aquila grinned mischievously as he sipped his soup. "Think whatever you wish to."

"I see," said Razzy glumly, adding, "so, how's the stew?"

"It's excellent! I feel honoured that you went through the trouble of making it for me."

"Ha! There there, you don't need to be so formal," she said before falling silent.

For a few minutes, neither of them spoke, and all that could be heard, was the pattering of food onto plates, the jingle of cutlery, and the muted sounds of grinding teeth.

Razzy's voice suddenly erupted from the silence. "If you're going today, I'm coming with you."

"I'm sorry?" Aquila looked up from his plate, puzzled.

"To the Black Lands, I mean."

"You're doing no such thing. I'll go in the evening, after you've left."

"No, that'd be a foolish thing to do. If we must go at all then let's do it right after lunch. It's way too dangerous to tread that way after the sun has set."

"I get it, but there's no *we*. I'm going there by myself."

"Don't be silly," Razzy said, straightening her back and wearing a severe expression across her face. "Even government officials go there in pairs. If you're exposed and incapacitated for some reason, then you need another person to call for help. A few minutes of delay could be the difference between life and death inside that forest."

"Alright, alright, but do you even have a hazmat suit?"

Razzy looked embarrassed. "Ummm … no. Don't you have a spare?"

"I'm afraid not," Aquila said sadly.

"Really? But aren't you the district's second in command?"

Aquila shrugged. "Power has nothing to do with it. We run this place like a democracy." He chuckled.

"Yeah, right! Don't even get me started. It shows that you've never been to see the farmers."

Aquila narrowed his eyes at this. "Have you?"

"Of course. It's my business to know everything that's going on here. Like the palm of my hand."

"For your book?"

"Yes, and also generally. As a journalist, this is what we do. Anyway," Razzy checked the time. "We should get going, if you want to get there before sunset."

"I thought we agreed that you can't come."

"I made no such agreement," Razzy said, standing up and smiling mysteriously. "I'll come with you till the edge of the corn fields, and wait for you there. So that you can call me if you need help."

"You really are assertive, aren't you?" Aquila laughed.

"You'll thank me later. Let's get going," Razzy turned to say, as she trotted to the living room.

* * *

It was late afternoon, when Razzy and Aquila arrived at the edge of the central farm where the Black Lands began. This was a different location from where they had been the previous day, when Aquila had first set eyes on this devastating terrain. Standing within the Project's controlled environment, Aquila got into his hazmat suit.

"Okay, I'm all set," he said, once he was suited up completely, except for the helmet and oxygen mask.

"Do you have a gun?" Razzy asked.

"No. Do I need one? I thought that area was deserted ..."

"Well, it is ... but you never know. Remember what I told you though. You have to start making your way back in twenty minutes, at the most. If your oxygen tank runs out in there, you're toast. Got it?"

Aquila rolled his eyes. "I get it, yes. Just stay here and stay calm. If I'm not back in an hour—"

"I'll seek help." Razzy checked the time. "Now, go! Quick! We only have about two more hours of daylight left, and I don't fancy hanging around this area after the sun sets."

Aquila strapped a pouch onto his waist that contained his vials for sample collection. He made sure to tighten all the straps on his suit, in order to render it airtight. Then, affixing the final two pieces of his costume, the helmet and mask, he gave Razzy a slight nod and made his way towards the jungle from hell.

He had only advanced a couple of steps into the barren stretch of land, that lay in between himself and the forest, when the temperature difference struck him. Despite his temperature-controlled outfit, Aquila could feel tiny beads of sweat forming insidiously around his neckline. There was a subtle sense of suffocation, and the fabric of his suit clung to his clothes like Saran Wrap, threatening to fuse with the layers beneath it.

Being a tall man, he lengthened his strides to cross this area, hurrying as fast as his cumbersome attire would allow. Cautiously, he entered the tar-black vestiges of the forest beyond. It felt like he was inside a charcoal sketch of a haunted fantasy world. Gnarled stumps of trees stood at random angles across his path, twisted, blackened and devoid of life. The soil beneath his feet was granular and dry, with patches of charred grass. Nothing stirred. Not a critter anywhere.

Aquila allowed himself to wander a little bit further into the depths of the wood, before pulling out some empty vials from his pouch. He kneeled on the parched earth and started collecting a few samples.

There was a rustling sound. Aquila stopped and looked around. He could see nothing. Perhaps a gust of breeze had stirred a branch. He bent his head again, focusing on his work at hand. He grabbed a fist full of dirt and let it flow between his gloved fingers. To get a feel for the texture. To the naked eye, the colour and texture felt unnatural.

What could have been in this soil? he wondered. *Factory waste of some sort? Acidic perhaps? Hopefully not radioactive.* He considered the options in his head. He would have to run some tests as soon as he got back.

There was another rustling sound. Louder and nearer this time. The sound rapidly escalated and morphed into a crunch of stomping feet. Aquila jumped up and whirled around in a quick motion. But before he could take stock of the situation, he felt it.

A violent kick to his stomach.

Aquila doubled over in pain. Another kick landed on his side. He fell down. Someone pulled off his helmet. Aquila's windpipe threatened to close up. He gasped for air, but his lungs burned with every breath he took. He tried to focus his eyes on his assailant but failed. His vision was blurring. It felt like there were several people—at least two—pummeling him simultaneously. Aquila leaned on his forearm, trying frantically to haul himself to his feet.

A solid punch rammed into his jaw, moistening his lips with a salty liquid. His head spun, and he fell back on the ground again. A shot was fired at close range. Then another. Was he struck? Before he could tell, he passed out.

CHAPTER FIFTEEN

Meanwhile, in Washington DC, the capital of the American Republic, the Armaments Resolution had been debated all day, in a special session of the International Conservation Council. Towards the evening, the member countries voted overwhelmingly to pass the Resolution. From now on, the use of weapons of mass destruction would be banned permanently. Carina had been there of course, representing Calamerica, along with Chancellor Cygnus and some of their staff.

The day's session had been long and soporific, but what awaited them that evening, promised to be a pleasant distraction. The Presidential Palace had been opened up for a cocktail party and dinner, to which Carina arrived right on time, accompanied by Gomeisa, her Chief of Staff.

It was one of those rare occasions that called for formal wear. So, Carina decided to show up in an evening gown of shimmering magenta with pleats of sliver, its skirt whisking around her bare knees like windswept smoke. Gomeisa, wore her best off-white pantsuit over a light green top with a purple scarf around her slender neck. She had glistening dark skin, as smooth as polished marble and crisp curls that fell around her shoulders like a cascade, beautifully offsetting the gossamer lightness of her scarf.

Entering the lavish lounge where cocktails were being served, they settled themselves in a couple of armchairs, around a floating side-table. A server-robot immediately appeared with a tray of hors d'oeuvres and left promptly with their drink orders.

Carina looked around the room, as she waited for her glass of White Zinfandel. At roughly the center, she could see the Chancellor nodding his head and pretending to be interested in whatever his companion, the President of the European Union, was telling him. Farther to the left, there were a group of bureaucrats, Carina didn't recognize. Probably, part of some of the world leaders' delegations. In a quiet corner, beside a wall-to-wall window overlooking the Presidential Garden, stood a man, who was staring at her with rapt admiration. She smiled as she recognized this man. It was Alrakis. She blushed at the realization. Alrakis smiled back and immediately turned around, to make his way towards the bar. Their drinks arrived, and Carina sipped her Zinfandel. Then, she turned to her Chief of Staff.

"What did you make of today's proceedings?" she asked.

Gomeisa let out a sigh. "I don't know, Ma'am," she said. "I don't know what to think."

"Oh? How come?"

"I mean, it's great that the resolution passed. But I still can't wrap my head around what they proposed to do with all the weapons."

"Each country has their inventory of weapons, and they need to get rid of it somehow, don't they? If they've pledged never to use them again, then they shouldn't be allowed to keep them either. Just think about it, today we may have a compliant government, and all might seem well. But who can say, that tomorrow a regime won't turn, and the new leaders change their minds about using these dangerous weapons? Better take them away, I say. Far out of the reach of individual countries."

"Why can't we destroy them? Get rid of them once and for

all?"

"Are you kidding? What about the environmental fallout? Or the radiation in some cases ..."

"But not if we detonate them in outer space."

"Oh, that's a whole different issue Gomeisa. Space is not our garbage bin you know? Remember how the mid twenty-second century was plagued with the space-debris issue from satellites? That was a huge debacle back then!"

"Right. And that's what led to the reduction in satellite communication. But still ... stashing all these weapons somewhere within reach, here on earth, bothers me."

"That's why they chose Greenland. It's a jurisdiction directly under the control of the International Conservation Council. No sovereign country would have access to these weapons any more."

Gomeisa leaned forward and lowered her voice to a whisper. "But what if the ICC is compromised some day? I don't rule out anything in the modern day and age."

"True. Me neither," Carina agreed, speaking softly. "Still, the options were limited, and Greenland is a neutral ..." Carina trailed off, noticing that Gomeisa was no longer paying attention, but looking intently in the direction of the windows. "What's the matter Gomeisa?" she asked in an anxious tone.

Gomeisa did not respond. Instead, she rose briskly and jumped forward, elbowing her way to the window area. Carina followed her. Alrakis was standing under the window again. This time, he was busy chatting with a delegate from the Republic. A server-robot stood in their vicinity, extending a tray with a drink. Alrakis picked up the glass and barely touched it to his lips, when Gomeisa plunged forward and whipped the glass from his hand, smashing it to smithereens on the sleek marble floor.

"Don't drink that!" she shrieked.

Alrakis shuddered. His eyes were rolling upwards, as he made some gurgling sounds from his mouth. The delegate in front of Alrakis wrapped his arms around him, to prevent him from falling. People hurried around the room in confusion.

Carina's mouth fell open in alarm. For a split second, she had no idea what to do. Then, collecting herself, she touched her wrist band to summon her body guards. In a minute or two, it was hard to tell how long, two tall and muscular, human bodyguards arrived.

"Your orders, Ma'am," one of them said in a gruff tone, addressing Carina.

"Ah, what? Yes ... please escort us back to our hotel. And you," she said to the other guard, "go with my aide Alrakis to the hospital, and stay with him at all times. Got it?" she added firmly. The second guard nodded and rushed to Alrakis' side.

There was a crowd of people around Alrakis now, including a first-responder, who was offering some preliminary care. Carina waited for them to carry Alrakis out on a stretcher, before motioning her bodyguard to escort them away from the reception hall.

No one spoke during the short drive back to their hotel. Carina cast an occasional glance out the heavily tinted windows of their armoured vehicle, to calm her flaring nerves, and Gomeisa fidgeted uneasily in her seat. Arriving at the hotel, Carina led Gomeisa to her own suite, with her bodyguard in tow. Once inside her quarters, Carina broke the silence.

Turning to Gomeisa, she grabbed her by the shoulders and asked in a low tone, "How did you know?"

"It was the server-robot." Gomeisa replied.

Carina looked confused. "What do you mean?"

"Didn't you see what all the robots were wearing around their arms?"

"Umm ... no, I didn't pay attention. Some sort of armband?"

"Yeah, exactly. With the flags of the host nations on them. But then, I saw the one that was going up to Alrakis, and it was different. It looked different ... but also, the armband. It struck me the most. When I focused on the band, I realized what it was. The flag on it was different. It wasn't a flag of the

American Republic, like the others."

"Oh? What kind of flag was it, then?"

"It looked like the Indochine flag. Which was curious. And there was something else too. Did you notice what it was serving?"

"I don't know … champagne?"

"Correct. That doesn't strike you as odd?"

"Should it?"

"Do you think Alrakis would have ordered a champagne? What's his favourite drink?"

"Oh, I see what you mean. We don't have access to much alcohol back home, but whenever I've seen him drink abroad, he has been partial to—"

"White rum."

"I believe you're right, yes."

"The champagne was served by the house. There were other robots carrying trays of it, all around the hall. Didn't you notice?"

"I … no. But if that's the case, then where's the problem? They were offering him the house champagne, like everyone else perhaps."

"Nope. That can't be it. Because there was only one glass of champagne on the tray and it was being offered to two people. Server-robots are trained never to do that. They'll never bring a tray over to a group, unless there's enough for everyone."

"Oh my! You certainly are observant," Carina said admiringly.

"Isn't that why you hired me?" Gomeisa asked, grinning triumphantly.

"It certainly is, and today you've truly done me proud."

"Thank you. I'm glad I could help. So, that's why I jumped up like that. It looked very fishy, the whole situation. My gut told me not to touch whatever was in that drink."

"Hmmm. You would've done well as a detective, you know! By the way, I'm wondering what would've happened if … if say for example, the wrong guy picked up that glass. How did they know Alrakis would drink it?"

"See, that's where I think this is part of an elaborate plan. Did you notice who Alrakis was standing with, when the drink was brought to him?"

"Some guy from the Republic, I think."

"Correct. Or in other words, someone from the host nation. If one glass of drink is offered to two people and one of them is the host …"

"Ah, I see where you're going with this. It's only polite for the host to pass it up, and offer it to his companion instead."

"And that's exactly what happened here."

Carina walked over to the nearest couch and sank into it, squeezing her eyes shut in concentration. "This is terrible," she said. "Looks like it was an assassination attempt."

Gomeisa hung her head and walked over to sit across from her boss on a low armchair. "We should check in with the Chancellor," she said quietly.

"Yes, we …" Carina began, but was cut short, when her phone beeped out an incoming call notification. Carina accepted the call. "Good evening. We were just about to call you," she said to the holo of the Chancellor, that appeared in front of her.

"Evening. You are safe? And your staff?" the Chancellor enquired in a hurried tone.

"Yes, we are unharmed. All but Alrakis. I am yet to receive news of his condition since the incident. And you, Sir? I'm hoping you're unharmed, and in a safe location yourself?"

The Chancellor nodded in the affirmative. His face showed clear signs of agitation. With jaw muscles clenched, forehead furrowed and eyes full of determination, he looked up at Carina and spoke assertively. "We need to leave. As soon as possible. How quickly can you arrive at the air-base?"

"I understand," Carina replied, and then after a moment's hesitation, "But I am afraid, I cannot leave without my aide, Alrakis. Unless he's fit to travel, I will stay back." She turned to Gomeisa and continued, "You and the others can go on ahead of me with the Chancellor's entourage."

"No! That is absolutely unacceptable!" the Chancellor growled. "I do not have the means or personnel here, to provide safe passage to anyone who's left behind. You must come with me. I plan to leave by midnight, at the latest."

Carina's face became as pale as the moon at dawn. She cleared her throat. "As you wish," she said softly.

"Good. I will expect you at the base, at least an hour before midnight. Please inform the rest of your staff," the Chancellor ordered, before hanging up the call.

"Not good," said Gomeisa, eyeing her Secretary of State with caution. "What are you going to do?"

"Well, Gomeisa, you know me. I'm not leaving without Alrakis."

"And how exactly are you going to pull that off? You heard the man; he'll have you removed if you disobey him. I'm sure of that."

"So am I. But that's not the point." Carina frowned and started pacing around the room. "I need to do what I need to do, and we don't have much time. So, inform the staff, that they're expected at the air-base before eleven. Get ready to go with them. And leave me to my business. Alright?" she finished firmly.

"But—"

"No buts. Now, go!"

Gomeisa turned to leave, when Carina called her back. "Oh, and one more thing. As far as everyone is concerned, I'm going to be on that flight with the Chancellor. So, tell them that. Including the security."

"Yes, Ma'am," said Gomeisa, as she hurried out the door.

Once alone in her suite, Carina summoned her bodyguard. "Do you know if the Canadian entourage is still here?" she asked.

"I believe they are Ma'am," the bodyguard replied.

"Good. Do you know when they leave?"

"The last I heard from my colleague; they don't have plans to leave today. Security has been assigned in their wing till tomorrow evening."

"Excellent. Please arrange for me to visit the hospital, where they have taken Alrakis."

"Right now?"

"Yes, as soon as possible."

"Certainly, I'm on it," he said, as he pulled out his tablet and got to work, following through with the order.

Carina grabbed her phone and dialled a number. "Dorado," she said to the person at the other end. "I need your help."

"Of course," Dorado replied.

"I might need to hitch a ride with the Canadian entourage."

"To Canada?" Dorado replied in alarm.

Carina lowered her voice. "Yeah. Can your father—" She stopped short, seeing her bodyguard approach. "Let me call you back," she said to Dorado, before turning to her guard. "What is it?"

"Ma'am your vehicle is here."

"Let's go then."

Carina rushed over to the armoured vehicle that was waiting for her outside the hotel, and getting into it, she immediately turned on the soundproof environment around her seat and called Dorado back, explaining the situation.

Dorado's father was the Canadian ambassador to Calamerica. He would facilitate a meeting between Carina and the Prime Minister. The goal would be an urgent bipartite discussion on the terms of the resolution. The meeting would detain her sufficiently enough, that she would miss her flight back to Calamerica. Due to security concerns with her continuing to remain in the Republic, she would therefore, be evacuated to Canada. Until, Calamerica was once again in a position to securely transport her back to her country.

Several more calls were made, and everything was arranged accordingly. The only unknown in the equation was Alrakis. If he wasn't fit enough to fly by tomorrow, her plan would fail.

Thus, with her scheme all worked out, Carina walked into the hospital, her heart throbbing with trepidation.

Alrakis was lying on his back with his eyes wide open when Carina entered his room. "You are awake," she said softly, sitting down next to his bed on a visitor's chair.

"From now on, I'm pretty sure I'm going to be perpetually awake," Alrakis said with a chuckle.

Carina smiled with a sense of relief. "So ... judging from your jokes ... can I hope you're feeling better?"

"Yep. I'm as fit as a fiddle. That was a close one though! The doctor told me it was a nerve agent."

"Oh God!" Carina exclaimed. "You have Gomeisa to thank, you know ... for—"

"My life. Yeah, I know. Where is she?" he asked, searching around the room.

Carina shook her head. "She's getting ready to leave with the Chancellor. On his orders."

"*She* is?" Alrakis exclaimed, sitting up. "What about us?"

"We're going to Canada."

"WHAT?" Alrakis almost jumped out of bed. "Why?"

"You shouldn't be flying tonight. The doctor doesn't recommend it."

"Then we can leave tomorrow."

Carina shook her head again. "The Chancellor wants to leave today. He was very firm." Then, lowering her voice to almost a whisper, "I have a bad feeling about you going back to Calamerica at all."

"Oh?" Alrakis' eyes widened.

"The Chancellor ... he ... suggested that we abandon you."

"You're not serious?"

Carina nodded, a pitiful look in her eyes.

"This complicates things," Alrakis said gravely.

"It does. What I'm wondering is ... what happened today ... why did they go after you? Why not me?"

"Oh, that's simple. They don't want us snooping around Area 51. I mean, that's pretty clear," Alrakis said, lowering his voice. "And you're too high profile a target to remove. It would cause international outrage. War even."

"Guess you're right. So, they chose you."

"Correct. Without me, the whole effort falls apart and their secret stays safe."

"Makes sense. That means we were right from the start. They have an ugly secret to keep."

"Yep, and now more than ever, we need to find out what that is. Did they really make those clones?"

Carina sighed. "Anyway," she said after a brief silence. "Try to get some rest, if you can. I have a meeting to attend. We'll head to Canada tomorrow."

"I don't think I'll be sleeping much. But I need to ask you something. Does anyone else know we're staying?"

"Just Gomeisa."

"Thanks. I should call to thank her, so I needed to know."

"Alright then. I'll leave you to it. Expect the Canadian guards to come for you in the morning," Carina said, as she turned to leave.

"I will. Goodnight and good luck."

"You too."

CHAPTER SIXTEEN

Aquila woke up in a police station with an oxygen mask strapped to his face. He blinked to gain focus. He was leaning back in a chair with his legs stretched to their full lengths before him. He was sore from head to toe and could recall the incidents of the last few hours, only in disjointed fragments—like wisps of torn clouds wafting through the sea of his consciousness.

Someone in a police uniform was leaning forward to get a better view of him. There were a few others in the distance, whose faces Aquila could not make out.

"He's coming around," a lady said softly from his right.

Aquila turned in that direction and met Razzy's gaze. Razzy smiled, looking relieved. Aquila smiled back instinctively, only to recoil with pain. His jaw was threatening to explode. He quickly realized he also had a mask on, and no one could see him trying to smile behind it.

"I don't need this anymore," he said hoarsely, as he removed the supplemental oxygen. "What happened? Where am I?" he asked, taking stock of his surroundings and rubbing the swelling on his jaw.

"You are at a police station," Razzy responded. "You were attacked. Inside the forest. The cops on patrol found you and

138

brought you here. When I saw them carry you out of the forest, I accompanied them …"

"We gave you a little something for the pain, and you slept like a baby on the way," the cop in front of them added.

"I see. Who attacked me? Did you catch them?" he asked, turning to the policeman.

"We gave them a good chase, but we had to get back to attend to you … you were in a pretty bad shape, and we were only two …" replied a husky voice from Aquila's left—a tall dark-skinned cop in an officer's uniform. Aquila had not noticed her until now.

"Oh! Well, thank you," Aquila said, smiling with the side of his face that was not injured. "Do you have any idea who they were? The attackers?"

The policeman standing in front of them shrugged. "Some local ruffians, I suspect. We catch them in the forest from time to time. That's why we were there. To keep watch."

"Ruffians? Just *ruffians*? It didn't seem like …" Aquila checked himself in mid-sentence and turned to the officer, "What do these ruffians want in the forest?"

"They try to escape, some of them," she responded.

"Escape from what exactly?"

"The law in most cases. Some of them deal in contraband or have other crimes against their names. They try to slink away into the forest and beyond."

Aquila clicked his tongue disapprovingly and said nothing. Somehow this explanation was not adding up. He fell silent, trying to formulate a question in his mind—a delicately balanced question, that would not give away his true feelings about the situation. After a short pause, he spoke. He wanted to ask why a bunch of outlaws and ruffians would beat him up black and blue, with the clear intention of killing him. But he refrained from taking that approach and said instead:

"What's beyond that forest? Where would the outlaws go?"

"Oh, they never get very far. They'll be caught, I assure you. There are other patrols out there." the male cop responded.

"No, I meant hypothetically. Where are they trying to go? To escape, I mean."

The two cops exchanged a meaningful glance between them, and immediately Aquila realized that he shouldn't have asked this question.

"There's a river beyond the forest," the officer responded in a measured tone. "It's beyond our jurisdiction. Maybe that's what they're aiming for."

"And how far is the river?"

This time the cops fell silent. Aquila scanned both their faces. And then Razzy's. She made a meaningful gesture with her eyes in response. Aquila stood up. Their silence was all the response he had needed. The forest was vast. Razzy had told him so, the first time he had set eyes on it. His gut told him that the river was hundreds of miles away. No fool would possibly attempt to cross over to it through a poisonous and fiery jungle, unless they were desperate.

The other explanation was that, his attackers were not a bunch of petty criminals at all. They were there for a purpose, and the attack on him today was not an accident. In fact, it lined up perfectly with their purpose, whatever it was.

As Aquila was ruminating on this, he jolted at the sound of commotion issuing from near the entrance. With a few long strides, he crossed the distance between himself and the station's front door, hoping to find out what was going on.

Just outside the station, a bizarre scene was unfolding. A police-vehicle was parked next to the station's paved front porch and two cops were dragging a handcuffed young man towards it with their backs turned towards Aquila. The man was walking quietly with his head bowed.

As the cops tried to advance with their captive in between them, a bent old man in baggy, faded pyjamas plunged forward and wrapped his arms around the legs of the shorter cop, screeching and wailing with agony. Aquila advanced towards the group, to better understand what the old man was saying.

"No Sir, he's a good boy, Sir ... please please forgive.

Noooo … pleaaaase," the old man sobbed.

"Get off!" the policeman huffed. "Get off I say, or I'll arrest you too!" he added, trying to shake himself free, but the old man did not relent. He let himself be dragged along the rough pavement, as he begged and pleaded for the young man's freedom. Aquila advanced a few steps further so that the cops could see him.

"What's going on here?" he asked, raising his voice above the ruckus.

"Good day Sir," the shorter cop responded with a little nod. "We're trying to take this little urchin into custody over here, and his old man won't let us."

"And what's his crime?" Aquila asked.

"We found him in the Black Lands, Sir. Must be dealing in something nasty or trying to run like the rest of them good for nothin's," the other cop responded—the taller, fairer one.

"No, no not true … my son is a good boy, very good boy … he was lost maybe," the father wailed. Then turning to Aquila and joining his hands together he said, "Please Sir, kind Sir, good Sir, forgive my Alan. He will never—"

"Alan?" Aquila interrupted, startled by these words. Hearing his name, Alan immediately turned his head towards the speaker, and Aquila's memory was jogged. The boy was wearing a long-sleeved T-shirt and dark jeans that were ripped in several places and covered with dirt, as if he had rolled in the mud wearing them. But his face was unmistakably familiar. "It's you?" Aquila said enthusiastically. "Our whiz kid, huh? What were you doing in that awful forest?"

Alan hung his head in embarrassment. "I … was lost," he stammered.

"He's lying Sir. Don't believe him," the shorter cop snapped, baring his teeth at the boy. "He had a—"

Aquila raised his hand to stop the cop. "I believe him," he quickly said. "Besides, it's not illegal to go into the Black Lands, is it?"

"For you, Sir, it isn't. But peasants aren't allowed. Unless

141

they work at a plant," the lanky cop explained.

"That fixes it then. He does work at a plant, this kid. He's an employee of mine and a damn good one too."

"But he never said so when we asked … and he didn't have a permit," the policeman objected.

"That's alright," Aquila assured. "I am willing to vouch for him. Please set him free right away. Clear him of all charges."

"But, Sir … we …" the taller cop started, but Aquila waved him off and advanced towards Alan.

"Remove his cuffs please," he said to the cops, holding Alan's bound hands up in front of them.

The taller cop grunted something incomprehensible, before setting Alan free. "Would you mind signing for him, Sir?" he asked Aquila.

"Of course!" Aquila grabbed the tablet that was extended to him. It gave him a sudden sense of déjà vu. The last time he had signed something like that it had landed him in deep trouble. He decided to read it carefully before signing this time. When he was done, he affixed his signature at the bottom and returned the tablet to its owner.

Alan's father broke down in tears, and taking Aquila's hands between his own, started kissing them relentlessly. "Thank you … thank you," he mumbled between sobs. "You saved him. You saved my son. You're an angel."

Aquila blushed crimson at these words. "I … you're welcome," he said.

Alan, who was silent through most of this interaction, scanned Aquila from head to toe and frowned. "You're hurt," he said. "Badly hurt. What happened?"

"Oh, it's nothing. I got into a skirmish. My bad, I shouldn't have wandered off into—"

"Here you are! I was beginning to wonder what was taking you so long," Razzy's voice interrupted from the vicinity. "Come, we should get going. I'll drop you home. You need to rest."

"Yeah, right. That's probably a good idea," Aquila agreed.

"Will you be alright taking your father back home, Alan?" He turned to ask his employee.

Alan was standing with his arms crossed across his chest and a studying, intense look in his youthful eyes. "I'll be fine, Sir. It's not me you should worry about, but you. You don't look well at all."

"I … I'll be fine," Aquila replied, but without much conviction. He was certainly feeling quite terrible. And the very strain of having to stand here and carry out a conversation was taking a toll on him.

"You know my sister is the best medic in town. Ummm … come with us, will you? She'll heal you in a jiffy," Alan continued, reading his superior's body language.

"Well … I don't know—" Aquila started to protest, but was interrupted by the old man's pleading voice.

"Oh, you must come, Sir. You must. You saved my son's life today, and I won't let you go home by yourself in this state. Those ghastly wounds! My daughter will fix it for you. Come. Please, come!" he said as he tried to pull Aquila along by his shirt sleeve.

"Oh alright, alright," Aquila relented. "It's mighty generous of you," he added with a smile.

"I'll call us a ride," Razzy chimed in.

"No, Razzy there's no need. I'm going alone. You need to get back. It's already been a stressful day for you," Aquila asserted.

Razzy opened her mouth as if to object, but the look on Aquila's face made her change her mind. She sighed and pulled out her phone. "I'll get us two rickshaws then. One for me and one for the three of you."

"Thank you," Aquila said with a smile, realizing at once, that it still hurt to do so. "Oww oww!"

"I hope it's not broken, your jaw," Alan remarked.

"Naw, I don't think so. Just a little sore," Aquila assured.

They didn't have to wait very long for their rides to arrive. Aquila saw Razzy off in the first one, before joining the others in the second, larger rickshaw.

"North side tunnel number twenty-five," Alan instructed the driver-robot, once they were all seated inside.

"Tunnel number twenty-five?" Aquila asked with a look of surprise. "Doesn't that lead outside the Project?"

"Yes, kind of. Outside the periphery for sure. But it's a tunnel, so it never reaches the surface."

"I see. It was not clear from the map I'd seen earlier. It seemed to be leading outside our borders. Where does it go exactly?"

Now it was Alan's turn to look surprised. "What do you mean?" he asked. "To the colonies, of course."

Aquila didn't know what to say, in order not to appear stupid. So, he just stared at Alan in confusion.

"You've never been to the colonies, have you? Where all the peasants live?" Alan asked, taking a hint from Aquila's expression.

"I'm afraid not," Aquila admitted. "I didn't arrive here too long ago, and it's been really busy ever since."

"That's alright. I understand. Management is discouraged from visiting anyway."

"Discouraged, you say? And might I ask why?"

Alan shrugged. "Probably the poverty. Or the squalor. It can be repulsive if you're not used to it."

Aquila cringed. "That sounds awful. I mean not the squalor … just that, people are stuck-up enough to avoid the very place, where all the people of this region have made their homes."

Alan smiled gratefully but said nothing. His father seemed to be dozing off in the seat across from them.

"How old is your dad?" Aquila asked the boy.

"Almost sixty."

"No kidding! He looks a lot older," Aquila mused. The shrivelled old man in front of him looked like an octogenarian at the very least.

Alan shrugged. "In our colony, people age fast," he said,

after a bit of reflection.

"It must be from the nature of your work, eh? All those long days in the fields, out in the sun, can't be good for you."

"Maybe. Father has been working these fields all his life. My sister and I also help out. Mother is too sick to work. So, the rest of us need to put in extra time."

Aquila clicked his tongue. "Sounds like a terrible situation," he said.

"They say it will be over soon. Father has been counting the days to our freedom, ever since he started working here."

"And what about you? You're not looking forward to going to Sanctuary City?"

Alan hung his head. "I don't know," he whispered.

Noticing how this question had saddened him, Aquila decided not to press it any further. Instead, he asked, "Are we almost there?"

The driver-robot heard the question and responded right away. "You will be at your destination in approximately two minutes and thirty seconds."

"Thanks," Aquila muttered as he looked out the window.

Dusk was starting to settle in. The mango trees that lined the road, cast their long, crooked shadows along the way like an intricate network of giant cobwebs. The fields were empty at this hour, and an all-pervading silence bore down on the surroundings. So deep was this quiet, that the softly snoring farmer in front of him, sounded like a roaring lion to Aquila's ears. The rickshaw jolted and braked, waking Alan's father.

"We're here," Alan said.

CHAPTER SEVENTEEN

A quila dismounted the rickshaw, followed by Alan, who then turned back to give his father a hand. In front of them, about a hundred feet away, they could see the ramshackle entrance to the tunnel. From the map of the Project Aquila had studied earlier, he knew that another hundred feet or so beyond that entrance, the climate-controlled environment of the Project would end.

"This way," Alan said, making for the tunnel.

As soon as Aquila stepped inside the underground passage, he knew exactly what Alan had meant earlier about the wretched conditions that prevailed in these parts. The tunnel itself was narrow and dimly lit, with something leaking down its walls and forming shallow pools near their feet. There was a rotting unpleasant smell in the air like that of a manure patch or a public urinal. Aquila crinkled his nose and plodded along, trying to ignore the nausea that was bubbling up inside him.

Alan noticed Aquila's expression and let out a chuckle. "See, I told you it's horrid in here," he said.

"Yeah well, I didn't doubt you one bit. But the squalor is no reason for anyone to shun the colonies. In fact, it's all the more reason for management to get involved, and fix this and ask the right questions, like why *is* it so bad in here?"

"The Project doesn't pay for the upkeep of the colonies. So, any cleanup here, is volunteer-based. We have a hard time recruiting volunteers, because people are working non-stop and have precious little time to spare."

"Oh! I didn't know that. I thought we had budget allocated for farmer housing. I'll have to look into where that money is going."

"It's probably going into keeping the air-circulation running in the colonies and our access to water. But not much more, I suspect."

"I see. And how *does* the air circulate in here?" Aquila asked, feeling embarrassed that he hadn't had the chance to research this beforehand. Having a high-level job such as his, came with the downside of distancing one from all the finer details behind the workings of each sub-unit inside a vast project.

"There are circulation pipes. That bring in fresh air from the Project. You see that vent over there, that's one of 'em." Alan said, pointing to an area just below the ceiling.

"Ah, okay."

"But these pipes are also quite old. They don't function very well. They were re-purposed from an underground Mars colony project, that failed a couple of decades ago."

"That's probably why they can't remove the stench in here," Aquila remarked.

"Yeah."

The passage was starting to broaden now, and a few paces ahead, Aquila could make out doors carved into the walls on either side, with streams of light trickling out of them. A muted buzzing sound, like that of chattering voices, emanated from that region. On coming closer, Aquila realized that the passage here was indeed a lot wider, with space enough for four people to walk side by side. Along the walls of this corridor, were the entrances to the farmer homes. There were no panels to the unit doors, just openings from which curtains of various colours were hung. The strong putrid air from near the

147

entrance was starting to clear up a fair bit as they progressed, being replaced by the pleasant odours of breads and soups. From far away, a melancholy tune played on a flute floated to their ears.

They kept walking in silence for a few minutes passing dozens of closely nested dwellings. Occasionally, they crossed a bifurcation in their path, with a transverse corridor bending out to their left or right. These lateral corridors were similarly lined with living quarters on either side. Finally, arriving in front of a door with a bottle-green curtain, Alan stopped.

"After you," he said, moving the curtain aside to let Aquila in.

Aquila cautiously stepped inside the poorly-lit little room behind the curtain. It looked like the entirety of their apartment. Along the farthest wall, in a rickety old cot, lay an emaciated elderly woman wrapped in a blanket. Beside her, a young lady sat on a stool, applying an ointment to the prone woman's head. In the center of the room, there was a table and four chairs, and along the walls were some additional sitting cushions. To the right of the dinner table, two hammocks hung from the ceiling, and to the left, a second cot rested against the wall. Right next to the door, there was a stash of little gadgets strewn across the floor, like bits and pieces found at an electronic repair shop. Towards the back of the room, Aquila could see a closed door with a wooden panel, behind which he surmised was the unit's toilet. On the floor close to the entrance, was a low-stove on which a gruel of some sort was brewing.

A chill went down Aquila's spine at the sight of this stark, minimalistic home. He swallowed down the tears that threatened to rise up from within. Instead, he tried to liven up the atmosphere by saying something upbeat.

"Mmm, something smells really good in here! What's cooking?" he asked merrily.

"Just dinner," the young lady responded from the back of the room.

"That's my sister, Elaine," Alan chimed in. "Come here, Elaine. Do you know who this is?"

Elaine stood up and squinted. She was in her mid to late twenties, tall and lanky like her brother but with a tanner complexion. Her black hair fell like a gleaming waterfall across her back and front, hiding her shoulders entirely. She was wearing a light summer dress of coarse cotton, hand-dyed in pastel shades. She looked careworn but pretty, with large intelligent eyes. She walked forward to get a better look at their guest, but recognition did not dawn.

"Someone from the plant?" she asked after a moment's deliberation.

"You're exactly right! And not just from the plant, he's our Chief Conservation Officer, himself!" Alan gloated.

"Oh! And to what do we owe this honour?" Elaine asked with a broad smile. "Please, do sit down." she added, pulling up a chair.

"He saved me from the cops today, you see. A very kind man. And dad asked him to come to dinner," Alan replied with a quick glance at his father, who had plonked down into a sitting-cushion against the wall.

"Oh no!" Aquila quickly corrected "I don't plan to stay for dinner. I'm just here for my injuries. I got into a little accident today, and Alan tells me you are an excellent medic. I'm Aquila, by the way," he explained, as he extended his hand to Elaine.

Elaine hesitated for a second before accepting the handshake. "But that cannot be," she said in a small voice. "If you are a visitor, you must eat with us. It's our custom."

Aquila blushed and scratched the back of his head. "If it's a custom … I wouldn't want to disrespect it. I'll stay for dinner then."

"Alan, come here," the old man called his son. Then he gave his kid some money and whispered something into his ear. Alan nodded and turned to Aquila.

"I'll be right back," he said. "In the meantime, why don't you show Elaine your injuries. She has a whole suitcase full of concoctions that she makes herself."

"Wait, no! Where are you going? If I'm staying for dinner, you're not going to make any special arrangements for me. I'll eat what you're eating."

"But it's nothing—" Alan started.

"No, I don't want to hear any excuses. This is *my* custom. So, you should honour it," he added with a sly grin.

"Ha! Nicely done, Sir," said Alan. "I guess I don't have anything to say to that."

"Good," said Aquila. "Now if Elaine can give me something for my aches and pains, I'll be ready for dinner in a heartbeat."

"Of course," said Elaine. "But I need to do some diagnostics first." She walked over to a corner of the room and retrieved a portable diagnostic center. Then she glided the device over to Aquila's chair. "If you don't mind Sir, please put your hands, palms-down over here," she said, indicating a glass panel.

"Wow, this is a nifty little thing. Must be pricey too! How on earth did you guys get it?"

Alan turned cherry-pink. "I put it together myself, actually. From some discarded parts Ramesh let me take home."

"Goodness! That's pure genius!" Aquila exclaimed.

"No broken bones. Blood oxygen-level ..." the diagnostic center started to pronounce, and everyone turned to listen to the report.

"Okay, I have the basics," Elaine said as she turned away. "I'll be right back with the treatments." She returned to the back of the room and started shuffling through some vials.

Alan pulled up a chair next to Aquila and sat down. Turning towards him, Aquila asked:

"So, Genius Boy, what was it you were *really* doing, when they caught you today?"

Alan hung his head and did not speak.

"You can tell me. I won't spill the beans. I promise," Aquila assured. "Were you collecting samples?" Aquila grinned mischievously.

Alan looked up and smiled a half-smile. "Maybe." He

mumbled.

"Then let me tell you a secret," Aquila said, lowering his voice. "So was I."

"Oh? Did you get any?"

"Nope. You?"

Alan nodded, indicating that he did.

"And? Where are they? Did the cops take them?"

"No. I hid them. Before they caught me."

"Smart. Did you even have protective gear on?"

"Of course. But they confiscated that."

"Is that right? Hmmm. I can try to see if I can get you a new one. But you have to promise me something. Never ever go in there without your permit again. I don't want to see you in another brush with the authorities. Got it?"

"But Sir, I don't have a permit."

"What? Why? You work at a plant, so you should be eligible."

"Maybe. But they don't let peasants have one either way. I've asked, but they don't want to listen."

"That's unacceptable! Did you ask Ramesh?"

"No. I asked the junior manager, who hands out permits."

"Okay, I'll speak with Ramesh myself and get this sorted for you. But once I get you a permit, you must promise to do what I say. Is that clear?"

"Yes, Sir! But why are you—" Alan started, but was cut short by his sister's arrival.

"Here, I think I have everything you'll need. Let me go over the doses for you." she said to Aquila. She took one vial at a time and placed it on the table explaining the dosage and contents. When she was done going through them all, she scooped them up and placed them inside a small box. "There you go," she said. "If you forget the things I said, then you can always scan the vials on your phone and get the details from there. Thankfully, you have no fractures or internal hemorrhages, those take much stronger stuff. Now, let me brew you some of my best pain-tea. It'll help with the soreness right away!"

As Elaine headed off to the stove in the corner, Alan started setting up for dinner. He placed four empty bowls in front of a steaming pot and ladled a mushy substance into it. Then, he brought out a large loaf of bread and arranged it at the centre. While he was doing this, Elaine brought some steaming tea in a chipped china cup and placed it in front of Aquila.

"Your tea," she said, before returning to the stove to make an omelette.

At dinner, they were joined by Alan's father and Aquila learned that his name was Mr. Shi. Mrs. Shi was lying in the back of the room, too sick to join them. She suffered from malnutrition and had not been able to get out of bed for months, Elaine explained. For dinner, each of them received a large bowl of porridge. The only omelette was for Aquila, as the others swore that they did not like eggs for dinner. There were also slices of bread for the table, but without any condiments. Elaine apologized profusely for this inconvenience and promised to make Aquila a jar of mango jam as soon as possible, to compensate.

"That's absolutely not necessary," Aquila said, as he dipped his bread in some porridge and took a bite. He immediately furrowed his forehead from the unfamiliar taste that hit him. "What is this stuff?" he asked.

"It's sorghum," Alan explained. "We grow our own in small patches."

"Oh, how come? There's enough rice and wheat to go around."

Alan and Elaine exchanged glances with each other and their father. "That's true. But we choose to export them." Alan finally said.

"Why? You're only required to export the produce that is left over, after meeting your own requirements. Didn't you know?"

"We *do* know. The thing is … the faster we reach our quota, the sooner we can leave this hell behind us," Elaine explained. "So, we export at maximum capacity. That means nearly hundred percent of the grain and over ninety percent of the remaining crops."

"You're not serious!" Aquila exclaimed.

"Everyone in our unit does it, Sir. You didn't know?" Alan asked.

"No, I didn't," Aquila admitted. He dipped into some more porridge and ate quietly while ruminating on the situation. Noticing his reticence, the others decided to give him some space and focussed their attention on their own meals instead. The only thing that could be heard in the room, were the slurping sounds from the dinner table and Mrs. Shi's occasional coughs. After a long while, Aquila spoke again.

"When do you think your unit will be done with exporting its full quota of produce?" he asked.

Alan cleared his throat before answering. "If we can keep up this rate, we're expecting to be done by the end of the year."

"Then you'll be one of the first," Aquila observed.

"Yes, that's the goal," Alan said.

Aquila rose from the dinner table, and the others followed. Carrying his plate and bowl over to Elaine he asked, "Where do I wash these?"

"Oh, please Sir, give it to me. We don't let our guests do the dishes," Elaine said, grinning broadly.

"Ha! Another custom, is it?" Aquila asked.

"You can say that."

"In that case, thank you for everything. I think I should be taking off now. It's getting late." Aquila grabbed his box of medicine and ordered a ride on his phone as he spoke.

"Let me escort you to the tunnel end," Alan offered.

"Oh, no need for that, really. I'm feeling better already, thanks to the healing tea."

"It's not that, Sir," Alan explained. "It's just ... not safe for you to go alone. They ... umm don't like you much around here."

"Seriously? But I'm new here, they can't possibly even know

me yet."

"No, I meant not *you* in particular. It's management folks they don't like. And you look like management. They'll know right away. Our community watch guards are out on patrol now. They can be very unfriendly to you. Dangerous even."

"And I'll be alright if I'm with you?" Aquila asked with a grin.

"They know me around here. If you come with me, they'll trust you," Alan assured.

"Okay then. Let's go. My ride is on its way."

Aquila turned to leave, but Elaine stopped him halfway, "Please Sir, do come visit whenever you like."

"I will. I promise," Aquila said with a smile, and looking up at her, he saw Elaine's features light up spontaneously at this remark.

Aquila and Alan walked silently back to the tunnel entrance and said their goodbyes. On getting home that night, Aquila went to bed right away, still sore from the day's adventures. But no matter how much he tried; he was unable to fall asleep. It wasn't the pain, no. Elaine's potions were working wonders to soothe his body, but his mind was still whirring away at full speed. The events of that day had left him with more questions than answers and certainly a great deal of dilemma.

CHAPTER EIGHTEEN

Having fallen asleep in the wee hours of the morning, Aquila slept till noon that Sunday. He had hoped to feel substantially better after some sleep, but it turned out that he was totally mistaken. For some reason, he felt much worse today than on the day of the actual attack. It was probably his body finally waking up to the full reality of the encounter and reacting in hindsight. He decided to give himself some more time to heal and ordered a sumptuous breakfast in bed.

Again, he had miscalculated the effect this breakfast would have on him. Instead of feeling contended with the meal he had been served, he felt a crushing sense of guilt and remorse with every bite he took.

Some people don't eat like this. Some people I know, he reminded himself. He looked at his plate and imagined Elaine's graceful sincere face reflected off it. He plunked down his fork and leaned back. Nothing tasted like it used to anymore.

As Aquila sat there, staring at his half-eaten breakfast, his servant-robot announced the arrival of a guest.

"Send her in," Aquila ordered, assuming it was Razzy.

The robot looked confused. "I believe the visitor is Mr. Orion," it clarified.

"Oh!" Aquila said, sitting up straight in his bed. "I wasn't expecting him."

"Should I tell him that you are indisposed to accept company then?"

"No, no. Just send him in."

"Alright Sir, as you wish."

The robot rolled out of the room and returned a minute later, accompanied by Orion.

"Ah, there you are!" Orion said jovially. "You don't look too bad. Not too bad at all. Am I here at an odd hour?"

"No, not at all. Thanks for coming," Aquila said. "How did you find out?"

"It was the police station. They called me last night. I came over to check on you, but you weren't home."

"Right. I came home late last night," Aquila explained, without elaborating where he had been.

"I heard you were at the colonies," Orion said lowering his voice. "Is that true?"

"Well yeah, in fact, I was. There's no escaping you, is there?"

"Like I've said before, it's my business to know what goes on inside my district," Orion said, laughing heartily.

"Hmmm. You're not mad then?"

"Mad? No. Why would I be?"

"I thought we were discouraged from going down there. To the colonies."

Orion shrugged. "I don't bother myself with petty stuff like that. You're my second in command. You can do as you please. Besides, what you did before that, was far more dangerous. If you had consulted me in advance—"

"You would have stopped me from going? To the Black Lands?"

"Perhaps not stopped you, no. Cautioned you for sure. And especially ..." here Orion lowered his voice considerably. "Especially, regarding the company you chose. I don't think it was a good idea at all, going with her."

156

"You really don't like Razzy, do you?" Aquila chuckled.

"It's nothing personal. But I try to keep my distance from the press, whenever I can." He shook his head absent-mindedly. "She gives me a bad feeling, she does."

"I'll keep that in mind. Anyway, since you're here … I think I might need the day off tomorrow," Aquila said. He stretched his arms to see if they hurt and cringed immediately. "Yep, still sore."

"You didn't have to ask. I came here to give you the whole week off. I heard about your injuries. They were pretty bad. Also, you inhaled a fair bit of toxic air in there, while your mask was off. They tested you at the station for poisoning and the levels are low. They injected you with an antidote, but it'll take two to three days minimum for the toxins to wash out of your system."

"Oh really, they told you this? The cops? How come they didn't tell me?"

"You never asked. They have it all in your file. All you had to do was request a copy."

"That's good to know. I'll send in a request then."

"Good. Alright, I'll leave you to your brunch. Get some rest and I'll check in later," Orion said, as he rose to leave.

"Wait, before you go," Aquila called. "I wanted to ask you something."

"Fire away," Orion said, sliding back into his seat.

"Did you know that some of the farm units are exporting nearly *all* of their produce and eating nothing themselves?"

Orion sighed. "Yes yes, I'm afraid I'm aware of that. But what can you do? There's no talking them out of it. Trust me, I've tried. Their union leaders are adamant. That sister of Alan's is one of them."

"One of what? A union leader?"

"Yep."

"I didn't know that. And what's their argument? Going early to Sanctuary City?"

"You got it."

"That's insane. If they kill themselves then what's the point? No, this won't do. This won't do at all! Hey, I have an idea."

"And what is it that you propose?"

"I propose that we enact a law to restrict the maximum amount they can export. Can we do that? Would the Project admin be on board?"

"Probably." Orion nodded. "But wouldn't that be an encroachment on their freedoms?"

"What *freedoms*? Freedom to die of starvation? That's not a freedom. That's like suicide."

"Hmmm. You have a point. I'll make a proposal to the board tomorrow. I might have to pull you into a remote meeting, if they agree. Are you okay with that?"

"Not a problem at all."

"Alright, stay tuned then. But be ready for the consequences. If you do this, it might make you really unpopular with some of the union leaders. Like they say, you should never help those who don't want to be helped." Orion laughed out loud with these words.

"I hear ya, and I'll keep that in mind."

"Good. I'll be off then. Get some rest!" Orion said, as he waved his hand and left the room.

The rest of Aquila's day passed lazily. Razzy came to visit in the evening, and they finally got to watch some of those movies Aquila had shortlisted for them earlier. Before leaving that night, Razzy told him that she was being called away on a work trip again. She could not tell him where she would be going but promised to call as often as possible. She was going to be away the whole of next week and weekend, returning only on the following Monday. Although the news upset him at first, Aquila eventually realized that it was probably a blessing in disguise. He needed this alone time, to heal from his wounds and introspect on the issues that were plaguing him of late. He slept better that night, withdrawing to a peaceful island within the cacophony of his turbulent mind.

* * *

The week passed a lot faster than Aquila had expected. Alan stopped by a couple of times, bringing refills of potions from Elaine. Orion visited too. They had a meeting with the board to enact new export limitations on the farmers. Aquila had Ramesh come over one evening to chat about getting Alan a permit for the Black Lands, and also to see if they could procure him a new hazmat suit. Razzy called a few times to check on him. Aquila finally caught up on his sleep. He also managed to watch quite a few movies. Overall, it was a successful week and by Friday, Aquila was feeling cheerful and rejuvenated, his injuries almost completely healed.

Bright and early on Friday morning, Aquila was in his verandah whistling a happy tune, when his kitchen-robot came in to take his breakfast order. Aquila ordered his breakfast, and then an idea popped into his head.

"Tell me, what do we have in the kitchen today that's fresh from the farm?"

"Well Sir, we just got a couple of Cornish hens and fresh mint leaves. Some parsnips and potatoes—"

"Perfect," Aquila interrupted. "Can I have the hens roasted with a side of your mint sauce, garlic mashed potatoes and pan-seared turnips, ready and packed by five in the afternoon?"

"Of course, Sir. Should I have them packed in auto-heat containers?"

"Yes please. And can you toss in some bread and butter with it?"

"How much would you like Sir?"

"Enough for four ... no, make that five."

"Not a problem."

"Also, can you order me a ride for around the same time."

"I sure can, Sir."

"Excellent. That will be all," Aquila said, dismissing his help.

At around six that evening, Aquila arrived at the entrance to the north side tunnel number twenty-five with all the food he had ordered, packed up in a large auto-heat container. Stepping into the tunnel, he found the stench a great deal more bearable than last time. Perhaps he was getting used to this, he thought.

Inside the tunnel there were a couple of others walking in either direction. In general, it appeared to be busier than last time. A short, broad-shouldered man gave him a dirty look as he passed by, and Aquila immediately averted his eyes, remembering Alan's warning from last time.

He walked onto the broader section of the tunnel, passing several doors on his way, as he tried to recall how many bifurcations there were, before the green-curtained entrance he was seeking. And then, a different thought struck him. He realized that he had not fully worked out what he would do, once he arrived at Alan's home. He could not knock since there was nothing to knock on. And it would be awfully rude to just barge in uninvited. While he was lost in thought, pondering all his options, he did not notice that he was in a collision course with someone heading his way. Before he knew it, Aquila bumped into the advancing denizen and almost dropped the parcel he was carrying.

"Oops, I'm so sorry ..." he started. And then he noticed who was standing before him. "Oh, Elaine! What a coincidence. I was on my way to your home actually. I did promise I'd stop by," he said with a broad grin. "Is this a bad time?"

"No, not at all Sir. I'm so glad you came. I was just on my way to bring Father back from the farm. But Alan is home. So, do go in, and make yourself comfortable," Elaine said, holding their curtain aside to allow him passage.

"Is your father still at the farm? It's rather late, isn't it?" Aquila checked the time on his phone. It was way past production hours.

"No, it's not that late. He often works longer. He has an after-hours' shift at the granary."

Aquila's heart filled with pity. "Oh!" he simply said. "I'll … go chat with Alan then."

"Yes, please." Elaine led Aquila into their home. Then, she quickly turned and walked off.

Inside the apartment, Alan was next to Mrs. Shi's bed, feeding her something from a bowl as she sat propped up by a pillow. He turned around as soon he heard Aquila's voice.

"Oh! What a pleasant surprise Sir! What brings you here?' he said enthusiastically.

"I thought I'd pay you a visit, like I promised. And I wanted to thank my healer, Elaine. I'm as good as new now, thanks to her!" He smiled whole-heartedly and set his package down on their table.

"I'm sure she'll be delighted to hear that you're better, Sir. What's in that package? It smells wonderful!"

"It's just some stuff for dinner. I thought we could eat together, like we did last time. I hope you don't mind?"

"My God! That's so kind of you. You didn't have to …"

"Of course, I had to. After all you and your sister have done. It's the least I could do," Aquila said, as he seated himself in one of the chairs. "How's your mom doing today? Do you think she can join us?"

Alan shook his head in dismay. "I don't think so, Sir. She's still very feeble. I was just feeding her some porridge."

"That's too bad. But please, give her the porridge. Don't mind me. I'll be right here."

Just as Aquila was finishing this sentence, Elaine returned with her father—the old man wearing a bright toothy grin across his round wrinkled face. "You came to see us! You came!" he said in welcome.

"I did indeed."

"And you brought … food?" Elaine asked in surprise. "Mmm … it smells so good. What is it?"

"Just some stuff that was in my home," Aquila replied politely. "I don't know about you, but I'm starving! Shall we eat?"

"Of course! Let me set the table. I also made some jam," Elaine said, as she got busy bringing over dishes and cutlery from their kitchen area.

Once the table was set and the food unpacked, they gathered around to dine together. Elaine cut up a piece of chicken for her old man and smiled with satisfaction. Then she turned to Aquila.

"Thank you," she said softly. "For doing this. It means a lot to us."

"No, thank *you,*" Aquila insisted. "I'm only trying to do my very least to repay the kindness you've shown. And also ... to make sure your unions don't hate me," he added jovially.

"*Hate* you? What on earth for?" Elaine asked.

"So, you haven't heard?" Aquila asked, looking at each of their faces in turn.

"Umm ... no," Alan replied.

"Oh, I see. Well, a new act was passed today, proposed by me. Effective immediately, it'll put a cap on the maximum amount of produce each unit can export."

Elaine went deathly pale at these words, and Mr. Shi simply stared at Aquila in disbelief. Alan however, did not show any visible reaction to this announcement.

Aquila's heart broke at the sight of their faces. He had not meant to hurt them like this. "I ... it'll be for the better, I promise," he mumbled.

"Why? Why did you do this?" Elaine asked, putting her fork down on her plate.

"I don't want you to starve, that's why!"

"But do you even know what this would mean for us?"

"It'd mean, you get to go to Sanctuary City a little later than expected, right? I know. But would it even be worth it, if you killed yourselves in the process? Years of genetic engineering may have made us all resistant to most illnesses, but till date there's no cure for starvation. I mean, look at your mother for crying out loud." Aquila spouted vehemently.

"Yes, that's exactly the point, isn't it? My mother. Have you seen her, Sir? I don't think she'll survive another winter in these conditions. If we get delayed beyond the winter, there will be no mother to take to Sanctuary City, I can tell you that," Elaine explained desperately.

Alan who had so far been silent, looked up at these words. "And you think our situation would somehow magically improve once we get there? To Sanctuary City?" he asked in a sarcastic vein.

"You don't think it would?" Aquila turned to ask the boy.

"I don't know. I have my doubts."

"How come?" Aquila asked sincerely.

"I have seen the life we have here. That the others have here. Sir, you have seen it too now. With your own eyes. Do you genuinely think a system that keeps us like this at the Project, is going to provide for us better, somewhere else? In some mythical city that we know nothing about? Have you even seen Sanctuary City, Sir? Because we have not. We don't even know where on earth it is. And that scares the shit out of me."

"Wait, are you telling me that you've never been shown a map or a plan of the city?" Aquila asked, shock written all over his face.

"Nope. Not once," Alan replied.

"Not even the union leaders?" Aquila asked, addressing Elaine this time.

"I believe we haven't, no," Elaine admitted meekly.

"Have you been given an overview of the facilities perhaps?"

Elaine and Alan shook their heads in the negative.

"Hmmm. That can't be right. We need to fix this issue. Let me see what I can do," Aquila offered.

"What *is* it like in Sanctuary City? You must have seen it. Does it really live up to the hype?" Elaine asked.

"That's a good question. And come to think of it, I don't really know. I assumed the folks who needed to go there knew all about it. So, I never tried to find out for myself. Why did I never try to find out?" Aquila mused, cupping his chin with his right hand.

"*I* certainly want to find out," Alan grumbled. "They're going to send us in batches with the sick and elderly going ahead of everyone else, and once there, they can't even call home. This doesn't strike you as odd?"

"No, that part isn't particularly unusual, given how difficult and expensive it is to call internationally these days. But I do agree, that you guys should be given all the details about the colony to which you're migrating. And well in advance too."

"Our union has been requesting this for some time now," Elaine chimed in. "We'd really appreciate it if you could make it happen."

"Definitely. I'll make it a priority. If only to be forgiven for brokering the new export regulation." Aquila grinned sheepishly. "By the way, speaking of priorities," he added, turning to Alan, "I have some good news. I got you a permit as promised. And your hazmat suit should also be here in a week. I had to pull a few strings, but it's done now!"

"No way!" Alan exclaimed. "That's brilliant. You're the best!"

"It was nothing. But remember what I said before. Use them wisely, and keep me in the loop. Otherwise, I'm going to take them away. Got it?"

"Yes, Sir!" Alan said with a mock salute.

"Good." Aquila checked the time. "I should get going now. But we'll be in touch."

Alan nodded his understanding and smiled gratefully. Elaine got up from the table and brought Aquila a large jar of home-made jam, before Alan walked him to the tunnel entrance, like last time. On getting home that evening, Aquila wasted no time and booked a Monday morning meeting with

Orion to discuss the Sanctuary City situation. It felt good to seem useful to the people who needed it the most.

Aquila was jolted awake on Saturday by the sound of thunder crashing outside his bedroom. Another torrential shower had been planned for that afternoon, so it was doomed to be a particularly dull day. Razzy was still away on business, and Orion was at the plant, monitoring the weather event. Realizing that he had already seen his favourite movies several times over, and not wanting to be bored out of his mind at home, Aquila headed over to the library before midday.

He was in the mood for a novel. His medically relaxed nerves, coupled with the stormy weather outside, provided the perfect excuse to kick back with an interesting story. Aquila searched through the catalogue and selected a wordy contemporary drama. He was about to curl up with the book next to one of the library's large windows, when he felt an urge to take it back to his little nook in the restricted section instead. He had grown rather fond of that space. It offered him an escape from the banalities of his everyday life—a seclusion and privacy he had long craved. He headed to the cozy little room with his book tucked under his arm and settled himself into the largest couch.

Just as he was about to lie on his back to read, he noticed a remote-control set on a floating table nearby. From habit, he picked it up and switched on the God of War collection. He stared at the menu and flicked randomly through its contents, like an addict who cannot seem to help himself. There were the familiar news reports, collections of documentaries, more files on Napoleon, some ancient movies. He went on browsing without looking for anything in particular.

About five minutes into this indolent scrolling, Aquila came across something unusual. It looked like a full-length novel in an ancient e-book format.

Why would a novel be in here? he wondered, as he sat up.

It was by some Russian author. "Leo Tolstoy," Aquila read out loud.

This piqued his interest. Nothing he had encountered in this repository so far, had been of Russian origin. Inside the folder, was a copy of the original work, but converted into a modern e-book. It had Ramesh's name in the metadata.

Orion must have asked Ramesh to convert everything into modern format, Aquila mused. He clicked on the pages read section. Zero pages read till date.

Why convert a novel if you aren't going to read it? What a waste! Aquila wondered, chuckling quietly. At once, he took it upon himself to do justice to this work. He downloaded it to the library's e-reader and opened the first page.

"War and Peace by Leo Tolstoy," he read. Then he looked at the page count. "Looks like I'm gonna be here all night!" he said, as he dug into the voluminous tome.

CHAPTER NINETEEN

"N o, you can't be serious! You're not leaving me behind in Canada!" Alrakis exclaimed, as Carina announced the news.

They were in a guest suite at the Ambassador's summer home in Western Canada. Located in the northeastern section of the house, it was a complete unit, with three spacious bedrooms and two and a half bathrooms, a living plus dining space and a large balcony overlooking the mighty Rocky Mountains. The house itself was vacant at the moment, apart from the staff on duty. So, Dorado's father had offered it to Carina and Alrakis, while they awaited their transportation back to Calamerica. Alrakis was seated on a soft, velvet couch next to the living-room window, while Carina perched herself on the window seat.

"Oh, don't be so dramatic," Carina insisted. "It's not that bad really."

"Not that bad? *Not* that bad? And how do you expect me to carry on with my investigations from here?"

"It won't be a problem. I have it all worked out with Dorado. The Underground is actually way more active in Canada than back home. They will help you."

"I don't trust that. They're too secretive for comfort."

"You're forgetting that I used to be one of them. I know how they work."

"Yeah, but that was ages ago. The word on the street is that, they have morphed significantly in recent years."

"Even if that's true, Dorado trusts them, and that means I do too. Dorado and I go way back—"

"Yes, you told me."

"No, but that's not all. You have to remember that we fought shoulder to shoulder in our days of activism. With our sweat and blood. We went into hiding together. We hid in caves and under-water storehouses, not knowing if we'd ever make it out alive," Carina paused to catch her breath. "And that … that kind of friendship creates a bond that transcends all trust issues."

"I get it. But he's not here anymore, is he? I don't know anyone in Canada."

"You know his father, and I think that should be enough. He's on our side. And I have a good feeling about their Prime Minister. After all, she was the only one to pull her country out of Project 15/8 in its early days. Why do you think that is?"

"Umm … I dunno. Maybe she suspected something was off, just like us?"

Carina nodded. "I can't be sure, but my gut tells me that this might have been the case. Anyway, since you're going to stay behind, that's another thing you could try to scope out. Where Canada stands on this issue. Depending on how your investigations unfold, we might need some powerful allies along the road. If we can enlist Canada, then I'd consider that a huge win."

"I see. So, leaving me behind is a strategy in disguise?"

"Oh c'mon, you *know* that's not the case. The Chancellor gave me a clear instruction to *abandon* you in the Republic. That sends a stark message. I hate to say it, but from his point of view you're no longer welcome in Calamerica. I cannot risk having you back in the country under these circumstances."

"But what about you? If I'm not safe, you aren't either.

Everyone knows that I don't act on my own. The Chancellor certainly realizes that anything I've done to upset him, was at the end of the day, commissioned by you."

"Of course, he does," Carina agreed. "But like you said before, getting rid of me isn't that easy. It'd send waves of shock through our nation and across the international community. That means, I should be alright for now. And with you out of the country, the Chancellor will soon think that our spying efforts are in disarray."

"Can't argue with you there," Alrakis agreed with a sigh. "So, when do you leave?"

"This evening. The Chancellor is sending his private jet."

"Does he know that I'm not going with you?"

"Nope. He doesn't. I'll tell him when I get there."

"How are you planning to frame it?"

"I have it all worked out. You requested a sabbatical and stayed back to travel and recuperate from the shock of your near-death experience. Can you go along with that?"

"For sure. I love it. It's brilliant!"

"Ha! Thanks," Carina chuckled. "I need to go now. But we'll talk soon," she added, as she turned to leave.

* * *

At the other end of the world, Aquila navigated his way through hallways and winding corridors to arrive at the district's central stadium, housed inside their largest office building. Halting in front of one of its large balcony doors, he peeked inside. The audience was already starting to trickle in through the lower-level doors.

The tiered, circular auditorium was massive, with seating for at least ten thousand, at full capacity. But today, they weren't expecting that many. Just the union leaders from all the farm units and some of their prominent allies. At best, there would be a thousand attendees in total. This explained why most of the upper levels were empty, and everyone was gathering in the few front rows nearest to the central podium. At the center, was a huge circular shape on the floor, from which the speaker's podium would rise bearing its occupant, when the time came for the presentation to begin.

Aquila stretched his neck to get a glimpse of the people walking in. Someone was waving at him from the second row. It was Alan. He was standing next to his sister, with his back turned to the podium area. Elaine did not notice Aquila and was focusing on the other leaders entering the stadium. She was dressed more formally than usual. Clad in a grey pantsuit and baby pink cotton shirt, she looked fetching and professional in equal measure. Aquila waved back at Alan, before stepping out of the balcony and closing the door behind him.

The presentation was scheduled to begin in less than fifteen minutes, and Aquila wanted to make sure everything was proceeding as planned. So, he trotted over to the rear elevators and made his way backstage. Entering the small room that served as the staging area, Aquila found Orion sitting alone at a coffee table, tapping his knuckles on its surface. Seeing Aquila come in, he stood up.

"Aquila!" he exclaimed agitatedly. "Any news? Where are they?"

"They aren't here?"

"Well of course not! Do you see them in here? Because I don't," Orion replied, rolling his eyes in frustration.

"Oh, that's weird. They promised—"

"Don't you even start about their promises," Orion growled, walking up to Aquila. "Didn't I tell you not to trust them? I've been trying to get them here for months, and not once did they keep their word. That's why I said it was a lost cause. But you didn't believe me! You thought Razzy knew better. Oh, those scumbag reporters. I know the lot of them, I do."

"Now now, don't jump to conclusions. I know you hate

reporters, but Razzy is different. She has arranged everything. I even spoke to her this morning. They're coming for sure. Even the top brass at the ICC are aware of this presentation. They can't skip it this time."

"Trust Razzy, you say, eh? And where is she, may I ask? Why isn't she here, if she's arranged everything?"

"It's not her choice, and you know that. She had business to attend to. Anyway, let's not get ourselves all worked up, over something that's a non-issue. Let me just call them to see where—" Aquila was cut short, as the door opened and two primly dressed officials entered the room.

"Good afternoon," the lady among them greeted, extending her hand to Aquila. "I'm Maia. We're here from Sanctuary City. You must be Orion."

"Umm … no I'm Aquila, actually. We spoke on the phone. This is Orion," Aquila replied, shaking the lady's hand, before gesturing to Orion.

"Nice to meet you," Orion said gruffly. Then checking the time, "You're late!"

"We are extremely sorry. Our vehicle got lost on the way here from the airport."

"I see. Did you not ride in one of our rickshaws?"

"No, Sir. We brought our own self-driving car. It's easier that way. We have all our equipment in it."

"Plus, you probably don't trust us," Orion mumbled under his breath.

"What's that?" Maia enquired.

"I was just asking if you flew first class."

"Ah, okay. Yes, we had to. Otherwise, we wouldn't be allowed a vehicle. Anyway, shall we start setting up? How much time do we have?"

"Yeah, I think you should hurry. We have under fifteen minutes left," Aquila cut in. "If you don't mind coming this way. The podium is over here," he added, as he walked over to a circular platform at the back of the room.

Maia and her companion hurried over to the podium.

Behind them, a self-navigating trolly rolled along with their equipment. Once the duo had started setting up their equipment, Aquila and Orion left them to it, and took the elevator upstairs to grab their seats in the auditorium.

The presentation began exactly at two. The glistening white podium floated up from the ground, like a reclining version of the moon. Atop it, were the two presenters with their holo projectors and microphones. The lights were dimmed, and a deathly quietude descended into their midst. Then a music started to play, a symphony, a rhythmic cadence that started slow, but gradually rose to a terrible crescendo. And then it stopped. Immediately, as if on cue, a holo filled the area above the podium, hiding the presenters behind it.

"Wow," came a synchronized gasp from the spectators.

"Ladies and gentlemen. Welcome to Sanctuary City," Maia said into the microphone. "Now, let me take you on a tour."

Aquila was amazed. What unfolded before his eyes was a city more beautiful than his beloved Moscow. Tall buildings housing luxurious apartments lined the broad avenues. Luscious greenery surrounded each tower, and creepers and wildflowers hung from their roofs and balconies. There were city squares for markets, decorated with statues and ornamental fountains. There were public and private pools and spas. Parks and gardens abounded, as did benches for weary pedestrians and flower beds along the sidewalks. It was a dream city. A sprawling paradise, just like it had been promised. All of it empty. Gathering dust as it waited for its lifeblood to arrive— the entire population from the Project.

"Questions, anyone?" Maia asked, as she ended the walkthrough.

"Yeah, I have one." Aquila raised his hand. A thousand heads turned in his direction, and muted whispers rose like ripples through the silence.

"Please, go ahead," Maia replied with a wry smile.

"Everything you showed us in the holos, is it all ready? Or is this just a model?" Through the corner of his eye Aquila could see several people nodding approvingly.

"Ah, great question! And kudos to you for your attention to detail. Your hunch is correct. This, in fact, is the final model. Much of it is already complete of course, and the rest is being built as we speak. We expect a completion date well in advance of the first journey out of here. Which I believe would be sometime in the winter, am I right?"

"Yes, that's what we expect. Late fall to winter at the earliest," Aquila confirmed. He leaned back in his seat and crossed his arms over his chest. "So, tell me something Miss Maia, why present a model? Why not actual footage?" Some people clapped at the question, and others murmured excitedly. Next to him, Aquila noticed that Orion was fidgeting in his seat and frowning with discomfort. He ignored his manager and continued. "You say much of it is already complete. Then what's the harm in showing us some of the real stuff?"

"Ah, another excellent question," Maia replied with mock excitement, but the smile across her lips had faded. "I'm sure you understand the security concerns, Mister Aquila. Real life footage would be too risky and—"

"Too risky for whom exactly?" Aquila countered, sitting up straight this time.

"For the colony of course. We fear that actual shots from the site would betray its location and other parameters, and make it vulnerable to terrorist attacks. We could take this conversation offline Sir, if you'd like a detailed discussion on the security issues."

"No, that's quite alright," Orion intervened. "I'll explain it to him later in private. Please go on with your presentation."

"Very well then," Maia said. "Anything else I can clarify for you Mr. Aquila?" she asked, smiling artificially.

Aquila glanced at his manager who was still wearing an uncharacteristic frown. "No. I got what I needed for now," Aquila responded gruffly.

Maia didn't seem convinced with this response. She looked

searchingly into Aquila's eyes, before clearing her throat and speaking to the rest of the audience. "Would anyone else like to pose a question?" she asked in a saccharine voice.

Several people raised their hands. The questions were all in a similar vein. They wanted to know where they were going, when they were going, how they would get paid and other such details about their migration. In Aquila's mind, most of the responses offered by Maia and her colleague fell short of being satisfactory. But having noted Orion's reaction to his questioning earlier, he decided not to express any more of his concerns. At least not here, in front of such a large crowd.

At the end of the question-answer session, just as the attendees were about to leave, Elaine elbowed her way over to Aquila.

"Thank you," she simply said. She was about to leave, but Aquila reached out and grabbed her elbow.

"For what?" he asked.

"You know for what." Elaine grinned. "For the questions. No one I know would've been bold enough to be so direct."

"You're welcome—"

"Aquila, when you're done here, can I see you in my office?" Orion interrupted, appearing stealthily by his side.

"Yeah, sure. I'll be with you in a minute," Aquila responded, and dismissing his boss, he walked Elaine and Alan to the door.

It was noisy inside the stadium, so none of them tried to speak over the ruckus. Once they were outside, Aquila thanked them both for coming and promised to catch up with them later regarding their viewpoints. Then he turned, and was about to walk to Orion's office, when someone grabbed him by the arm. He whisked around defensively and shot a dark look at his attacker, who let go of his arm immediately. It was a burly looking man in his mid-forties. But he was not alone. Quite a group had gathered around him. Men and women of various ages, their faces serious and expressions unreadable. The man who had grabbed him, spoke in a deep husky voice.

"Thank you," he simply said.

"I'm sorry, who are you?"

"I'm Ming, I lead one of the unions. You did well back there. We appreciate it."

Another woman walked up to them from the gathering crowd. "And I'm Kiara from Unit 5. A union leader, I mean," she said. "I agree with Ming. You seem to get us."

"Oh gee, thanks," Aquila said, trying to hide his embarrassment. "I just asked what I felt were the right questions."

"I know," Kiara agreed. "But no one else ever has. No one from management at least."

"Well, I hope to be on your side going forward." Aquila said firmly.

"We hope so too," said Ming. "We have a proposition," he continued, pausing to glance at the others, who nodded their heads in encouragement, "we would like you to attend our monthly meetings, if that's okay with you. Would you be willing?"

Aquila smirked. "Do you usually invite the management?"

"No. Never. You ... you'd be the first," Kiara responded nervously.

"Then I'd be honoured." Aquila smiled. "But right now, I gotta run. I have a meeting. It was nice chatting. See you at your next meeting!" As he waved and walked away, he noticed that some of them were smiling and waving back. Aquila grinned internally at this minor victory, as he sauntered off to his manager's office in the adjacent building.

When he arrived at Orion's door a few minutes later, Aquila was slightly breathless and his heart was racing from anticipation. He walked into the spacious office and shut the door behind him. Orion was standing with his back to the door, staring out the picture window behind his desk. He whisked around at the sound of the door closing.

"What do you think you were doing today?" he barked, before Aquila could even open his mouth in greeting.

"Nothing. Just asking questions. Legitimate questions. Did

I upset you?" Aquila drawled.

"It's not about upsetting me, no. It's just ..." Orion clicked his fingers, as he searched for the right words.

"Is it about upsetting *them*, then?" Aquila asked, raising his eyebrows meaningfully.

"Look," Orion said, taking a pace closer to his subordinate. "There are some alarms that are worth raising and others that are not," he continued, lowering his voice somewhat menacingly. "Let's just say, you've raised an unnecessary one today."

"I see. Do you think there'll be consequences?"

Orion flipped around to face the window again. "Maybe. They might mark you as the nosy one, and keep an eye on you. Can't say what'll happen, but you should be on your guard."

"Are you saying I'll have a target on my back?"

Orion turned to face Aquila. "No. Not if you keep your mouth shut going forward. Just," he reached over and clasped Aquila's shoulders, "stay under the radar, will you? That'll keep us all out of trouble." There was a passionate sincerity in his eyes that Aquila could not ignore.

"I get why you're worried, and you're probably justified. The ICC scares me too. But there are some things I need to know. *We* need to know. Before we send even a single worker to Sanctuary City. Don't you agree?"

"Yes. Of course!"

"Then who do we ask?"

"For starters, you can ask me. If I don't know myself, I'll try to find out through my sources. But asking a challenging question to an ICC delegate is never wise. Never. It's foolhardy, do you understand?"

Aquila nodded; his face flushed. "They didn't even tell us where that bloody city is. Did you notice?" he asked through gritted teeth.

Orion sighed. "Yep. But I know. I've already done plenty of snooping of my own."

"Oh really?" Aquila asked as he sat down across from Orion.

"And? Where is it?"

"In International Waters. My sources say it's Greenland."

"GREENLAND!"

"Shhh!" Orion cautioned. "Keep your voice down. Yes. They don't reveal any specifics related to the location, because of security reasons, like the lady explained."

"Security reasons, huh? What a load of bullshit! Do you believe them?"

Orion shrugged and sat down at his desk. "I'm only relaying what I know. What I believe ... is a different issue. They have the island cut off from the grid, with all kinds of security features. At least, that's what I've heard from my contacts."

"Maybe Razzy would know—"

"No!" Orion stood up abruptly. "Don't even think of it," he said wagging his finger. "No sharing any of this info with anyone. Not even her."

"I wasn't going to give away any of what you said. You can count on me for that. I was probably going to just broach the subject and see if she knows anything more. She's writing a book about this, after all."

"Well, you're a smart fella. Be discreet, and remember never to reveal your own misgivings, if any."

"I will. Thanks for the words of caution."

"Good. Now, if you don't mind, I have to get some work done. Do you want to have dinner later? I'm in the mood to dine out tonight."

"Sure, that'd be great! I'll stop by at the end of the day."

"Excellent! See you then," Orion said, smiling for the first time since their conversation began.

CHAPTER TWENTY

Aquila lay on his back on a bed of sun-kissed grass, that brushed like muslin against his reclining form. His arms were folded behind his head, his eyes closed, as he breathed in the fragrant moisture-laden air. Something tickled his face. His eyes shot open. He blinked to adjust his vision. Leaning over him, was a beautiful, teasing face, chuckling like a child.

"Scared you, huh?" Razzy said. Perched on her elbow, she was dragging a fallen leaf along the line of his jaw.

"Ha! You can never scare me," Aquila said, playfully tapping her on the nose. He sat up and stretched. "It's a beautiful day," he added.

"How would you know? You had your eyes closed."

"Hmmm. I can see better with them closed sometimes."

"Really? And what did you see?"

Aquila smiled as he gazed into the horizon. In front of him, a gentle breeze was drawing sparkling ripples across the surface of the river Gomti. Between the twinkling ripples, its azure cool waters gurgled with life and vitality. Aquila remembered the documentary Orion had shown him, about the Gomti's restoration. Before the Project, there was no life, no colour, no reason for the river's existence. Its muddy water was more toxic than industrial refuse. The Project had transformed it completely in body and soul.

"Hey! Where are you? What are you thinking?" Razzy asked, waving her hand before his eyes.

"Hmmm? Nothing. I'm thinking ..."

"Tell me," Razzy insisted, resting her head on his shoulder.

"You know what I'm thinking."

"No! I don't. But I want to know."

"It's already December."

"Are you chilly?"

Aquila laughed out loud. "No. And I wish it was that simple."

"Your thoughts are never simple."

"I can't help it. I'm anything but a simple man."

"And that's precisely what I love about you!" Razzy gushed, her cheeks colouring up as she spoke.

Aquila wrapped an arm around her shoulder and squeezed it gently.

"Well ..." Razzy said, looking up at him.

"Well, what?"

"What's bugging you?"

"It's almost time for the first group to travel."

"We still have a month, but yeah you're right, we're nearly there."

"It worries me."

"Why?"

"It feels too soon."

"The sooner the better, no? These people deserve to have a decent life, finally. Away from here. Somewhere safe. Why should you be worried?"

"Yeah right!" Aquila huffed sarcastically. "In a safe place we know nothing about. Convenient."

Razzy frowned and sat up straight with her legs folded on the grass. "Not nothing. We do know a lot of things now."

Aquila shook his head. "It's far from enough."

"What do you want to do then? Delay the flights? Do you

have a plan?" Razzy became suddenly serious.

"Nope. No plan. Nothing concrete. And that's what keeps me up at night."

"Would it help if we had footage? You know, from location …"

"Of course, it would. You know I've been asking for it for a while now. But how are we going to get it. I've tried every—"

"I have a plan," Razzy said, standing up in a hurry. "Let's discuss it over lunch," she added, before breaking into a sprint. "Race you to the rickshaw!"

"Hey, wait!" Aquila exclaimed. He jumped up and rushed after her.

CHAPTER TWENTY-ONE

It was January at last. The weather was bright and sunny with a crisp wind whistling through the tress, when Aquila arrived at Razzy's office in the district's main shopping strip. There was commotion everywhere. Loaded carts were moving back and forth from the shops and restaurants. Some shop owners were clearing out their inventories and closing down for good. Others were busy making last minute bargain deals with the farmer families that had gathered on the strip.

Aquila pushed past the throngs of people and made his way to the little retail space Razzy was using as her make-shift office. They had already said their goodbyes the evening before, just so that they could avoid this exact scenario. Razzy had important things to settle in her office before her afternoon flight. So, she didn't want Aquila stopping by that day. She had also forbidden him from showing up at the airport.

"It might make me cry, and that would be bad omen," she had said.

Nevertheless, Aquila broke his promise. He had to. Razzy had left her holo-recorder behind at his place. She wouldn't be able to send any footage without it, which was the sole purpose of her trip. He packed the recorder in his backpack and rushed to her office, as soon as he discovered it this morning. Now he was here. He walked into the lobby and stood in front of a set of automatic glass doors. The doors didn't open as they normally did. He realized there was a doorbell, and rang it.

A minute went by. Two minutes. Nothing happened.

"Hello! Anybody home? Razzy?" he hollered. Pin drop silence greeted him in response. He reached inside his pocket for his phone. "Damn it!" In his hurry to get here, he had left it behind. Dejected, he walked out of the lobby, wondering if he should go back home for his phone, when the lady who ran the café next door walked by.

"Excuse me." Aquila waved at her as he jogged over. "Hi, good morning! I was wondering if you've seen Razzy at all this morning. I'm looking for her. It's urgent."

"Good morning! Razzy? Oh, no. Haven't seen her here in two days. She cleared her office and left."

"What? When?"

"On Saturday. I heard she's flying with the first unit. To Sanctuary City," the lady explained, lowering her voice conspiratorially.

"Yes … yes, she is," Aquila replied sounding distracted. "Anyway, thanks a lot. Have a good day! I gotta go," he finished, as he waved goodbye and took off.

Aquila hailed a rickshaw and drove back home. He found his phone on his coffee table where he had left it. He hastily dialled Razzy's number. The call didn't go through. No signal.

Weird, Aquila thought. *There's signal everywhere inside the Project, and her flight doesn't leave until three.*

"Now what do I do?" he murmured to himself.

"Sir, Mister Alan was here to see you," Aquila's domestic robot said, interrupting his train of thoughts.

"Oh hey, didn't see you there … who did you say was here?"

"Mister Alan Shi, Sir. Your employee."

"Ah Alan … that's it! That's who I need," Aquila blurted in a moment of clarity. "When was he here?"

"Just moments before you got home."

182

"Did he say where he was going?"

"No Sir. But not to the plant."

"Oh? How do you know?"

"Because Mister Ramesh is not at the plant today. I saw him at the market this morning, and he told me to let you know."

"I see. Well, thank you. Anything else?

"No Sir. That's all from me."

"Okay. You can go now," Aquila said dismissing his robot and making his way outside. Stepping out the door, he reached for his phone and booked himself a rickshaw. He had Razzy's equipment safely stowed inside the backpack across his shoulders.

"If he's not at the plant, he should be at the farm," he muttered to himself as he checked the time.

His ride arrived within five minutes. Razzy's flight wasn't until that afternoon, and Aquila knew that Alan's dad was gong to be her co-passenger. Alan would probably accompany his old man to the airport, later that day. So, he could take Razzy's equipment with him. That way, Aquila wouldn't have to break his promise of not showing up to say goodbye. The plan was simple enough, and there was ample time to execute it. Having worked it all out in his head, Aquila boarded the rickshaw and made his way to the farm unit number one, where the Shi family worked.

His rickshaw sped past the lively activity that unfolded all around. The entire district seemed to have woken up from a deep slumber. Apart from the scheduled travellers, there were numerous others in the streets. The observers. Those neighbours and family members, who were being left behind for now. They were gathered in small clusters here and there, animatedly discussing the momentous event that was underway—the maiden voyage to Sanctuary City.

Peering out his window, Aquila became magnetically drawn to this bustling spirit. Overcome by the infectious vitality in the air, he lost all track of time. And before he knew it, he had arrived at his destination.

He scrambled off the rickshaw and hurried to the paddy field, where Alan was assigned for the day. At the field, everything was functioning as always. The farmers were busy at work, seemingly oblivious of the feverish excitement spreading through the district elsewhere.

Aquila ran around the area, searching for Alan. Several times, he called out his name. The boy was nowhere to be seen. Just as Aquila was about to turn around and leave, he saw three people approaching from the bee house. They were dressed in full bee-suits with their faces hidden behind veils. Noticing Aquila in the distance, one of them broke away from the rest and advanced in his direction. She removed her veil and revealed her lovely familiar face.

"Mister Aquila, what are you doing here?" she asked.

"Elaine, I'm so glad to see you. I'm looking for your brother actually. Have you seen him?"

Elaine frowned. She grabbed Aquila by the sleeve and pulled him away from the others. Then lowering her voice, "He isn't here. I don't know where he's been all day. I thought he was with you …"

"Well, he did come to see me this morning but … I missed him. Where's your dad?"

"Mom and dad are already at the airport. They have some stuff planned for them before the flight. An orientation of sorts."

"Oh, I see. So, your mom is also going? I thought she'd leave later, with you two."

"Yes, that was the plan, but our plant manager insisted that she leave with the rest of the seniors. He didn't want to risk leaving her behind during the winter."

"But your dad can't possibly care for her alone … she's too frail!"

Elaine shrugged. "Alan thinks so too, but they assured us it'll be alright. They have good hospitals there. We've seen images."

Aquila became thoughtful. "This is strange," he said finally.

"What is?"

"This. Everything. Look," he checked the time, "it's pushing past noon. I need to find Alan. I wager he's at the airport. He'll probably want to say goodbye to his folks. Is there anything you'd like me to tell them?"

"Uhmm …" Elaine hesitated. "Please tell them … that I love them."

Aquila smiled affectionately. "I will," he said.

* * *

Aquila arrived at the airport a couple of hours later, to find the area completely surrounded by the military and paramilitary personnel he had seen there before. He walked up to one of them and presented his credentials, wishing to see the passengers waiting inside.

"Do you have family travelling today?" the soldier asked.

"No. I have friends."

"Friends?" A look of incredulity flitted across the guard's face. "I'm sorry Sir, friends aren't allowed. Only family."

"Okay, whatever, but I'm the Chief Conservation Officer here, and I need to go in. I'm sure I have the authority—"

"No exceptions, Sir. We can't let you in."

"You can't be serious! There's something I need to give to one of the passengers. She's left it behind, and it's very important."

"We can hand that over for you. What's the passenger's name?"

Aquila was about to object, but the guard furrowed his brows menacingly, making him think twice about triggering a confrontation. "Her … name is Razzy," he blurted.

"What was that?" The guard grabbed a tablet and started searching the passenger-list.

"Razzy."

There was a minute of silence as the list was being scanned. Then, "Nope. No such passenger here."

"That can't be right. Can you please search again? She's with The International Gazette."

"The only reporters travelling today are over there." The soldier pointed to a couple of folks standing about a hundred feet away from them. "Is she one of 'em?"

Aquila swerved around to look at the group. There were two men and one woman. The woman wasn't Razzy. He shook his head. "Nope."

"Then I can't help you." The guard said firmly.

Aquila stood there for a while, looking flabbergasted. He opened his mouth a couple of times, but no words materialized. In a bit, the guard took pity on him and spoke again, a little more gently this time.

"Maybe you could ask them if they know her. The tall one is also from the Gazette."

"That's a good idea. Thanks," Aquila replied with a nod, as he headed over to the group.

The reporters were engaged in animated conversation when Aquila caught up with them. Noticing him behind them, they stopped.

"Mister Aquila, isn't it?" the tall one asked, tilting his head to the side. "We met at the—"

"Yes, yes, I remember," Aquila lied, not wishing to waste any time on small talk. "How are you?"

"I'm doing great! And you?"

"Me too. See, I don't want to take much of your time here. I just had a quick question."

"Sure! Fire away!"

"I was actually looking for a colleague of yours. I have some business with her. Can you tell me if she's on your flight?"

"Of course! What's her name?"

"Razzy."

"Razzy?" he asked in surprise.

"Yeah … you know, petite lady with black eyes, dark hair …"

"He probably means Razim," the lady reporter chimed in, walking up to their side.

"Oh, right! Yeah Razim. No, I don't believe she's scheduled to be flying with us today. What do you need her for?"

"It's … nothing. But thanks!" Aquila said, as he shook the reporter's hand. "Anyway, have a safe flight," he added.

"Razim?" Aquila mumbled to himself as he left the group. "I guess that makes sense. Razzy is short for Razim. But why didn't she ever tell me?"

"Pssst," someone called to him from nearby.

Aquila pivoted on his heels in one swift motion. There was no one in the vicinity. Several feet away, he could see an automatic luggage-cart heading for the tarmac. The cart stopped abruptly.

"Yo Aquila, over here," the same voice called again. It was coming from the cart and sounded oddly familiar.

Aquila rushed over in the direction of the caller. As soon as he approached the baggage carrier, its rear door opened. Someone extended a muscular arm and pulled Aquila into the dark belly of the vehicle. The door closed behind them.

"What the hell—" Aquila began.

"Hush. Not so loud," his kidnapper responded in a raspy voice. The baggage cart started to roll along.

"Orion?" Aquila whispered in disbelief.

"Yes, obviously."

"What's going on?"

"It's that good for nothing friend of yours."

"Oh, c'mon! You don't mean Razzy …" It was still dark inside the luggage carrier, but Aquila's eyes were starting to adjust to the change in luminosity. He glanced at his manager's face and noticed an irritable expression written across it.

"Quiet! We're almost there. Follow me," Orion replied, as he crawled on his hands and knees, making his way towards the vehicle's anterior.

Aquila followed close behind. The cart came to a halt and a portal opened up in the front. Beyond it, was a low tunnel extending into the darkness.

"Is that … a cargo loader?"

"Yeah. Come on now. We don't have much time," Orion insisted, stepping into the tunnel, his body bent double inside its constricted space.

"Woah there … are you suggesting … you can't be—"

"Are you coming or staying? I won't be responsible for what happens to you when I'm gone!" Orion threatened.

At that moment, the rear door to the vehicle started to open, and Aquila heard the gruff voices of military men on the other side. In a panic, he curled up like a ball and rolled into the tunnel, the portal closing behind him. Once inside, he had to squint to make out Orion's outline, a couple of feet ahead. Orion held a finger to his lips and lowered his breathing to a minimum. Aquila held his breath and waited for the cue to start moving. They sat there for what seemed like a millennium, frozen to the spot like carvings on a wall, daring not to move a single finger. Voices of the military men outside, continued to drift into the passage in bursts. There was some laughter.

And then, a door closed. The voices disappeared. There was a beeping sound. The cart had rolled away. Orion motioned for them to plough forward. There was no luggage inside the loader at the moment. Aquila did not know if that was because they had already been loaded. But he did not ask—wary of making any additional sounds that could invite unwanted attention. What they were doing was unnatural. Therefore, he had no doubt it was highly dangerous.

After several steps, the tunnel became an incline—intended for the luggage to tumble down along it, aided by the now motionless conveyor system. Orion sat down at the edge of it and let himself slide into the aircraft's hold. Aquila waited a second, so as not to crash right into his manager as he landed. And then he followed suit.

The hold was fairly spacious, with a ceiling high enough for them to stand up to their full heights. Aquila realized it was a massive craft. Probably, several stories high. It was slightly brighter in here than in the loading tube. In the semi-darkness, Aquila saw heaps of luggage in all directions. In front of him, Orion sat perched on a rather sturdy-looking crate. He was dressed as if on a back-packing trip, ditching his usual office-wear for a durable pair of jeans and all-weather boots. A light green polo shirt peeked from underneath his brick-red windbreaker.

Aquila removed his own black jacket and tossed it to the floor in frustration. "*Now* are you going to tell me what the hell's going on?" he asked, walking up to his superior.

Orion threw his arms up in the air. "If I knew, would I be sneaking in here like this?"

"Wait, what?" Aquila looked exasperated. "What is this? A wild-goose chase?"

"Maybe. We'll have to find out."

"You're not making any sense!" Aquila howled, as he plunked down on the floor next to Orion.

"Look, none of this makes any sense, okay. For starters, where is Razzy, eh? Have you seen her all morning? Because I haven't!"

"No ... I mean ... I've been looking for her too—"

"And that's why you're here."

"Yep. How did you know?"

"I knew it the moment you didn't show up at your desk. Razzy has been missing since last night. Ever since she left your quarters."

"Hey! Have you been stalking me or something?"

"Not *you*. Her. Like I said before. I never liked her. I had someone keeping tabs on her phone. But since late last night, she's off the grid. She's not inside the Project."

"I had a hunch that might be the case. But why?" Aquila mused, scratching his chin.

"Well, you tell me!"

"You think she might be in trouble?"

Orion broke into a sarcastic chuckle. "She's got you wrapped around her little finger, hasn't she?"

"That was completely unnecessary! I have had no reason to distrust her so far. I find your opinion of her biased. And unfounded."

"No reason to distrust her, eh? Then how do you explain her mysterious absences? The things she's hidden from you. Like her real *name,* for starters?"

"Oh c'mon! There are often professional constraints ... anyway that's besides the point. Whatever her mysteries, I don't see the logic of hitchhiking to Sanctuary City, hidden in the hold like a bag of potatoes, for that. Do we even know we'll find her there?"

"Of course not. Sanctuary City is the last place on earth where I expect to find her, to be honest."

"What? Why the hell are we going then?" Aquila screamed, tugging fistfuls of his hair in frustration.

"Shhh! Not so loud! We aren't out of the woods yet."

Aquila stood up and started pacing. "Please tell me you have a good reason for this," he muttered, shaking his head.

Orion clicked his tongue disapprovingly. "You know, sometimes I can't even recognize you anymore, Aquila. Weren't you the guy who always questioned the secrecy around Sanctuary City? Weren't you of the opinion that sending all these people down there to a secret and heavily policed private location, would be against our better judgement? Didn't you always smell something sinister afoot? What changed?"

"Sure, yeah. But over time, some of my fears have been quelled—"

"BY HER!"

"Ummm ... in part yes, and others too."

"Stop lying to yourself Aquila. She has been constantly doing everything in her power to bring you on board. Right from the beginning. From back when she organized that presentation. You were the loudest voice of dissent. Rather stupidly, you let everyone see your reservations. She saw it too and took action. Don't you see a pattern here?"

"I'm sorry to say this, but when you harbour a pre-existing bias against someone, you tend to see patterns everywhere. I had no such bias, so I saw none. I just saw a sensitive person listening to my concerns and trying to address them to the best of her ability. In fact, that was exactly why she was travelling today—to send me footage."

"And *did* she?"

"Well, something must have happened to her for sure, and that makes me kind of worried."

"Don't be a fool! Her name wasn't even on the passenger list. She never planned to go. If that doesn't alert you to her deception, then I don't know what will."

"I … I mean—" Aquila was cut off when there was a loud jerking motion, the engines had turned on. "Looks like, we're taking off. We should probably hold—"

The craft swerved to the side and a few pieces of luggage glided towards Aquila, trapping him between them.

"Ouch!" came a feeble sound from nearby.

"Orion, was that you?" Aquila whispered from behind the boxes.

"Nope."

There was silence, as they lifted off. Aquila held on to a large metallic container next to him in order to prevent another tumble. None of the flight announcements reached the hold. In the dark silence, Aquila waited with bated breath for the telltale signs of a steady flight. When they were fully airborne, he crawled out from behind the boxes and started looking for Orion.

The jerk at liftoff had tossed the various pieces of luggage at odd angles over one another, in a way that it was difficult to walk between them. Aquila had no choice, but to move forward on his hands and knees, through the zigzag of strewn packages.

He had only made it a few paces, when his elbow struck a shoulder.

"Ah, there you are!" he said, grabbing the shoulder and turning it towards him. The face that greeted him was not Orion's. "Alan! What are you doing here?"

Alan's face puckered up. He leaned against a box and broke down in sobs. "I couldn't Sir, I couldn't," he whimpered between tears.

Aquila wrapped an arm around him comfortingly. "There there," he said. "Couldn't what, kiddo?"

"Couldn't ... let them go alone ..."

"In that case, you're in good company," hollered Orion, who had walked up to them in silence.

CHAPTER TWENTY-TWO

A brief interview with Alan revealed that he had come prepared. In fact, he had been planning this for weeks. Orion had done the same. They had carefully packed a prudent assortment of essentials—food, equipment, some tinctures, tents and a whole camping kit. That left Aquila as the one least equipped to face this journey, and whatever was to befall them thereafter.

"How long is the flight?" he asked dejectedly, once their stories were shared.

"Ten hours," said Orion. "It's a massive craft. Super slow."

"And what's the plan when we get there?"

"Plan? I don't have a plan. Do you?" Orion asked, turning to Alan.

"Umm ... for starters, we need to get out undetected. I have a feeling that's not going to be easy."

"Hmmm. For sure. And what happens when they come for the luggage?" Aquila asked, glancing at both of his companions in turn.

"I have a plan for that," Alan replied.

"You do, eh?" said Orion, raising an eyebrow.

"Oh, I don't doubt it," Aquila chimed in. "He's a real wizard. Go on, what's the plan?"

"Well, Mister Ramesh had sent me to do some maintenance work on this particular craft, when they were getting it ready, a month ago."

"And?" Aquila urged.

"And … I found an oxygen cabinet right at the back of this hold. It's rather small for the three of us, but we could probably squeeze in, right before we land. Provided we get the timing right, we won't be there long enough to suffocate."

"Smart kid!" said Orion, with a friendly pat across his back. "Besides, we'll have the oxygen tanks in there if we suffocate."

"True," Alan agreed.

"Doesn't it have a lock? Aquila asked.

"Yes. But I can pick it," Alan confirmed.

"Brilliant! I think we should all try to take a nap, if we can. We're gonna have a hell of a day ahead of us when we touch down."

"I agree. I can set an alarm on my phone to wake us up before landing," Orion offered, before finding himself a cozy spot for a snooze.

* * *

Orion's alarm did not go off as intended. The party woke up to a terrible beeping sound that rang through their bones.

"I think we've landed," Alan said, pulling at Aquila's arm. "Quick, this way!"

"What? Oh right." Aquila rubbed his eyes and looked around. It was still dark inside the hold. The luggage door had not opened. There was still time. "Where's Orion?"

"Over there," Alan replied, pointing to a crouched figure a few feet away.

Orion straightened at the mention of his name and hauled a fairly large backpack onto his shoulders. "Let's make a move," he said.

Aquila realized; he had not noticed that backpack before. "How come I didn't see you bring that here?" he asked.

"Because ... I didn't! I had it loaded the night before."

"So, you knew this whole time that you were going, eh?"

"We don't have time for this," Orion urged, seizing Aquila by the sleeve. "We have to *move*. NOW!"

Alan had already started making for the oxygen cabinet at the back. He too had a large pack slung over his shoulders. Orion hurried one step behind, pulling Aquila along with him. Just as they reached the cabinet, the baggage door started to open. The trio hid behind a stack of suitcases, as Alan worked the lock.

"Hurry," Orion urged. His voice a hoarse whisper.

"I can't ... it's not. They must have changed the system."

"Shit!" Aquila cursed under his breath. Beads of sweat started forming on his brow. "What now?"

"I don't know," Alan said meekly.

The luggage door was halfway open by now, and the hold was starting to brighten up. They could hear the conveyor belts whirring to life outside. Any minute now, the hold would be boarded by the airport staff.

"We are trapped," Aquila said under his breath. "Orion ... where's Orion?" He turned around to look for their missing companion. Orion was about ten feet away, waving for them to join him. The duo rushed in that direction.

"There's always an emergency door with these holds," Orion said through gritted teeth. "I've found it. It's here. It will lead to the rear of the craft and likely not be guarded. If we could only hop off."

"That's a great idea! Alan, can you pick the lock?" Aquila asked. They heard a security robot mounting the hold from the other end.

Alan was sweating profusely. He stammered incomprehensibly as he inspected the lock. "Umm ... I dunno ... I'm not familiar—"

"It's palm activated. Hang on. Let me try something," Orion said, as he reached into his backpack and pulled out a small packet. From the packet, he delicately plucked a single glove and wore it on his right hand. Then, he placed his palm on the touchpad. A door opened before them.

"Jump!"

They jumped. It wasn't a terrible distance for a jump. About twenty feet. Still, it could have done some damage, had they landed on bare concrete. But Alan and Orion had shoved their bags down before them. The bags auto-inflated upon impact, providing a cushioned landing pad. No bones were broken.

"Parachuted landing bags!" Aquila said, chuckling softly. "You weren't lying, when you said you came prepared."

"There's no one on this side," Orion reported, surveying the area around him. "And we're shielded from view by the propulsion system. But where are all the passengers?"

"There's no passenger within a fifty-kilometre radius. No human, in fact," Alan said, observing the vicinity through a pair of scanning vision glasses.

"They must have de-planed them a while ago," Aquila concluded.

"We probably over-slept." Orion looked up and saw a roof over their heads. "Yep, we definitely over-slept! We're not on the tarmac, but inside a hanger."

"Jesus! You're right," Aquila exclaimed, noticing the walls all around. The hanger was massive, but it was enclosed all the same. Other than their own vessel, there were a couple of other carriers parked in the distance. "What about the luggage? Are they still unloading?" he asked, after he took stock of his surroundings.

Alan, who was hunched up beside an engine and peeking around from behind it, trained his glasses on the other end of the craft. "Looks like they're done. They didn't unload anything. Just a couple of boxes."

"That can't be right," Aquila said, walking up to Alan. "Can I take a look?"

"Sure." Alan handed his glasses to Aquila and stepped aside.

"And … what do you see?" Orion asked after a couple of minutes.

"They're leaving."

"What?"

"Yep. They only took a handful of boxes. Probably the crew's … or the journalists', I dunno."

"But the hold was still full when we left!" Orion objected.

"Yes … I know," Aquila murmured, as he watched the single luggage cart roll towards the open door with two security robots in tow.

"Is there security?" Orion continued to quiz.

"Not really. Only two robots. They're probably armed, but they're alone."

"Should we follow them out?" Alan asked.

"I don't think that'd be a good idea. Once they see us, they'll raise alarms, and their heavily armed counterparts won't be far behind," Orion cautioned.

"What do we do then? Just stay behind?" Alan asked, looking completely bewildered.

"Unfortunately, yes. That's our only option for now."

"What if they come back for the rest of the luggage, and find us here?" Alan quizzed.

"I have a feeling they won't," Orion said, shaking his head in dismay.

"I hate to admit it, but I agree," Aquila remarked, joining the conversation. "When does the next batch get here?"

"In a couple of weeks," Orion replied.

"We might be left alone in here until closer to that date," Aquila said.

They watched, as the moonlight trickling into the hanger from its lone open door, gradually faded away and its gigantic panels closed like a monster's maw, immersing their world in total darkness.

"I think you're right," Orion said, softly into the ensuing silence.

CHAPTER TWENTY-THREE

It was rather late in the night, when Aquila and company found themselves completely alone, locked up inside a hanger at Sanctuary City. Aquila recalled that he had not had anything to eat since breakfast that morning. His companions were just as starved. So, they set up a tent for the night and immediately got busy putting together a meal.

"I can make some porridge," Alan offered. "I packed a hotplate and some sorghum."

"I have some lentils," Orion said, rummaging through his own supplies. "But we should probably save those for later, when we'll be in want of protein."

"Later, eh?" Aquila sighed deeply. "How much stuff did you guys bring? Can we last a week?"

Alan scratched his head. "If I were alone ... then yeah. A week. Maybe even ten days. But now we're three ..."

"Right," Orion nodded. "I have some high protein stuff. Including pills that will go longer, and give us some raw power. Say, a couple of weeks."

"If we put everything together, I guess we can last ... at least one week. Right?" Aquila asked.

"Yeah," Orion and Alan blurted simultaneously.

"Good. Although, I doubt we'll have to go that long. There

has to be food in Sanctuary City somewhere. Now, we just have to find a way to get out," Aquila mused.

"Right," said Orion as he helped Alan prepare the porridge.

Aquila screwed up his face and tapped his forehead with an index finger, as he tried to formulate a plan. "Wait a minute," he said, clicking his fingers triumphantly. "Hey Orion, what was it you did back there that got us out of the hold? You used a glove ..."

"I did. An impersonation glove. It's cloned to mimic a high-profile individual."

"Perfect! Then maybe that'll do the trick."

"I dunno ..." Orion said tentatively. "We were lucky the last time. It was a desperate situation, so I gave it a shot. But if we had the wrong credentials, then we would've set off all kinds of alarms."

"Oh! Whose credentials did we use?"

"That's the other problem. I don't really know. A bunch of these gloves were stolen from a high security facility in the Republic, and pirates have trafficked them everywhere. Since they were obtained from the black market, they didn't exactly come with instructions. They belong to high-ranking individuals in the ICC. That's all I know." Orion ended with a chuckle.

"I see. And how many do you have?" Aquila enquired.

"About a dozen, but there could be duplicates in there. Meaning gloves cloned against the same person."

"Hmmm. Do I dare ask, why you even *had* these to begin with?"

"Now is not the time to explain that. We have bigger issues. If we ever get out of this alive, I'll explain everything."

"The porridge is ready," Alan interrupted. "I have some bowls we can use."

"Great! I'm famished," Orion said, grinning ear to ear, as he walked over to grab a bowl.

There was a beeping sound. "What was that?" Aquila whispered; his eyes wide with fear. "Security cameras?"

"Nope," Alan confirmed, shaking his head violently. "I took care of those as soon as we jumped."

"How?"

"This." Alan reached into his pocket and pulled out a small object that looked like a key fob.

Aquila took the object in his palm and bounced it up and down. "A memory device?"

"Not at all. It's an all-purpose jammer. Made it myself." Alan grinned exuberantly exposing all of his glistening front teeth.

"See, I told you he was a genius," Aquila said turning to Orion, only to discover that his manager was no longer by his side.

Just as Aquila was about to get up and look for Orion, the latter emerged from inside their tent, carrying a backpack. Aquila's backpack.

"It's coming from in here," he said, as the beep sounded again. "What have you got in there?"

"Nothing! Just a holo-recorder and ... oh, I forgot this was in here," Aquila said, digging inside his bag.

"What? What did you find?" Orion asked enthusiastically.

"My hazmat suit. It was a gift from Dorado." Aquila pulled out the suit and petted it lovingly.

"Bingo!" Orion exclaimed, his face colouring up. "That's exactly what we need!"

"Huh?"

"Okay, this is a long story, but first let me check if I'm right. Can I see the suit?"

"Sure." Aquila handed the garment to his companion.

Orion inspected the rim of the suit, pressing it lightly between two fingers. Then he checked under the hood and inspected the buttons near the neck. Finally, he set it down on the floor and laughed triumphantly. "That Dorado! Sly as a fox that one."

Aquila threw up his arms in frustration. "Sooo? Are you going to explain, or no?"

"For sure, but not on an empty stomach. Let's have some dinner first. Here, grab a bowl," Orion said tossing a bowl to Aquila.

Alan ladled them all, generous helpings of the steaming gruel, and they sat down to slurp through their dinner as fast as they could. Finishing his bowl before the others, Aquila wiped it with a cleaning towel and set it down next to Orion. "I'm ready when you are," he said, urging his manager to start his story.

"Ah yes, the story ... fist thing's first, your suit has a built-in communications and alarm system. That's what was beeping. I turned it off."

"Why was it beeping?"

"Because you are here. In Sanctuary City. It's designed to go off whenever you are in a territory controlled by the ICC. Like when you were at the ICC's satellite station."

"You *know* about that?"

"Of *course,* I do. Who do you think got you out of there anyway?"

"I'm pretty sure that wasn't you!"

"Maybe not me per say, but our allies."

" *What?* You're in alliance with the leaders of Calamerica?"

Orion shrugged. "Some of them. It's complicated. But back to the topic at hand ... your suit, it's a special variety. Used by the rebels of The Underground for when they are abducted by the ICC or stranded in hostile territory. We used to have some at the Project, but they raided us about a year ago and confiscated any suit they didn't recognize. They also limited our access to hazmat suits in general. That's why, we have such a paltry supply in our district. Dorado knew about this, and he brilliantly managed to smuggle one in with you."

"So, do the ICC officials know what these suits can do?"

"No. I'm told they never figured it out. It's a highly sophisticated technology that can masquerade as a regular safety alarm."

"What else can it do? Other than beep in enemy territory?"

"Ah, yes! That's the best part. It can establish a communication link with allies."

"Allies? Allies of what?"

"Of The Underground."

Aquila stood up abruptly, his face agitated. "I don't like the sound of this. We should get rid of that suit."

"Are you crazy? This may be our only way out of here, and you want to toss it out? What the hell is wrong with you?"

"What's wrong with *me*? What's wrong with *you*! Don't you know that The Underground is a very dangerous and secretive—"

He was cut off mid rant, as Alan walked up to them looking truly excited. "I think I did it. I established a link!" he said, grinning triumphantly, as he held the hazmat suit in his hand.

"Ummm … what?" Aquila didn't understand.

A gurgling sound emerged from the protective suit, and then a voice was heard. "Received SOS. Where are you and who's on the call?" A choppy voice enquired.

Orion rushed to Alan's side and spoke swiftly into the garment's hood. "This is Azure13. We are in Deep Base."

"Roger. I'll send help. Over and out," said the voice as it flickered out.

"Azure13? You are a member of The Underground, aren't you?" Aquila asked, confronting his manager head-on.

"What if I was?" Orion stared sternly into his employee's eyes, who held his gaze without blinking. Neither of them spoke. Their jaws rigid, eyes fixed on each other, noses inches apart. Finally, Orion sighed and pulled away. "I'm not, by the way. But like I said, they're an ally."

Aquila cleared his throat. "Against the ICC?" he asked, his voice calmer than before.

Orion nodded. "Yes."

"And you trust them?"

"Of course."

"Despite their notoriety?"

"Yes. I have my reasons. And later, I might share them with

you. But right now, we have a mutual foe in the ICC, and The Underground will help us out. I'm sure of it."

As he spoke, the neglected hazmat suit emitted a buzzing sound and within seconds, the holo of a finely dressed handsome young man emerged in front of them. "Good evening, Orion," the man said.

"Ah, Alrakis! Good to see you. Thanks for calling."

"Likewise, and of course I'd call. What did you expect? How long have you been at Deep Base?"

"I dunno ... a couple of hours?" Orion replied, glancing at Aquila for confirmation.

Aquila nodded in agreement.

"Ouch. That's too long. They must be looking for you. The cameras—"

"Excuse me," Alan interrupted. "I took them out. The cameras."

"I see. Smart move but ... not quite enough. If they lose camera feed for too long, then you can be sure, they'll come down to check."

"I know," Alan agreed. "But the jammer I used is very sophisticated. It doesn't block the feed. It just loops the image, playing it over and over again. That means, they'll just see an empty room with the parked aircrafts."

"Sweet!" Alrakis grinned. "Is it a temporary pulse?"

"Yes. It resets in roughly three hours. If we're stuck here beyond that, I'd have to jam them again."

"Now that I'm here, I hope that won't be necessary. Okay, let's get to work. Quick. Do you know where you are?"

"Inside a hanger, most likely. Other than that, we don't know much," Aquila replied.

"Okay. Let me pull out the plan of the city." Alrakis waved his hand, and a 3-D plan of Sanctuary City appeared in front of him. "Do you see it?"

"Yes," Orion confirmed. "But how accurate is it? They've never released the detailed plans."

"Oh, this one's authentic alright. Our spies stole it straight from Area 51."

"Quite a feat!" Orion said, as loud gasps were heard from his companions. "So, where do you think we are, based on the map?"

"I reckon, right in this building over here," Alrakis said, pointing to a dome-shaped structure set in the middle of nowhere, at a great distance from the city center. "This is the main airport hanger."

"Splendid. And how do we get out?"

Alrakis chuckled. "That's the real question, isn't it? Well, what I know is that, the hanger door is probably retina-activated from the control center, which is over here." He pointed to a small shed at the edge of the tarmac. "But how do we get to the control center?"

"How about with a drone?" Alan prompted.

"Sure. But where would you get one?"

"I brought one with me."

"No way! What model?"

"It's a FirebirdXS," Alan explained, pulling out the device and turning it on.

"Perfect. That'll do the trick. What's your name, kiddo?"

"I'm Alan, Sir. Nice to meet you."

"Nice to meet you too. You seem really smart. I'll need your help setting this up. Can you do as I say?"

"Certainly. What do you want me to do?"

"Okay, I want you to take the hazmat suit, and remove its top two buttons, from right below the neck."

Alan jumped over to where the suit was lying on the ground and quickly obeyed the instruction. "Got them. What now?"

"Good. One of them should be red, and the other one is black, am I right?"

"Correct."

"Okay, the red one's a camera, and the black one's a retinal image bank. It stores retinal images of important individuals and can flash it at a scanner. Both can connect to the satellite, just like your drone. What you need to do now, is slap the two devices on your drone's device ports. That'll power 'em up."

"Done."

"Excellent. Now can you connect your drone to the satellite, and make it discoverable? That way, I'll send you a request for control, and take over."

Alan picked up the drone's console and navigated through the steps. "It's connected. You should see it now."

"Yeah, I think I do. Its location is masked, so it must be in Sanctuary City. No other place on earth hides its coordinates like that. I'm sending you a request ... tell me if you see it?"

"Ummm ... not yet. Ah, there it is. I accepted. She's all yours now."

"Wait, but how are you going to fly it out of the building? I don't even see any window ..." Aquila jumped in, as he searched for an opening along the walls of the giant dome.

"Ah, that's the easy part," Alrakis said. "There are portals on the ceiling that open automatically to drones. We just need to fly it across the room, staying close to the roof, until one of the portals open. And then, we can zoom right out of it."

"Sounds good," Orion said. "So, what are we waiting for?"

"I'm ready," said Alrakis. "Alan, please release the drone, and I'll take it from there."

Alan did as he was instructed. In the wink of an eye, the little airplane swooped out of his hands, turned in mid air and dashed for the ceiling, faster than a hawk launching towards its prey.

"I'll sign off now," Alrakis said, his eyes glued to the drone hovering above their heads. "Pack your stuff, and wait near the door. As soon as it opens, you run, heading east. When you're at least a kilometre out from here, you can set up camp. Got it?"

"Yep," everyone said in unison.

A tiny portal on the roof flew open as the drone zoomed out of sight, and Alrakis' holo disappeared.

CHAPTER TWENTY-FOUR

It was nearly dawn, when the three intruders arrived at a spot about two kilometres east of the airport hanger in which they had found themselves stranded. Breathless and panting from the terrible sprint, they pitched their tent as soon as they were able to gather themselves, and then huddled inside for some much-deserved rest.

Outside the domed hanger, Sanctuary City was deserted. This had to be an illusion. They knew for a fact that thousands of their very own farmers had arrived from Indochine less than twenty-four hours ago. So, where were they? And the others? There were no security guards in sight. No airport staff. No vehicles. No civilians.

Aquila felt an eerie premonition take hold of him as the hours wore on—an augury of insidious evil. He lay inside his sleeping bag and tried to gather his thoughts in vain. His brain was working away at full speed, and there was no quieting it. Beside him, his companions were fast asleep, snoring rhythmically. After tossing and turning for a couple of hours, he too fell asleep.

Aquila awoke at around midday, to a whirring sound outside their tent. He blinked his eyes and noticed that he was the only one still sleeping. The others were already outside, conversing in an excited tone. Sitting up, Aquila poked his head out of the tent to see what was going on. Their drone had returned, and Alan, who was holding it in his hands, seemed to have made a discovery.

"It's not just a camera," he could be heard saying, "it's a camera phone!"

"Can you dial Alrakis from it?" Orion quizzed, leaning over the drone.

"Perhaps. That's probably how he'd called in last night. But I'm not sure how it'd work from our end. He'd called in from an encrypted band."

"What if we use the hazmat suit again, to ping The Underground and ... maybe they can—"

"Morning guys!" Aquila interrupted, as he emerged from the tent.

"Good morning, Sir," Alan greeted.

"Morning? More like afternoon!" Orion laughed, gazing up at the yellowish-orange sky, across which a sleepy looking disc was making its way up to the center.

"Guess I overslept," Aquila said, somewhat sheepishly. "Anyway, what have we learnt? Any word from Alrakis or The Underground?"

"Nope. Nothing yet," said Alan. "But it looks like we can call him from the drone, once I figure out how ..."

Before he could finish the sentence, as if on cue, Alrakis' holo appeared. "Hello all," he said. "I returned the drone."

"What took you so damn long?' Orion growled.

"I just wanted to make use of it, to look around first. As you probably already know, Sanctuary City is completely cut off from the Satellite camera grid. We've had access to no live images whatsoever. Just the plans I showed you earlier. So, we know precious little about the entire island."

"It's deliberate," Orion grunted.

"You bet. But now that you guys have landed, their secret's no longer safe."

"You surveyed the city, you say?" Aquila jumped in. "What did you find? And more importantly, where *is* everyone?"

"That's a great question. I don't exactly know."

"What? How is that even possible? What did you see from the drone?"

"Well, I saw all the buildings we'd expected to see. The tall residential towers, the parks and squares, the granary, the protein factory, the armoury, the water plants, the commercial hub. Everything as per plan. But ..."

"But what?"

"No people. None. Some robots here and there. Mostly near the factories and plants. Not many though. But not a single human."

"That can't be right. Someone must've jammed your camera," Orion said.

"I don't think so. I saw everything else. Even the birds in the trees."

"What are you trying to say then? That they simply vanished *thousands of people*? Kaput? Just like that?" Orion snapped his fingers for emphasis.

"No, that would be absurd. That's why I checked the western-most corner of the city which had a huge gated community. The map says it's a hospital complex. But it's too huge to be just that. Almost a city of its own."

"Really!" Aquila exclaimed; his arms akimbo. "And did you find the folks in there?"

"Not really. Mostly because I couldn't fly over it. I sensed safety systems all around the perimeter that'd shoot the drone down on sight. But FirebirdXS has a built-in human-activity sensor that was picking up signs of life. We were too far away to be confident, but yeah, they're probably in there."

"Oh, they're most definitely in there!" Orion shouted. "I know those bastards. They wouldn't have had that kinda security in there for nothing."

"What do we do now? How do we get in there?" Aquila mused, while pacing around in a frenzy.

208

"Do you have any weapons?" Alrakis asked, glancing at each of them in turn.

"No," Alan said meekly.

Everyone turned to Orion, "I packed a laser shooter. Heavy duty," he said grimly. "But that's not an option. We can't possibly win against their trained security guards in an encounter."

"No, I wasn't suggesting an open—" Alrakis started, but Orion cut him off.

"I have a better idea," he said. "Can we get in through the plumbing?"

Alrakis shook his head vehemently. "I wouldn't risk it. It's a hospital, remember? There might be sick people in there and the waste could be contaminated."

"That's a risk I'm willing to take," Alan volunteered unexpectedly. "I'm young and fit, and my frail parents are in there. I'll go in to look for them."

"You're a brave young man," Alrakis said with a smile. "And I feel you. Trust me, I do. I lost my parents when I was very young. But how about we keep your offer as our last resort? Give me twenty-four hours, and I'll come up with something better. I promise."

"If not, the kiddo's right, we should take a chance and enter through the drains. They probably have the folks in there for a routine health screening on arrival. I'm not too worried about getting infected. I'd gladly go with Alan," Orion announced.

"Me too," Aquila said.

"Okay, let's keep that as our back-up plan, unless I find an alternative," Alrakis agreed. "For now, I recommend that you move closer to the hospital zone, and set up camp. Right now, you're too far away to breach it. Here, let me show you on the map." Alrakis waved his hand and the 3-D plan of the city appeared once again. "You are roughly in this area now and … *this* is where you'd need to go. It's at least fifteen kilometres to your west. I'll send the map to your drone's drive so that you can find your way."

"Sounds good," Aquila said with a nod. "Also, before you leave, please tell us how we can call you back."

"Ah, right! I forgot about that. You can use the drone's console. I installed a soft-button on it that will go straight to my phone."

"Perfect," Aquila said. "We'll call you, once we're camped outside the hospital's security perimeter."

CHAPTER TWENTY-FIVE

The area around the hospital was inaccessible. A motion-activated, optical fence equipped with death lasers defended the complex like a medieval fort. Alan studied the fortifications through his scanning vision glasses and recommended, that they pitch their tent at least two kilometres from the entrance. Here, they waited patiently for nightfall.

Aquila tried to call Alrakis a couple of times, but there was no answer. At around midnight, he set out to do something more productive. If sneaking in through the sewers was to be their only option, then they would have to figure out where the drains led. Aquila took it upon himself to find out. On the map of the city, he had seen a compost plant. It was in the vicinity of their current location, and Aquila was certain that the hospital's sewage system would lead up to it. With this in mind, he was making his way to the plant, when Alan came running up to him.

"Mr. Aquila," he said breathlessly. "Come back, quick! We have news."

"What is it?" Aquila asked, turning to face his companion.

"Come! Hurry! Mr. Alrakis is calling." Grabbing hold of Aquila's arm, Alan dragged him back towards their tent at full speed.

At the tent, Orion was sitting cross-legged on a patch of grass, with the holo of Alrakis speaking animatedly in front of him.

"Alright then," he said to Alrakis, as Aquila and Alan approached, "how much time did you say we have?"

"Fifteen minutes to get to the cliff. You should leave NOW!" Alrakis ordered, before vanishing into thin air.

"Let's go," Orion said, once the call had ended. "Alan, pack the tent. Aquila, we're going southeast. You see that hillock over there?"

Aquila strained his neck in the indicated direction and saw the greying outline of a grassy mound. "Yeah, I see it. What is that place?"

"Just a park. With a clear view of the road below it. C'mon, we need to get to it fast. I'll explain everything on the way," Orion said, as he slung his backpack over his shoulders.

"I'm ready," Alan said from behind them. He was stuffing the tent inside Aquila's luggage.

Aquila walked up to him and lifted the pack in a haste. "I got it," he said. "Let's go."

The path they followed winded forward, rising slowly with every step. The park wasn't at a great distance, but the uphill hike along with the weight of their backpacks was slowing them down. Alan raced ahead taking the lead, while Orion and Aquila panted to keep up.

"What's the deal? Why are we going up there?" Aquila asked, huffing from the exertion.

"A set of hospital robots are going to pass by this way real soon. They just arrived from Calamerica, so Alrakis knows all about them. He told us how to hack one," Orion said breathlessly.

"I can see the summit!" Alan hollered from a few meters away.

"Hurry, let's go. We have work to do, before they get here," Orion urged.

In the darkness, the trio dashed through what felt like decorative flower beds and neatly trimmed patches of grass, often trampling saplings under their feet, by accident. Running at breakneck speed, they reached a sharp cliff at the summit, from where there was indeed a clear view of a broad highway, several meters below. Orion set his backpack down and immediately turned to Aquila.

"We need your hazmat suit," he said. Then he swivelled around and started digging inside his own bag for additional equipment. "Okay, here's my laser gun. Alan, do you remember all the instructions?"

"Yes Sir, I do."

"Good. Then start setting up. Aquila, can you look out for the robots? It's a dispatch of five hundred units, and they should be coming from that direction," Orion said, pointing due north. "Oh, and lie low. Get down on the grass. They have three-sixty-degree infrared vision."

"Roger!" Aquila crawled up to an advantageous spot, where the elevation seemed appropriate, and lay down on his belly with his eyes fixed on the northern horizon.

"How do I turn on the projectile mode?" Alan asked, with Orion's gun in his hand.

"Ah, yes. Let me change it for you," Orion said.

As Orion was tinkering with the weapon's settings, Alan got to work on the hazmat suit. "Alrakis said that the piping comes open ... and inside is a thin strip ... ah found it!" he muttered to himself.

"They're coming!" Aquila announced agitatedly.

"Hurry," Orion urged.

Alan grabbed the laser gun from Orion and deftly loaded it with a strip of the rubbery material, that he had extracted from the hazmat's piping. Then he put on his scanning glasses and dropping to his knees, slithered forward. "I'm good to go," he said.

"What are we doing exactly?" Aquila asked in a low whisper, when Alan had positioned himself prone on his belly alongside him.

"Well, I have Mister Orion's gun loaded with a masking polymer. Your hazmat suit has a lot of secret weapons, and this was one of them. Now all I have to do, is shoot at the backplane of the last robot in the train. That'll cut it loose from the grid."

"You mean, the polymer will attach to the robot's satellite port and block remote communication?"

"Correct. If I can hit the right spot."

"I see. And then what?"

"Then, the centralized command that's driving them forward, will no longer reach that particular unit, and it'll stop moving. After that, we'll have to try to go up to it, and control it locally."

"Using what?"

"My drone—"

"Shhh," Orion hissed. "They're too close."

The first row of robots passed directly under them as he spoke. The robots were less humanoid than the ones in Project 15/8. They appeared to be specifically designed for hospital service. Each unit had a rounded head, capable of turning in every direction, a pair of shoulders and two arms equipped with hands and fingers. The rest of the body was shaped like a large, closed trolley, capable of carrying medical supplies inside. They were marching past the hillock in perfect formation, like a military parade. There was no human in their midst. No guide or guard. Which implied, that they could certainly defend themselves from thieves and hackers without any external assistance.

The procession was like a massive, humming, droning, living river raging towards the sea. Aquila was in awe of the scale and organization of whatever it was they were witnessing, right in front of their eyes.

"Why the hell do they need so many? And where are all the humans?" He mouthed to Orion in the darkness.

Orion held his index finger up to his lips to encourage silence, but in his eyes, Aquila saw a tinge of raw horror. It took several minutes for the last row to arrive directly below their observation point. Alan immediately took aim. Behind his scanning vision glasses, he squinted to narrow in on his subject.

"Now!" came Aquila's whispered command. A shot was fired in silence.

The robot procession kept moving, as if nothing had happened. For a minute, it felt like nothing had, in fact, happened. But then they saw the straggler. The lone unit that had sputtered to a stop and was now being left behind by its fellows.

"Yes!" said Alan, throwing his arms up in triumph. "It's cut off. Let's go to it. Quick."

Orion crawled up to his knees and cupped a hand over his eyes, as he scanned their surroundings. "This way. There's a path over there that'll take us down," he said, as he scrambled towards a trail, a few feet to their east.

Aquila sped after him. Alan grabbed his drone's console and the pair of scanning vision glasses, before joining them. It took them no longer than ten minutes to get to the bottom of the hillock. Alan was ready to sprint towards the stalled robot, when Aquila grabbed his arm. "Wait." He looked around for traps and sensors, before giving Alan a thumbs-up. "All clear," he said softly.

Alan made his way to the isolated robot with the enthusiasm of a kid in a toy store. Reaching it, he dragged his right thumb along the edge of its backplane, as his eyes stared intently into the screen of his console. There was a flash of light on the screen, but it quickly disappeared. Alan made a clicking sound of disappointment with his tongue and switched hands. This time, he thumbed the robot's back panel with his left hand and repeated the exercise. Within a moment, his drone's console lit up. Alan grinned broadly and clicked on the console screen. He tapped on the screen a few more times and then he was done.

"It's connected," he said, walking up to Aquila, who was standing a few feet away. "Locally, I mean. We can control it with my console now. But I have one more thing to set up before we go. Do you have a flashlight?"

"Umm … yeah. Have one in my phone. Hang on." Aquila fumbled in his pockets for his phone. "Here you go. Where do you need it?"

"Follow me," Alan said, as he walked to the front of the robot. "Under here. I need the light right below its neck. I'm gonna open the front panel. "He indicated the spot with his finger. As he spoke, his deft hands swiftly got to work, tapping here, probing there, right under the robot's head; his own face scrunched up in concentration.

"Aha! I have it," he finally said, grinning ear to ear, as a panel opened up between the robot's shoulders, a couple of inches below the neck-joint. Alan reached into his pocket and pulled out his scanning vision glasses. He turned quickly and extended the glasses to Aquila. "Do you mind putting these on and telling me what you see, when I give you the signal?"

"Sure." Aquila nodded, putting on the glasses and leaning forward to get a better view of what Alan was doing under the robot.

"No, not here," Alan said, looking over his shoulder. "You should stand facing the road. I'll tell you when it's time."

Aquila nodded and turned towards the road. With his back to Alan, he could no longer see what the kid was doing, but from the corner of his eye he noticed, that half his body had disappeared underneath the robot's head, and some wires were being tweaked down there.

"Hurry up, folks! What's taking you so long?" Orion's voice called from the base of the hillock.

"Almost done!" Alan hollered back.

"If this unit is off the grid too long, someone's bound to come looking. We need to get it inside the hospital as soon as possible."

"I know, I know. I think I got it, though. Just give me a sec," Alan assured.

"What the hell are you trying to do anyway?" Aquila

whispered, cocking his head slightly to the side. His voice was laced with concern. "Can we skip it?"

"I … we could but … we wouldn't see where … yes! Okay, I got it. Do you see anything, Sir? Through your glasses, I mean."

"Oh, hey! This is weird," Aquila said, reaching to adjust the angle of his glasses. "My view just changed. Is it supposed to? I no longer see the road in front of me …"

"Good. Yes, it's supposed be like that. What exactly do you see?"

"I see a head. The back of a head actually. Wait! It's *my head!*"

Alan laughed out loud. "Perfect! That means it's working. I paired the scanning vision glasses to the robot's eyes. So, you're seeing through its eyes now. Come, let's head back up and get this baby on the road!"

"Wow, that was brilliant!" Aquila exclaimed, patting Alan on the back, as he sped towards the knoll.

They clambered back up the hill, to their vantage point from before and turned to face the robot, several metres below. "So, what now? How do we do this?" Aquila asked.

Alan passed his console to Aquila. "I can't do it, Sir. My parents could be inside and … you go ahead," he said, a pleading look in his eyes.

Aquila accepted the console, and coughed to clear his throat. "Okay," he said. Adding, "your parents are fine, Alan. We'll find them. And get them out."

"I know … but I wouldn't be able to bear—"

"We get it, boy. We get it," Orion cut in, patting Alan gently over the shoulder. "Now, let me pull up the map Alrakis gave us. I can use it to give directions."

"Sounds like a plan," Aquila agreed. "While I'm driving this thing, will I be able to hear any sounds?" he asked, turning to Alan.

"Oh yes! We'll hear the sounds. All of us. These glasses have built-in speakers, that'll play every sound the robot picks up."

"Perfect! Here we go then. I'm going straight ahead, till you tell me where to turn." Aquila nodded to Orion.

"Yep. You need to go more than a kilometre along this road. Do you see the rest of the consignment? Through the robot's eyes, I mean."

"Yeah, I got that. Nope. No sign of the others. Although the range on these eyes is mind blowing. Oh, and I'm travelling at 50 kilometres per hour, by the way!"

"Whoa!" Alan's eyes were wide. "That's incredible for a delivery trolly!"

"I know, right? Okay, when do I turn?"

"Mmm ..." Orion studied the map and counted something out on his fingers. "You'll see an intersection in about a minute ..."

"Okay ... yep, I see it."

"Good. Turn left."

"Gotcha."

"How's the road? Any sentries?"

"Nope. None whatsoever. It's just as empty as everywhere else on this goddamned island."

"Everywhere, except perhaps—" Orion started to murmur.

"Made the turn," Aquila announced, cutting him short. "How far now?"

"You're halfway there. I suggest you slow down. The other units were probably cruising at around 20. I'd say that's a safe bet for us to avoid standing out."

"Roger."

"This road should lead you straight into the facility, according to the map. But once inside, we'll be on our own. The map only shows me the perimeter of the hospital. Nothing inside." Orion's face became thoughtful as he spoke.

"Got it."

"So ... do you see a gate yet?"

"Am I supposed to?"

"If not now, then soon, I'd say. You should be close."

"I … hmmm …"

"What?"

"I see something ahead. It's huge."

"Fortifications?"

"Could be—" There was a sharp beeping sound.

"What was *that*?" Alan jumped to his feet.

Aquila squinted and scrunched his face, as if trying to read something in front of him. "There are some coded messages in the robot's field of view. I can't understand them."

"Oh, it's probably asking for a password," Alan replied.

"It?"

"The hospital."

"Shoot! What do we do now?" Aquila asked, his voice laced with concern.

"Don't worry, Sir. The robot is programmed with the response. It will answer on its own. But I suggest, you bring it to a stop while it responds. Otherwise, it'll slam right into the door before they open it."

"Yikes. We wouldn't want that, would we now?" Aquila barked out a dry laugh, as he maneuvered the robot to a stop.

There was another beep. "That must be the response," Alan muttered.

"Ah, I see movement ahead of me," Aquila said.

"Movement? As in people?" Orion sounded horrified.

"No, not people. A gate. It's opening. It's *massive* and metallic, like the kind you'd have in—"

"Prison." Orion completed. Aquila nodded. They fell silent for a moment, absorbing the revelation that emerged.

"Okay guys, I'm going in!" Aquila said at last, breathing heavily—a rasping kind of breath.

A moment passed, and then a strange buzzing sound burst through the eyeglass speakers. It had a watery feel to it, like a swarm of bees splashing through the rain. "What *was* that?" Orion exclaimed.

"I dunno. But I can't see anything." Aquila's voice quivered, as he spoke.

"Shit! Are you inside yet?" Orion blurted agitatedly.

"I have no idea. It's dark all around. Looks like the eye sensors went out."

"Are you sure they went out or—" Alan was interrupted mid-sentence, as Aquila huffed a sigh of relief.

"I can see again. Something must have temporarily clouded the trolly's vision. Like it was sprayed down by a mist."

"Hmmm, well what do you see? Are there guards? Other trollies?" Orion asked.

"Nope. It's just me. There's a low building just ahead. Like a loading area. And … a vehicle parked against it. A transport van. This might've been how they brought the folks down here." Aquila turned to remark.

"Anyone in the van?"

"Hang on, let me get closer … umm no … but it's filled with luggage. *Their* luggage you think?"

Orion shrugged. "Could be. But why is it still in the van? Strange."

"Stranger things have happened," Aquila mumbled. "Okay, I'm entering the loading area. It's like a large lobby. Completely empty. I see a couple of doors. One on either side of the lobby."

"Open doors?"

"Closed. One marked 'ladies' and the other—"

"Gents."

"Yep. But they're not washrooms. A small sign below the gender label says, 'screening area'. I dunno man … this place … it's giving me the creeps. Besides …" Aquila trailed off.

"Besides what?" Orion asked tentatively.

"It feels oddly familiar. Like a déjà vu."

"Maybe you've seen it in a holo-movie?" Alan suggested.

"Unlikely," Orion objected. "This place doesn't even have any map. It's top secret. No one could possibly have filmed it."

"Alright, I'm at the end of the lobby. There's a huge concrete courtyard in front of me. Still no sign of movement anywhere. I see several buildings at the far end of the courtyard. Stark-looking, gray structures. Grim, like a bunch of row houses in a run-down neighbourhood. They could be the hospital wings, but who knows? So, where do I go now?" Aquila asked.

"Oh right!" Alan exclaimed. "Maintenance mode."

"*What?*"

"Quick, give me the console, Sir! Alrakis taught me how to set it up."

"I don't get it. How's that gonna help?" Aquila looked perplexed, as he turned to Alan and passed the console.

Alan didn't immediately respond, choosing to focus intently on the console's screen instead. When he was done, he raised his head and smiled. "All set, here you go," he said, handing back the control. "When in maintenance mode, the trolly will navigate itself and head towards the repair shop, which is usually located at the very end of complexes, such as these. And in order to do that, it will have to pass through the other wings and possibly through all the patient wards as well. That way, if we see something that looks like a ward, we can seize back control and investigate it. Besides, a trolly in maintenance mode will look less suspicious passing between the wards, so no one will disturb it. At least, that's what Alrakis told me."

"Smart!" Aquila replied, flashing Alan a half-smile. "I'm almost at the end of the courtyard. Soon we'll be inside the first building. Now, the real heist begins!"

Orion and Alan huddled close to Aquila, breathing heavily down his neck, the muscles on their faces taut with anticipation. "So ... are you inside? What do you see?" Orion rasped.

"Shh!" Aquila hissed, his finger rising involuntarily to his lips. "I'm in the building. I see other robots."

"They can't hear you, Aquila. You don't need to shush us." Orion chuckled. "How many robots are there?"

"Just a couple. They're rolling down the corridor. There are doors on either side."

"Could they be the wards?"

Aquila shrugged. "Can't tell. All the doors are closed. No people anywhere. Or voi …" He paused, becoming instantly alert. "Wait, I hear footsteps. Someone's coming," he continued in a hoarse whisper. "Two people. Probably hospital workers. Coming straight at me."

"Have they seen you?"

"I dunno. Their eyes are hidden. Behind full hazmat suits!"

"Whaaat?" Alan shuddered, as if a gust of icy wind just brushed over him.

"Doesn't look good, does it?" Aquila whispered apologetically.

"No, it—" Orion began, when Aquila grabbed his arm to stop him.

"Hush! They're saying something. I wanna catch the words …"

They heard a mild crackle through the speakers, as the personnel moved closer, and then a low rumbling of voices seeped through.

"Time to take them off the grid," said a baritone male voice.

"You mean Ward 32?" a mewling female voice responded.

"Yep. You do that, and I'll notify the in …" The voice faded rapidly, as the man hurried away.

Aquila puckered his face and trained his ears to catch the man's departing words, but without any luck. Near him, he could almost hear Alan's heart pounding at a thousand cycles per second. "I … I can't hear him anymore. He left in a rush. The woman's heading my way." He inhaled a deep breath, before speaking again. "I know what to do," he announced decisively. "I'm gonna follow her."

"Good idea. She'll probably lead you straight to Ward 32," Orion agreed.

"Yep. Okay, she just passed by me. How do I do take back control?"

"Here, let me do it for you," Alan offered, snatching the console from his outstretched hand and tapping it furiously, before returning it with a fluid motion.

"Thanks. I'm turning around. I'll follow at a distance, so that she doesn't suspect anything."

Aquila turned the robot around and cruised along the corridor at an even pace, keeping at least a couple of meters away from their quarry. The woman with the mewling voice quickly turned a corner, and Aquila hesitated, before continuing to give pursuit. Around the corner, there were evenly-spaced doors on either side of what seemed like a dimly-lit, never-ending corridor. The woman was already ten doors ahead and hovering like a shadow, over a door handle to Aquila's right. She pressed some buttons, waited a second for the door to open and let herself in, to what one could only assume was ward number 32.

"She just disappeared into the ward," Aquila said softly. "Should I follow?"

"NO!" Orion clasped a hand over Aquila's shoulder in warning. "That'd be too dangerous. We should wait till she comes out."

"We don't have time for that. How 'bout I enter one of the other wards? This corridor seems to be lined with them."

"Yeah, that'd work too. All we need are some patient data, and any occupied ward should have it."

"Good. Let's try the door just to my left. It has a kind of traffic light sensor on it. Sensor's glowing red. Does that mean it's empty? Or restricted access perhaps?" Aquila sounded confused.

Orion became thoughtful. "My guess is that, it's occupied. But like you said, 'restricted access' At least for now. Maybe wait a bit? And see if the light changes?"

There was a clicking sound.

"Someone's coming out ..." Aquila whispered. The others huddled around him, straining to pick up any additional sounds. There was silence. Pin drop silence. "Nope. Looks like they aren't," Aquila sighed.

"What about the light?" Orion asked.

"Huh? Oh, you mean at the door ... yeah, let me check. It's

changed to yellow. That's interesting. What could that mean?"

Orion shrugged. "No idea. But I'd say, it's still not our cue to go in."

"Maybe they're prepping the room or something," Alan volunteered.

"Could be," Aquila agreed. "How long do you think I should wait? I'm pretty sure we're gonna start raising suspicion soon."

"Good point." Orion nodded. "I'd give it another minute or two. And then, we need to drop it and keep moving towards the repair shop."

One minute passed. Two minutes. Aquila felt beads of sweat trickle down his neck, but he didn't dare to stir. As if stirring would make his presence known. The light hadn't changed. It was time to move on. Yet, Aquila couldn't get himself to drive the robot away. Something in his gut didn't feel right. He *had* to go into that room. That *particular* room. "I'm going in," he said with absolute resolve.

"What? No, don't be rash—" Orion grabbed at Aquila's arm.

"The light just changed to green!" Aquila interrupted, his face brightening up.

"It did?"

"Yep. Let's see, how do I get in …" Aquila mumbled, while his fingers glided over the console, "ah, here we go. The door opened by itself!"

"Maybe because it's a delivery trolly," Orion mused. "Well, go on then. Get your ass in there. We don't have much time."

"Roger. Okay, I'm in. It's mighty dark in here …"

"The trolly should have a night light," Alan prompted.

"Found it. It's a weak light, but I can see shapes …. beds. Two, no three beds. Occupied. What now?"

"Can you roll over to the nearest bed?" Alan instructed.

"Yeah, I'm there."

"Good. Do you see a control panel next to it? Or near the headboard? The bed should be hooked up to one. That's where all the data is."

"Ummm ... I see ... there is ... it's like a column next to the bed, and it's beeping. It has a screen on top—"

"Yep. Sounds like a control panel to me. Quick, get the robot to connect with it and start the transfer."

"I ... I ... can't figure out how," Aquila stammered, sweat pooling around the folds of his neck.

Alan extended a hand and snatched the console from him, as if on cue. His face transformed into something unrecognizable. Like a hunter focusing on a kill. His fingers moved effortlessly over the console, as he got to work on the file transfer.

There was a loud bang, and then a shrill sound emanated from the speakers—a rhythmic ringing. It was deafeningly loud.

Aquila instinctively covered his ears and screamed out. "What the hell is *that*?"

"I dunno, but it doesn't sound good . . ." Alan began.

"Alarm. It's an alarm," Orion blurted out, looking horrified. "C'mon, we gotta go. Now! To the coast." He got up and broke into a sprint, heading east.

Alan scrambled to his feet in an instant, dragging Aquila up by the arm as he rose. "What coast?" he hollered, cupping his hands around his mouth to amplify his voice.

"There's a water purification plant near the seashore to the east. Alrakis told us to run that way in an emergency." Orion turned around to respond. He was already a few paces ahead, so his voice was barely audible.

Grabbing their bags, Aquila and Alan picked up speed and joined Orion, as he raced furiously towards the shore.

CHAPTER TWENTY-SIX

This area of the city was like a peninsula. The eastern shore, where they were headed, was not that far off from the western edge. Alan being the lankiest, quickly overtook his companions and disappeared into the distance. Aquila with his long strides tried to catch up. Orion took up the rear, trailing behind the group as he stopped to pant every few minutes. Aquila glanced up at the sky as he ran. Dark ominous clouds were gathering near the east, and just as he was about to warn the others, a terrible bolt of lightning ripped through the horizon, followed by an angry growl of thunder.

Alan had stopped a few meters ahead and was beckoning them forward. Aquila turned to Orion. "C'mon, let's go! It's gonna rain..." He barely finished his sentence, when the sky burst open and fiery torrential rain came gushing down. As Aquila was about to extend his hand to help Orion over an incline, Alan rushed back, gasping for breath as he spoke, "we're there, nearly there, I've seen it, the shore."

"Where?" Aquila screamed out over the howling wind.

Alan pointed east. "Right behind the rocks where I was standing just a minute ago," he said, as he hurried in that direction.

They kept running as fast as their legs would carry them, slipping and sliding on the muddy earth for a few more minutes, until they arrived at a downward slope laden with boulders, just as Alan had indicated. Beyond it, they could see a vast expanse of emptiness, fringed with frothing waves—the open ocean. Alan had already made it half way to the beach, when Aquila stepped on the mossy rocks that led to it. He immediately skidded and nearly toppled over.

Turning, he waved to Orion. "Watch your steps!" he cautioned. Orion nodded and balanced himself carefully, with his arms outstretched like an acrobat on a trapeze.

In a couple of minutes, they were both on the beach and still in one piece, but Alan was nowhere to be seen.

"Where did he go?" Orion asked, squinting against the sheets of falling rain.

"No idea. I'll search that way, you go the other," Aquila said, pointing north as he spoke.

"Maybe, we should wait for the rain—" Orion began, but was cut short by a familiar holler.

"Hey, over here. I found a recess behind these rocks. It might lead to a cave." Alan waved, his dis-embodied head poking out from a fissure between two massive pieces of rock.

Orion and Alan headed in that direction. The fissure was narrow enough that they had to turn to their sides to gain passage. They lumbered on through the gap, clasping their backpacks tightly to their chests. Rain soaked their clothes and made its way to their skins, its freezing touch sending shivers down to their bones. After what felt like an eternity, Aquila stumbled over something to his right and toppled to the ground.

"Ouch," someone squeaked from underneath him.

It was Alan. They had fallen into a cave. It was fairly large and sheltered from the rain. Aquila apologized and staggered to his feet. Orion was right behind him. He had managed to avoid a fall.

"Finally, a cave!" he said, grinning from ear to ear. "That rain was real nasty."

"It was," Aquila agreed. He had removed his jacket and was ringing it out as he spoke. "But it's not over yet. We need to figure out what to do next."

"I'm on it," Alan replied. He was crouched on the floor, drying his drone's console with a T-shirt. "We'll call Alrakis from here as soon as it's dry enough."

"Quick thinking," Aquila said with a pat on Alan's shoulder. "Didn't he tell you he had a plan, if things went awry?"

"He mentioned something like that. We need to find out what exactly it is though. Okay, I'm calling him now." Alan pressed the call button, and held his breath in anticipation.

All eyes turned to the console. The call kept ringing. After about fifteen rings it stopped.

"Try again," Aquila urged, his voice cracking slightly.

After two more attempts with the same result, Alan sank to the floor, his head between his hands. Aquila sat down next to him, while Orion started pacing around the cave, hunching slightly so as not to bump his head against the roof.

"Quite a pickle, isn't it," Orion grumbled. "I say, we keep trying every couple of minutes."

"There's no point." Aquila sighed. "He should be able to see the missed call, and call us back. If he isn't …" he trailed off.

"How long do you think before the security on this island finds us?" Alan asked.

"Your guess is as good as mine," Orion responded. "We don't even know if they're onto us. Though it's likely they'll search the island for intruders either way, since the alarms went off like that."

Aquila was hearing this conversation, but his attention was not quite there. Ever since his arrest by the ICC, he had become wary of expecting other people's agendas to align with his own. He pulled Alan's backpack between his folded legs and was digging through the contents absent-mindedly. Then, finding what he was looking for, he pulled it out. It was the drone, onto which Alrakis had loaded a map of the city.

"Alan, how do I get the map to pop-up?" he asked, fiddling with the gadget.

"Oh, let me help you." Alan leaned forward and quickly obliged.

The map appeared in its full glory, suspended between them like a wisp of smoke.

"Now. Where do you think we are ..." Aquila mused, rubbing his chin. Stubbles had started growing there, he noticed.

Alan pointed with a nimble finger. "See that? It looks like a beach. This beach. It's pretty long. I suspect, we are in the southern side. Right around these rocks."

"Good guess," Aquila said. "And ... those buildings over there, right next to the coast. They look like—"

"Water purification plants," Orion interrupted. "I've seen enough of those in my lifetime, to know exactly what they are."

"That means we're not very far from where Mr. Alrakis wanted us to go," Alan observed.

Aquila did not immediately respond. He was hunched over the map, studying it closely, his face twisted in concentration. After a moment of silence, he pointed to a low elongated building, about a kilometre further south of the water-purification unit. "What do you think that is?" he asked, addressing no one in particular.

Orion stepped forward. "Looks like some kind of factory. There are chimneys—"

"That's exactly right, isn't it? Too many chimneys! Can't be a factory." Aquila shook his head.

"What? You're not making any sense—" Orion began, but was cut short by a ringing sound. Alan's console had lit up and was displaying an incoming call alert.

Alan rushed forward to pick up the console, his heart throbbing. Before accepting the call, he turned to the others for approval. Orion nodded, making eye contact. "Hello," Alan said in a quivering voice. Immediately the holo of the caller appeared, suspended in front of him, and he jerked back in surprise. It was not Alrakis.

Orion and Aquila were equally startled. Orion took a moment to collect himself before grinning amicably. "Why Carina! What brings you here? Where is Alrakis?" he asked the stately dark-haired lady, whose holo stood in front of them.

"Hello Orion, Aquila and who is this young man?" Carina replied, turning to each of them as she mentioned their names.

"Oh, he's from my District, this lad. Name is Alan. A bright little chap indeed." Orion smiled.

Aquila's face had turned completely white, as if he had just seen a ghost, "I ... I have ... *seen* you!" he finally stuttered.

"Yes, I believe you have. I'm the Secretary of State of—"

"Calamerica," Aquila completed.

"What!" Alan simultaneously exclaimed.

Carina smiled at them both. "No need to panic. I'm friends with Orion, and Alrakis is my aide. You can trust me. You have nothing to worry about. In fact, Alrakis is on his way to Sanctuary City, as we speak."

"Hang on," Orion interrupted. "You're sending a rescue party? How? Sanctuary City is inaccessible."

"I know. That's why his submarine will be waiting for you about a hundred kilometres off the coast of the city, in international waters. I have a plan for you to get to him, but you must act immediately."

"I'm sorry to interrupt Ma'am, but the patient data, we lost them ..." Alan was trembling.

"No. We didn't. They uploaded before the alarms went off," Carina said glumly.

"Oh, and what did you fi—" Alan started, but Carina raised her hand to stop him.

"I'll explain later. We don't have much time. You need to get out of there as soon as possible. They're aware of the security breach, so they've sealed the airport, and the Chairman is on his way."

"The Chairman?" Orion looked puzzled.

"Of the ICC," Carina clarified. "We have intel that he's an extremely dangerous man. My sources tell me, he's about to land in Sanctuary City in roughly forty-five minutes. You have to reach Alrakis at his submarine before he arrives."

"Wow, is that even possible?" Aquila interjected.

"Like I said, I have a plan. I need you to get to the water-purification plant right away. It has an onshore unit for fresh water harvesting. It should be lightly guarded, if at all. The plant's other unit is about half a kilometre offshore. The two units are connected by an underwater tunnel for maintenance. This tunnel is probably unguarded, and so is the offshore unit. If somehow, you could breach the tunnel and get to the second unit, they should have amphibious jetcrafts there, for patrolling the area. They're super fast but don't travel far. That's why, Alrakis will bring his submarine as close to the city's security perimeter as possible, which is about a hundred kilometres offshore. You should be able to make it to the submarine just in time, before the craft's power drains out."

"And all this in just forty-five minutes?" Orion asked.

"Correct."

"Sounds like a stretch," Aquila mused. "And what about the others, by the way? We just leave them here?" he asked.

"Unfortunately, you must. For now, at least."

"When can we come back for them?"

"We don't know. They are gravely ill—"

"Gravely ill? What the hell!" It was Orion this time, unable to contain his anger. "What's wrong with them? What did you find?"

"It seems they've been infected with some sort of a virus. A prehistoric strain. Something that might have been buried in the permafrost here, for centuries. When the region thawed recently, it could have gotten mixed with the ground water."

"And they *knew* about this? The ICC?" Orion growled.

"It's likely," Carina replied lowering her eyes, her voice like a wisp of wind.

"Those bastards!" Orion yelled, his right fist punching an imaginary target in front of him.

"So, is there a cure? How are they treating it?" Aquila asked.

"Well, the patient file we received was that of one Mr. Shi, and it didn't seem promising—" Carina was interrupted by a loud thud inside the cave.

Aquila and Orion whisked on their heels to find Alan lying on the floor behind them. Orion rushed to his side. "My boy! It's going to be alright …" Orion's voice fell to a low whisper, that Aquila could no longer hear. His ears were buzzing, and his head felt heavy. He realized, he had to make some difficult choices and fast. He turned to Carina and spoke breathlessly.

"This Mr. Shi, is he alive?" he asked, lowering his voice.

"Yes, but—"

"What happens if we delay our escape by just a little? We need to get Mr. Shi out!" he explained.

"No! That'd be suicidal. Believe me, you would *not* want to encounter the Chairman at any cost."

"Why? I mean, how bad could he be? Just another ICC thug, I'd imagine."

Carina sighed impatiently. "I'm afraid not," she warned. "He's … he may not exactly … be human."

"Not *human*? How's that even possible?"

"We have a hunch that he may be a clone. A historical person of great notoriety, resurrected from the grave."

"Noo!" Aquila panicked, his face as pale as death. Carina was about to elaborate, but her image flickered. There was a terrible clap of thunder outside that shook the earth beneath their feet. As it subsided, the call dropped, and Carina's holo disappeared as swiftly as it had materialized.

CHAPTER TWENTY-SEVEN

Aquila slid to the floor in horror. Orion and Alan walked up to him. Orion had his arms around Alan's shoulder. Even then, the boy was shaking like a leaf in the wind.

"What happened? Where did she go? What did she say?" Orion blabbered agitatedly.

Aquila turned slowly towards his manager. His lips quivering as he spoke, "Hitler. They've resurrected Hitler," he said.

"Who's resurrected who now?" Orion asked.

"You know, when I said that the loading dock inside the hospital looked familiar? Like I've seen it before somewhere?"

"Yeah ..."

"Now I remember where I'd seen it. In the videos about Auschwitz. A concentration camp, built by Adolf Hitler, during the Second World War."

"Holy shit!"

"And Carina said that the Chairman of the ICC might be a clone of some notorious historical figure."

"So, you think it's Hitler?"

"I do."

"This is bad! Very bad. We need to get out of here immediately."

"No!" Alan shouted. "I'm not going anywhere. Not without my parents."

"He's right," Aquila agreed. "We can't leave them here to die."

"And the alternative is that, we stay here to die with them?" Orion looked incredulous.

"Not we, just me. You and Alan need to follow through with Carina's plan and head to the water-purification plant."

"No way, Sir. I'm coming with you," Alan objected.

Aquila turned Alan around by the shoulders and looked him straight in the eye. "Look kiddo, I know what this means to you. But you gotta trust me, okay? Someone needs to figure out how to get in to the underwater tunnel, and Orion can't do it alone. We're a team, remember? We're in this together."

Alan hung his head and nodded wearily. "Now, here's the plan," Aquila continued. "Do you guys swim?"

"I used to, when I was younger," Orion grunted. "A bit out of practice though."

"What about you, Alan?" Aquila asked.

"I'm a deep-sea diver, Sir. I brought a diving suit."

"See, that's what I meant! Orion needs you. *We* need you."

"So, you want us to breach the offshore unit of the plant?" Alan asked.

"That's exactly right. Get in there, get a jetcraft, and turn back to the shore." Aquila checked the time on his phone. "Wait for me near the bank in twenty-five minutes. If I'm not there by then, contact Alrakis, and head as fast as you can to his submarine. Don't look back. Got it?"

"And what if I can't figure out how to get us in? To the plant I mean?"

"You will. I know you. Believe in yourself."

"But if something goes wrong—" Orion began.

"If something does go wrong, make contact with Alrakis, and swim back to the shore. I'll meet you there in twenty-five."

"I don't have a spare diving suit for Mister Orion. I just packed a small refill oxygen tank," Alan said, shuffling through his bag.

"Even if you did, I'm not much of a diver," Orion said. "I'll have to hang close to the surface. We'll figure something out. Let's go!" he added, as he made for the cave opening.

"Mr. Aquila!" Alan turned to say. "Here, take my jammer and console. You'll need it!" He dropped the two items into a small sachet and tossed it over to Aquila, before following Orion out.

CHAPTER TWENTY-EIGHT

Once Orion and Alan had left, Aquila felt a sudden jolt of terror course through his body. He had no idea what he was going to do despite the confidence he had shown earlier, while sending his companions away. Numbly, he took the sachet Alan had tossed him and shoved it into his backpack. Then he wiped his forehead with his still damp shirtsleeve. In the 3-D map of Sanctuary City, he had seen a low elongated building with multiple chimneys that had struck him as peculiar. This was his only lead. He vaguely guessed what that building might be, but if he were wrong, then he would hit a dead end. He took a deep breath to calm himself, put on his jacket that was still drying on the cave floor, and ventured out into the cold, fragile night.

The rain was no longer pounding down with its earlier vigour. This made it easier for Aquila to take stock of his surroundings. The dark beach lay in front of him, the sand wet and hardened by the receding waves. The tide was turning. But this also meant, that a new dawn was drawing nigh. He would have to act fast to execute his plan and make for the open seas, before the sun came up and blew his cover. Without wasting another second, he scanned the horizon and started sprinting in the general direction where he expected to find the building he was looking for.

In a couple of minutes, he could see a large parking lot to his left, just next to the beach. Several cargo trucks were parked there in rows. A wide path led out from the lot and extended to the shore. Right at the end of this path was the low, narrow building Aquila was looking for. It was a menacing structure with its numerous chimneys hard at work, expelling billowing coils of smoke. This was exactly what had struck Aquila as particularly odd. Modern day factories did not have that many chimneys, or any chimney at all, for that matter. Who designed this unit, and to what end? Also, why was it the only industrial activity to be seen anywhere in this city? Everything else Alrakis had seen with their drone, had seemed unmanned and lifeless.

Aquila trotted down the path—which appeared upon closer inspection to be track marks made by the cargo trucks—making his way for the building entrance. He was nearly there, when a roaring sound behind him, made him spin on his heels. A truck was heading his way. He dived to his side and fell crashing onto the packed sand. Luckily, the truck was unmanned. No one had seen him lunge out of the way.

The truck moved closer to the building, before making a U-turn. It stopped with its rear facing a pair of roll-up automatic doors. The back of the truck opened and to Aquila's surprise, a hospital trolly similar to the one they had hijacked earlier, glided out of it, followed by another. The two trollies slid onto a moving walkway—fitted with rails, custom-built for these particular units—and rolled towards the building entrance. The first trolly's head turned towards him and he froze, expecting an alarm. These units were equipped with three-sixty-degree infrared vision, Orion had said. But the eyes stared at him blankly. After a minute, nothing had changed, no alarms were triggered. The eye sensors seemed to have been deactivated.

Without thinking, Aquila threw himself at the second trolly, grabbing on to its neck with his arms. The roll-up door in front of him was opening, and the first trolly had almost disappeared behind it. Quickly, Aquila mounted his trolly's closed rectangular cart, and lay flat over it. In doing so, he realized for the first time, that the length of the cart was exactly enough for a grown human to lie on. He felt suddenly nauseated. His hunch had been right. He knew where he was going.

* * *

Alan ran like the wind in the direction of the water-purification plant, forgetting to check behind him to see if Orion was still following. A minute later, he was running out of breath. He halted next to a row of palm trees, and bent over double, to fill his lungs with much needed oxygen. The beach was a lot narrower here despite the low tide, and he could see the frothing surf crash against a rocky coast. Orion was diagonally across from him, heading towards those rocks. Taking a moment to regain composure, Alan ran in that direction.

"I think I can see the building from here," Orion shouted, noticing Alan. "Those twinkling lights beyond the rocks," he added, pointing northeast.

Alan clambered on to a rock next to Orion. From here, he could see all the way to the horizon. He saw what Orion was pointing at. It did indeed, look like a plant of some sort. Apart from the couple of lights glowing on its roof, a tall building stood there, looking abandoned and forlorn.

"Okay, I see it now," he said. "There should be a similar one, its twin, somewhere out at sea."

"Correct. But it's too dark. I can't spot it."

"I can. Through my scanning vision glasses," said Alan, who had already dawned this speciality equipment.

"Excellent. How far is it?"

"The glasses say, it's about a kilometre from here."

"That's a long way to swim."

"Yep. But we won't have to. If we find the tunnel that connects them." Alan clambered off the rocks and came to Orion's side. "I have an idea." He dug into his backpack and pulled out a tablet. Quickly, he punched in some numbers, before looking up with satisfaction. "I imagine, the tunnel will connect the two units in a straight line," he explained. "I was able to roughly calculate where it'll be. If we swim from here in a straight line, then we should reach it in about two minutes, accounting for the water current, which will be in our favour."

"Sure, but there's no way we'll know where we're going with that much accuracy, once we start swimming."

"Of course not!" Alan grinned, his perfect teeth flashing in the darkness. "That's why we'll need my drone."

"That would've been a brilliant idea, if you hadn't given your console to Aquila earlier."

"I won't need the console. I can still set it up to fly in a straight line and hover. Just need to punch in the exact distance." He held the drone level with his head and keyed some numbers into its side panel. "Done. When I release it, it'll reach its destination and remain suspended in mid-air to mark the spot. All we need to do is swim towards the drone. When we're near, I'll dive, and look for the tunnel entrance. If I can get us in, I'll come back up and get you. Grab this life-jacket. It'll keep you afloat, while I'm down there," he added, tossing the jacket to Orion.

The jacket fit snugly around Orion, once he tightened the buckles. He thumbed a touchpad on the side, and it lit up. "Inflate," he commanded. The device lustily sucked in air and bloated up like a blowfish.

"No, not yet!" Alan cautioned. "It'll slow you down, if you inflate it now. You'll need it, once we get there. When you wait for me close to the surface."

"I was just trying it out," Orion grunted. "Deflate." The lifejacket reverted back to an innocuous looking regular jacket.

"Okay, let's go. Ready?" Alan removed his shoes, dropping them next to his backpack and padded into the ocean in full diving gear.

Orion nodded and followed close behind.

* * *

Aquila lay flat on his back, as the trolly rolled under the automatic door. It was a low door Aquila noticed, when his head was barely able to squeeze through, without being crushed like a walnut between its jaws. Past the doorway, the ceiling was higher, but not high enough for him to stand up. He scrambled onto his hands and knees for better visibility. Yet, he saw nothing. It was too dark inside. Soon, his eyes began to sting, like they had been pepper-sprayed.

The trolly trudged on for a few more minutes, before he smelt it—the strong acrid vapours, the stench of mortality. Right at that moment, a door opened in front of him, blasting him with a terrible heat. Beyond that door, was a ball of fire, licking the walls of the chamber like a dragon's breath. In that moment, he knew that wherever he was going, would surely be his ultimate destination.

For the first time in his life, Aquila panicked. He wanted to move, wanted to jump, wanted to do something, *anything*, but his body refused. Every single muscle felt leaden.

The trolly in front of him decelerated. It had nearly reached the furnace. It adjusted its position slightly and drove into the incinerator, belly-first. Once the entire length of its trolly cart had disappeared into the furnace, the robot stopped, its head and arms remaining outside. A few feet behind it, Aquila's robot trolly also came to an abrupt halt, lurching forward slightly and almost toppling him over. There were two distinct sounds, "thump, thump," of objects being ejected from the first trolly, and dumped into the furnace. Unloaded, the trolly backed up slowly and U-turned onto a parallel set of rails that lead to the exit. On cue, Aquila's trolly started to move again.

Aquila turned his head towards the retreating trolly, gliding towards him along the parallel path. Its cart looked red hot. There would be a moment very soon, he realized, when it would pass right by him on its way out. But mounting its cart was out of the question. It would burn through his clothes in an instant.

An idea flashed through his mind. Just then, a searing gust from the furnace hardened his resolve like a slap to the face. Of all the terrible ways to die, burning alive to death seemed like the worst. In that moment, every cell in Aquila's body violently rejected that fate. He sprung to his side and jumped on to the passing trolly's back, straddling it from behind, his legs latching on to its robotic arms. In doing so, his feet accidentally grazed the edge of the cart. Aquila screamed out in pain, as the heat burned through to his socks and blistered his skin.

The pungent vapours of charred flesh emanating from the furnace had filled the tunnel by now, and he struggled to breathe against it. Bile rose up in his throat, as he resisted an urge to throw up. He closed his eyes and began counting his heart beats. One. Two. Three. It helped him calm his nerves. The smoke was starting to clear. He clung on to his robot, with all his might, without looking back. Finally, a cool refreshing breeze wafted across his face, and he opened his eyes to a lightening sky, dotted with gradually disappearing stars. They were outside again.

Aquila hopped off the trolly with a spring in his step, despite the angry welts on his feet. This near brush with death had filled him with a newfound relish for life. He saw his trolly heading back to the truck that had brought it here. He followed it with his gaze and knew exactly what to do.

He was familiar with these trucks. They were Russian made, and if his memory served him right, they could be operated either manually or on autopilot. All one had to do to take back control, was to jump into the driver's seat and disable the autopilot. As the hospital trolly maneuvered its way to the cargo compartment, Aquila climbed into the front of the

241

vehicle and did just that. He waited for the other trolly to return from the furnace and roll into the truck, before setting his destination.

Luckily, the truck's front panel had a list of pre-programmed destinations to choose from. It took him a few seconds to scroll through its contents. The list included ward numbers, loading docks, and a host of important landmarks in the city. A ward number drifted into his mental space. Twenty-seven. That's where they had found Mr. Shi, lying on a bed in a dark, gloomy room. He punched Ward 27 into the truck's control panel and sat back, waiting for his vehicle to take him there, praying it wasn't already too late.

* * *

It took Alan longer than he had expected, to swim to where his drone was suspended, a few feet above the surface of the waves. Reaching it, he noticed that Orion was not far behind. From the buoyancy of the water, it felt like they were in a relatively shallow region. He turned to Orion.

"I don't think we are more than ten feet from the bottom over here," he said. "It should be an easy dive."

"Let's find the tunnel then," Orion gasped, while inflating his life jacket.

"You stay here. I'll be right back." Alan breathed through his helmet. Then he disappeared into the gently undulating waters.

Below the surface, the cold, arctic current was very dark and had a heavy, viscous quality. Alan extended his right arm to feel his way forward. In a moment, his eyes adjusted better, and he could see the outline of a huge cylindrical shape in front of him. He paddled forward in a swift motion, reaching to touch the structure. His outstretched hand struck a rock-solid surface. The tunnel.

His heartbeat quickened. He palmed the side of the tunnel expectantly. It felt smooth to his touch. No unevenness or protrusions anywhere. Nothing that could resemble an entryway for divers. An idea popped into his head. He reached inside his diving suit and retrieved his scanning vision glasses. He dawned them over his headgear. The glasses illuminated a tiny spot on the tunnel's side. It glowed in the dark, but was invisible to the naked eye. He touched the tip of his right index finger to that area and bingo! With a roaring sound, a cylindrical capsule began to slide out from the main body of the tunnel. Quickly, he touched the switch again to reverse the process, and swam back to the surface. Orion was waiting for him.

Alan removed his helmet as he approached his companion. "I found it. The entrance. We have tunnels like this at the Project, and I know how they work. There's a watertight capsule that'll come out perpendicular to the length of the tunnel. One diver can get in and stand inside it. Then the capsule will be sucked back into the tunnel and disengage from its wall. After that, the tunnel door will close, and the capsule door will open. Then the diver can get out." He ran out of breath and stopped.

"Good. We can go in, one by one," Orion replied.

"Yep. But once one of us is in, he'll have to admit the other from the inside. The switch outside, will no longer work."

"Interesting. You go first then. I'll wait for you outside."

"Can't do that. I don't have a diving suit for you. You need to go in, and I'll wait."

"Okay ..." Orion hesitated, momentarily unsure of himself. "Err ... tell me what to do from the inside."

"There should be a way ... maybe a lever or something ... to latch the capsule back onto the tunnel wall. Unless that happens, the tunnel door can't be opened again. It's a security feature, so that excess water can't get in."

"If I can pull that lever, then you'll be able to open the door and get in?"

"Yeah, I think so."

"Okay. Let's do this then!"

Alan dived back and swam quickly to the tunnel. Orion followed at his heels. Arriving at the spot, where he had found the entrance capsule, Alan thumbed the switch that would disengage it. With a whirring sound, the capsule began to slide out. They moved out of the way. Once the cylinder was completely extended, Alan motioned to Orion.

"Now, a door will open in the front. You should slip in. Go!"

Orion swam around the protruding capsule and waited in position as its door began to open. He cast a glance at Alan, before wiggling in through the opening. As soon as he disappeared inside the cylinder, the door closed promptly and the entryway retracted. Alan sucked in a breath, waiting for his companion to make the next move. He checked the time. They had to act fast.

* * *

The truck rolled into the hospital compound from a side entrance, which Aquila had not seen before. He ducked under the seat, while it cleared the gates, just in case there were guards or security cameras around. For good measure, he did not emerge from there, until his vehicle had come to a complete halt.

Raising his head slightly, he noticed that the truck had pulled over to a vacant lot, in what looked like the rear of a hospital building and stood with its back facing the wall. Thus positioned, the truck opened its back door, through which a single trolly gilded out from its hold.

Aquila knew where it was headed. Ward twenty-seven. What he did not know however, was what it would bring back. While he waited for its return, he continued to remain as hidden as possible, with only his eyes peeking out over his seat.

Perhaps only a minute had passed. Perhaps two. But to Aquila, the wait seemed to stretch on forever. Finally, a mechanical head bobbed out of the building, followed by arms and a metallic protruding belly. The trolly was backing up into his truck. Quickly, Aquila's hands reached the control panel and pulled up the list of destinations. He selected his destination. Incinerator. Then he crouched below the dashboard, like a hunter waiting to pounce.

* * *

Five minutes. Alan checked the time again to be doubly sure, but there was no denying it, five minutes was way too long for Orion to have been in there and not been able to find the lever that would reengage the capsule. Waiting any longer would be futile. If Orion had gotten into some sort of trouble, then waiting could in fact, be dangerous. Alan thought about his options. He could collect his drone, head back to the shore, and try to make contact with Alrakis. Report the situation. Ask for his help. Or, there was the other much more dangerous choice. Going after Orion on his own without consulting anyone. Given his natural instinct, he obviously chose the second.

Scrambling to get a foothold on the slippery surface of the tunnel, Alan made his way to its roof. His hands skid along the walls, as he clambered up slowly but surely, his clunky diving gear working against his efforts. He took advantage of the natural buoyancy of the saline water to buoy his weight up, as he climbed. Finally, he surfaced. Breathing heavily, with his feet firmly planted on the solid tunnel wall below.

Taking a moment to catch his breath, he searched the sky above him. He moved forward a few steps, before leaping with his right hand outstretched, to pluck his drone out of the sky, like a sea-monster, devouring a bird in mid-flight. He landed unsteadily on his feet, against the persistent pressure of the breaking wavelets. Then, he turned off the drone and shoved it into his backpack, before diving back into the water.

Alan swam towards the pinkish horizon, hoping to reach the offshore unit of the plant, before the imminent sunrise. He could see a dark mass in the distance, sticking out of the ocean, like the hull of a gigantic ship. If he got there soon, perhaps he could break in and rescue Orion from wherever he was inside the plant. But time was running out fast. Aquila would be waiting for them on the beach, and Alan's parents might be with him. Alan could not linger at mid-sea for much longer.

With his heart racing furiously, Alan made his way towards the looming structure ahead of him and was almost half way there, when he saw something heading towards him. Like a speck of dust over a carpet of waves, the object zoomed forward in his direction. A jetcraft. Alan sucked in a breath as a sudden realization dawned. He was in open water with nowhere to hide.

* * *

The horizon was turning a brilliant blood-orange and the stars were winking out fast, as Aquila's truck rolled onto the sandy track, leading up to the incinerator. Halfway down the track, it stopped and its rear door flew open. Without wasting another second, Aquila sprang out of the driver's seat and landed in a crouch on the pillowy sand. The trolly carrying the occupants of Ward 27 had slithered out of the truck and was making its way to the furnace. Aquila rummaged inside his backpack for Alan's jammer. In an instant, he had retrieved it and was pointing it like a weapon at the receding trolly. He clicked, and the trolly stopped dead in its tracks. Aquila heaved a sigh of relief before rushing to it.

The cart of the trolly had a switch on its side, that was glowing bright red, indicating that it was full. Aquila had a hunch, that pressing that switch would open the cart, enabling him to reach whoever was inside. He was about to do just that, when he remembered the virus. He hurried back to where he had left his backpack and retrieved his hazmat suit. When he returned to the trolly in full protective gear, he felt a sudden wave of panic overcome him. He was ready to open the trolly, but remained frozen to the spot. He could not face what was inside. He willed his arm to extend itself, to reach for the switch, but nothing happened. He stood motionless in the light of dawn like a disembodied soul, without any control over his motor skills.

A shrill ringing sound jerked him back to his senses. An alarm had gone off somewhere. Aquila's pulse quickened, his reflexes kicked in, and without even realizing he was doing so, he was pressing on the glowing red switch, like his life depended on it.

* * *

The jetcraft was growing larger by the minute in Alan's field of view, and he had no way to avoid a head on collision. The current was so strong now, that it took all his effort to simply stay afloat. He thought about what he had on his person. Something, anything he could use as a weapon, if need be. All he could think of, was his oxygen cylinder. It was relatively heavy and could be hurled at an attacker, in the event of an encounter. But if he had to face down a robot, then his chances of success were negligible. He reached around his waist to unbuckle the clasps that attached the cylinder to his back.

He had almost gotten it unfastened, when something shot at him from the craft. It landed with a gigantic splash right in front of his face, sending a ripple of waves that propelled him backwards. Alan spat out salty water from his lungs and blinked to clear his vision. The blurred shape of a hulking figure rose from the jetcraft, and shouted out to him.

"It's a lifebuoy. Grab it! Hurry! The sun's rising." It was a familiar voice. Orion. Relief washed over Alan like a healing balm. He reached out for the buoy and slung it over himself. He felt a tug towards the vessel, as Orion drew back the cord that tied the lifebuoy to the jetcraft, hauling Alan along with it.

* * *

There were two bodies inside the hospital trolly, wrapped from head to toe in body bags. Probably safe to touch, even without a hazmat suit. But since Aquila had protective gear on anyway, he decided to take a peek inside the bags, before recovering them from the cart. His fears were confirmed. It was Mr. Shi and another rather shrivelled old lady–Mrs. Shi perhaps. Aquila couldn't remember exactly how Alan's mother had looked, having seen her only from a distance, while she lay groaning in the corner of their dingy living quarters. But it had to be her, given the likeness of her features to her children's.

It was hard to tell if they were still alive. If they were breathing at all, it was imperceptible to Aquila's untrained eyes. Regardless, he knew that there was no way they would survive much longer, without clinical attention. But first things first. He had to get them to the shore and signal to Alan and Orion somehow, so that they could come to the rescue. Aquila left the couple's faces uncovered, to help them breathe, and proceeded to heave them out of the trolly cart. He laid them side by side on top of the trolly and retrieved Alan's console. He would have to replicate what Alan had done before, and drive the trolly locally. That was the only way he could get himself and the elderly couple to the rescue party, before the security personnel caught up with them.

* * *

"I think, I see him … or them … or someone," Alan stuttered, peering through his scanning vision glasses as they approached the coast.

Orion, who was busy navigating the vessel, looked up for a second. "Where?"

"Eleven o'clock." Alan pointed. Indeed, there was activity in that direction. A few huddled shapes against the lifting darkness. Orion reacted promptly and steered towards their right, heading straight for the indicated spot.

"As I move closer, make sure it's really him, will you? Otherwise, we're in trouble!" Orion shouted over the sound of the craft and the splashing waves.

"Of course. I ... can't see his face ... but it's definitely him."

"What? Are you sure?"

"I'm positive. I recognize his hazmat suit. It's unique."

"Alright then, hang on tight kiddo. We'll be there in a minute."

Suddenly Alan froze. Mr. Orion!" He turned to say, his face ashen. "Hurry! I think they found us."

"Shit!" said Orion, looking up. He doubled their speed, and the craft swerved sharply as it jerked forward. Through his scanning vision glasses, Alan could see a speck at the edge of his vision. It was growing larger by the second and making its way towards Aquila, head-on. Aquila had his arms raised over his head and was waving frantically, as he jumped up and down to attract their attention. He was not alone. There was a hospital trolly parked behind him. Alan's heart skipped a bit. He couldn't see what was in the trolly, or on top of it, but in his mind, its very presence was an augury of evil.

It may not have taken more than a few seconds to reach Aquila, but to Alan it felt like the longest few seconds of his life. Up close, he could see what lay atop the trollies—two bodies wrapped in body-bags, with only their pale greenish faces uncovered. Every muscle in Alan's body seized up. He wanted to rush off the vessel and run towards the prone figures, knowing instinctively who they were. He wanted to hug them viciously and haul them onto the craft. But his body refused to cooperate. He just stood there like a statue with his eyes wide with horror. Through the daze that had clogged up his mind, he could hear voices around him, speaking in agitated tones. The words were in fragments, his brain barely registering their meaning.

"Into the cabin, right now!" someone hollered. "You don't have a hazmat," the same voice continued.

"No! I'll help you lug them."

"Absolutely not! Do as I say. Take Alan with you."

Soon, there were a pair of strong arms around Alan, gripping him by the waist and tugging him down a set of stairs. Alan stumbled along, his feet struggling for purchase on the wave-soaked steps. A couple of more steps brought him to the dim interior of the jetcraft. He was pushed into a comfortable chair. He collapsed into it, and let out the breath that he was not aware of holding in. With a lurch, the craft moved forward, and silence fell all around him.

CHAPTER TWENTY-NINE

A quila stood at the helm of the jetcraft and donned Alan's scanning vision glasses. Orion had tossed him the glasses to assist with his navigation. His pursuers were at the beach now, and were preparing a jetcraft of their own. They were getting ready to give chase.

Without taking his eyes off the beach, he lowered his head slightly and spoke into the vessel's intercom. "Did you make contact with Alrakis yet?"

"Just got off the call," Orion responded in a gruff voice.

"And?"

"He sent a location. You need to feed it into the vessel's control board, and it'll take us there. Is your phone on?"

"It is."

"Okay, I'm sending the location."

Aquila's backpack started to beep. He grabbed his phone from it and yelled, as he saw the map. "Yikes! We're totally off course!"

"Well, turn around then. We have fifteen minutes tops, before the craft loses power."

"Doing just that. Hang in there. Can't promise we'll make it," Aquila huffed, as he programmed the craft to take them to their destination. "I'm going for top speed, but that means we might lose power sooner."

"Well, do we have a choice?"

Aquila sneaked another peak at the jetcraft, now trailing them. "Nope. Hold tight!" He set the speed and sucked in a breath. The craft flew like the wind, threatening to catapult him into the open sea beyond. Aquila grabbed on to the deck railing and gazed back at their pursuers. They were falling behind, having misjudged the abrupt change of course.

Good, maybe there is still hope. "We've confused them," Aquila said into the intercom, after a moment's pause.

"But it won't be for long. Can you see who's chasing us?" Orion asked from the cabin.

"Nah. The deck is empty. Whoever's in it must be downstairs."

"Or it could be a robot."

"Could be. But unlikely. What we pulled was too huge a heist for them to trust a robot with our capture."

"I have to say, I agree … ah oh, what's happening?" The vessel was sputtering.

"The power's going," Aquila panicked. His words crackled, as they came out of the intercom.

"Are we nearly there? How much farther?"

"About five miles."

"That's not too bad. The current is in our favour, and inertia will keep us going. We can make it, even if the engine stops."

"I see it! I can see the submarine. The top of it!" Aquila yelled triumphantly, just as the craft's power went out completely. But like Orion had predicted, they were still moving along and staying their course. As they drifted closer, Aquila could see a flag imprinted on the roof of the submarine. It looked like the Canadian flag. Aquila blinked, frowning at the oddity of this observation. Before he could reflect on what he saw, however, a capsule was ejected from the body of the submarine, and it zoomed forward towards their craft. It stopped a couple of feet from their deck and hovered within

Aquila's reach. Then its top flung open.

"Is this Orion? I can't tell," the capsule asked in Alrakis' voice.

Aquila saw the tiny communication device fitted to the top of the capsule and cleared his throat. "Umm, no ... I'm Aquila. We spoke—"

"Yes, I know who you are. Hurry now, load the infected persons into the capsule as fast as you can."

Aquila noticed that Alrakis had called them infected persons and not bodies. This was a good sign. Although it did not mean much, but Alrakis was one of the few, who were fully aware of the nature and extent of this infection. The fact that he was still optimistic, gave Aquila a flicker of hope. He lifted Mrs. Shi up into his arms and lowered her gently into the capsule. Her wispy frame felt as light as a whisper against his strong arms. Then he did the same with her husband, who did not seem any heavier. Once loaded, the capsule closed automatically. Then Alrakis spoke rapidly, blurting out instructions.

"Now, listen carefully. We're taking the patients back to the submarine, and while we do that, I need you to remove your hazmat suit, without touching its outer surface. Leave the discarded suit on the deck and head for the cabin—"

"Wait," Aquila cautioned. "I hear something." He turned his head to look behind them. The pursuing craft was catching up fast, and now Aquila could see something emerge from its hold. A robot. It looked dangerously armed. Aquila let out an audible gasp and stood staring at the robot in awe.

"Aquila! Are you even listening to me?" Alrakis' voice jolted him back to his senses. "Don't worry about the robot. It won't shoot to kill. They need you alive as a witness. Now, where was I? Right ... there's an emergency exit downstairs, that I want you to open. Take the others, and swim out of there. Head straight for the submarine. Got it?"

"Got it," Aquila echoed hoarsely, as he watched the capsule pull away from their vessel. He quickly removed his protective gear and rushed to the door that led downstairs. Just as he was about to climb down, he felt another urge to glance back at the enemy vessel. This time, someone else was coming up the stairs, two individuals actually. Definitely human. They looked familiar.

No, it can't be! Aquila told himself, before ducking through the door and making his way down the steps. It was dark in the cabin, but he could hear the murmur of voices. When his eyes adjusted to the light, he saw Orion already on his feet, frantically searching for something.

"Did you hear us?" Aquila asked turning to him.

"Partly, yes. Now where's that damn emergency—"

"Found it!" Alan shouted. He was already working on getting the door open. "Quick, through here," he continued, motioning them forward.

Aquila nodded and hurried along. Alan had already pushed the hatch open, allowing a large wave to crash right through, soaking them up to their knees in an instant. Aquila reached for a handgrip, in an attempt to steady himself. Alan had already dived out; Orion was ready to follow. With measured steps, Aquila took a deep breath and wobbled forward. Before following his companions, he poked his head out of the hatch, to get one last look at the pursuing boat. The robot was still standing guard on its deck, and behind it were two female figures. One confident and alert, scanning the surroundings. The other gagged and bound to a post behind her. There was no mistaking their identities from this angle.

It was Razzy in all her glory. Her soft feminine features scrunched up with concentration. Behind her, writhing and struggling against her bindings, was the slender frame of Alan's sister—Elaine.

Noooo! Aquila felt bitter bile rise up in his throat. But before he could allow himself to be crippled with horror, he swallowed it down and plunged forward into the water.

CHAPTER THIRTY

A quila glanced around him. He was sitting inside what looked like the control room of the submarine. It was a fairly large, open space with a huge screen at the very end and the various controls located in and around that area. Through the corner of his eyes, he could see Orion standing there, waving his hands and chatting animatedly with someone, possibly one of the crew members. However, none of that conversation seemed to make any impact on Aquila's mind.

The events of the last few minutes had happened in a sort of daze. He remembered reaching the submarine, climbing up its side, and then arms pulling him through an opening right into the belly of the beast. Just before he had disappeared inside the submarine, Aquila recalled seeing a huge explosion behind him and flames engulfing the remains of their sinking jetcraft. That fire blocked out everything as it licked its way up to the sky with its monstrous greedy tongue—his emotions, his pain, the image of Razzy standing there on the boat, her hair tossing in the wind. And now, he was here in this control room with Orion, tapping his feet anxiously on the cold metal floor. Alan was nowhere to be seen. A door opened in front of him and a dapper looking young man stepped through. He had a prim sophisticated air about him.

"Mhmm," he said, clearing his throat. "You must be Aquila." He smiled gently. Before Aquila could respond however, Orion padded over and started speaking rapidly.

"Oh, there you are Alrakis! You were gone forever. Thought you'd never be back! What happened then? Are they dead?"

The beautiful young man turned his blue eyes up at the speaker. "Not dead. But pretty bad. We have nurses on board. They are treating them as we speak."

"And Alan?"

"He's outside the room, waiting for them to wake up." Alrakis sighed and looked at his feet, a grim expression across his face.

Aquila coughed to attract their attention. "What happened to our jetcraft? I saw it blow up. Did they fire at it?"

Alrakis was shaking his head. "No, that was *us*. We blew up your hazmat suit. It had your DNA all over it, so we didn't want it falling into their hands." He smiled a half smile and extended his hand. "I'm Alrakis by the way, pleased to meet you."

"Pleased to meet you too," Aquila replied, shaking the offered hand. "I ... I have something to tell you. Something I saw," he began, eyeing his manager warily through the corner of his eyes. "Ah ..." he hesitated.

"Go on," Alrakis encouraged.

Aquila opened his mouth to speak, when a terrible howl ripped through the room. He stopped dead in his tracks. "What was that?" he rasped, almost inaudibly.

Alrakis had turned and was making for the door. He gestured for them to follow. "The hospital room. This way!"

Aquila followed Orion out the door. They made their way through narrow winding corridors and reached a set of stairs. Alrakis was already at the bottom of the steps, standing in front of a translucent wall, speaking with a woman in medical gear. From here, Aquila could hear parts of the conversation.

"… in there, crying …" the woman said.

"And the mother?" Alrakis asked.

The woman shook her head. "… maybe," was all Aquila heard. He took two steps at a time and reached the bottom step. Walking up to the chamber in front of them, he pressed his face against the translucent wall. Inside, he could see several beds, with only two of them occupied. A figure in a protective suit was crouched near one of the beds—Alan, Aquila realized with a sinking feeling. He had his arms tightly wrapped around the reclining form of his father and was swaying back and forth, letting out soul-shattering yowls of pain.

Aquila's right cheek felt moist. A fat drop of tear had leaked quietly onto it. He palmed his face dry, before turning to the others. "We couldn't save him then?" he asked, his voice barely a whisper.

Alrakis shook his head. Although he could never have known Alan's father, his eyes also shone with unshed tears. "And his wife?" Aquila asked.

"Hanging in there."

Orion was seated on a chair with his head between his hands, trembling slightly. Aquila approached him with caution, and placed a hand on his shoulder. He looked up. "I know this is a bad time, but there's something you need to know." Aquila paused to glance at Alrakis, before adding, "Both of you."

"What is it?" Alrakis looked up.

"They have a captive. Alan's sister. Alan mustn't know."

"What? How?" Orion growled.

Aquila shrugged. "And there's more. You were right, Orion."

"I'm always right," Orion snapped. "Spit it out."

"I … umm Razzy. She was there. On that jetcraft."

"As a captive?" Orion asked.

"No. She was free. Keeping an eye on Elaine, who was bound and gagged. I can't explain it."

"I'm sorry."

Aquila shook his head. "No, *I'm* sorry. Sorry that I refused to listen to your premonitions about her. In the end, you were right."

"It's not always good to be right," Orion said matter-of-factly.

"Hang on. I'm confused. Who the hell is Razzy?" Alrakis chimed in, looking lost.

Aquila eyed his manager for support. Orion got the hint and nodded. "I'll tell him. I know you want to go to Alan. Go ahead."

"Hazmat suit's in there," Alrakis added, pointing to a cupboard to their left. "We are due to arrive in about half an hour, so you should still have a few minutes alone with him."

"What do you mean we're arriving in half an hour? How fast does this thing go? Calamerica—"

"We're not going to Calamerica," Alrakis interrupted. "I'm in exile. In Canada. That's where we're headed."

CHAPTER THIRTY-ONE

When Aquila stepped off the submarine at around mid-day, the surreal beauty of a pristine wilderness stretched before his eyes. He had no idea that such splendour existed anywhere on this planet. It was like being transported back to a simpler, more primitive time.

"Is this geo-engineered?" He turned to ask Alrakis, who was walking beside him.

"It isn't. Although some parts of the country are. The south mostly. But here in the north, they managed to preserve nature in its more natural state, somehow."

"It wasn't an accident," Orion quipped, and Aquila immediately remembered that his manager was in fact, Canadian. "It was a result of years of deliberate effort. Facilitated by the First Nations' people, mostly."

"Ah, that makes sense." Alrakis nodded. "Considering that their current leader hails from the First Nations' community."

"But we digress," Orion began. "Where is Carina? I thought she'd be here."

"Oh no, she's not planning to be here personally. That would be too brazen. No one knows about Canada's involvement in your rescue. And we hope to keep it that way."

"I thought you said she had news," Orion wondered out loud.

"She does. She'll deliver it to her Canadian peers, and we'll listen in. Don't ask me what it is though. She didn't tell me. Oh, we're almost late for her call. Let's hurry," Alrakis concluded, checking the time.

They rushed past a beautiful tulip garden and onto a winding gravelled path up a slope. In front of them, on a mild elevation, stood a lofty building with many rooms. Alrakis hurried towards its paved ornamental porch, with Orion and Alan following close behind. Alan was mostly silent, staring dejectedly at his feet as he walked. Aquila hung back a little to gain perspective, before speeding to catch up. An idea was forming in his head, but it was too early to share it with the others.

* * *

The meeting room was crowded. Aquila slunk in after his companions and found himself a seat near the back. They were in the Canadian Parliament, Aquila had learned. Which meant, that being a fugitive from the ICC did not seem to matter much to the Canadians. Unless of course, no one here actually knew what they had just done. Alrakis had not had time to explain. He just told them not to speak to anyone at the meeting.

A dark haired, middle-aged woman rose to the podium at the front of the room. She had a light brown complexion and glowing kindly eyes.

"The Right Honourable Malina, the Prime Minister of Canada," a booming AI voice announced.

"Ahem." She cleared her throat. "Can I have order in the House please." She paused and looked around. A hushed silence fell around her. "Thank you all for joining us at this emergency meeting at such short notice. A few minutes ago, a snap announcement from the ICC went out to the Permanent

Member Nations. Canada not being a permanent member, was excluded from this missive. Therefore, we have invited the Secretary General of Calamerica, to fill us in on what was discussed. Now, let us welcome the Honourable Carina, to address the subject." She turned to her left, where the air flickered and a semi-solid outline began to take shape. In a minute, the image had congealed into the figure of a tall stately lady, who Aquila immediately recognized as his saviour from the ICC debacle.

"Good afternoon, ladies and gentlemen of the House," she said with a ghost of a smile. "I'm sorry to say that I bear grim tidings." Her face became unusually stern, in a way that made Aquila jump in his seat. He quickly flicked his head around, to glance at Alrakis at the very end of their aisle. But Alrakis' seat was empty. Aquila swallowed hard and turned back to Carina.

"... therefore, an international arrest warrant has been issued by the ICC, encouraging all nations to promptly apprehend the perpetrators," she was saying. Aquila glanced at Orion, who had his eyes trained on Carina's holo and didn't return his gaze. "Anyone with information regarding the whereabouts of these individuals, must report it immediately to the ICC or risk being found complicit in the crime." Carina's face was impassive as she continued to make her speech. Nothing about her allegiances could be gleaned from her expression.

Aquila shifted nervously in his seat, and averted his eyes from the podium. It was then, that he noticed an armed security robot enter through the tall double-doors and march up the aisle to their seating area. Walking straight up to Aquila's seat, it stopped in front him and spoke in a low rumble.

"Mister Aquila and Mister Orion, please come with me."

Orion jumped and turned around. "What? Where?"

The robot did not respond. Instead, he looked up at the back door, from where a second, similar guard was making its way towards them.

Holy shit! Aquila thought. *Does this always happen when Carina is involved?* Orion nudged his shoulder, encouraging him to step out of his seat. Aquila stood and nodded at Alan, who was sitting between him and Orion.

"Does he need to come?"

"All of you. This way," the robot replied curtly.

Without daring to voice any further objections, they walked out in a single file, with one of the guards leading the procession, and the other bringing up the rear. Outside the meeting room, the sprawling building was mostly deserted. They glided down a never-ending corridor, before arriving at a set of capsule elevators with a glass interior. Their escorts led them inside and gave a cryptic verbal command to its AI.

The elevator started to plummet on cue, traversing scores of floors as it went. Through the glass, Aquila could see floor after floor fly by, each one different from the next. Some of them featured hanging gardens, the others were lined with meeting rooms. Soon, Aquila was absolutely sure that they were in the basement, because the building they had entered, had not been this tall. When it seemed like they had reached rock bottom, the capsule stopped abruptly. If they had been in a pre-historic building, this would have been its dungeon, Aquila reflected, not without a hint of terrible premonition.

The robots expertly navigated the constricted passageways of this level and brought them in front of a set of ordinary-looking metal doors. The doors opened, and the robots stood aside to let the people pass.

"Phew, not a prison then." Aquila exhaled, as he entered the small office room beyond. Alan was the last to step in, when the door snapped shut with lightning rapidity, blocking out the trickle of light from the passageway. Aquila swerved on his heels and rushed back, banging his fists on the metal panels. But the door was firmly shut, without any means of prying it open. "Shit! I spoke too soon."

In the darkness, Aquila felt a warm touch on his shoulder. "Calm down." Orion whispered in his ear.

"No! I can't. Where's Alrakis, by the way? How do you know we can trust him?"

"Well, we'll soon find out. Because someone's coming." Orion was staring at the back of the room, where an office desk stood, flanked by several chairs. Behind this arrangement, was a sliding door which had begun to open, illuminating the room with a dreamy light.

Three figures entered—one of them was Alrakis, the other Aquila could not recognize, and between them, the Canadian Prime Minister.

Malina lowered her head and spoke softly to her companions. "You may leave." They immediately turned around and disappeared into the shadows, leaving Malina alone with the occupants of the room. The sliding door shut behind her, as a couple of lights went on above her head.

Aquila opened his mouth to speak, but Orion raised his hand to stop him. "Malina, it's a pleasure." Orion said, bowing his head politely.

"You ... you ... *know* her?" Aquila gasped; his eyes wide.

"Of course, I know her. I'm Canadian." Orion said.

"So, should I assume that everyone in this country is on a first name basis with their Prime Minister?"

At this Orion chuckled. "No. I don't believe so. Malina and I go way back. She's like ..." Orion searched for the words. "... family," he finally said.

"What do you mean we're *like* family? We *are* family, Orion—" Malina began.

Orion put a finger to his lips, indicating that she should stop. To Aquila's surprise, Malina was not offended. She quickly changed the conversation.

"I understand that you heard Carina's message?" Now she was looking straight at Aquila.

Aquila nodded meekly. "Then you know that there is a manhunt," she continued.

"For us, yes," Aquila replied.

"Not specifically. They don't suspect anyone in particular. Not yet, anyway." Malina's lips curled into a lopsided smile.

"And we want to keep it that way," Orion added.

"But my point is not that," Malina clarified. "My point is something else entirely. I believe Mister Aquila here, had said something about Auschwitz."

"How did you ... I never told ..." Aquila stammered.

"I told Alrakis," Orion cut in. "When you were with Alan in the submarine. Anyway, you were saying ..." He turned to Malina.

"Yes, I wanted to tell you that it's not what you think. The Chairman is not Hitler."

"Oh! How do you know?" Aquila asked.

"We saw him. By we, I mean Carina, and the other delegates from the Permanent Member Nations. Until now, no one ever had. Seen the Chairman of the ICC, that is. But for this particular announcement, he appeared in person via hologram. And Carina confirmed that he's definitely no clone of Hitler or any other infamous tyrant, for that matter."

"Then we were wrong?" Orion gasped. "They didn't create a notorious clone after all."

"They could still have. But if they brought back someone of extraordinary caliber, then they'd most likely be in a leadership role. Unfortunately, we've seen all the other top ICC officials, and none of them are clones of famous historical personalities." Malina sighed.

"So, what do we do now?" Aquila whispered almost to himself.

"First, we listen to a recording of the Chairman's announcement. Then, we figure out a plan to keep you in hiding, until we can gather enough evidence to show the world, what's really going on in Sanctuary City." Malina paused to touch a spot on the wall behind her. "After that, we take the ICC down." As soon as she finished this sentence, the door behind her opened and Alrakis walked in. "Do you have it?" she asked him.

Alrakis nodded, and produced a thimble-sized storage device from his pocket. Plugging it in, Malina motioned for the others to sit down. She clapped her hands and the room went dark.

The recording began to play. Aquila stared at the blank space in front of him, where a human form was slowly materializing from the darkness. The arms came into focus, a couple of sturdy shoulders, stocky legs, well-built body, short height, dark hair and a face—definitely not Hitler's, but familiar. Aquila's eyes widened with horror. He leaned forward to get a better look and fell from his seat with a thud.

CHAPTER THIRTY-TWO

"What do you mean, he's a Napoleon? What the hell is a Napoleon, anyway? Is this some sort of a harebrained plan you're cooking up, so that you can get to Razzy? I bet you still don't believe she tricked you, do you?" Orion was yelling, as he paced around the room. He was irate. Aquila had never seen Orion this incensed before. He always had that warm and fuzzy, neighbourhood Canadian vibe. Aquila's ears buzzed like they were being attacked by swarms of angry hornets.

Orion was not unjustified in reacting this way, Aquila realized. After all, he had not been able to explain the whole story to his manager yet. All he had done so far, was blurt out the words Napoleon a few times, and fall from his chair. So, he gathered his wits about him and began to speak.

"You would know all the answers Orion, if you actually let me *speak!*" He yelled out the last word for impact. He could still hear his manager muttering incoherently behind him. But this had gotten his attention.

Orion whirled around to face Aquila. "Go on then," he said curtly.

Aquila coughed to clear his throat. "First off, it's not *a* Napoleon. It's *the* Napoleon."

"And? Is that supposed to mean something to me?"

"Okay, do you remember the files? The ones you showed me in the library?"

Orion's eyes popped out. "Yeah … what about them?"

"I've seen them."

"*The whole thing?*"

"No, but most of it. And that's how I know who the Chairman is. He's Napoleon Bonaparte, a nineteenth century military general, a conqueror, a commander and later *Emperor of France*—a legend really."

Orion's hands shot to his head to clasp fistfuls of his hair between his fingers. "Holy, mother of …" He restrained himself, eyeing the Prime Minister.

"Will someone kindly do the honour of explaining to me what's going on here?" Malina asked, watching them in confusion.

"Well …" Aquila cast a surreptitious glance at Orion.

"Go ahead," Orion urged. "You can tell them about the files. Now's not the time for secrets."

Aquila sat up straight and asked everyone to take a seat. He explained to them about the God of War files, and how they were discovered accidentally from a wreckage. He gave them an overview of who this famous general was and his many accomplishments. He told them how mentions of Napoleon had been meticulously erased from all contemporary historical records, and how much that had surprised him. In the end, he told them about Tolstoy's War and Peace, which might contain some insights into Napoleon's methods and therefore, the keys to defeating him.

"But how?" Alrakis said at last, looking lost.

"How what? There's a lot to unpack here. Can you please be specific?" Aquila asked.

"Oh, sorry. How did they erase him completely from our collective memory?"

"It must have been a concerted effort, spanning decades. They obviously knew they wanted to resurrect him. Therefore, they had to make people forget that he ever existed." Orion ventured a guess.

"I agree." Aquila nodded. "And that's why, once they succeeded in creating the clone, they were going to destroy their own records as well. So, they made that plane crash into the Indian Ocean. Lucky that Orion's divers found it in the end."

"Why Napoleon though? If they wanted to bring back a psychopathic mass murderer, then why not Hitler?" Alrakis looked puzzled.

"I think I can answer that," Malina chimed in. "Hitler's remains were never found. Not really. The Russians had some charred remains that were unrecognizable. In the end, it's believed that his body was identified by tooth samples. But the evidence around this is murky. Besides, he was tossed into an unmarked grave, so there was no way to retrieve him later anyway."

"Whereas, Napoleon was revered as a hero by the French and given a mausoleum at the Les Invalides in Paris. I've seen footage of his tomb being raided during the tsunami. His remains must have been stolen at that time. A lot of treasures were lost during the floods, along with Paris itself. And for many years, no one noticed that all items pertaining to Napoleon were among them. After that, as the years wore on, the world gradually forgot his name," Aquila explained.

"And you say that you know how to defeat him? This Napoleon?" Alrakis asked.

"I … no I didn't say that. But I've read War and Peace five times already—"

"*Five tines?* Dear me!" Orion exclaimed. "Remind me to give you more work when we get back."

Aquila chuckled, despite himself. "As I was saying, the book, details Napoleon's war against the Russians—the war that ultimately brought him to his knees. Before that, he was a feared and undefeated ruler. But it all went downhill after the

Russian War. So, by figuring out how he was defeated then, we can defeat him now."

"No!" said Malina, with an air of finality. "There will be no defeating anyone. This is not a war. And even if it was, I'm not going to risk sending Canadian troops up against the ICC. It would be the most reckless and unpopular decision in Canadian history. The only way to deal with this is through diplomacy. If the ICC is corrupt, we must expose them and enlist the support of other nations to oust and prosecute their leadership."

"*Diplomacy?*" Aquila sad bitterly. "Do you even understand what's at stake here, Madam Prime Minister? Thousands are going to die. And soon! Alan's sister Elaine ..." he glanced at the boy in question, to find him fast asleep with his head on the desk. All eyes turned to Alan.

"The boy is tired. Poor thing," Orion said, steering Aquila away from a possibly dangerous confrontation. "Look Malina, I agree with you. And I also agree with Aquila to a certain extent. Besides, we don't even know where the other nations stand. How many of their leaders are in cahoots with the ICC, for example. Why don't we discuss this in the evening? I think we can all use some rest right now. And lunch."

Malina opened her mouth and closed it quickly. She flashed Aquila a stern look, as if to say, this conversation was not over. Then she nodded slightly. "Alright. Stay here for now. I'll send someone to take you to your rooms." Then, she promptly turned and walked out the door.

CHAPTER THIRTY-THREE

It was almost twilight in Lucknow, and Ramesh was ready to get off work. A few days ago, Orion had come to him, wanting to share a secret. He was going to travel to Sanctuary City and possibly take Aquila with him. He wanted to see first-hand, whether this fabled city really met expectations. At that time, Orion had entrusted Ramesh with the oversight of the Project's key operations during his absence. This was a huge responsibility as far as Ramesh was concerned. He was honoured to have been chosen for the task. Yet, it also meant, he would need to put in longer hours.

It goes without saying that Ramesh's manager Sabrina was not too thrilled with this arrangement. She did not enjoy being brushed aside in favour of her underling. So, she had made it a point to meet with him every evening after work, to get a status update on plant operations. That is where Ramesh was headed this evening, when he sauntered out of the Central Control Unit and made his way to Sabrina's office across the town square. He was running a few minutes late, because of the pesky weather-event they had to schedule for midnight. It was a massive event and project-wide in scope. Naturally, some of the parameters were acting up, and Ramesh had been busy fixing them.

Ramesh had his head down and was walking briskly across the deserted square, when he heard a mechanical thumping sound in the distance. He stopped to take a look. It was coming from the direction of the Farm-robot Unit. He checked the time. He was already ten minutes late. But if something was going awry with that unit, then it needed urgent attention. Reporting to Sabrina could wait.

As soon as he had turned to walk in that direction, the unit's doors flew open, and a noisy procession began to emerge. Ramesh's eyes widened with horror. His worst nightmare seemed to be coming true. Through the gates of the Farm-robot Unit, he could see at least a hundred robots marching forward in perfect unison—like a military regiment. They were advancing quickly. He started running across the square at full speed, ducking for cover, when he saw a portly figure emerge from the building in front of him—Sabrina.

"No!" he shouted, flailing his arms wildly. "Get back in!" Sabrina did not seem to heed his warning and advanced stubbornly in Ramesh's direction. She had her arms crossed over her chest and face scrunched into a grimace. "What are you doing? Look to your left," Ramesh continued. "Run!"

This got Sabrina's attention. She turned her head in the indicated direction and saw what Ramesh was seeing. "Oh my God!" She gasped. But instead of seeking cover, she stomped over to the robots. "Stop!" she said, holding up her hand. "I *order* you to stop. Right now!"

Ramesh had nearly reached one of the office buildings, when he heard her shrill voice. He stopped and turned around. Sabrina was still there, in the middle of the square, unflinching, undaunted, facing up to a battalion of killer robots—a trusting warden of the ICC. To Ramesh's surprise, the robots came to an abrupt halt. Sabrina turned her head and smirked at him triumphantly. Ramesh could feel his vision clouding, with large drops of sweat leaking into his eyes. He rubbed his face with the cuff off his shirt and looked up again. This time, he saw a different scene. The robot closest to Sabrina had raised its arm.

Shit! Ramesh was about to plunge forward, but it was too late. In the blink of an eye, a white-hot beam shot out of the robot's arm and catapulted Sabrina's charred, lifeless body beyond a parked rickshaw outside of Ramesh's field of view. Then the rogue robot broke formation and began to charge towards Ramesh. A rush of adrenaline overtook him, triggering his fight or flight reflex. He immediately flipped around and flung himself at the building's front door. He heard metallic footsteps behind him, as he ran down the lobby and made his way through dimly-lit corridors. Luckily, it was after-hours, so the offices were completely deserted. If only he could get into a relatively secure room and lock himself in there, until his pursuer gave up and left him alone. It was unlikely, but worth a shot.

There was a blasting sound, followed by a familiar burnt-metal smell. The robot was on his tail and had blasted something out of the way. Ramesh did not turn to look. He kept barrelling along the seemingly endless corridor. Until, he hit a dead end. He had arrived at a section of this building, that he had never seen before. And there was a sturdy-looking metal door right behind him, where the corridor ended. A palm-plate embedded in the wall next to it, granted access to the area. Ramesh was not sure, if his credentials would allow him to enter.

Around the bend in front of him, he could see a shadow growing larger and the sound of crushing robotic feet. He had a split second to make a move. He reacted on impulse and touched his palm to the door's access plate. It opened with a jolt. If he went in and the robot could still blast through, he could potentially be trapped inside, with no where to run. But what choice did he have. He sucked in a breath and glided through the door, which snapped shut behind him. He was inside a dark tunnel. It looked pretty secure, but death lasers could cut through most things. He turned on his heel and began to sprint towards wherever this tunnel led.

Five minutes later, Ramesh was still running, but no one seemed to have followed. Leaning against his knees, he stopped to catch his breath. Suddenly, he remembered something he had learned at training, many years ago. The Project had a hidden underground control centre, that was practically impregnable. It was built to protect the operations of the Project from the extreme weather events that would ensue, once the geo-engineered bubble around it was discontinued. It also protected against wars and terrorist attacks, his trainer had said. He had probably made it inside the very passage that led to this control centre.

This realization calmed him. He slowed down and allowed himself to think. He needed back-up and needed it quick. There were many lives in danger, with these killer robots on the loose, and he did not have the background or training to handle a situation like this by himself. He was considering all his options carefully, when he reached another closed door. His credentials were enough to unlock it. His hunch was correct. This room was indeed, another control unit for the Project. The lights turned on as he stepped inside. His first thought was to find the communications area. He located it along the left wall and rushed forward.

"Call Orion," he said to the panel in front of him.

There were a few seconds of silence and then, "Call failed," came the response. Ramesh sank into the chair across from the phones and smacked his head down onto the kiosk in frustration.

* * *

"Will you stop pacing already? It's making me dizzy." Orion had his boots off and was lying on a single bed next to the window, in the room he and Aquila were asked to share.

The Canadian guards had taken Alan to the hospital wing to check his vitals, because he looked very feeble and weary.

Aquila turned to his manager. "Remind me again, why Canada withdrew from Project 15/8?"

"I already told you all I know. For the rest, you need to speak with Malina."

"You said The Underground didn't approve and Malina, she …"

"Has connections to The Underground, yes. She trusts their gut. But why do you want to know, anyway?"

"Because, do you realize what this means?"

"What?"

"That we have no other allies. The leaders of the other countries that signed on, are fully aware of what's going on. They will have no qualms when the ICC goes through with their plan."

"It doesn't necessarily mean that. But you're right, it's a distinct possibility. Otherwise, someone would've gone sniffing, found out their real agenda and walked out."

"Exactly. And even if they didn't find out earlier, they'd definitely figure it out *now.* As soon as they see that people are dying in droves. Only an idiot would assume that the permafrost virus just simply *appeared,* that no one had known about it in advance."

Orion nodded grimly. "I don't disagree, but what do you suggest is our action point here?"

"There's nothing we can do about it now. It's just something we should keep in mind, before reaching out to anyone for help."

"We can still get help from The Underground. But it'd be trickier, now that the Chairman told the world that our recent break-in was engineered by them."

"Can he prove it though, that The Underground had something to do with our escapade at Sanctuary City?"

"He pretty damn well can, if he wants to. Remember, how we reached Alrakis in the first place? By pinging The

Underground from your hazmat suit. That signal went through Sanctuary City's dedicated satellite. Hence, they know whoever's helping us, is backed by The Underground."

"Hmm." Aquila cupped his stubbly chin in his hand and became thoughtful. "I was wondering—" He was cut short by a loud knock on their door.

"Come in," Orion said.

It was Alrakis. He looked like someone had just slapped him. "Orion, Aquila, you must come with me. Back to the basement office. Carina needs to speak with us. It's an emergency!"

Without saying a word, Orion jumped off the bed and made to follow him out the door. Aquila was close behind. Silently, they took the elevators down to the lowermost floor and arrived at the prison-styled office room, tucked away on that level. Malina was already waiting for them. Alan was by her side. They were chatting softly.

"Elaine, have you heard from her? She's back at the Project," Alan was saying. He stopped to look up, as the rest of the party entered. Aquila's stomach contracted at the mention of Elaine's name. But he did not have the nerve to correct Alan. To tell him, that she was no longer at the Project.

Malina stood up, seeing them walk in. "Please come and grab a seat. Carina will be calling in shortly."

Aquila had barely gotten himself into a chair across from the Prime Minister, when the phone rang. Malina swiped her finger in front of her face, accepting the call, and Carina began to appear before them.

"Good afternoon, everyone," she said curtly. "I don't have much time, so I'll try to keep this short. The Chairman has called for an emergency session of the ICC, and the delegates of the Permanent Member Nations must report right away. I need to leave for the Republic, to attend in person, within the next hour."

"What the hell!" Orion exclaimed. "What does he want *now?*"

Carina glanced at him before continuing. "He wants the permanent members to vote on declaring an emergency and instituting martial law, effective immediately. He has offered to send ICC troops, who are far more effective and numerous, to take over regional command, in order to protect the member countries from an imminent guerrilla invasion by The Underground—"

Orion rose from his seat. "This is absolutely ridiculous! He's trying to take over the world!"

"Just like the real Napoleon would have," Aquila muttered.

"Please gentlemen, let her finish," Malina said. "Carina, this sounds very disproportionate. Declaring world-wide emergency, just because two people broke into their secure city! How is he justifying this to the heads of state?"

"I was going to explain," Carina said. "There has been an attack. Project 15/8 was besieged."

"*Besieged*? By what or whom?" Malina asked, her jaws dropping to the floor.

"By killer robots apparently." Carina shrugged. "And they are pinning this on hackers, backed by The Underground."

"Shit! Shit! Shit! I knew this was going to happen." Aquila banged his fist on the desk.

"You did?" Carina looked puzzled. "Why didn't you tell us?"

"He did, actually," Orion jumped to the rescue. "A while back. I mean, he was the first to notice that the ICC was sending us killer robots, to repurpose for farm-use and— "

"No that was Ramesh, he spotted it. I just confirmed it," Aquila corrected.

There was a ringing sound. All eyes began to dart around the room, looking for its origin, when Carina cleared her throat. "I'm getting another call. It's urgent. Please hold." Her holo became still, frozen like a wax doll in a museum. A minute later, life returned, and Carina's confident, musical voice spoke again. "It was Dorado. Your deputy plant manager is trying to reach you, Orion."

Orion looked up. "Ramesh?" Carina nodded. "Speak of the devil! Is he safe? Where is he?" Orion's voice was shaking with agitation.

"Yes, he's safe. For now. He has locked himself inside some bunker, but he needs help and soon."

"That's it then! We're going back to the Project. Come on Aquila, Alan, let's go." Orion stood up abruptly.

Malina reached out and grabbed Orion's arm, pulling him back. "What do you think you're doing? Do you believe you can just walk out of this door and take a flight back to Lucknow? You're wanted criminals, remember?"

"Everyone's going to this summit, like Carina said. No one's going to pay attention to us, while that's going on," Orion explained.

"Sit down, Orion." Malina's voice was firm. "Even if they don't, we need to be cautious. And under no circumstances can we fly you there in a Canadian craft. Also, we need a strategy first," she said. "So, tell us Mister Aquila, what does your famous Russian writer say about defeating Napoleon? How did they do it?"

All eyes fell on Aquila, and he looked visibly flustered. "I … umm … well. Napoleon was … very confident. Overconfident, actually. He had underestimated the odds against him—"

"Hang on," Orion interrupted. "Let me write this down. Does anyone have a tablet?"

Alrakis nodded and reached into a drawer underneath the desk. "Here you go," he said.

"Overconfident. Underestimated the odds. Okay, go on …" Orion urged, as he made notes.

"As I was saying. He was beaten by his hubris, you can say. He threw all his men at the Russians, without considering all the parameters."

"What parameters in particular?" Orion quizzed.

"For starters, the weather. The harsh Russian winters were unlike any Napoleon's men had ever encountered in their homelands. Most of them froze to death traversing the vast nation."

"Okay, weather," Orion jotted down the point. "Greenland is cold, but the Project isn't, so we can rule out freezing the killer robots," he mumbled, as he wrote. "What else?"

"There was also … the solidarity of the common Russians. They fought back in a way that surprised Napoleon's generals, abandoning cities and letting their capital burn … Oh right! That was another thing—scorched earth. They burned everything down as they left their homes, their crops, their supplies, everything."

"Okay back up," Orion said, looking up from his tablet. "How did burning their own towns help?"

"Ah, that's the most brilliant part!" Aquila's voice rose with excitement. "See, when the French army invaded Russia on foot, travelling thousands of miles through frigid terrain in the middle of winter, they couldn't have possibly carried enough supplies to last them till the end. So, for obvious reasons, they'd planned on looting the conquered towns and villages for food and supplies later on. By burning everything in their wake, the surrendering Russians prevented this from happening. In effect, they depleted the French army of food and resources. Soldiers died in the thousands; their horses lined the streets—"

"Alright, alright, that's enough," Orion said, smiling a little at Aquila's enthusiasm. "I think we get the gist. Although, I don't know if we could fit any of this into our current situation here … if we burn down the Project—"

"No!" Alan screamed, attracting attention to himself for the first time.

"Don't worry," Orion assured. "I said *if* … no one's burning down anything. Even if we manage to evacuate everyone, we'd destroy the entire world's grain reserves, which is definitely not an option."

"Aquila, since you've obviously studied this man, what do you think were his strengths?" Alrakis asked out of the blue, surprising everyone.

"Umm … do we really need to know his strengths, in this context?" Aquila was thrown off guard.

"In order to know one's enemy, to truly understand them that is, we need to know both their strengths and weaknesses and act accordingly," Alrakis explained.

"Alright. If you want my opinion, I'd say his most winning trait was his personal charisma and his ability to win the loyalty of his people, in particular, his soldiers. He was a most admired general and undoubtedly a French icon, even after his death."

Malina started speaking and stopped short. "Where's Carina?" she then asked, raising her eyebrows.

"Oh, she left a while ago. She had to get to the summit," Alrakis noted. "I didn't want to interrupt your strategizing, to point this out earlier."

"I see," Malina said. "Anyway, so where does this leave us?" The question was directed at Aquila, who blinked a few times before responding.

"I don't know."

"Okay, tell me this then," Malina said. "What happened to Napoleon in the end? Did he win back lost ground? Did he recover from his losses?"

"No. The Russian War turned out to be pretty much his undoing. He tried to make a comeback and failed. In the end, he died, rotting away in an island prison."

"I don't get it. Why would the ICC resurrect such a man, in that case? One who was eventually outmatched? If they needed a successful leader, there were many more choices, long-lived monarchs who reigned and conquered vast kingdoms. Queen Victoria of the nineteenth century for example."

"I think I can answer that," Aquila said. "They needed someone with charisma and passion. A natural-born leader, who rose from the ranks and won the adulation of millions.

Besides, there's a big difference between that Napoleon and this. The Chairman of the ICC may have all the genetic characteristics of Napoleon Bonaparte, but he doesn't have his *soul*. What happened to the French Emperor, was the result of his soul's baggage. It was *his* destiny. The Chairman does not have to share that fate. In fact, those who created the clone, may not even have told him, who he really is, or was. Which gives me an idea actually ..." Aquila paused to collect his thoughts. "Okay, I have it. I have a plan. I know how to defeat The Chairman!" he finally said.

"Well, spit it out then!" Orion asked impatiently.

"Here's what we need to do. You," he pointed at Malina, "need to turn me in. And you," now he looked at Orion, "need to go to Project 15/8 and handle the situation there. Buy me some time, while I work my plan on the Chairman." He paused. "Oh, and take Alan with you. He knows how things work at the Project." Alan's head snapped up, and he was going to say something, when Orion stood from his chair with a jerk.

"*Turn you in*? What—" He began in an agitated tone.

"Hold on Orion," Malina said. "I think it's a brilliant idea, if Aquila has a solid strategy in mind to back it up. Turning someone in for the crime of breaching Sanctuary City, would be a great way to prevent the Chairman from escalating the situation and persuading the other nations into supporting him. It would also take everyone's suspicion off Canada and Carina. That way, we can continue to use our powers to assist you, without being watched."

"Exactly," Aquila agreed. "Now, Madame Prime Minister, can you arrange for Orion and Alan to travel to Project 15/8 immediately?" he asked.

"I think I can. The Underground would probably send us a craft and a pilot," Malina said. "In honour of their fallen leader, Sakari." She looked meaningfully at Orion as she said these words.

"Sakari?" Aquila asked.

"My sister and ... Orion's late wife." Malina sighed.

CHAPTER THIRTY-FOUR

Aquila arrived at the lobby of the Canadian Parliament shortly before dawn, dressed in a neatly pressed white shirt and black pants. The clothes belonged to Alrakis, who was standing solemnly to his right. Orion stood to his left. Alan had been sent to the hospital wing to be with his mother, before they left for the Project. The massive lobby was surrounded by a semi-circular glass panel and elegantly decorated with clusters of sofa sets and matching centre tables. Dreamy dawn-light filtered in through the glass, reflecting off the various vases overflowing with lilies and wild orchids, imparting an aura of other-worldliness to the setting. Through the glass double doors, Aquila saw three shadowy figures approaching from a distance.

"Are you ready?" Orion breathed into his ear.

Aquila nodded. "Don't forget about the files," he said softly. "The God of War files. Our life depends on them."

"I won't," Orion assured, as the front doors opened and Malina walked in, flanked by two robotic body guards.

The Prime Minister arrived in front of their party and looked Aquila straight in the eye. Her expression was gentle, kind even. "You know the drill, Mister Aquila. You've been arrested before."

"That is correct." Aquila agreed.

"I should remind you however, that they might not take you to Sanctuary City at all. If you were hoping to rescue Elaine …" she trailed off, shaking her head from side to side.

"I'm aware. They're going to try me under the ICC's jurisdiction and detain me at a satellite station."

"That is the law. And you'll remember nothing of your journey from here to there."

"I'll be drugged. Yep, I know all that."

"Alright then. Let us proceed outside. They are waiting to arrest you, just beyond our gates." She began to turn around but stopped mid-way. "Good luck Mister Aquila. You are very brave," she said with a sad smile.

* * *

Orion got off the phone with Alrakis and made his way to the front of the craft that Malina had arranged for them. Alan was in the control room with the pilot, guiding her to Lucknow.

"What did he say?" Alan asked, as Orion entered.

"We don't have much time. At the emergency summit, they passed a resolution to send a fleet of ICC warships to Project 15/8. To gain back control over its operations."

"Which is crazy," remarked the pilot, a strapping young recruit of The Underground. "Take back control from whom exactly? The Underground didn't unleash those robots. The ICC did."

"We know that, they know that, but the world doesn't. They have to cook up a story. Make up an excuse for the invasion. In the end, the ICC wants to control the entire produce. That way, they'll control every nation. Don't you get it?"

"But how can they?" Alan screamed. "All that food belongs to the world. Every country has a stake in it."

"When do megalomaniacs ever play by the rules? Anyway, we need to hurry. The vessels will arrive in less than twenty-four hours. And we lost contact with Ramesh. How soon can we land?"

"In five minutes. But the airport looks surrounded ..."

"No! Don't go to the airport. When we last heard from Ramesh, he was in the special control bunker underneath the forest. It has a hidden access inside a clearing, where a small craft like ours can land. Here, let me find it on the map for you." Orion placed his fingers on the navigation map displayed on a screen in front of them and began to zoom in. "There. See that patch? We need to land there." He indicated the spot with his index finger.

"Roger. Prepare for landing."

* * *

Aquila opened his eyes to pitch-black surroundings, inside a grimy room with water dripping from its ceiling. He rubbed his tired eyes. The room was a cell with bars lining the front. Slowly, as his senses began to wake up, he smelled something foul in the air, reminiscent of death and disease.

This is not a satellite station, he realized to his horror and rose quickly to his feet. He tiptoed to the front of the cell, almost skidding on the wet stone floor beneath him. "Hello!" he yelled, gripping the bars so tight that his knuckles turned white. "Hello there! Anyone home?" The corridor ahead, narrow and gloomy, was silent as a graveyard. In the pervading silence, he thought he heard a low but distinct whimpering sound. It was not coming from the corridor, but from right behind him. He swivelled around defensively. "Who's there?" he said into the darkness. There was no response. Now Aquila could hear the sound of breathing. Harsh rasping intakes of breath and then, what sounded like a sniffle.

"Mi ... Mister ... Aquila?" said a woman's shaky voice, drifting through the shadows.

"Elaine!" Aquila gasped. He sank to his knees and blinked to adjust his vision. He could see a figure, crouched in the corner of their cramped cell. She was raising herself up slowly, struggling into a sitting position. "Are you hurt?" he said, as he rushed to her side.

Elaine's face was as white as a sheet, she looked drained of life, barely hanging on. She swallowed painfully and raised her head. "I ... she tortured me."

"She?" Aquila's eyebrows shot up. "Razzy?"

Elaine nodded weakly.

"Where is she?" Aquila's eyes darted to the squalid corridor beyond their cell.

"Gone." Elaine shrugged. "I'd followed you. To the Airport. She found me. And brought me here."

"She did what? I thought she wasn't even on that flight!"

"She was." Elaine closed her eyes, as she slid back to support her back against the wall. Aquila could see tear tracks lining her sallow cheeks, and on her forehead, what looked like dried blood.

"I ... am sorry," he blurted out. "Did you eat anything?" Elaine shook her head so imperceptibly that Aquila would have missed it, if he had blinked. He edged tentatively towards her and gently touched her shoulder. She winced and drew away. "Does it hurt?" Aquila rasped.

"Everywhere. It hurts everywhere."

Aquila could feel frothing bubbles of anger well up within him. He clenched his teeth to tamp it down and reached out to place his hand on hers. This time she did not pull away. "You need to eat something. What are they feeding you?"

Elaine shook her head. "Nothing. They brought me nothing to eat. Just water."

"That's outrageous! But don't worry, they're going to bring us something soon." Aquila squeezed her hand comfortingly.

"I doubt it. The city is deserted. Everyone left. Just us and the patients in the hospital."

"Trust me," Aquila said, his hand still on hers. "If there aren't people. There will be robots. I was sent here by the Canadian authorities. They can't just starve me to death, without raising a maelstrom of questions."

"But what then though? They'll kill us anyway. I heard them talk about it."

"You did? What did you hear?" Aquila straightened his back, his voice becoming tense.

"About a planned accident. At the nuclear arsenal. They're gonna blow it up."

"The nuclear wha—" Aquila paused mid-sentence, as his memory was jogged. "Oh! The Armaments Resolution"

Elaine looked up at him with barely concealed puzzlement. "It's ... complicated," Aquila explained, noticing the question in her eyes. "The bottom line is that the ICC is now in possession of the entire world's nuclear arsenal, and they have it stored in Greenland, because it's neutral territory. That's where we are now, in Greenland. Sanctuary City is in Greenland. That means, the confiscated nuclear weapons are probably being stored nearby. An accident at that facility, would be a convenient way to destroy Sanctuary City, along with all the evidence of their crimes."

Elaine sucked in a sharp breath and sat up with a jolt. "No!" Aquila said. "Lie down. Please. You're weak. I shouldn't have told you this." He leaned forward and tenderly wrapped his arm around her shoulders. She allowed herself to fall back against his embrace and close her eyes. Tears were dripping down them. Uncontrollable tears. Aquila watched her as she breathed. Not daring to speak another word, lest he break her completely. But Elaine was strong. She had always been strong; from the day Aquila had first met her. Somewhere in his heart, he knew that there was still a lot of fight left in her. As if answering his thoughts, Elaine opened her mouth.

"Alan? Where is he?" she asked.

"Safe. With Orion."

"And my parents?"

"In Canada. In the hospital." Aquila didn't have the heart to tell her about her father. Not now. Before he had left for Sanctuary City, Elaine had asked him to tell her parents that she loved them. Now she would never get the chance. But they had to keep it together, if they were to make it out of this alive.

"If they kill us, if they kill *you,* what are they going to tell the world? You were handed over by Canada, you say?"

"I was. And you're right, it wouldn't be easy to explain away my disappearance, since it was an International Prisoner Transfer. It was well publicized. Your case was different. You weren't supposed to be on that flight, and no one is keeping tabs on you, so they can do whatever they want, technically. Sorry, no offence meant."

"None taken." Elaine sat up, appearing livelier than before. The fact that her family was still alive and protected seemed to have given her that extra dose of adrenaline, which was all she needed to continue the fight. "How did you get here? Do you remember the journey?" She swerved around to ask.

"Nope. I was drugged the whole time. Woke up in this cell. It's standard procedure apparently. You?"

Elaine nodded. "Nothing about me was standard procedure of course. So yeah, I do remember it. Every step of it. Being tied up. Gagged. Razzy and someone else beating me up …" She choked. "Anyway," she continued, collecting herself quickly, "before they shoved me in here, they took blood samples. Don't ask me why, but they did. That was the weirdest bit. That's why I wanted to know if they did the same with you."

Aquila pulled back from Elaine and rose slowly to his feet. "Maybe," he said thoughtfully. "I wouldn't have known if they did. I was unconscious. But the question is, why?"

"Exactly," Elaine echoed.

They fell silent. Aquila walked up to the front of the cell and rested his head against the bars, as his brain worked away at their conundrum. Nothing was making sense. Yet, in a weird sort of way, everything seemed to fit perfectly together, like a puzzle with just a few critical pieces missing. What were those missing pieces? After an extended period of silence, Elaine spoke again.

"I heard that they found impersonation gloves in the City. Did you use them?"

"Yeah, we did, when we first arrived here. Me, Orion and Alan."

"I knew it. From the moment they mentioned an intruder, I knew it'd be the three of you. How did you get those cloned gloves?"

"I … we," Aquila began to answer when his eyes lit up. "That's it! That's the answer! Clones!"

"What?" Elaine looked at him like he was a lunatic.

"They're planning to clone us. You and me, and that's why they collected those blood samples."

"Wait, they can't do that. No one has ever created a fully functional clone so far and—"

"Oh! But they have. Look, we know from reliable sources that the ICC can, in fact, create fully functional clones. They already have, and that's what they plan to do with us. They'll probably put our clones through a televised trial, make them implicate themselves and sentence them to death, while they quietly get rid of our real versions here, along with the rest of Sanctuary City."

"Oh my!" Elaine's hands shot up to cup her face. "What do we do now?"

Aquila had his arms akimbo as he paced up and down the cell. "I have an idea. But you have to do as I say."

Elaine nodded. "Okay. Let's hear it."

* * *

Orion looked out the window as they edged closer to the circular clearing below. The sky was turning a stormy orange, with dark clouds gathering near the horizon. They were hovering over a patch of grass enclosed within a faintly glowing ring.

"Land inside the ring," he said, leaning towards the pilot. "It's a landing pad."

The craft touched down with a soft thud. The contact triggered a sensor, and the landing area began to descend below the surface of the earth. Once they were completely underground, a hatch closed above them, hiding them from view. Orion was the first to disembark. Alan followed tentatively, and their pilot took up the rear. They were inside a short passage at the end of which was a closed door. Orion rushed to the door and placed his palm against the authentication sensor. The door swung open into a large control room, surrounded by life-sized displays. A tired looking man was crouched in front of a screen, listening intently to what sounded like a camera feed. He bolted upright at the sound of advancing feet.

"Orion! You made it! When you left me Dorado's contact deets, I didn't even know if I should use it to reach you," he said. "I'm cut off here. Completely cut off. They took down all the comms."

"Woah there. Slow down, my friend. How are you, anyway?" Orion tried to smile, but didn't quite succeed.

"I ... not good," Ramesh replied. "They have the Project surrounded, and now they're herding people to the airport."

"To the airport, you say?" Orion walked over to Ramesh's side and stared into the screen in front of them. "How do you know that?"

"Look. Do you see this procession over here?" Ramesh pointed at a convoy of rickshaws, winding its way to the eastern edge of the Project, guided by a contingent of killer robots. "That's the road connecting the tunnels to the airport."

"Interesting." Orion's brows puckered into a frown. "Where could they be sending them?"

"To Sanctuary City. It says right here, in the airport logs." Ramesh pointed at a flashing display to his right.

"No way! We have to stop them. This is a parallel control center. We should be able to override that command."

"No, we can't. I've tried. When they took over the main control center, they must have set it on autopilot. It'll carry out everything that's been programmed in. It can't be stopped."

"What about the other plant activities—"

"They're continuing as per usual," Ramesh interrupted. "The water purification, harvesting, food processing, everything's going on. I had a thunderstorm planned for midnight, even that seems to be proceeding right on schedule. We can see it all from here, but we can't change the parameters. Not anymore."

"We're doomed." Orion slumped into a chair. He eyed Alan, who was leaning against a wall, his arms crossed. "Any idea, kiddo?"

Alan made his way towards them. "Hmmm," he said, crouching below the panels to inspect the hardware. "I might be able to hack in to the main control center from here, if you give me access. No guarantees though." He stood up. "But first, what are we looking to do?"

"Preventing the planes from flying would be a start," Ramesh suggested.

"No, that's not good enough." Orion was tapping the panel in front of him—a nervous gesture. "Even if we stopped them from sending everyone to Sanctuary City, we can't really protect them here either. With all those killing machines on the loose. Hang on." He bent to pull out a tablet from his backpack, that was lying on the floor. He flicked it on and started reading aloud from it. "Over-confident, underestimates the odds, weather—"

"What are you doing?" Ramesh looked baffled.

"Oh right, consulting my notes about the Chairman of the ICC. What his weaknesses are, how we can defeat him etcetera."

"I don't know how it helps to know that he's over-confident, but hey, you're the boss. And it's not like I have a better idea." Ramesh threw his arms up in frustration.

Alan leaned over Orion's shoulder and peered into the tablet. "Weather ... hmmm. There might actually be something useful in here," he muttered, his eyes lighting up. "You know what killer robots can't stand?" he asked Ramesh with a grin.

"What?"

"Drowning. Didn't you say you had a weather event planned tonight?"

* * *

"It seems like your plan isn't working," Elaine said, leaning her head against the moss-covered wall. "We've been here forever and you've been screaming yourself hoarse. No one's coming. No one's coming for us."

Aquila was still standing near the door of the cell, leaning against the bars. Through them, he could see a dim, narrow passageway winding away into darkness. The only sounds he could hear, were that of dripping water and his heart beating at a hundred cycles per minute. "No. I don't believe that," he whispered. "They have to feed us. The world is watching."

"The world ... has too many other things on its hands—"

"Shh! I hear something ..." Aquila raised a finger to his lips in warning. There was a mild rolling sound, like that of tiny wheels. It faded and then rose again, becoming louder. The passage began to light up, and a glowing figure emerged, about four feet high with a mild halo around it—a robotic prison superintendent. It swung around the corridor and stood to face Aquila at the cell door.

"I am here with your dinner," it said. In that moment, Aquila was transported back to another prison cell, half way between the earth and the moon, where he had stood facing this exact model of robot, speaking exactly these words. A triumphant smile lit up his face.

"Thank you," he said, accepting the plate of cold mush, through a small opening between the bars. "And for her?" He pointed at Elaine, who was sitting up now and staring at him in awe.

"Yes Sir." The robot nodded and reached into its belly to remove another tray of food. Aquila passed it on to Elaine, who pounced on it immediately.

"Do you have a lawyer, Sir?" The robot asked.

Aquila considered his next words carefully. "No," he replied.

The robot made notes. "Would you like me to request one for you?" If Aquila felt a sense of déjà vu at these words, he did not give it away.

"No," he said again. "However, there is something I *would* like to request."

"Go ahead." The robot made further notes on his tablet and looked up.

"I'd like to request witness protection. For myself and Elaine. But I have one condition."

"State your condition," it urged in a monotone.

"I will deliver my testimony in person, to the Chairman of the ICC and to him alone, with Elaine by my side to corroborate my claims."

"Anything else?"

"No."

"Your request has been submitted." The robot tucked away the tablet it was typing into, but it did not turn to leave.

"When will we hear the response?" Aquila ventured, tentatively.

"Soon," it said and fell into a meditative silence. A string of colourful lights along its chest started to blink on and off in rapid succession, and a beeping sound filled the room. Aquila stood there, holding his breath and grasping onto the prison bars with both his sweaty hands for an incredibly long time.

And then, as suddenly as it had begun, the light and sound display ended. The robot lowered its head and spoke in its boring, soporific voice.

"The Chairman has granted your request." It touched its hand to the cell door which flung open. Two magnetic handcuffs flew out from its belly and attached themselves to the prisoners' wrists. "Now, if you will follow me, I must take you to him at the International Satellite Station," it said, before turning to lead them out.

CHAPTER THIRTY-FIVE

Orion was leaning against the wall of the control room, anxiously tapping his foot on the floor. "A cloud burst, you say? Do we have enough time?" He frowned at Alan; his eyes enquiring.

Alan was hunched underneath a control panel, twiddling with the hardware, trying to gain access to the plant parameters. "If the thunderstorm is planned for midnight, then much of the activity is already underway. All we'd need now, is to send the system into overdrive, and it'd react by triggering a massive precipitation."

"But we have to time it to when they have everyone on the planes, ready to leave, and only the robots are outside, exposed to the elements. Otherwise, we risk drowning some of the citizens," Ramesh chimed in from across the room, where he was busy staring into a large screen.

"Where are they now?" Alan asked.

"There's a huge convoy on its way to the airport. It should be there in about half an hour."

Orion walked over to stand beside Ramesh. "Hmmm. That looks like all the residents. And look, the robot guards are leaving the tunnel gates. Meaning the tunnels have been evacuated, and all the citizens are out."

"You're right," Ramesh echoed. "I'd say the aircrafts will be ready to leave in a couple of hours tops."

"Shoot! That's not enough time," Alan exclaimed.

"Unless …" Ramesh walked over to Alan's side. "… unless we limit the perimeter of the event. Localize it to the airport area. All the robots are going to be there anyway, guarding the airport."

"Good idea. Okay, I did it. I hacked in!" Alan stood up, a wide grin across his youthful face. "We can control all the parameters from our location now. Mister Ramesh, do you want to take it from here?"

* * *

Aquila woke up shackled to a chair with magnetic clasps around his waist and arms. Whatever they had used to drug him this time, must have been strong. Because, he felt himself swimming in and out of consciousness, like a dead weight floating to the surface of an ocean, before getting swallowed up by the waves again. When he opened his eyes, the room swung like a pendulum in front of him.

"Mister Aquila," a tender voice whispered from his left. "Are you alright?" The words seemed to come to him from a great distance. He shook his head to clear his mind and turned to the side, struggling against his bonds. Elaine was strapped to a chair next to his. She looked pale and wispy like a morning mist, with worry lines etched across her delicate face.

"I … how long have I been out?" Aquila groaned.

"I don't know. But I've been awake for quite some time, and you weren't waking up. I was worried …"

Aquila blinked and looked around him. They were inside a dark room without any obvious doors or windows. A faint glow rose up from the floor, like moonlight reflecting off a lake. He opened his mouth to respond, when a blinding flash erupted from the wall in front of him. He closed his eyes reflexively, and when he opened them again, the room was no longer dark.

The floor was studded with small oval lights that had turned on, illuminating a short, stocky figure standing across from them—Napoleon Bonaparte in the flesh. He looked exactly like the holos Aquila had seen in the restricted section of the library—closely cropped dark hair, olive complexion, muscular build and confident, alert eyes brimming with combat readiness. The clothes he wore were more modern and military grade—close fitting gray trousers and jacket made of leatherine, a durable and practically impenetrable material.

"Mister Aquila," the new Napoleon said, a wry smile across his face. "You are famous!" He paused, as if expecting Aquila to respond or react in some way. But when Aquila remained silent, he spoke again. "First you try to break in to a top-secret ICC database. You get caught, acquitted, and then you flee. But you don't stop there. You come back for more. Hitchhiking to Sanctuary City on your own, followed by your little friend." He gestured towards Elaine. "If you think you will not be sentenced to death, then you are a fool." He broke into a cruel and gravelly laughter. He stopped to catch his breath. "But you don't look like a fool to me, Mister Aquila. So, tell me … what is it that you want?" He spoke the last few words softly, almost like a caress, before pulling up a chair to sit across from them.

"I told you what I want," Aquila replied curtly.

"Indeed. You want to turn in your accomplices like a traitor. A traitor who makes a last-ditch effort to save a poor farmer girl." Again, he pointed at Elaine. "No. Something isn't adding up. The Underground might be foolish or reckless or simply wrong in what they desire, but they're definitely not traitors to their kind. Therefore, my question is, who *are* you?"

Aquila, who was staring intently at his upturned right wrist, looked up at these words, his lips curving into a grin. "Maybe I could ask you the same thing, Honourable Chairman. Who are *you*, exactly?"

* * *

295

Carina's hands were shaking as she held her phone, waiting for Alrakis to answer her call. She had snuck out of the meeting room for five minutes, right after the last round of voting, and was standing inside a VIP bathroom, sweating profusely.

"Carina!" a familiar voice blurted. "What's wrong? Why are you calling?"

"The Summit is on recess. They voted unanimously in favour of declaring martial law and handing over military control to the ICC. We don't have much time. The ICC armies are arriving within hours. What news do you have from the others?"

"I ... Orion has been completely cut off since his flight landed in Lucknow, but I know he isn't dead."

"How?" Carina's voice quivered.

"I can see satellite images of the area, and their hideout looks intact. All the entrances are sealed. The robots aren't anywhere near its perimeter."

"Okay, but are they making progress with their plans?"

"There's no way to know."

Carina sighed audibly. "What about Aquila?" She felt a tickling sensation on her cheeks as she spoke his name, and a wet salty aftertaste. She tried to hold in the tears, now pouring freely.

"He ... I activated the chip on his wrist and uploaded the files he had requested before he left Canada. He was right. Area 51 had all the documents we needed. Beyond that, I have no idea."

"Is he ..." Carina made a choking sound.

"No. The chip is organic, and fuelled by his nervous system. It wouldn't have accepted any information if he were dead."

"Okay. I have to get back to the meeting. I'll call you again when there's another break." With that, she hung up and washed her face at the sink, before making her way back to the meeting room, looking like an expressionless wax doll.

* * *

Orion felt the ground shake above them, as claps of thunder tore across the horizon. They stood frozen in front of a display screen, watching the sky above the airport rip apart, as rain gushed down like heaven's fury, flooding the tarmac in an instant.

"Do you think this bunker is watertight?" Alan asked meekly.

"I guess we'll soon find out," Orion whispered.

"The radius of the storm is large enough to reach us," Ramesh clarified. "I couldn't make it any smaller. But we are somewhat in the fringe of it. We won't get the full impact."

"And if we did?" Orion asked.

"If we did, then there's no way our bunker would hold. It's mostly weather proof, but it has its limits too. What we unleashed tonight is something no engineer would have foreseen. I can guarantee that much."

"Should we get out then? While we still can?" Alan was looking nervous.

"I can't fly in this weather, if that's what you're suggesting." It was the pilot, who responded this time.

"We should think of something else then. It's likely, we'll get flooding above our heads, and when that happens the ceiling might give," Ramesh warned.

"I have an idea." Orion bent over to gather his backpack and jacket from the floor. "Let's go upstairs to my office on the top floor. We should be safe in there."

"But it also means that we'll lose access to this control room. And there'd be no way out of your office, except by air, when the lower floors are flooded," Ramesh said.

"Well, that's just a risk we're gonna have to take." Orion shrugged, as he walked towards the door.

* * *

Napoleon shot out from his seat and glared at Aquila. "*How dare you question my authority*! I have the power to—"

"Arrghhh!" A shrill cry pierced the room, as Aquila bent over double in his chair, writhing with agony.

"Wha ... what happened? What are you playing at?" The Chairman's face was flushing an angry crimson.

"I'm not ... my hand ..." Aquila coaxed out, glancing at his right wrist, where a bluish welt had begun to appear out of nowhere. "Please ... release my arms ..."

"There's no way—"

"Oh c'mon! What do you have to fear really? He's still tied to the chair by his waist," Elaine spoke up, her eyes filling with horror.

Napoleon gave her a stern look, before tapping at a bracelet around his own wrist. "Alright. Your hands are free, Aquila. Explain yourself. And quick, because I don't have all day."

Aquila breathed a sigh of relief as his arms snapped free. Quickly he grabbed his right hand with his left and began to massage at the bruise, soothing it till the throbbing went away. "Napoleon," he began slowly, chewing on each word, "you are a warrior. A general. A KING!" He paused. "And if you will allow me, I can show you."

"Show me how?"

Aquila's fingers clasped around his right wrist, as he closed his eyes in concentration. A tiny gasp erupted from Elaine's lips. He let go of his wrist, and looked up immediately. The Chairman was still standing across from them, his features drawn. But now he was staring up at a figure, suspended in midair right at the center of the room—a mirror image of himself, garbed in ancient military attire, complete with his signature bicorne hat. "What—"

"Napoleon Bonaparte, born in Corsica in the year 1769, was a military general, later Emperor of France, and beloved of his people ..." began a narrator voice, as the image of the real Napoleon rotated slowly along a vertical axis.

"Turn it off!" The Chairman ordered. "I'm not falling for this. I know who I am, and it is certainly not *this* man."

Aquila chuckled, and did as he was told. The narration paused, but the figure of the French Emperor continued to hang motionlessly before their eyes. "No, you aren't this man, Honourable Chairman. You are, in fact, his clone."

"That's impossible!"

"Is it? Then tell me, Sir, who are you?"

"I am from Indochine. Born into poverty and wretched circumstances, I always yearned to save my people. And then, I was spotted by the ICC and groomed for my position. I was lucky. Not everyone had the opportunity I had—to join the ranks of the world's most powerful organization, to contribute towards making a real difference. So, I took it on eagerly, but it wasn't easy to rise through the ranks. After many years of diligent service, I became what I am today. And now, I can finally save my people. From years of drudgery and strife. That is why I created Sanctuary City, where they're going to be safe at last, and more importantly, they're going to be free."

"Free indeed. Free from life itself," Aquila said bitterly. "I can prove to you that none of what you said right now is true. It's just the backstory they implanted when they created you. They lied to you Chairman; you have to believe me."

"Well, I don't. Anyone could have created a doctored holo like that. So, unless you have any testimony to provide, I must—"

"Wait!" There was a hint of desperation in Aquila's tone. "Let me show you something else." He scrunched his eyes shut, concentrating hard. Soon, Napoleon's image faded, while another figure emerged from the blankness—an elegant lady in a flowing high-waisted gown of white silk with gilded embroidery.

The Chairman glanced at it and then did a double take, his eyes wide with astonishment. "No! How did you—"

"So, you recognize this woman, do you Sir?"

"Of course, I do … that is … she's Kamalini … my wife."

"What if I tell you, she isn't? That Kamalini doesn't exist, except in your memories. Memories that were deliberately implanted to mislead you." Aquila touched his wrist again and took a deep breath. The audio began to play as he did so.

"Empress Josephine was Napoleon Bonaparte's first wife and the love of his life—"

Aquila paused the narration. "The woman you see before you, is Josephine," he explained. "Not Kamalini. Josephine, Empress of France. *Now* do you get it? Tell me something Sir, the Project that you love so much, why is it called Project 15/8? Why? Where did that number come from?" There was harshness in his voice as he spoke.

The Chairman was startled. "I … everyone knows that it stands for Independence," he replied, but without much conviction. "When India was a nation, it had gained independence on that very day. So, the naming is a homage."

"Really? But that date means nothing to the erstwhile nation of China, which is now a part of Indochine. Didn't that strike you as odd?"

"What are you trying to say?" Aquila noticed that the Chairman had gone quite pale during the course of this conversation.

"Let me show you." Aquila paused to play another file. "Born on the island of Corsica on August 15th 1769, the boy Napoleon was—" the narrator's voice began.

"I've heard enough!" the Chairman growled. "None of this proves I'm Bonaparte's clone. It's just a bunch of coincidences, cleverly arranged to confuse—"

"Oh no, it isn't. And neither is it *all* of the information I have to show you. My sources have also sent me classified files from Area 51, containing specific information on how you were created. It outlines everything—how you began, and how you're going to end."

"How I'm going to end? You mean … my death?" The Chairman's lips trembled, with anger or fear, Aquila could not tell.

DIE TO SEE TOMORROW

"Exactly. It has been preplanned. You have a chip embedded in you, that will cause your self-destruction, once the ICC forces take over Project 15/8. You're not even a real person Mister Chairman, just a means to an end.

"If you care to see this information with your own eyes … and verify its authenticity, I can give you all the files. They have been uploaded to my wrist-chip by my allies. All you have to do is transfer them to a storage pin, and go through them yourself." Aquila extended his arm towards the Chairman, exposing the welt on his wrist.

The Chairman took a step forward and hesitated. For several seconds no one moved, or even breathed—the scene looking like a page from a book, frozen in time.

Finally, the Chairman dug into the pocket of his blazer and pulled out a small object, before approaching with caution. He swiped the object quickly over Aquila's wrist and pivoted on his heels. "I'll be right back," he said over his shoulder, as he walked out the door, shrouding Aquila and Elaine in darkness.

* * *

Orion stood at the picture window of his ninth-floor office, peering through an antique telescope. There was very little to see in this weather, except for storm clouds and sheets of terrible rain. Through the haze, Orion could discern the outlines of drowning killer robots, scattered around an otherwise deserted city.

"Woah, it's rough out there," Ramesh remarked from next to him. "Where do you think the plant employees are? Their apartments are dark."

"They're in those aircrafts too, I suspect. Along with the farmers. Ready to leave for Sanctuary City." Orion pointed at the airport area to their northeast, where massive Airwhales, several stories high, could be seen on the tarmac.

"But why? That was never part of the deal."

"And neither were the mass murdering robots. But here we are, aren't we?" Orion replied, without bothering to hide the sarcasm in his tone.

"Look, the horizon is clearing up to our west. I think I can see the river."

Orion turned his telescope around. "Yeah, you're right. I do see the river … and something else."

"What is it? What do you see?"

"Battleships. Several. Heading our way."

"Shit! That's not good!"

"Nope. Not good at all." Orion sighed.

* * *

The emergency summit was over, and the delegates from the ICC member countries were gathered on a rooftop patio of the Republic's Parliament for refreshments. Carina bent over a low ornamental parapet, distancing herself from the others. Her mind was restless as she looked around her. The streets below were empty, with intermittent police patrols. Everyone had been ordered to stay indoors, awaiting the arrival of the ICC troops.

"What are you thinking?" said a soft voice behind her shoulder. It was Gomeisa, her Chief of Staff.

"Nothing. I … I'm just wondering when the army will arrive," she replied cautiously.

"Didn't you hear? They landed about an hour ago. Have you heard from Alrakis?"

"Not since our last recess." Carina's response was absentminded. Her eyes were roving around, scouring the city for the signs of activity. "What's taking them so long?" She wondered out loud.

"The army, you mean?"

"Yeah. If they've already landed, then they should've sent their commanders to report to us immediately."

"I don't know, maybe we should ask … oh look, I think I see something." Gomeisa pointed at a speck in the horizon, growing larger as it rolled up the broad avenue leading up to their building.

"You're right. It's a tank. Four tanks actually—" Carina was cut short by the sound of a commotion behind them. She turned around quickly to find a small crowd leaning over the parapet at the other end of the roof. They were pointing fingers and speaking animatedly. "What's going on?" She asked no one in particular.

A man holding a slender wine glass darted past her. "More tanks! That's too many," he was saying.

Carina eyed the President of the Republic. He was a tall, grey-haired man with a mousy demeanour, and now he looked paler still, as if he was fading into the background. His bodyguards rushed to his side, and one of them said something into his ear. The President nodded and asked for a microphone, which the guard immediately supplied. "Ahem," he said, and everyone fell silent, turning their heads towards him. "I have been notified that the ICC army has finally sent its officers to report to us. Their tanks, as you can see, are already on the streets …"

"We are surrounded," someone remarked from the audience, which the President ignored and forged ahead with his speech.

"The commander of the contingent is on his way upstairs. He will formally introduce himself to us, any moment now. And then, with our permission and blessing, his forces will take their positions at different strategic locations around the city." He paused, as the commander in question entered through the door, followed by at least 30 armed officers, who spread out into the crowd, encircling the congregation. The commander was wearing plain clothes, but his troops were in full military gear. "Ah General, nice to meet you," the President greeted with a slight nod.

"Nice to meet you too, Mister President. However, I am not a general. In fact, I'm not with the army at all. I am an officer of the International Satellite Police. And we have come here under the direction of the ICC Chairman with a mandate to make arrests." Gasps were heard all around the room and the sound of shuffling feet. Then, dozens of handcuffs whirled through the air, clasping onto the wrists of all the attendees, including Carina and Gomeisa.

"You have the right to remain silent," the officer said at last, and proceeded to lead them out.

CHAPTER THIRTY-SIX

Aquila squinted as the door slid open with a blinding burst of light. He was expecting the Chairman to have returned, but instead it was someone else entirely—a handsome young man in a dark brown, knee-length coat and beige trousers. His immaculate white shirt was partially unbuttoned in an uncharacteristically casual style.

"Alrakis!" Aquila rasped through a dry throat.

The younger man beamed and walked towards him. "You did it!" he said. "Your plan worked!" He touched the side of Aquila's chair releasing his bonds, and then bent to do the same for Elaine. "Here, I brought you some water." Alrakis reached into the pocket of his overcoat and pulled out two water bottles.

Aquila took a few swigs of the cool refreshing water, savouring each soothing gulp. "Where's the Chairman?"

"He's with Carina. Making all the arrangements. Cleaning up this mess."

Aquila nodded. "Carina is here too? At the satellite station?"

"Oh yes. They arrested all the delegates and brought them here, Carina included. As soon as I got the news, I hurried here. Arranged for her release. Explained what we had been doing in the background this whole time. That settled, now we can get back."

"Get back where?"

"To Calamerica, of course. Orion and Alan are being brought there as well. The ICC warships rescued them from the roof of Orion's office."

"WHAT? What were they doing on the roof? Are they alright?" Aquila stood up so quickly, he got a head rush.

"Relax, they're fine. Would I be so calm if they weren't? Anyway, let's get you outta here. You look like you could use some food. There's an aircraft waiting for us, and dinner is about to be served."

* * *

Aquila looked into the mirror as he adjusted his shirt collar. He was wearing an auburn shirt that beautifully set off his eyes. Although he had just shaved and moisturized his face, the lines on his forehead were deeper than they had been a year ago, his complexion was a shade darker and the silver in his hair more abundant. He buttoned his cream-coloured suit jacket and sighed deeply. His age was catching up to him fast.

Dinner on the aircraft had been a quiet affair earlier, with only Elaine and Alrakis joining him. Elaine had barely spoken and focussed mostly on attacking the contents of her plate like a hyena. Alrakis had been cheerful and somewhat shyer than usual. Then again, Aquila had never seen him in an informal setting before, and wondered if he was always this shy in private. After dinner, Aquila had fallen asleep in his cabin, waking up only after they had landed inside the floating Reception Hall above Calamerica. Although he was not drugged this time, ironically, he had once again missed the entire flight back from the International Satellite Station. After landing, Alrakis had shown him around the Reception Hall, which hovered in the sky about a thousand feet above sea-level, offering panoramic views of Calamerica from all its windows.

Then, always the gentleman, he had lent Aquila clothes fit for a gala and left him to his grooming.

Now, Aquila stood dressed in borrowed clothes, a tad tight for him in places, getting ready for the imminent cocktail party. He brushed his longer-than-usual hair one last time. Made sure no stray strands fell into his eyes. Then, he headed to the party.

A short, tastefully decorated corridor led from his room to the ballroom, where guests had already begun to assemble. It was an oval shaped hall with white skirted tables scattered about at regular intervals. Waiters, both human and robotic, hovered between the guests, carrying loaded trays of refreshments and hors d'oeuvres. At the far end, stage lights illuminated a semilunar area of the floor, where musicians were starting to gather.

Aquila saw Orion in the crowd, leaning against a table, chatting animatedly with Ramesh. They had their faces turned towards the stage and did not notice him in the background.

"Gomeisa, wait," someone said from the other end of the hall. Aquila turned to find Alrakis sprinting to the side of a lovely young lady in a gossamer golden gown. The woman stopped in her tracks, allowing Alrakis to approach and take her by the hand towards one of the tables.

Behind them, a woman in a wheelchair had entered. Aquila immediately recognized the skinny young man pushing the chair along. Alan waved at him, a grateful smile across his lips, and his mother nodded feebly from her wheelchair. Before Aquila could reciprocate, someone shot from Alan's side and threw herself at him in a warm embrace. She smelled of soap and lavender, her hair a silken curtain of inky rain, falling gracefully around Aquila's shoulders as her arms wrapped around his neck.

"Elaine." Aquila said, breathing in her soft fragrance. He held her by her shoulder and bent her backwards to stare into her face.

She blushed, lowering her eyes and smiled. "Thank you," she whispered. "For everything."

"I … it was nothing." Aquila felt a flush of emotion rise up to his cheeks. He let her go and quickly averted his face to hide his embarrassment. "I hope you're feeling better," he said to the floor.

"Mhhm. And you?"

"Yeah, I'm fine …"

"Come Elaine, the show is about to start." It was Alan. Aquila looked up. There was slow music playing in the background, and the stage at the end of the room was filling up with pairs of professional dancers. Elaine nodded and followed her family towards a table, turning to wave at Aquila, before she disappeared behind a waiter. Aquila waved back.

The dancers began to swirl to flamenco music, their flowing dresses twirling around their legs, their heels tapping the floor in rhythmic unison. Aquila watched, transfixed by this mesmerizing spectacle.

The guests had mostly assembled at the tables. Some of the faces were familiar and others unknown. Among the faces, Aquila searched frantically for someone, his eyes roving, scanning each table twice, just to be sure.

"She's not here. The one you're looking for," someone said from his side.

"Who?" Aquila turned to the speaker. It was Carina. She was wearing a knee-length, navy blue evening gown and had her hair tied up in a chignon. She had one robotic bodyguard by her side. "Oh, Madame Carina, good evening."

"You can call me Carina," Carina said with a dismissive wave of her hand. "Good evening to you too. Have you been enjoying yourself?"

"It's quite lovely, all of these arrangements." Aquila spread his arms out to indicate his surroundings. "But there are still some nagging questions—"

"I figured as much," Carina interrupted. "In that case, come with me. We should chat."

Aquila nodded and followed Carina down the hall to a set of elevators in the corner. They took the elevator to the floor below and arrived in front of a set of curved metallic doors. Carina touched the door sensor to allow passage and nodded once to her bodyguard, which it promptly interpreted as its cue to leave. Then, she stepped inside the room. Aquila followed her and gasped as he took in the sight.

They were standing in a room surrounded by glass on all sides, apart from the ceiling. A glittering array of luminescent snow globes dotted the azure blue waters below. Upon closer examination, Aquila could see a pattern forming from the arrangement—two huge eyes with blue irises staring up at the sky.

"Wow! Is that—" he began.

"Revolution City. The capital of Calamerica." Carina grinned. "All those bubbles down there are the houses and building complexes, the floating farms too. They are joined to each other by passages, our main thoroughfares. Together, they look like a pair of eyes, watching over our nation like sentries."

"Impressive."

"Come, have a seat." Carina indicated towards the middle of the room, where plush sofas were set in a lotus arrangement around a circular centre table.

"I didn't see you at dinner tonight," Aquila said, as he relaxed into his seat.

"I was in meetings with the Chairman. We were figuring out how to cure the infected farmers at Sanctuary City."

"And did you. Figure it out?"

"We have a plan. Thanks to you, we were given a chance to treat Alan's parents already, and we gleaned some antibodies from their serum, which we could use as a treatment. The hurdle is the international ban on developing and using allopathic treatment procedures. However, I was able to convince the Chairman to lift the ban temporarily, to address this extraordinary situation. This was no ordinary illness; it was a biological warfare of sorts. So, the considerations are unique."

"That's excellent news. Does that mean we can save the remaining patients?"

"That's the hope. The ICC is in the process of evacuating them to various hospitals across the globe as we speak."

"I'm so glad. What about the world-wide emergency? Is that going to be lifted soon, now that we have the perpetrators behind bars?"

"No, not right away. Most of the nations are without leaders at the moment. Until elections can be held again, the ICC will be filling in the leadership vacuum."

Aquila laughed out loud. "That means Napoleon got to be an Emperor after all. Albeit temporarily."

At this Carina smiled. "It was smart of you to remember what Bonaparte's strengths were, and to use them to our advantage. He was revered by his men. By his army. If we didn't know that, then we couldn't have leveraged him to make his army turn around and arrest the very leaders, who had requested its presence to begin with. But that was not the only reason you surrendered to the ICC, was it? You wanted to confront Napoleon yes, but also someone else. Am I right?"

"I suppose you are."

Carina raised her hands to her neck and removed what looked like a necklace from around it. It bore a sliver locket that flipped open at her touch. "Do you recognize this woman?" she said, handing him the open locket.

Inside, was a picture of two women, hand in hand, looking at each other, their faces radiant. One of them was clearly Carina and the other … "Razzy!" Aquila exclaimed, dropping the locket.

Carina shook her head from side to side. "Mizar. Her name is Mizar. She had disguised herself as Razzy, short for Razim, which is Mizar spelled backwards."

"How did you find out?"

"When you spotted her on the jetcraft that was pursuing you, Orion showed us her picture. We looked into it further and found out that she was acting as a spy for the Republic. I know this is no consolation, but she did not just betray *you*. She also betrayed *me*. She was my wife."

Aquila's face went pale. He struggled to find words. "But ... I ... why? Why would she do that?"

"I don't know. But I suspect, it had something to do with her past. She descended from a long line of heartland farmers, who felt like they were becoming disenfranchised by the influx of cheap grain from the east. Their family had led a revolution and were expelled from the Republic as a result. But somewhere deep down, their seething anger may not have been quelled. So, when the current President of the Republic came into power, they worked in collusion with him to usurp the grain supplies from the Project. In the end, what she did, wasn't personal. Still, it hurts like hell." Carina's eyes were welling up.

"It does, indeed. But why are you telling me all this? We hardly know each other—"

"I know. But I would like to get to know you better."

"And why is that?" Aquila raised his eyebrows in surprise.

Carina pulled out a dainty little handkerchief from her purse and dabbed at her eyes. Then, sniffling, she looked up. "Aquila, did you ever wonder why you, of all people, were arrested by the ICC before this whole fiasco started?"

Aquila sat up straight. "Of course, I did. But as things started to unravel, I realized, it had something to do with The Underground trying to impersonate me, to break into ICC records."

"Yes, you're smart. That's exactly how it went down. But ask yourself this, why did anyone bother to make impersonation gloves using *your* DNA to begin with? Why did they *chip* you too? You are a nobody. Sorry, no offence. But implantation and DNA mapping are not procedures that apply to civilians like yourself."

"Yeah, I know. And no offence taken. Do you know the answer then?"

"I didn't at first, but I figured it out." Carina stood up and drifted to the window. When she spoke next, her voice sounded like it was coming from beyond the clouds. "When I was a child, my parents were leaders of The Underground. My father was from Calamerica, and my mother was born in Russia. She came from a generation of Americans, who had fled to Russia during the Deluge. My folks met in Revolution City, got married and had me. At that time, the Chancellor had given out orders to chip all the children of the revolutionaries and to enlist them in special schools. Their DNAs were also collected and experimented on. The idea was to monitor them as they grew up, so that they didn't follow in the footsteps of their parents. My parents fought fiercely against this oppressive regime, and they were identified.

"When I was around five years old, my father came home one night and told us we must leave. Immediately. We fled in the dead of the night to a safe-house—the home of my father's best friend. We stayed the night, and in the morning, my parents left, telling me to wait with our host's family until their return. They never came back." Carina paused for breath.

"I'm so sorry," Aquila whispered. "But—"

"You don't see the connection, do you?" Carina flipped around. She had a sad smile across her lips. "I found out later, that my father was caught and killed that night. But my mother escaped to her childhood home in Russia. She had my baby brother with her, only nine months old. He had already been chipped, but his chip hadn't been activated yet. When I grew up, I tried to track my mother, my brother. But it was futile. They had hidden themselves well. For my safety and theirs. I ended up being raised by my father's friend, here in Revolution City. And then, many years later, I heard about you, when you were arrested by the ICC. A man about my brother's age, whose DNA had been collected somehow, and turned into impersonation gloves. I had to find out who you were."

"So, you came to rescue me."

Carina nodded. "And in order to free you, I had to inject you with illegal drugs to serve as an alibi for your infraction. I couldn't throw away the needle I used to drug you." Carina smiled again. A radiant smile this time.

"Let me guess," Aquila began. "You got it DNA-tested when you came home. And the DNA matched yours."

Carina broke into a giggle. "Correct again. You are my little brother Aquila, and now we can at least have each other."

Aquila sighed deeply and leaned back in his seat. All his life, he had felt a vapid sense of loneliness, a lack of purpose and direction that had estranged him from the rest of humanity. This alienation had grown especially strong since his mother's demise. Still, somewhere deep down, he had held on to hope for a day such as this when he would finally find acceptance and belonging. So, Carina's revelation did not surprise him as much as it should have. In fact, it felt natural and long awaited—expected even. He glanced at his sister and smiled.

"So? What do we do now?"

Carina walked over to him slowly and perched herself on the armrest of his couch. "You can … come live here, if you wish," she hesitated. "With me. I mean."

"Ha!" Aquila laughed. "I do. I wish it," he replied softly.

ABOUT THE AUTHOR

Poulomi Sanyal has been writing poetry since she was ten years old. She created her first literary magazine when she was twelve. Sanyal was born in India but has lived all over the world, including Hong Kong. For the last couple of decades, she has called Canada home. She is fluent in English, Bengali, and Hindi, and she also speaks conversational French.

Sanyal received her master's degree in engineering from McGill University in Montreal and has spent a good number of years working in engineering in Toronto. In her free time, she enjoys writing, painting, acting, volunteering and traveling.